THE SEARCH

DALE PEROUTKA

Primix Publishing
11620 Wilshire Blvd
Suite 900, West Wilshire Center, Los Angeles, CA, 90025
www.primixpublishing.com
Phone: 1-800-538-5788

Published by Primix Publishing: 08/01/2024

ISBN: 979-8-89194-078-9(sc)
ISBN: 979-8-89194-079-6(hc)
ISBN: 979-8-89194-080-2(e)

Library of Congress Control Number: 2024901269

CONTENTS

PROLOGUE

A *nd the universe began!*

Suddenly, there was light, but no light we could see.

Suddenly, there was matter, but no matter we could feel.

Suddenly, there was energy, but no energy we could perceive.

There was an enormous nuclear and subnuclear reaction, an explosion that encompassed and comprised the known universe. A person, if such a person existed at that instant, would have no frame of reference for the enormity of the explosion. As the minuscule brain of an ant cannot comprehend the solar system, the galaxy, or the distances between such galaxies, such a person could not comprehend what has frequently been called "The Big Bang!"

Many forms of life were created and immediately extinguished in that initial millisecond in time. The great thinker Einstein proved that time itself and the level of space were warped by the stress of the forces of the explosion. Some very primitive forms of life lived through this event and were later modified or extinguished. Strange elements were modified by the violent passage of mesons, quirks (both two up and one down), pions, W and Z bosons, and other subnuclear particles yet to be discovered. Only the strong survived, although sometimes, the strong was an imprecise definition because some life developed a memory that allowed it to modify itself to survive that caustic, hostile environment.

Among this later form of what loosely might be called life, was a virulent form of absorption that existed on energy, electrical energy given off by nuclear reactions, explosions, lightening and the rubbing of one positively charged piece of matter against a negatively charged piece of matter.

In the first micro millisecond of "The Big Bang," this form of life or absorption was instantly created; within the next micro millisecond it was destroyed; unfortunately, within the third micro millisecond, it was immediately recreated, but not destroyed.

This form of absorption or life permeated certain parts of primeval matter. Much formed around itself. Most of this life was ultimately attracted to, absorbed by, and decimated by larger energy sources such as suns, novas, and later the universe's abundant black holes.

A small amount remained dormant in undisturbed primal rock, floating in uncharted space between galaxies. This rock, irregularly and roughly shaped with little refraction, was about the size of half of a small compact car and, if on earth, would weigh about two and a half tons.

Eons passed.

Gravitational waves ebbed and flowed.

Galaxies continued their unrelenting rotation around the center of the universe, some traveling through space faster than the average of approximately .02 percent of the speed of light, some traveling slower.

Some galaxies slowly collided with cataclysmic violence! A small part of the original dust and rock coalesced into planets; most such planets remained cold, grey, and lifeless while other planets condensed liquids out of the original dust and rock to start the long, painful journey to support life.

The forefathers, or more accurately, the forethings of thinking, reasoning beings poked their heads (or upper part of their bodies) out of ancient slimy mud and slowly evolved.

Years, multiples of millions of years passed.

Civilizations were born, rose to heights of glory and died. Some civilizations never progressed beyond the nuclear age, choosing instead to decimate themselves through an inability to compromise and peacefully resolve their differences. For life to survive, it must compete and win at any cost!

Slowly, ever so slowly, the rock was nudged out of its solitary position between galaxies by infinitesimal gravity waves. It was passively drawn to *a flat spiral galaxy thought to be in the middle of the universe of millions of such galaxies.*

Gradually, it drifted into the edge of this galaxy. Gravitational waves caused by the violent collisions between stars influenced its movement more and more. Its speed increased due to the faint pull of gravity. Gravitational waves, as infinitesimal as a grain of sand on a planet, still had an influence upon its movement.

No intelligent, reasoning eyes or senses saw its movement. It passed through the edge of this galaxy and plunged through first one solar system and then another, narrowly missing a star here and a planet there, all the while having its course altered and modified.

It reached a solar system with nine planets, one of which is a huge gas giant. It skimmed this gaseous planet and due to the planet's huge gravitational pull, it received a change in its direction and a radical lessening of its speed. It missed a red planet. It approached a beautiful greenish blue and brown, practically all water covered planet and at an altitude of just under a hundred miles, slightly penetrated its atmosphere.

This planet, with its attendant atmosphere, was rotating about eleven hundred miles an hour at its equator. Again, gravity exerted its pull and pulled the object closer to the planet, bouncing the object several times at the outer edge of the atmosphere like a thrown pebble skimming the surface of a smooth pond. Its speed was slowed even more; the blue and green planet's gravity exerted a greater and greater influence upon the object.

The friction of the atmosphere heated the rock and rubbed off tiny particles like sandpaper rubbing against a brick causing the object to become electrically charged. It eventually burned and submerged itself through the planet's heavy atmosphere.

As things sometimes occur, the rock unfortunately passed through a thunderstorm. Since it was part ancient metal, and electrically charged, it attracted lightning and was struck, not once, not twice but with many violent strikes before it crashed into the ground with a shattering impact. The ancient rock, and the life inside, received jolts, charges of millions of volts of lightning like a comatose human body receiving an electrical jolt from a defibrillation machine. The place of impact was in the south-central part of Central America near a lightning scarred, metal filled mountain.

It slowly awakened. It started ravenously feeding on the electricity, its food, because of its starvation all those eons of years. It was frenzied in its search for food, food! It terrified the local natives whose primitive direct current electrical generators attracted life.

It reproduced itself. The original self, the original "life" was eaten, although, eaten is a poor description of being devoured by your starving offspring, who are multiplying and being devoured by their offspring.

Ah . . ., rain, thunderstorms, lightning, electricity, the essence of life! More, more, it multiplied and broadened its mindless search for more electricity.

A long night began. . ..

THE INDIVIDUALS

JOSEPH DAVID ROBINSON, Just over six-foot, crew cut brown hair, brown eyes, wore military clothes, but is civilian. Over-all operations and supervisor/leader of his group of military men who were in considerable legal trouble with the Army. For legal purposes, Joseph's group were treated as civilians. All men in great physical condition.

SPENSER GERRY, Private First Class (one stripe with rocker).

ALVIN SWANSON, Private First Class.

COLONEL REGINALD DEVONSHIRK, III, United States Army, Special Units Division, wears half-moon glasses, short, last duty assignment, age, bum right leg and refusal to be a yes man. Receives assignments that cannot be given to the regular military nor the CIA or FBI, usually require some activity, usually illegal and always confidential, to protect the United States.

SERGEANT DEAN MORRIS, Sergeant First Class: three stripes with two rockers, dark haired, hard bodied, had made Army his career, but because of a mistake in a conflict the Army had been involved in, rather than discharge him, he is assigned to this detail of misfits. Most, if not all, are escaping being court martialed facing probable federal prison.

THOMAS TRINKO, Private Second Class, formerly drove stagecoaches at Knott's Berry Farm, knows horses. He and several of his group were facing mandatory prison sentences for being in places they were forbidden to "visit."

ROBERT JONES, Private First Class, one stripe

ION FLANNERY, Private First Class, one stripe

SAMUEL KLEIGHORN, Corporal, two stripes, from Texas, raised on horse ranch.

EUGENE HARRISON, Private First Class, one stripe, Buddy of Trinko, both accomplished in picking locks, breaking into places not for profit, but simply being curious.

RON JEFFERSON, Corporal (two stripes), medic, significant E.M.T. training. Was facing charges of insubordination to an officer, a doctor with the rank of Major. Ron knew more about emergency procedures than the doctor, and to the delight of his fellow suffering enlisted men, called the doctor a "Horse's Ass" to his face and proved him wrong!

JOSE GONZALEZ, Corporal, two stripes, degrees in computers and electronics. Charged with hacking into highly restricted systems.

HERALD GOLDSMITH, Corporal, Joe's unofficial accountant who not only spoke great Spanish, but also Hebrew, French and a little Polish.

LEROY JOHNSTONE, Sergeant, three stripes, expert shot and could repair any gun he ever saw. Several gunsmiths and Master Sergeants in charge of gun-ranges did not like being told to their face what they were teaching was unconditionally wrong.

Note: the above three considered themselves the "token minorities" and the only thing that kept them in control and quiet was the threat of a court martial. Unspoken, but deeply felt was the later enjoyment and sense of belonging they felt with Joseph's group.

The above enlisted men had been in significant trouble in the Army. All had unique abilities such as lock picking, and an ability to break and enter nearly every secured building (stealing nothing). They were mostly guilty of being where they had no right to be with unproved allegations of burglaries, trespassing, excited violations of security restrictions, insubordinate demeanor, general inability to conform to Army nitpicking rules and regulations, etc. They were given the choice of being court martialed or joining Col. Devonshire's outfit under the direct and only command of Joseph Robinson, a civilian, and Sergeant Morris.

JANE OSTMARK, Major, United States Army, pilot of C-130s, blonde, very attractive.

PAUL WEAVER, Capt. United States Army, co-pilot of C-130s, accomplished chef.

Dr. SAMUEL ICRONIFF, PHDs in Astrophysics and Astronomy.

Dr. RUDOLPH SAMUELSON, PHDs in Inorganic Chemistry and Cosmology, Both with genius level I.Q.s.

CHAPTER ONE

The vacant, deserted, one-story house, with its equally poor, lonely, and totally neglected neighbors waited for someone to take them out of their misery. One moonless night, four vans full of 2-kilogram packages, arrived with lights out to the house's back-side two car garage. A garage door was lifted, six guards were posted, and nearly two tons of packages were quickly and quietly unloaded into the garage. When the door was closed and securely locked, guards left, knowing that no one would think or believe that the items were stored in such a destitute location. Both vans and the guards disappeared down the street.

Unseen eyes calmly watched the unloading. Two clicks, then three clicks, and finally, four clicks. Soon, five masked men dressed totally in black, quietly approached the front of the house, picked the locks, and made their way to the garage. They spread twenty-two pounds of C-4 and twenty pounds of white phosphorus with two detonators over the packages and a single detonator with two pounds C-4 in the interior of the lonely house. Two clicks and then four clicks; they disappeared too.

After a 30-minute delay, unseen eyes quietly opened a small box, flipped two switches, and pressed two red buttons. The deserted one-story house exploded with the garage roof disintegrating up and then downward, adding fuel to the violent fire burning below. After 20 minutes, the entire house totally collapsed within itself-destroying the huge supply of cocaine with a street value of millions of dollars. Satisfied, the unseen eyes also disappeared!

TWO YEARS LATER, EARLY SPRING, SOUTHERN CALIFORNIA

"Would somebody locate Mr. Robinson and have him report to me, now!" Colonel Regional Devonshirk, III, United States Army, Special Units Division, yelled from behind his desk as he slammed down the phone.

"Yes Sir," Sergeant Dean Morris replied from the front office.

"Anyone know where Mr. Robinson went?"

"Sure, Sergeant, he's over at the computer center helping them to get the system hooked up with the military computers."

"Swanson, go get him. The Colonel wants him. Pronto."

"Sergeant Morris, when he gets here, think about rounding up your men. We'll have something for you," ordered Colonel Devonshirk.

Private First-Class Alvin Swanson, five feet, five inches, crewcut brown hair, and weighing only one-hundred-forty-five pounds from running five miles a day, barely breathing heavy from the half mile run to the unit's computer center, burst through the pressurized front door.

"Mr. Robinson, the Colonel wants you right now."

"OK, run back and tell the Coronel I'll be right there, please."

Joseph turned to Jose Gonzalez, a five foot, six inches, black hair, with dark eyes, clearly an East L.A Mexican of one-hundred-fifty pounds with his required tattoos, "This is a good setup, agree?"

"Yes Sir! Plus, it gives us access to a whole series of Internet information for sneaking into C.P.A.s and bookkeepers' records because you know that drug cartels and others need to keep track of their money."

Jose didn't know that about four months ago, Sergeant Dean Morris had approached Joseph after being told that Jose and his family were living in a one room shack. The Army, in an unusual fit of efficiency, had allowed Jose to keep his stripes, but fined him most of his Army salary. Apparently, Jose's wife was out begging for food because there was no money coming in for the family.

Joseph had shaken his head, "He is one of ours, we can't have that!"

Joseph thought for a moment, "I have an idea, first, take this, I only have three hundred dollars on me, do you know Jose's wife?"

"Sure, that will help a little. Then what?"

"We are planning on hitting that narcotics house near Interstate 15, just north of San Diego, either tomorrow night or the next night. It is supposed to hold a large amount of cocaine, and if so, they always have a lot of cash. What do you think of us first grabbing as much of that cash as we can, and then, destroying the place?"

"OK, but we can't just give them the cash. Jose is too proud of a man to accept that."

"I thought you knew me better than that. I need to make a phone call. Then, we'll UPS or FED EX the boxes of cash to a church in Santa Fe, New Mexico. Remember, they don't have to account to the IRS where and when they receive money. Then the church will purchase stock of certain corporations. You and I, as employees or subcontractors of such will receive credit cards of quite high value.

Seeing Dean Morris' look of astonishment, Joseph continued "Oh. Didn't I tell you that you had another employer?"

Dean stood there, his head shaking.

"Don't you remember?" asked Joseph. "I had your taxes done last year and you signed the tax return. Didn't you read your tax return? All income, taxes and deductions were legally accounted for. There is a small retirement program set up for you, too.

In about a week, we'll receive the credit cards and then go shopping for Jose and his family. We will need to find a better place for them to live and probably furnish most, if not all of it. To change the subject, the three cars we have, all used, will have to go. We've used them in too many assignments. I'm thinking of two old SUVs and maybe a van of some kind in good condition."

"My God, Joe! You never told me all stuff."

"Well, true; however, during our first conversation that seems a long time ago, I told you and our guys that I wanted and we were a 'one-for-all and all-for-one' secret group. You remember our first 'assignment' where we collected a large award? A couple of guys really needed money to pay off nasty debts and to support their families. I made sure they got it! I took none of it except a little to buy that computer center. Well, now, Jose needs help and he will get it!"

Dean recalled the meeting that night where Joseph explained what they were doing. He explained that he wanted about three boxes of cash. Someone thought that handling heavy duty trash bags would be easier to handle and they could fill the boxes later.

At O-dark hundred, as practiced, seven armed guards were quietly captured, eyes and mouths duct taped, arms and legs zipped tied, and placed, not gently, on a ton-and-half truck parked at the location, driven nearly two miles away and dropped at a local police station. Most had arrest warrants anyway!

Three trash bags full of cash were thrown into the trunks of two cars. Explosives were triggered a block away; one narcotic dealer's house was destroyed!

Two credit cards arrived five days later at Joseph's post-office box. Joseph took Jose aside and told him, "Listen, just listen, we are going house-hunting for you and your family. I will not allow you or any of my men and their families to suffer because they are here. So, just go along, OK?"

Jose, surprised, simply nodded.

The men gathered Jose and Mrs. Gonzalez with their two little, cute, black-eyed boys and went house-hunting after Joseph explained what they would be doing.

The first was a dump where a few pounds of explosives would have improved it.

The second was a mansion which was rejected without even looking inside.

The third was about 1800 square feet, three bedrooms minus beds, a dining room minus table and chairs, the kitchen, minus a refrigerator, and a living room with a working fireplace, but no chairs or sofas. Next to the attached two-car garage was a laundry room minus the washer and dryer. The Gonzalez family wandered through the house and after the third tour, Dean saw Jose's wife's black eyes shining; she wanted it!

She approached Joe and touched his arm, "Sir, this is so beautiful, but, but we can't afford it."

Joseph took Jose and his wife aside. He told them, "OK, this is yours! The lease will be in your name with the payment being made by a church in Santa Fe, New Mexico. It will be paid in full before you move in, which will probably be tomorrow. I will try to arrange a two-year term which means you wouldn't have to worry about a house payment for two years. However, the water, gas, electricity and maybe telephone are your responsibility."

Mrs. Gonzalez just stood there, her mouth open, shaking, her eyes watering.

"Mrs. Gonzalez, what is your first name and what was your unmarried name?"

"Rosa. Rosa Maria Munoz," she stuttered, grabbing her husband.

"Rosa, put those orders for the utilities in your unmarried name; the lease will also be in your unmarried name or better yet, a sister or aunt with a different name. It would be better if they didn't know about it. It might be best if your sister or aunt live in Mexico, so no one knows where she is located. Is that OK? Jose, you know the reason why. Oh, by-the-way, you will be getting a raise from me/the group, so you'll be able to handle the bills."

Joe motioned to Dean, "Take a couple of guys, Rosa and Jose and the kids, and go down to Best Buy, Macy's, or a similar place, and get them a new refrigerator, and a washer and dryer. Have Rosa and Jose pick out new beds for the entire family, dressers, and a dining room with table and chairs, and whatever else they need. Buy some sheets and blankets for the beds, and a bunch of towels! Get the stores to deliver and set the stuff up as soon as possible, preferably tomorrow since we are paying for it now! The sellers will complain but if you threaten to cancel our entire sales, they will do it. With two little ones, the Gonzalez's need it as soon as possible. Can you think of anything else they could use?"

"Sure, how about a nice B-B-Q. Everybody else has one. I'll check with Home Depo. They have decent ones. And maybe a freezer for the garage. With two little boys, they will need one."

Trembling, Rosa looked at Joseph with tears from her eyes, "*Senior*

Joseph, why, why?" She gestured at the house as she clutched his arm and held her two boys with the other hand.

Joseph reached over and placed his hand on Jose's shoulder.

"This man, Rosa! That's why! You can be proud of him. I can't tell you what he does, and he and we can't either, but he is a very important member of our group. And we take care of our own!"

"Rosa, for both you and Jose, this is important! If someone asks who your landlord is, tell them he or she lives in Mexico and Jose handles all that. Jose, if someone is asking those kinds of questions, let me know immediately! Ok?"

"Dean, when that stuff is delivered, get the guys to help the Gonzalez family move from the old place. Let's make it easier for them-find a decent grocery store and fill up the kitchen with groceries."

"Joe, on behalf of our men, thank you!"

"Aw! You are welcome. You and I take care of our men!"

Joe didn't realize or think about the issue later, but his unit, and Dean Morris too, subconsciously felt that because of Joe's leadership, concern, and loyalty for his men, they would follow him anywhere!

On the way to see his Coronel, Joseph Robinson paused to talk to Alvin Swanson.

He knew that Al Swanson had received several nasty letters and a humiliating and skeptical phone call from his parents and a few family police officers who didn't believe, because he had been in MP custody for some time, that he had not been officially charged and convicted of various violations of the Uniform Code of Military Justice. It took a long letter from Mr. Robinson to calm their fears.

"Things are ok, now, Sir," replied Al Swanson. "They were impressed with what you had to say. Thank you very much, Sir."

P.F.C. Alvin Swanson, one of the first enlisted men assigned to the unit, remembered the second time he saw Mr. Robinson.

The first time was a personal interview in an unmarked office in some headquarters building on an Army base in Texas. After being handcuffed and escorted by two burley M.P.s from the pre-trial confinement barracks, where he was confined before being criminally charged for trespassing into top-secret areas (and getting caught!), to see a civilian with no name or form of identification. The questioning was hard and very personal.

The second time, the Colonel had introduced Mr. Robinson to the group and Al Swanson was still not impressed. He recalled the first two leaders, both second lieutenants of the group; the first couldn't find his rear end without it being written somewhere in a manual; and the second believed that strong military discipline with much spit and polish was how to run this unit. Al Swanson never knew that they were only very temporarily assigned to the Colonel. The men realized, however, that almost immediately after Mr. Robinson arrived, the two lieutenants were history.

Mr. Robinson showed up wearing what appeared to be rejects from the bargain basement in a Good Will store, and a floppy hippy hat. He carried a box full of Winchell's Donuts. The Colonel had walked in, called "Attention" and stated, "Mr. Robinson is a civilian and your new leader."

At that, the Colonel turned and walked out. Mr. Robinson looked at "his" men, all dressed in the general Army Combat Uniform (ACU) most having a digital camouflage pattern, known as the Universal Camouflage Pattern (UCP).

Mr. Robinson's opening statements, "Good morning. Relax! Sit down. Help yourself to the donuts. If you don't, I will be forced to eat that whole dam box," raised questions in their mind.

He sat on the desk at the front of a non-descriptive room in an equally non-descriptive building in a low-middle class part of Orange County, California, not far from the John Wayne Airport.

"All right, I am not of the military, and you do not salute me, the Colonel, yes, but not me. Also, we're getting a Sergeant named Dean Morris. He is at least a Staff Sergeant or probably higher. Importantly, he and I do not care what you wear or how polished your brass is. He and I both agree that the only clean and highly working things are your weapons. I will do whatever I can to supply you with the best possible weapons and the training thereof. However, they are defensive weapons only, we will not invade a county or city and blow up everything.

But" he grinned, "We will have the most fun when we blow certain bad things up, including buildings, and probably do away with bad guys."

Mr. Robinson bit into a donut. "I have met each of you, reviewed each of your personal records, read the various actual, planned, and a few trumped-up charges against you and know why you are here and not in a state, federal or military prison!"

There was absolute silence from the men in the room.

"I have some bad news and some good news. First, the bad news, for most, if not all of you, according to the U.S. Army, this is your last chance! Each of you don't know why you're here and not in a jail or prison someplace. I and Sergeant Morris have specifically selected each of you. That, gentlemen, is the last time we will talk about your history.

The silence continued-seemingly waiting for the ax to fall!

"Now, for the good news, this is your chance to do something worthwhile for our country. Sergeant Morris and I believe that you are just like the Sergeant and me; in other words, regardless of your criminal charges, each of you is intensively patriotic! You, we, love our country! There is better news. After a certain time with us, your criminal history will be forgotten, period."

"Do you understand what I just said?"

He received surprised nods from the group--the ax fading away.

"We, gentlemen, are a unique unit. There is no other unit like us in the entire American military organization. We will be doing things that are certainly barely legal," he grinned, "probably totally illegal, but could be fun. But and this is a big but, what we will be accomplishing is unquestionably needed for our country. We will bring down bad situations and worse people that hurt our country and the people we protect."

Mr. Robinson paused; he had the undivided attention of the entire unit.

"Now, what am I talking about? As you may or may not know, one of the biggest problems facing our county, and more precisely, our fellow citizens, including our military, is drugs. I'm not talking about marijuana, which may become somewhat legal in most states. What I'm referring to is cocaine, heroin, methamphetamine, and a whole bunch of newly manufactured drugs, none of which has any medical value. A newer stimulant drug is Khat which was originally grown in East Africa, but now is generally banned in the U.S. and U.K. Most of these drugs come from Mexico, Columbia, Peru, China, and several other foreign countries. The so-called U.S. War Against Drugs has been a huge economic and social failure. Many upper-echelon people consider it a joke! We-you are not interested in the low-level user or pusher; that we leave to the local police department."

Mr. Robinson paused to bite into his donut.

"I need to give you a little background. The FBI and DEA, in their fight against drugs, developed a three-level process. The first level is source; where the dope comes from, in other words, Peru, Columbia and Mexico, China, and others. Apparently, the FBI, DEA, CIA, or other types of secret units, have experts or undercover people in each level. The second is transit, how does the narcotics get to their destination or in other words, to here in the U.S. The third is consumption. We in the United States have the horrible history of purchasing almost all the narcotics the drug cartels and others make. Do you understand so far?"

Upon receiving nods, he continued, "However, here is where we come in-each manufacturer and/or upper-level dealer of drugs, including drug cartels, must, repeat, must deal in significantly large quantities to make their business profitable. And therefore, each must have some way of transporting or smuggling their products into our country. They also must find a place to store that stuff. There have been estimates that more than thirty metric tons of cocaine are illegally transferred into the U.S. each year! Interesting word: illegal. I don't know of any cocaine legally transported into my and our county. Methamphetamine, smuggled into our county by the thousands of pounds, is worse. Several billion dollars are lost in America and sent to the drug people in the various foreign countries."

Joseph paused, "Men, one of the worst drugs all around us is fentanyl! It is so potent, so dangerous that a teaspoon of the drug will kill blocks of people! It is quite cheap and apparently quite easy to make and becomes attached to legitimate medications that nearly every cartel is delivering to America. Around 5722 people died in 2021 because of this drug. It was estimated that about 230 California kids, ages 14-16 died in the same year from the drug. If I receive information that there will be fentanyl in our "locations," we/you will be double masked, double gloved, and will not touch the containers. We will be sure to put phosphorus on/near the containers. We will discard the masks and gloves and if necessary, outer clothes if we must touch the stuff to protect all of us."

Private Jose Gonzales blurted, "My favorite cousin, Delores OD ed on some narcotic about six months ago. She had a needle still in her arm when they found her body." He choked back a sob, "There was nothing I could do to help her." Supporting hands from several members of the group grabbed his shoulders to show support.

Joseph Robinson nodded, he had known of Jose's cousin's death, but he could not and would not divulge that information.

He paused, "Gentlemen, between other assignments, our task, our duty, is to destroy those storage places with all of the narcotics in them!"

Mr. Robinson hesitated for a moment; he could sense the heightened interest in his group, a feeling of potential accomplishment other than the horrible, certain future that each had personally faced. And as important to Joseph Robinson, a developing feeling of togetherness! He looked at his specially chosen men: Spencer Gerry, Alvin Swanson, Thomas Trinko, Robert Jones, Ron Flannery, Samuel Kleighorn, Eugene Harrison, Ron Johnson, Jose Gonzales, Harold Goldsmith, and LeRoy Johnstone.

"Each of you has some, let us say, unique, talents that we will use. I had the final say in choosing each one of you and I know what you can and can't do.

Two of you are experts in explosives and I know your prior accomplishments. We will probably use C-4 and white phosphorus with wireless detonators. A couple of you can pick any locks around. A couple of you can secretly sever, hack, or override electric alarms wherever they are. And some of you can walk very quietly, or in other words, can sneak past guards. One last thing, we will practice disabling guards and removing them because we don't want to blow them up with the building."

Mr. Robinson paused for a second and smiled, "Plus most of the guards are wanted by our law enforcement and officers look very favorably to having a bunch of wanted individuals dumped on their front lawn or steps."

One man whispered to another, "This is going to be interesting!"

Mr. Robinson continued, "Finally, you heard me say 'we.' I mean that! I will tell you everything I can about our assignments and Sergeant Morris and I will solicit your input on what, how, and when we accomplish that task. Neither Sergeant Morris nor I will B.S. you! If your suggestions make sense, we'll do it your way. If you all believe we cannot accomplish our mission, we will decline the assignment. I don't care what some higher-ranking nitwit demands, if you say no, that is it! Note that what we will do are requests, assignments are the wrong word because we have the right to reject the requests, and as importantly, we will not do orders! The interesting part is that no-one, no-one knows of us, who we are, where we are, and what we can or refuse to do!"

"By the way, the Chain of Command is Sergeant Morris, and then me. While the Colonel gives us most of the assignments or requests, the Sergeant and I are it. Notice the word: requests. They are not orders that we must obey. I want, demand (!) that we work together as a team to solve the problem. If we cannot accomplish it or don't want to do it, we simply will not do whatever it is. Just to make my point clear, the decision is up to us, no one else!"

Mr. Robinson bit into a second fruit-filled donut. "Ahhh! As you know, each of you signed a non-disclosure, high security agreement. We/you will <u>not</u>, repeat not, talk about what we have done or are about to do to anyone else without my express permission. Ever! Do you understand?"

Sergeant LeRoy Johnstone rose, "Sir, permission to speak?"

"LeRoy let's get two things straight: first, sit down! You don't need to stand when I enter the room. Second, none of you will ever need to ask permission to speak."

"Sit down, I said!"

Leroy sat.

"What was your question?"

"Sir, why us? It seems to me that the various specialty units of the Army, or the Navy such as Seal Team Six, or Seven or whatever they're called, or the Marines or the Air Force or someone might be more qualified?"

"Good question. Because of what you are or were. All these other units crave publicity and occasionally their feats are documented in films or other media. Plus, each of the regular military is top-heavy with brass, each of whom crave seeing their faces on tv. As for us, the assignments, note I did not say orders, are requests that may not, will not, and cannot be publicized because how we handle such requests will be illegal and unconstitutional as hell. But we help get rid of the horrible drugs invading our country. And do you want to know the best part of what we accomplish?"

The entire group nodded.

Joseph grinned, "The enemy doesn't know anything about us; they will think and believe that their competition blew up and destroyed their storage places and maybe kidnapped their employees. So, we get them fighting between or among themselves much more than they do now. Remember, there are no written or documented records kept about what we are doing. Your personal records are kept in a totally different location. The person in charge of your personal records will, if necessary, testify under oath that he/she knows nothing about such records, and then, they both will disappear. So, that is why you don't talk to anyone, repeat: anyone, about what we have done, or are doing in person or especially on the phone. You do not, repeat Not, talk to your wife, girlfriend, or both, or your family, about what we have done or are presently involved in. If someone really presses you, tell them that we are assigned a top-secret survey of the Army on several different supply topics which you cannot tell anyone about, period."

"But, if someone starts asking any of you questions, I want to know about it immediately. Understand?"

"Also, if you see the same car or truck going by more than once, let me know immediately. Got it?"

After receiving nods, Joseph Robinson paused for a moment, thinking: *"I've got to tell them."*

"Gentlemen, there are only three people in the entire United States military and civilian hierarchies who know the entire structure of us. No one else knows who we are, where we are located or what our duties are. Remember each of you flew into the John Wayne airport in civilian clothes and then disappeared. Our so-called sources don't know how or when or with what we accomplish their requests, note-not orders, just that eventually something happens. And Top-Secret information flows through or near them and always, information is given orally to us. Remember, nothing in writing! Understand?"

Nods.

"One final point. If you are going to write a letter to anyone, including your parents, or whomever, I'm not censoring your letters, but give your sealed envelope to Sergeant Morris and they will be postmarked by a post office in Denver, Colorado. Do not, ever, tell anyone where you are stationed. If someone asks you, I suggest that you tell them that you are in one of those jobs which requires a lot of traveling, and then, change the subject.

Upon receiving agreement, Joseph continued, "If someone asks you who you are and/or what you are doing or where you are assigned, you know nothing! There is no appeal, no Article 15, no summary court, or general court proceedings or whatever for doing so, except me. If I even think you are talking to someone about what we have done or are about to do, that conversation could harm or even kill members of our group. Our assignments, or missions are too important, too sensitive, to allow any publicity. And my decision for the sake of the other members of the team is final, period."

Joseph continued, "One last issue. If you're sitting a restaurant or bar some place and a young, good-looking blonde with large baskets that she is advertising but not willing to sell, or touch, and she says, "Oh my goodness, you are the most handsome man I've ever seen!"

Two points: one: We are not that handsome!"

He didn't smile. "And two: Let either me or Sergeant Morris know the approach immediately! And stop the conversation as soon as possible and exit the bar, restaurant or wherever you are."

"Any questions?"

Coldly, his brown eyes caressed the group as he fondled 9 .mm automatic on his belt they hadn't noticed before."

His point was made. "Let's take a little break. Eat the dam donuts! I've got a few photos to show you about our enemy."

After a few moments, Joe said, "OK, grab a donut and gather around me. I want to show you a few photos and maps showing where the drugs came and come from."

Joe pointed, "This map is possibly two years old map of Mexico essentially showing the locations of the major drug cartels. Keep in mind that these locations change almost monthly based upon who is trying to claim someone else's territory. And these are not friendly "claims." These are fought with deadly consequences, not single killings, not tens of killings, but frequently hundreds of killings including innocent citizens. All for control of narcotics!"

"Will we be going into Mexico?" asked Jose Gonzalez.

"Maybe only once in a while, but most of our time will be spent in the U.S." Joe smiled, "Some of you guys simply don't look like a Mexican and I wouldn't, and we wouldn't, take that chance."

The group looked around, one was very black, several were very white, even in a uniform, two looked like cowboys, a few looked Mexican and one even looked middle Easterner.

Joe continued, pointing, "The top part of Mexico from essentially Tijuana to about halfway between Nogales and El Paso is, or was, where most of the narcotics came from, Jose. My contacts told me that Sinaloa and Los Zetas are probably the two most dangerous cartels in Mexico, today! However, I heard a rumor that a group coming up out of Baja, California, is attempting to control that part of Sinaloa's territory, but how successful they are or will be, no one seems to know. It may be that the best our country can do is count the bodies. I don't know anything else about that fight. Anyway, from just East of El Paso going south to the border of the Mexican state of Coahuila is or was the Juarez Cartel's territory. Continuing South," Joe pointed, "is the

Los Zetas area, which has extended part by part into lower Mexico as they take over smaller cartels. On the gulf is or was the Gulf Cartel."

Joe moved to the West side of Mexico, "Down here, Cartel Jalisco Nueva Generation which may or may not have combined with the Templar Knights. Keep in mind, guys, that there is a huge amount of money at stake here. Some of these cartels have developed international agreements and receive and develop pipelines through Mexico to the U.S. Please keep in mind that these cartels change almost monthly."

"That's it for today, men. Either tonight or tomorrow you will meet our new Sergeant. See you then."

Private Swanson also never forgot the first time he met Sergeant Dean Morris. He was the hardest and nastiest looking Non- Commissioned Officer Swanson ever met. There didn't appear to be a friendly bone in his body. His face looked like it would break if it smiled. When he growled, his voice would terrorize a rock crusher. His voice sounded like two gravel trucks mating in a closet.

Swanson recalled the saying, "He looked like he could chew nails." Wrong, this N.C.O. looked like he made nails, not bothering to chew them! Swanson didn't know this N.C.O. routinely did 60 plus pushups every morning, half on his fingers before his warm-up run of five miles! This five-foot-ten-inch crew-cut, brown haired, 175 pounds of all muscle, simply radiated power, and potential meanness.

Sergeant Morris' opening words were something else he never forgot, "I will be your Sergeant. I am not your girlfriend, your wife, your sister, or your mother, so, don't try to screw me. If you do what Mr. Robinson and/or I ask you to do, note I said ask, your future will be interesting and rewarding."

"Mr. Robinson and I will train and practice with you on how to silently enter a house or room, how to tape a suspect's mouth and eyes shut, how to handle and tie up his body, how to place explosives, and in other words, get in, get it, get out, and blow it up with the bad guys never knowing we were ever there. We will practice shooting out in the desert, but that is defensive shooting only, stealth and sneakiness is the word! If you do not perform what we asked, keeping in mind that you will have an input in our assignments and how we accomplish them, and if you refuse to cooperate," at that, Sergeant Morris drew his 9 mm. handgun, racked a cartridge into the firing chamber, and raised it to his lips, and said, "Don't worry baby, you will not have to work today."

"Any questions?"

Everyone in the room knew, knew, with fear in their stomachs, precisely what Sergeant Morris meant. Each were also very aware that they could have gone back to their original base/camp/or whatever and face a certain several decades in Leavenworth or some other hellhole!

Alvin Swanson fondly remembered their first "assignment," one of many. They received word, via the Colonel, that a certain individual was wanted by the F.B.I., and a ton of city police and sheriffs' departments, for multiple alleged, but not proved, murders, assaults, and other felonies.

Somebody said, "This guy is a real rat!"

Joseph Robinson replied, "Oh no! Don't insult rats, they are better than this guy."

The problem, however, was that intelligence said this person was hiding in a house in East Tijuana, Mexico. And that the Mexican government was refusing to extradite or release him to the American authorities. Apparently, a lot of money exchanged hands in Mexico.

Mr. Robinson told the unit a major court case held the U.S. Courts didn't care *how* the defendant came to the courts, just that he was there and that was that. He said, as an example, that some wanted suspect was kidnapped in Mexico, blindfolded, gagged, taken to an airport, and thrown on a plane. Upon landing in the Miami airport, he was dumped on the runaway, dazed, where the FBI captured him. No one believed or were concerned about his and his attorneys' continual complaints he had been kidnapped in Mexico. The judge commented, "That is out of our jurisdiction; take it up with the Mexican authorities." And of course, Mexico cooperated by denying any knowledge of the suspect.

Mr. Robinson obtained wireless communication devices for each of the group. He told his men that they could not talk over the "net" because much of what they were going to do required absolute stealth and quiet; if someone was talking, maybe the culprits could hear them. They developed and practiced a system of clicks: one click-at the location and entering, two clicks-guards were in custody or disabled (usually by duct tape), three clicks-inside, and four clicks-suspect in custody or explosives set. Four clicks and an immediate four clicks-come and get us. One long click meant help!

Mr. Robinson emphasized that under no circumstance was anyone to touch the duct tape with their bare hands or skin. In other words, no fingerprints or DNA traceable to them. The result was that each person was given dual surgical gloves to wear on an assignment. And nothing was to be left at any location except the duct tape attached to a low life. Or sometimes, a little something, maybe a match book that could lead to a different cartel. And most importantly, no voice or talking within our group and no talking ever to the suspects or guards.

Al Swanson remembered that after much discussion and planning, they had simply driven into Mexico and found the house. Before that, however, during the planning stage, Sergeant Morris surprised both Al Swanson and his buddy, PFC Spenser Gerry, when he asked them what they thought and how they would accomplish the assignment. They thought for a moment and suggested that they both act as armed lookouts across the street and if necessary, back-ups if the capture didn't go as planned. Both PFCs were even more surprised that Sergeant Morris agreed with their thinking and complemented them. That was the first time anyone in the Army said something nice and agreeable to them!

That night at "oh-dark hundred," after crossing the border, and hiding in an alley, each of the group changed clothes: dark sweaters covering bullet-proof vests, dark pants containing extra magazines for their 9 .mm Glocks, black ski masks covering faces, black single soled tennis shoes with black socks, some pockets containing lock-picking tools or duct-tape, two had Taser equipment, each belt held a K-Bar knife, and perhaps more importantly, two of the men carried hypodermic syringes loaded with a fast acting sedative.

In Mexico, across the street from the suspect's house, Swanson and Gerry split and acted as lookouts in case anything went wrong. Each carrying a silenced M-16 with night scopes.

Robert Jones, Private Second Class, (one click), very quietly "picked" the lock on a side door and slowly opened it. With hearts pounding, six of the group quietly captured two sleeping guards, tied and duct-taped their mouths and eyes, hands, and feet, as practiced! Both guards were duct-taped together with perhaps excessive amounts of tape. (two clicks). Leaving one to control the guards, the remaining five slithered into a bedroom, tranquilized the sleeping suspect, duct-taped his mouth, eyes, hands, and legs, made sure they had the right suspect, and four clicks.

He was carried outside and dumped into the trunk of a waiting car being driven by a grinning Mr. Robinson with Sergeant Morris in a second car behind him. Swanson and Gerry were collected, and they all returned to an alley. The group made a quick stop to change clothing and wipe their faces; they couldn't even attempt to cross the border looking like bandits.

Then said suspect, safely unconscious in a trunk of Mr. Robinson's car, was taken across the border and dropped on the front steps of the local F.B.I office on Vista Sorrento Parkway in San Diego, California. His wanted posters were taped to his chest- if the office didn't know who he was. After banging on the front door, the group retreated to make sure someone opened the door and found the suspect. Joseph Robinson confirmed in an anonymous phone call that the F.B.I. had the suspect in custody but that the F.B.I did not know, or care, how he got there, he was simply there!

The celebration of the retrieval was heady and solidified the unit. To add frosting to the celebration, in three days, Mr. Robinson obtained and divided the reward money with the unit which helped pay off some heavy personal debts and helped a few needy families. The rest went into purchasing a very sophisticated computer system by Mr. Robinson, Jose Gonzalez, and Corporal Herald Goldsmith, Mr. Robinson's accountant.

Private Swanson, not for the first time, admired the four nearly incomprehensible consoles in the computer center. There were enough dials, buttons, switches, knobs, blinking lights, disk drives and levers to give a 747 pilot an erection. He had heard that they could talk to any police agency in the free world including most officers in the street, and that they could talk to any airplane in the air anywhere in the world. Joseph told the group that the Los Angeles County Sheriff's Department's central radio room was even more sophisticated.

Swanson knew, but could not and would not talk about the source of the funds paying for Joe's center.

About twenty minutes later after the summons, Joseph David Robinson strolled into Colonel Reginald Devonshire's office, wearing the traditional army uniform, without insignia, and plopped his just over six-foot frame in a chair. He took off his battered Angel baseball cap and brushed back his crew-cut brown hair. He looked around the intentionally non-descriptive office on an equally boring office building next door to a vacant Air Force recruiting office.

The only furniture in the front room was three empty secretaries' desks and a half-dozen beat-up chairs. The front office was usually manned by part of the group when they weren't in an assignment or training. Both rooms were surprisingly very clean with polished floor and no dust anywhere. The front windows were intentionally left very dirty and covered with various pieces of newspaper so no one court see inside! Joseph smiled; his men were finding something to do between assignments.

The Colonel's office held a decrepit desk with a highly sophisticated phone system, a powerful computer, no printer, and a large circular table with fourteen equally dilapidated chairs. No fax machine was needed because both the Colonel and Joseph Robinson believed this unit should have no paper records, period. A seldom-used shredding machine was on the side of the desk.

On a small table was the Colonel's *de rigueur* coffee pot. The odor of his personal combination of extra strong and well-boiled heavy Columbian and Costa Rican mixture with some military rotgut nearly undrinkable coffee permeated the room.

Joseph remembered the first, and only, time he tried to drink a half-cup of the Colonel's coffee. He swore that the coffee hit the bottom of his cup with a kerplunk. It tasted like a combination of rejects from the county's sewer system and battery acid; never-the-less, the Colonel happily drank at least several cups a day, stating, "This puts hair on your chest!" Joseph thought that the Colonel's stomach was made of cast-iron to even smell the stuff, and it would probably put hair on his shoes!

Joseph's men refused to touch the stuff!

Joseph also knew that the reason the Coronal hated drugs and the drug cartels was that he lost part of his right leg in the dirty desert of Iraq while chasing suspects involved in drug transportation.

Joseph recalled the effort involved in concealing the purpose of the office and leasing an entire enclosed floor of a neighboring apartment building with ten separate units by a Captain from Kirkland Air Force Base. Joseph was told that the building and office were leased by a corporation in Nevada which was owned by three other corporations, each in a different state. Three older used cars with California plates registered to the corporations made up their local transportation needs. All any citizen ever saw was an occasional Army person walking by who usually was not very friendly. Food was a neighbor Denny's, drive ins, or more frequently, cooked in one of the men's kitchens.

"You wanted me, boss?"

His first meeting with this Colonel crossed his mind. More than two years ago, he had been summoned from his no-future graveyard security job at a Southern California drug company to a meeting in a Hilton hotel room with no number on it. After introducing himself in his Class A uniform complete with seven rows of ribbons including a Silver Star, a Bronze Star, and a Purple Heart, the Colonel told him, "Mr. Joseph David Robinson, we have searched for and researched over 1500 people, and you came out as most interesting. Do you know a Mr. Sam Restig?"

"Why, yes Sir. He's my supervisor where I work; I think he is a retired military officer."

"I've known him a very long time. He strongly suggested that I talk to you."

Surprised, Joseph Robinson nodded, but said nothing.

After a moment of silence, Colonel Devonshirk took a deep breath and went on, "We have an offer for you. If you decline our proposition, this conversation never took place, this room has no recording devices of any kind, we never heard of you and that is it. If you talk to anyone, repeat anyone, about our offer, you will be branded a kook and treated as such. If you insist on going by "the book," this meeting is over! That's the bad news. The good news is that I have a most interesting job proposal for you. Oh yes, are you happy bring a futureless simple guard?"

"Absolutely not, Sir. However, Mr. Restig is a very interesting supervisor."

"This position, Mr. Robinson, is so classified that it does not exist on any paper. Your background investigation shows that you can keep your mouth shut, that you take a promise of confidentiality seriously, and that you are fiercely patriotic. We know as much as possible about you, including your so-called criminal background. In my opinion, what you did in nearly killing your nude wife in bed with the next-door neighbor shows a certain degree of humanity. We also know that you are currently not involved with anyone else."

He paused for a moment, waiting for a response.

Surprised, Joseph Robinson made no comments, his face expressionless. He had heard from friends that someone was asking questions about him but didn't know anything else.

The Colonel smiled and continued, "In addition, you show leadership qualities that we/I need. Your Mr. Restig was impressed with the way you straightened out and ran his security outfit. Now, the position entails that you lead a group of men whom you will select. Each man has, shall we say, a highly checkered past and all are facing heavy court martial charges with considerable prison time. Each one has unique abilities, usually involved in sneaking into and out of places where they are prohibited or doing things that while not harmful, are certainly illegal. Two of them are certified lock-pickers, two others are explosive experts, and most are very good with a rifle."

The Colonel paused for a response, but Joseph simply nodded.

"Periodically, you and your men will be tasked to perform probably illegal and normally unconstitutional assignments that are frequently highly dangerous. However, no other unit in the U.S. will be able to do what I ask you to do and importantly, you will certainly help our country and our citizens. All I can promise your men is an ultimate reward of a very clean record."

Joseph thought for about a minute which seemed much longer, his face could hardly contain his excitement, "Sir, I've read a lot of fiction books that have as their foundation a unit such as the one you are talking about, but is this the real thing?"

Colonel Reginald Devonshirk simply nodded once.

"Sir, a question, is this involved with fighting terrorists?"

A single shake of the head, "Generally, not you."

Joseph had a sudden thought and gave voice: "Sir, another question, exactly how well do you know Mr. Restig? He told me there were a few times wherein someone saved his life in Iraq, and in other conflicts, and vice versa, and he wholly trusted that person."

Then an epiphany hit Joseph, "*Was Mr. Restig training him for this job?*" He gave voice to the thought.

Again, Colonel Reginald Devonshirk slightly smiled, surprised, thinking "H*e was not supposed to know about the secret training,*" simply nodded once.

Joseph took a deep breath, thinking fiercely. "Sir, I have four questions. Number One, how much equipment or support can I count on or in other words, how much explosives, weapons, transportation, etc., will be available? Number two, do I have any help in leading this bunch or in other words, some NCO or such? Number three, location or where are we stationed? And Number four, chain of command, it must be an NCO or whatever, and the chain stops with me. Respectfully Sir, I remember Mr. Restig quietly, but strongly teaching that I must have absolute authority to either perform or decline an assignment if this job is what I think it is. If I, we, you, will be second guessed by some Monday morning nitwit, whatever rank, I'm out. My supervisor, Sam, in a few of his many war stories and our discussions, warned me about that, I guess the words are plausible deniability by anyone in Washington, D.C., if something goes wrong. Also, I am assuming that we'll get paid through third parties somehow."

Surprised, and pleased at the quick positive response, Colonel Devonshirk knowing he had the authority, responded, "OK, one: whatever equipment, or support in the way of supplies, explosives, weapons, and transportation will be arranged on a priority basis. You ask for it, I'll get it."

He paused for a second, "two: I have an NCO named Dean Morris.

He has been around, managed to irate a few of his former inflexible nitwits- I love that definition- Captains, and essentially takes no crap from anyone. He is tough, despises paperwork and 'informally' handles disciple issues. In other words, he takes his stripes off, and beats the stuffing out of a subordinate until he behaves. I would like you two to meet and see if you can work together. By the way, your decision on him is final, I will not force anyone on you. If you two get along, you and he will pick your men, and again, your decisions are final.

Three: Your station will be near John Wayne Airport in Santa Ana, California, because you'll probably fly to your assignments. We don't have the actual location picked out, essentially waiting for you.

He paused again, looking sharply at Joseph, "And four: I don't understand your question on absolute authority."

Joseph, attempting not very successfully to conceal his excitement, explained, "Sir, if we're going to be doing what I think, I, and my men must have final authority on whether we can do an assignment or not. With Mr. Restig, I told my men everything I possibly could, and seek and honor their thinking and suggestions. I did that with my men on the front lines under Sam and it worked! I've researched and read of too many so-called assignments, duties and/or commands that go totally haywire because the lower person didn't understand the big picture and/or he/she didn't comprehend his duties or even if the order/command was doable. In some of his war-stories, my boss, or I guess former boss, Sam Restig warned me of the traditional Army lack of downward communication."

"Two final conditions, Sir, my sole chain of command is you and only you. Most importantly, since my men will probably be wanted in different states, camps or bases, our location must be top secret. Their records must be maintained outside of this location because no-one here has ever heard of them. Beards welcomed. These points, Sir, are deal breakers because I'm sure you know this unit cannot survive with any publicity!"

Coronel Devonshirk sat back in his chair thinking, his heart happily pounding: *"At last! Oh My God, Thank You! At Last!"*

He stood, smiled, and held out his hand, "Deal!" Joseph Robinson, excited, happily shook "his" Coronel's hand.

The rest was history!

Some two years and many "assignments" with a surprising number of destroyed drug houses and locations, later, "Yes, I've got something, something unusual for you," Colonel Devonshirk said, his eyes concerned behind half-moon reading glasses.

"Unusual? You mean there is something 'usual' about our office here?" Joseph Robinson thought for not the first time this squat Colonel was himself unusual because it took a special person to run his band of misfit and unique personalities. Joseph also knew this command was the last duty assignment for his Colonel. Age, a partially missing right leg (deposited on the dirty desert of Iraq) and a refusal to be a 'yes' man to his superiors did not engender him to the Army's superior brass or his chances for promotion.

Joe remembered that his Colonel never wore his uniform telling Joe, "I don't need my uniform to get my job done. My staff, including you, know who and what I am, and I don't want anyone else watching people saluting this old dude. So, no saluting!"

"Before we get into why I called you, here, look at this." He handed part of a San Diego newspaper showing photos of a severely burning house just south of the San Diego city limits. Two nights ago, it simply exploded. The reporter writing the article said that the firemen took a long time to control the blaze; it looked like something blew up inside and the huge amount of water didn't seem to help. The article mentioned several neighbors had warned police that the house was a narcotics location, but no one did anything.

"Good job, Joe! Any fatalities?"

"No sir. There were six guards, all captured and dumped about three blocks from the house." Joseph smiled, "My men only spoke Spanish and tried for a southern Mexican accent. I didn't even know there was such an accent. There was about a ton of cocaine and about a dozen wrapped and protected jars. I don't know what they contained. We used exactly thirty-nine pounds of white phosphorus and ten pounds of C-4. It was quite effective." He grinned, "The more water they poured on the house, the larger the fire. Also, one of my guys made a couple of book matches from a different cartel town and one of the books, minus a few matches, simply fell next to where we dropped the guards."

"Very nice touch!" Colonel Devonshirk said, "Well, the reason I called you is that this is strange. I received a request from General Fox via a General Douglas in our headquarters who received an appeal from the State Department by way of a rumor from the CIA."

"Really?" Joseph Robinson said as he brushed a heavily tanned hand over his crew cut hair. "I didn't know that the State Department talked to the CIA and am surprised that both even knew the mere mortals over in the Pentagon."

"Just listen for a second," Colonel Devonshirk said testily. "The State Department is requesting technical investigative help. One of their ambassadors to a Central American country and that government is apparently hysterical over some form of life. If I understand correctly, some natives saw a huge flash in the sky and then felt an impact as if something heavy hit the ground."

"A missile?" Joseph Robinson's clear shiny brown eyes narrowed.

"I don't believe so. No country, particularly the Russians or us, fired a missile anywhere near Central America during that time. The problem is that this site is about in the middle of the jungle. I've been told there is a small airstrip along a small river which is their main access to that area."

Colonel Devonshirk paused for a moment; his eyes lost in the memory of the startling telephone call. "The reason I need you to go down there is that the natives found a new form of life."

"A new form of life?" Joseph Robinson asked, his concentration narrowing on his boss, a rare flash of ice running up and down his spine.

"Yes. The local natives took the least of two evils and complained to the area authorities when that so-called life attacked their old John Deere tractor and primitive electrical generators."

"So what? Their engines probably polluted the hell out of the environment anyway."

"What I didn't tell you," Colonel Devonshirk said impatiently, "is that this life completely destroyed the natives' tractor engine and whatever they had for electrical generators. This same 'life' later followed, attacked and destroyed the vehicles that the local authorities rode in on."

Another shiver ran up and down Joseph Robinson's frame. "What do they want from us? And more importantly, are our 'cut-offs' in place? I don't want the whole world to know about us."

"They want someone to fly a couple of scientists down there to investigate that life form. This request was only by secure telephone and only oral. Only very few people know anything about this mission. And they only think "someone" is going to do this, certainly not who, when and from where! You and your men are to provide security to protect the scientists while they do their research."

"Why not just send the Air Force or Regular Army?"

"Because the State Department insists that this should be a civilian operation," Colonel Devonshirk said. "They will allow us to use the big C-130s with military personal as a crew, but no other military presence. If you remember, all these Central American countries have always been overly concerned about their sovereignty, particularly since the U.S. Congresses shortsighted Watergate, Contra gate, Iran gate, Trump gate, and all the other idiot political investigations. That is why you, a civilian leader, gives credence to the State Department demands. They don't know of you, or that you even exist, or anything about you and your men, just that they hope someone will go down there and figure out what happened."

"Am I in charge of this operation?" Joseph asked. He had learned the hard way if the State Department or any other governmental agency had direct control of any of his operations, some unknown and worst, unknowing expletive-deleted horse's rear- end would micromanage his every step, after notifying his favorite reporter. He remembered that he and his group had walked away from several requests because the referring persons demanded control and constant communication on what was being done and insisted on knowing when, how, who, etc.

Several "requests" never made it down to Joseph's group simply because "Joseph's group simply didn't exist!" In addition, in response to a phone call from some nosey reporter, the Coronel had "no idea" what the caller wanted and all he (the Coronel) knew was that he was semi-retired in a nothing supply position. Smiling, he told Joseph later that he continually asked if the caller wanted women's shoes which made the caller disconnect the call, swearing.

The first time that occurred, the Coronel had received a phone call from a reporter about an assignment or request he had just received. The Coronel knew nothing about whatever the reporter was talking about and refused to give any more information about his full name, assignment, and rank. The reporter refused to divulge his informant's name. The Coronal made a quick phone call to his General. Last the Coronel heard; a certain captain was reassigned to be second in charge only of a guardhouse on an Army base in Alaska. The assignment request for Joseph was cancelled.

The Coronel remembered that of the many houses tasked, there were four slightly different "Assignments" that came down to him, and his men rejected them! One was to check a whole block re: drug sales. That was refused because it belonged to local police. Two of the remaining had insufficient information. The last was rejected because the men felt that it seemed like a set-up or seemed suspicious: too much specific information about the locations; and the sources seemed distrustful or dubious!

"Once you get airborne and at the location, you'll have total command. I'll run interference for you here and help you obtain whatever supplies you need. "

Joseph Robinson thought for a second knowing that running interference meant just that: his Colonel would do everything possible to support him. He remembered a situation where he and his men blew up a house on a street in South Tucson that had held about three tons of cocaine and a few more tons of marijuana. The Colonel had commandeered two "black" (no identification on them) helicopters to retrieve Joseph and his men from being arrested by the local police and/or shot by the upset owners of the narcotics. Joseph remembered that both helicopters were on the ground for a total of seven seconds.

"Thank you, Colonel!" came from Joseph's men!

"Well, our people are all in the military, but I suppose they could go in civilian clothes. I'm going to insist, however, that they be allowed to carry their regular weapons including their M4A1s and so on. Where are the scientists that we must take along?"

"They are in-route and should be here by 0200 hours tomorrow."

"Tomorrow?"

"Yes, Tomorrow! I have a C-130 landing at John Wayne Airport at about 0300 hours tomorrow morning. You need to schedule your E.T.A. shortly after sunrise so that you'll have as much daylight as possible."

"A C-130 landing at 0300 hours! That will irritate the hell out of Southern Orange County and Newport Beach. You know they B.M.G. (Bitch, Moan, and Groan!) if a local dog barks. A C-130 landing and reversing its props will wake up all of Santa Ana and Fountain Valley."

"In a word: tough! It will land and take off before anyone can figure out what happened. The plan is that you meet two other C-130s in the Gulf of Mexico, and they will follow you. You and one other will land at that airstrip. That first plane will carry a couple of small old jeeps plus additional supplies. You'll need JATO (Jet Assisted Takeoff Rockets) to get out of there, but we'll keep one of the C-130's in the air as a cover."

"Jeeps?" Joseph asked. "Why not Humvees?"

"Good question. I was told that access to the area where the object landed is only by a small road or more of a trail that the natives use for their carts. The thinking is that a couple of small jeeps are better able to get through the jungle down there, and if something happens, you can leave them there without much of a loss. The Humvees are expensive."

"Typical. Some bean counter will get a promotion while my men going on a mission get old or used gear."

Accustomed to Joseph Robinson's sarcastic analysis, Colonel Devonshirk paused for a moment, "Joe, something about this mission concerns me. Not only is this being done so quickly, but it's also quite unusual for the powers-to-be to authorize the use of three C-130s. And landing one of them at 3 A.M. tells me that somebody is truly concerned, aka scared. Running those aircraft is expensive! It's not normal for the State Department to get excited over something like that life form. They prefer to talk something to death before they'll do anything. I've met the current ambassador down there and he is a cool, calm, almost unflappable diplomat. For him to become excited requires an extraordinary occurrence."

"Who is the ambassador?"

"Ambassador Lewston. Why?"

"Kirkcade Lewston?" Joseph asked.

"Why, yes, do you know him?"

"Not well, but I agree with your description of him. He's the only person I've heard of who keeps his black socks and bow tie on during sex," Joseph said.

"What!?"

Colonel Devonshirk glared at Joseph's wide innocent eyes. The thought crossed his mind: "*How the hell does he know that?*" The thought of "*No, don't ask! I don't want to know,*" made more sense. He had learned through around two years' experience and several harrowing situations that Joseph Robinson had strange and more importantly accurate sources of information.

He locked eyes with Joseph Robinson's deep brown eyes, "You be careful down there. Those people are scared! The State Department suggested that we take only one C-130, but after hearing the whole story, I insisted on three C-130's, hoping for two planes. It was informative when they didn't complain at all about the three planes."

Joseph Robinson was startled. This was a side of his white-haired hard-nosed boss dealing with the U.S. government he had hardly seen.

"I am planning to have you on the ground for only a day, Joe. Let's treat this mission as highly classified until we find out more. I don't care what the State Department says, you and your people take along enough supplies to last for at least a week or two, and whatever weapons you think you need to protect yourselves. I apologize for the short information and request, but I didn't think you and your guys needed much planning."

"No problem! All right, sir," Joseph Robinson nodded. "I'll get right on it, and we'll be ready."

After briefing Sergeant Dean Morris and the rest of his squad, Joseph was asked, "Sir, what weapons can we take with us? We can take the M-16s or the M4A1s we have been practicing with?"

"I think we should take the M4s. They only weigh about seven and three-quarter pounds not including their 20 rounds. Plus, we're going to a jungle area and the about 300-400 yards range should be sufficient. In addition, since the Army signed contacts with FN Herstal, they both will want to know how the weapons operated, assuming we ultimately use them. We will not tell them much, but we can give them a little information."

Joseph continued, "You guys take anything that you think you need but keep it undercover. And wear civilian clothes. You can easily hide the M4s under your clothes since they are only about 14 or 15 inches long. I can't see someone from the State Department getting his tuxedo dirty by inspecting that big load of food and drinks that you're going to need in all those sealed boxes. But when I inspect those boxes, we should have enough weapons and ammunition to invade a small country. Food and lots of water for a week, too, it's hot down there. Understand?"

Sergeant Dean Morris and his staff exchanged glances. This was something they enjoyed: right at the edge of legal. . .

Early the next morning, after getting Sergeant Morris and his men in civilian clothes, their equipment together and transported down to the John Wayne Airport flight-line, Joseph Robinson watched a graceful brown and green camouflaged C-130 Hercules float over the 405 freeway, land (reversing its pitch propellers and waking up the entire neighborhood), turn at the southern end and taxi back to them at the northern edge of the airport, passing lines of parked civilian planes.

"Don't look at the landing lights, you'll lose your night vision," Sergeant Morris warned. He could feel vibration from the two live propellers, two were shut down for taxiing purposes. Upon being waived to a stop by one of Sergeant Dean Morris' men waiving bright orange colored landing wands, the remaining rumbling engines shut down and the back door ponderously lowered itself.

"Anyone see our scientists?" Joseph asked.

"Yes Sir, they're coming now," Sergeant Morris pointed at a Humvee racing up the runway. As they crossed the landing lights of the C-130, they could see a man in the front right seat with a frayed sport jacket that once could only be charitably called loud. Thick glasses were being held precariously on his nose by a brown stained finger. Sitting stiffly in the back seat, wearing a three-piece dark wool suit was an elderly man with a mop of white unruly hair.

"Do you know who they are?" Joseph asked.

"Sure, the man with the coke-bottom glasses and goofy looking sports jacket is Doctor Isaac Icroniff from Jet Propulsion Lab up in Pasadena," Sergeant Morris said. "The other guy, I think, is Doctor Isabel Samualson from M.I.T. in Boston. He apparently was visiting Doctor Icroniff at J.P.L. when this all happened."

"Wait a second, I know of these men," Joseph said. "Doctor Icroniff is a famous physicist with heavy degrees in astrophysics and astronomy, if I remember correctly, Doctor Samualson has his degrees in astronomy, inorganic chemistry and in cosmology. I remember reading some of their materials, but most of their writings are beyond us normal humans."

Sergeant Morris glanced at Joseph Robinson with considerable respect in his eyes; his leader never failed to surprise him with the Jeopardy-like breath of his knowledge and that he knew these scientists.

Private Eugene Harrison who was standing near the Sergeant exclaimed, "Cosmology? Why do we need a beautician with us?"

"What are you talking about?" uttered Sergeant Morris, surprised.

"Sure, Sergeant, don't you know that a cosmologist is someone who cuts women's hair?" replied Eugene Harrison.

Sergeant Morris stared at his Private, disbelieving what he heard. "A cosmologist studies the universe, a cosmetologist cuts your hair. Didn't they teach you that in high school?"

Embarrassed, Private Harrison mumbled, "Well, I kind of didn't make it through high school. I'm sorry Sergeant."

"That's all right, Eugene. Now you know that these scientists are important. Why don't you join the rest of the crew loading stuff on the plane?" Joseph Robinson said.

"Ok, the rest of you, get those small forklifts and load our gear," Joseph Robinson ordered. "Remember, you're all civilians now."

"Oh, yes sir," Sergeant Morris said. "You know of course that all civilians clank when they walk, run five miles before breakfast, smell of gunpowder, and have strange bulges in their clothes."

"Well, I always knew that 'my civilians' were different anyway," Joseph chuckled.

As the men climbed into the back of the C-130, secured their equipment and boxes to the central tied downs, and sat in the canvas seats on the inside sides of the aircraft, Master Sergeant Thomas T. Westlund, the plane's loadmaster, asked, "Where are you guys going?"

"We're here to rescue you," Corporal (in civilian clothes) Roger Samson said.

"What?"

"Sure, didn't you get the word?"

"What the hell are you talking about?"

"Didn't they tell you, Sarge? You must be rescued. Aw crap, there's always someone who doesn't get the message."

The glare from the Master Sergeant would have intimidated any normal person in uniform, but his silence said he knew enough he would be told whatever he needed to know whenever he needed to know it. And he didn't know who this wise ass was.

While loading the men, their equipment, and supplies (which seemed to have doubled overnight) and the two scientists, Joseph and Sergeant Morris were approached by a blond-haired female in a faded green flight suit with gold major insignia on her shoulders and command pilot wings on her chest. Her flight suit did little to disguise her well-formed body.

"Dam!" mumbled Sergeant Morris to Joseph Robinson through his salute to her. "Why did she have to be an officer? She's just plainly so beautiful." Joseph noticed that Sergeant Morris' salute was near parade ground perfect even though he was in civilian clothes.

"You Joseph Robinson?" the major said as she returned Sergeant Morris' salute with a smile.

"Yes. This person standing beside me with his mouth hanging open is Sergeant Dean Morris. Are you our pilot?"

"Major Jane Ostmark, United States Army, at your service," she replied as she shook hands. Her handshake with Sergeant Dean Morris lasted longer than it had with Joseph Robinson, their eyes meeting and holding for a second longer. Something moved inside of her at that handshake with this tough, rock-hard sergeant.

"Are you about ready?" she asked. "I was told that this mission has priority."

"Sure, do you know where we're going?":

"Yes, some little strip west of the coastline of the Gulf of Mexico in the middle of nowhere. My co-pilot has the coordinates. And I was told to push it." She looked at Joseph with bright blue eyes. "That's all the information I was given."

"Let's get this show on the road and I'll brief you in the air, O.K.?"

"Roger."

Thirty minutes later, somewhere over the southeastern part of California, after telling his men to get some sleep, Joseph and Sergeant Dean Morris crawled up into the C-130 cockpit. It was quiet with the constant not-unpleasant background rumble of four Allison T56-A-15 turboprops, 4,300 horsepower engines. Joseph gave the aircrew what information he had but advised, "I would suggest that you keep this plane ready to take off at a second's notice. Tell the other plane to land first so they can start unloading their jeeps. Are your J-Pods loaded?"

"Roger. Both of us are."

"Call signs, boss?" asked Sergeant Morris.

"Oh yes," Joseph Robinson said, "I'm Gander, my troops are Ducks, Dean here is Duck-Sam, you are Home Plate One, the other supply plane is Home Plate Two and our communications air cover is Home Plate Three."

"Well, when we get there, it'll probably be another wild goose chase to investigate some loin clothed native's mushroom dreams," Captain Paul Weaver, the C-130's co-pilot said after writing down the call signs on his knee pad. "I think that the commander of this plane should exercise her command authority and personally examine those loin clothed natives."

"That's a good idea," Major Jane Ostmark replied. "And while we're at it, you can examine those bare breasted native women. That way, you'll know what you haven't been getting all of your life."

Joseph could hear slightly suppressed laughter from the crew master. This banter apparently was normal in this air crew.

"Sir, why didn't the local authorities handle this?" Captain Weaver asked.

"Well, I suppose that they didn't want to risk their plane," Joseph drawled.

They quickly laughed, but it was a somber laugh. Joseph said, "I really don't know, and we didn't have time to do any investigation. This mission came down through the State Department and was approved 'at the highest levels,' whatever that is. This is supposed to be a strictly civilian operation."

"If your men are civilians, I'm a monkey's uncle."

"I am, and that suffices to make this a 'civilian' operation."

Later, the crew chief woke Joseph Robinson. "We've refueled and we're about twenty minutes out and coming down to 1500 feet."

"Thank you. I'll make sure everyone is strapped in."

They made a circle over the airstrip at about 500 feet waiting for the other C-130 to land. The approximately 3500-foot dirt airstrip looked like a brown gash cut into the dirty green jungle. To the sides, the dirty green jungle stretched as far as the eye could see. On the north side of the airstrip and airplane parking area, they could see what looked like a whole village of natives standing around. They were pushing carts and carrying backpacks. A few forlorn looking pigs and four chickens were tied to the two-wheeled carts.

The co-pilot pointed down, "Anyone speak their language?"

"I was told that the chief speaks some English and about half of our people speak Spanish. Between us, we should figure out what happened and where," Joseph Robinson said.

Their huge plane drifted over the jungle canopy, touched down, bounced, and stayed down. The front end was quickly "pushed" down while the propellers were forcibly rotated into full reverse. The noise was enough to awaken anyone around for several miles. They stopped in a cloud of dust and taxied to the west end of the field where the other plane had its rear door down and jeeps were being cautiously driven off.

The heat and humidity hit them immediately. Perspiration rolled off their foreheads and their civilian clothes were soon soaked.

"This place stinks like a jungle, rotting trees and Heaven knows what else," exclaimed Jose Gonzales.

Jose Gonzales mentioned to one of his men, "It smells like your old girl-friend's cooking."

"Yes, but that was on one of her good days!" was the response.

"Where's the chief?" Joseph asked.

Someone pointed, "I think that's the big guy with the bones in his ears leading that bunch of natives coming toward us."

The chief, a tall loin clothed dark skinned native with two white three-inch bones pierced through his ear lobes and heavy scarring and rough tattoos on his naked skinny chest trudged up to Joseph on blackened feet-feet that had never seen or known shoes.

"I didn't think they had these kinds of natives around here," murmured Sergeant Morris to Joseph.

"I didn't either, but we're so far out in the middle of nowhere that only anthropologists or explorers looking for lost pyramids ever get out here. That's the reason for this modern airstrip. Herald (Goldsmith, Corporal, 5'7", 170 pounds, shaved head, Van Dyke reddish beard), you speak a bunch of languages, give us a hand here."

After much hand waving and broken languages, Joseph Robinson figured that a large fireball crashed through a wild thunder and lightning storm and impacted near a hillside about ten to fifteen miles further west. The natives were scared. The chief refused to return to the impact area. They were leaving for the coast as soon as the planes arrived, and they could tell their story. He said that they had two old tractors they used for gardening and maintenance of the air strip, but that the force had destroyed the tractors. They called it "The Green Ghost" because it looked like a green transparent life form.

In broken Spanish, the chief pointed to a rough road hewn out of the jungle. "Down there," he said. His dark brown heavily calloused hand trembled as he told them the Green Ghost just went through their tractors' engines like a sharp knife through a piece of cloth.

Joseph Robinson and his squad members exchanged glances. Unsaid was the thought this chief did not frighten easily. He was the scariest man Sergeant Morris had ever seen. Two dark round objects that looked like shrunken heads hung from his right shoulder while the jagged scars covering his chest and arms were clearly not self-inflicted.

"All right, listen up," Joseph said. "They gave us four jeeps and I want to take all of them, three men to a jeep. One driver, one radio man and one gunner. The point jeep, called Duck One, will be about 200 yards ahead of the second, called Duck Two, and the third, called Duck Sam, will be about 200 yards behind, and I will be Gander and will be bringing up the rear with the scientists. We will all be about 200 yards apart but be sure to keep your distances. I'll also carry a few picks, shovels, bags, and containers if we must dig something up. We'll stay in constant live radio contact with each other. The rest of you will guard our planes, but I don't think we have to worry too much about hostile natives."

He looked around, "Sergeant Morris, have one of our radios run over to Major Ostmark's plane. Tell them to keep the radio on and monitor us. I suggest that they have someone sit on top of the plane because I don't know how far these things will reach in this jungle. If something happens, I want those planes ready to roll."

They stripped off their sweat soaked shirts and tossed them into the back of the jeeps. Under their shirts, each carried regulation 9mm's in shoulder holsters. The radioman and the gunner each carried M4s with four twenty round clips. Out of a box marked Campbell Soup came a dozen grenades; two were snapped on the lead gunner's chest strap and the remainder were gently placed in an open box between the front seats of the jeeps.

The first jeep containing Roger Jones, LeRoy Johnstone and Thomas Trinko departed, laboriously plowing its way through the fern and brush overgrown local version of a road. The jeep's engine growling in low four-wheel drive quickly disappeared in the trees supporting the high jungle canopy.

"Duck One, this is Gander," Joseph Robinson radioed to the first jeep. "Is the road passable?"

"Gander, Duck One. Somewhat roger. We're making slow progress.

The Hummers could not have made it. We can see where the natives came through here, but it's been some time since any regular vehicle made it. So far, it looks like any other jungle."

The second jeep, Duck Two was sent, Ron Jefferson, (Medic), driving, Sergeant Morris (who rode the second jeep) riding shotgun and Jose Gonzales in the back seat. Ten minutes later, the third jeep, Duck three, containing Flannery, Kleighorn and Swenson growled into the jungle.

Minutes later, Joseph radioed, "Ducks, this is Gander. Radio check."

"Duck One."

"Duck Sam."

"Duck Three."

"Ducks, Gander is moving. Advise conditions."

"Gander, Duck One, the road is still as bad as before, but it's awfully quiet here. It got quieter the closer we came to that hill. No birds, nothing. It's strange - as if the whole jungle shut down."

Joseph exchanged glances with his scientists, Duck One were men that were nearly fearless.

"All units, stay on the air," Joseph Robinson ordered.

"Gander, Duck One, Roger," came the reply. "You're starting to break up with heavy static. We've come about two or three miles and. . . Hold on, I see their tractor ahead of us."

A moment passed.

Silence

"Duck One?"

Nothing.

"Duck One, this is Gander. Advise conditions!"

Still nothing.

"Duck Sam, do you see anything?"

"Gander, negative, but you're breaking up with heavy static."

"Duck Sam, Duck three. Stop! Do not take your vehicles any further. Proceed on foot!" Joseph Robinson suddenly warned, tension filling his body.

"Gander, Duck Sam, Roger. Be advised that you're still breaking up with heavy static."

"Duck One, come in!"

A static filled silence filled the air.

Suddenly, far ahead of them they heard several faint explosions.

"Grenades!" The driver of Joseph's jeep, Private Spencer Gerry muttered, hitching the M4 on his side a little tighter.

Then a static filled voice shouted, "Gander, Gander, Duck Three, do not come any closer! This is Duck Sam. We have injuries. That life force attacked us and burnt the hell out of Duck One's jeep. Jones was burnt pretty bad, and Johnston got it on his arm and leg. Nothing stops that stuff. Don't come any closer!"

"Duck Three, did you copy that?"

"Roger, we'll wait here for them. We're about a half mile from them."

Joseph locked eyes with his driver, Private Spenser Gerry.

"What the hell is that stuff, sir?"

"I don't know." Joseph picked up his radio, "Sam, advise conditions when able."

A tension filled silence filled the air.

Then: "Gander, Duck Sam here. I have my men and we're retreating. That green stuff destroyed Duck One's jeep and it keeps flying around here. . . Oh My God, Get Away From Here!"

Joseph heard a microphone hitting something metallic, then a vicious static and then silence. In the distance could be heard the bark of M-4's firing!

"Gander to Home Plate One," Joseph suddenly called the planes.

"Home Plate One by."

"Home Plate One, get Home Plate Two off the ground, now! Home Plate One, be ready for an immediate emergency takeoff!"

"Roger."

"Gerry, take these scientists back to the plane and get them loaded. Lend me your weapon, I'm going ahead on foot. Make sure we're ready for an immediate takeoff."

Joseph, wearing his 9 .mm automatic in a hip holster and carrying the M4 in his left hand, trudged west toward his men. Shortly, he heard the pounding of four huge C-130 engines in full throttle, and then felt on the ground the rumbling harsh thunder of the C-130's JATO units pushing the huge plane out of the jungle. As the thundering plane fled eastward, the all-encompassing jungle around Joseph fell deathly silent, the humidity and heat penetrating him as if he was in an overheated sauna.

About thirty minutes later, he heard the growl of an overheated jeep engine. Around a bend in the dense jungle, the jeep appeared, nine men hanging onto a four-person jeep. They ground to a stop, steam hissing out of the radiator.

"What the hell happened?" Joseph demanded.

"That Green Ghost life force is real, Sir," Sergeant Morris reported, his eyes wide and hard. "It burned through our jeep like fire through tissue paper. It attacked the engine and our radio equipment, but nothing else! It looked like it just went through Jones to get to the radios. He is burnt on his right leg and side; Johnstone is burnt only on his left arm and leg. We threw grenades at that stuff, Sir, but nothing stopped it. We fired a few M4 rounds at it, but the rounds had absolutely no effect on that force!"

"Can they walk, or can we carry them?" Joseph asked. "I don't want to take these jeeps any closer to our plane than we have to. It looks like that force followed you. If that stuff hits our plane, we're out of luck."

"We'll carry Jones, but Johnstone can walk," Sergeant Morris said. "Back up there about a mile and about a hundred yards or so off in the jungle, we could see what looked like a crashed helicopter, but we didn't have time to examine it."

"The State Department didn't bother to tell us that a helicopter had been sent here. That figures! Let's go. Shut your jeep off and turn off all your electrical equipment," Joseph ordered. "Leave all of your radios here."

Nearly an hour later, out of breath, their bodies dripping with heavy perspiration, thirst burning their throats, hearts pounding, they struggled back to the plane with occasional fearful glances back at the jungle. All four propellers were turning, the rear tailgate was lowered to about a foot above the ground. Private Gerry and two more of Joseph's men jumped out of the back of the plane, grabbed Jones and Johnstone, and hustled them into the back of the plane.

Joseph collapsed on the floor, "Have we got everyone?" he grasped.

Sergeant Morris looked around, counted bodies, and said "Yes Sir."

"Get this plane off the ground, now, As Soon As Possible!" Joseph yelled at the crew chief.

"Roger. Tail gate almost finished coming up," yelled the crew chief. "Go!" he signaled the pilot.

"Major, get the hell out of here," yelled Joseph over the increasing thunder and pounding of the four engines.

Suddenly, the plane lurched forward and gathered speed.

"Everyone, grab ahold of something or belt yourself in. It's going to get rough in a second," Sergeant Westlund yelled as the plane started to bump over the uneven dirt airstrip. "As soon as the front end goes up, cover your ears!"

Suddenly, the front end of the plane went up.

All hell broke loose!

It sounded like enormous, ear-splitting rockets were trying to pound their way into the sides of the big C-130. The pilot had triggered the JATO units!

What wasn't tied or belted down flew backwards to the tail. The plane, now at about a 45 degree up angle, clawed for speed and height.

At about a thousand-foot altitude, the JATO units shut off. The big C-130 suddenly floated down to about eight hundred feet while its propellers grasped for air. The effect was like riding in a roller coaster except this roller coaster had four huge screaming engines.

Sergeant Westlund touched his earphones, then pointed at Joseph Robinson, "The Major wants you up front, pronto, Sir."

"Roger. Dean, come with me."

"Did you want to circle over that area?" asked Major Jane Ostmark when Joseph and Dean climbed up to the cockpit.

"Hell no! Get away from there as fast as possible!"

"Can you patch me into Home Plate Three on a secure circuit?"

"Sure, just a second. Here, put our headset on and all you have to do is press this button to talk."

"Home Plate Three?"

"Home Plate Three by, what happened down there?" drawled a very Texas voice.

"Home Plate Three, contact Colonel Robert W. Devonshirk and advise him that we had to escape from the jungle. That force is real, the reports are true that nothing stops that life. See if you can report to your own base after you get through to Colonel Devonshirk."

"Ah, roger, Home Plane One. You should be advised that we just received a garbled emergency classified message that much of the electrical power is going off in Northern Brazil and Southern Mexico from unknown causes, and something seems to be wrong with the Panama Canal, too. Two ships are stuck in there and they can't move them."

"Roger Home Plate Three, Home Plate Two, you copy?"

"Home Plate Two, roger."

"All right, Two, Three, I suggest that you return as fast as you can to your home base and land. If we're lucky, we can beat that Green Ghost life home before it attacks us. It burnt a couple of my men when it went right through them trying to get to any electricity generating object."

"Are you serious?"

"Absolutely! We think it attacked a helicopter and a couple of farm tractors down there and just flat destroyed them. It followed our jeeps and destroyed them when we tried to escape. Now, you're telling me that Brazil and Southern Mexico is losing its electrical power; that means that green stuff is spreading. And fast! I don't think we have much time."

"Would it help if we climbed to our ceiling altitude?" A tight Texas voice asked.

"I simply don't know," Joseph Robinson said. "If I had to guess, I would think that it might not make any difference. Distance is probably the operative word."

"Roger Gander, this is Home Plate Three going to full power."

"Home Plate Two, also roger."

"Give me full power, Paul. I'm climbing to 30,000; that should give us the best speed," Major Jane Ostmark anxiously ordered, pulling back on the control yoke. "It's a dam good thing we refueled before landing down there."

"Come on baby, you can do it!" exclaimed Paul pushing four engine levels past the stops.

Later, after watching the medical corpsman treat their burnt men and trying to make everyone comfortable, Joseph said to Dean Morris, "Come with me, I want to talk to our pilot and the other air crews."

After climbing up into the cockpit area, Joseph asked, "Can I talk to Home Plate Three?"

"Sure. Here, use this headset."

"Home Plate Three, this is Gander."

"Home Plate Three by."

"Have you heard anything from your base or my Colonel on the conditions in Brazil or the Panama Canal?"

"Affirmative!" A worried, tense voice replied, "We lost almost all contact with Brazil and Columbia less than an hour or so ago. The secured connection with NORAD seems full of static. Our ETA with our home base is about 45 minutes. We're over the northern part . . ."

"Home Plate Three, repeat, you broke," Joseph transmitted.

Nothing.

"Home Plate Three?" Major Ostmark nearly yelled at her microphone.

Suddenly, "Mayday! Mayday! Mayday! This is Home Plate Three. Our number one engine has been attacked by a green something and it's on fire. We're losing power. . . "

"Major, you copy that?" Joseph asked Major Ostmark.

"Roger. Home Plate Three?" Major Ostmark transmitted, her face white and taut.

"Gander, this is Three," came a shouted reply. "We're losing altitude fast! I'm getting the crew out. My number two engine is losing power and the flames and green life is spreading. I'll try to save the plane. Please try to get someone to pick up my crew."

After failed transmissions attempting to contact anyone, Major Ostmark turned in frustration to Joseph Robinson, her eyes brimming, the cockpit tight with tension, "We can't contact anyone and the air is full of static. I want to put this ship down as soon as possible."

"What is your ETA to Orange County?"

"About an hour," the co-pilot said.

"Try to get us there, if you can," Joseph ordered.

"We have enough fuel. Paul, give me emergency power," Major Ostmark ordered. "We'll keep our speed until the last possible minute."

"Roger, emergency power coming up," responded Paul as he unsnapped the emergency locks, pushed, and snapped four throttles forward to their absolute limit.

Forty minutes later, Paul said, "We're about twenty miles from John Wayne Airport, Major. We need to reduce speed and altitude, now!"

"Roger, Paul, give us a hot landing checklist. We'll put the gear down about ten miles out but watch our Rate of Descent speed. Give me flaps at four thousand feet, but we'll save full flaps until final. We'll land in from North to South because I know where that runway starts."

To the left, they could see an electrical farm with 66,000-volt transformers and heavy-duty connectors exploding and on fire. Over the farm was a green mist flowing up and down through the smoky air. Far to the left, they could see spots of fire with a green substance circulating above the fires.

"Give me full flaps," ordered Major Jane Ostmark as she fought the rapidly decreasing speed of her airplane and sudden air turbulence.

Seconds later, on final approach, as the big brown and green C-130 was slowing from its frantic high speed, about two miles from the 405 San Diego Freeway dotted with burning cars, a light flashed red in the cockpit and a horn blared. "Christ, our number four is on fire!"

"Feather it! Pull fire retardant! Give me a little more power on three," Major Ostmark yelled. The big plane started to slew to the side because of the drag of the burning engine.

"We're on final! Dam, we're hot!" Captain Weaver exclaimed.

"Get everyone in back braced for a rough landing," Major Ostmark ordered. "I hope we can stop this old girl."

Two hundred feet from the runway, passing over a parking lot, approaching the 405 freeway, another red light flashed and another horn blared.

"Number three engine on fire," Captain Weaver yelled. "Pulling fire retardant, shutting her down, feathering the props," as his hands flew over controls.

The big C-130, smoke streaming from two destroyed engines, flattened out over the end of the 5200-foot runway, bounced, went airborne, crashed back to the runway, and stayed down.

"Don't reverse the props! That will throw us sideways. Just shut us down! Paul, help me with the brakes," Major Ostmark grunted, her aircraft shaking violently under her.

"Sergeant Westlund, get the back gate down, now. I want everyone off this plane as soon as we stop."

The huge plane rumbled to a stop after running out of runaway and skidding into the left turn, the brakes, and tires smoking. "Shut down all electrics, all engines, I want nothing electrical running on this ship," Major Ostmark yelled."

"Grab what you can, men, and get the hell off," Joseph Robinson shouted as the rear gate slowly dropped. "Get some ground transportation and get those men to the hospital."

As Sergeant Dean Morris got his men out of the plane, it started to fill with smoke from the overloaded electrical wires.

He screamed, "The aircrew is still in there,"

He climbed back into the dense smoking interior looking for the aircrew. He fought his way through the dislocated supply boxes and thickening smoke inside the plane to the cockpit.

"Get out of here," he shouted at the pilot and co-pilot, coughing heavily. "Come on," he grabbed Major Jane Ostmark's arm, "This is too dangerous in here."

She looked at him wide-eyed, her body and hands shaking from the nearly crashed landing. "Come on, please, Major," he pleaded grabbing her around her waist, unsnapping her safety belts. "This plane is history!"

She grabbed her overnight bag; Sergeant Morris, his arm around her waist, carried and pulled her and her co-pilot through the all-encompassing smoke.

All three jumped out of the last aircraft they would ever fly!

Outside the plane, holding a vomiting and grasping Sergeant Dean Morris, Major Ostmark dragged him away from the smoking plane.

Two of his men ran up with an oxygen bottle, quickly attached an oxygen mask to his face and dragged him further to safety.

Minutes later, Joseph Robinson, his men, and the aircrew from the C-130 were standing about fifty yards away from the plane, two of its four engines still smoldering, the odor of burnt tires, brakes and electrical internal wiring flooding the air.

Above them floated a green transparent substance, violently twisting and turning. "That's the Green Ghost!" cried one of the men, pointing above the downed C-130.

Major Ostmark knelt beside Sergeant Dean Morris sitting on the concrete runway, gasping oxygen from the O2 bottle.

He struggled to stand, but she commanded, "Sit down!"

He sat.

Major Ostmark looked at Joseph Robinson, her hand shaking on Dean Morris' shoulders, her flight suit stained with sweat from the landing. "What now, Sir?"

CHAPTER TWO

SOUTHERN CALIFORNIA

"Well. Let's see," Joseph Robinson thought out loud.

"Swanson, get yourself and our two guys to the hospital. I think they'll be all right, but I want them checked out by a regular doctor or emergency room. Jefferson, go with Swanson, you did a great job taking care of them."

"On the way, Sir."

"Dean, how do you feel? Did you want to see a doctor? How's your lungs?"

"I'm all right Joe." Sergeant Dean Morris said weakly. "That smoke got to me a little."

"You listen to your boss," Major Jane Ostmark interrupted, her arm around his shoulders. "If you feel at all dizzy or woozy, you let him," she paused, "or me know immediately, understand?"

"Yes, Major," Sergeant Dean Morris said, his leaking eyes locking on hers.

Joseph Robinson looked at his sergeant with surprise. It was one of the few times that Dean ever quietly agreed to an order from an officer.

Joseph Robinson told his remaining crew, "OK, it's now close to 1800 hours. Let's have a meeting in our offices at 0800 hours tomorrow morning. I'll try to find some information. Everyone is dismissed until then. Try to get some rest. Dean, if you're feeling up to it, see if you can find someplace for Major Ostmark and her crew to sleep. We have two vacant rooms in our apartment complex they can use. A couple of you guys help the Sergeant, he can't walk too well yet. The rest of you men start unloading the plane if you can, but be careful!"

"Doctor Icroniff, Doctor Samualson, you two come with me," Joseph Robinson ordered. "I need an explanation for what happened."

During the ride to his headquarters, the V-6 engine in his van seemed to run on about five cylinders. While trying to coax the sputtering engine through the gates of the airport, Joseph Robinson roughly quizzed the scientists, "What the hell is that Green Ghost force?"

Both scientists looked at each other nearly blank faces.

"I, I've never seen anything like that before," Doctor Samualson stumbled with his words. "Albert Einstein and the great Steven Hawking theorized that there would be other forms of life, but they never thought of something like this."

Doctor Icroniff nodded, "Steven Hawking in one of his lectures at Cambridge postulated that there were no reason particular forms of life could not exist that at certain times were uncontrollable."

"Can we protect ourselves from that force?" Joseph asked after thinking through the triple negative statement.

Both scientists shook their heads.

"At this moment, I don't think so. I would like to do some research and check with Livermore and Los Alamos," Doctor Samuelson uttered, his old body shaking. "I hope we can get through. There is that large group in Europe that is heavily involved in quark research if we can still reach them, but it appears that when anything generates or utilizes electricity, it gets attacked by that life force. I could see a large transformer and electrical location east of the airport and it was being attacked by that force. I also want to try to contact the group in CERN because they were looking for some kind of anti-matter."

Doctor Icroniff agreed, "If that force penetrated the metal of the tractor engine, the metal of the jeep engine and the metal of the airplane engines which all have different types of material, I, I don't know of anything that could stop it."

"Well, as soon as we hit headquarters, I want you both to try to contact anyone that might have an answer to that force," Joseph ordered. "Immediately! I have to report to Washington and they're going to demand some answers."

After reporting to Colonel Robert W. Devonshirk, they opened a direct speaker-phone secured connection to Brigadier General Robert W. Grippand, United States Army, in Washington D.C. Their terse report to General Grippand and General Fox included the attack on their plane and the loss of the other C-130.

A disbelieving Lt. Colonel in General Grippand's office asked sarcastically, "You guys been smoking some of that California strange weed out there?"

Colonel Devonshirk leaned over and whispered in Joseph's ear," That's Lt. Colonel Tierton Templeton. Grippand has to signal before making a turn, Templeton's nose is so far up his rear end."

They ignored Colonel Templeton. "General, please check with General Douglass. Also, General, check with the State Department on what's happened in the Panama Canal. Better yet, see if you can raise them," Joseph said flatly, commanding, "Do it now!"

"I beg your pardon," came the exclamation of a United States Army Brigadier General; a General not accustomed to receiving orders from someone he considered a mere civilian and thus, inferior.

"Do it now!"

"Stand by," leaving the distinct impression that Joseph had better be right.

A minute later came an order, "Call back in sixty minutes."

Joseph quickly met with his scientists and when he returned to Colonel Devonshirk's office, his face was pale.

An hour later, through a static filled transmission, General Fox came back on the line. "I'm putting you on the speaker. Repeat your report."

After Joseph Robinson and Colonel Devonshirk finished their report, they could hear angry and even fearful voices on the speaker.

"At Ease!" yelled a voice. Colonel Devonshirk, impressed, leaned over and whispered in Joseph's ear, "General Spencer, Chief of Staff of the Joint Chiefs." Colonel Devonshirk waived four fingers over his shoulder indicating a four-star general.

"Mr. Robinson," rumbled General Spencer, "What do your scientists tell you about this force, this life?"

"Sir, they think it feeds on electricity, or in other words, electricity is its food and reproductive source. Nothing stops it, Sir! It apparently destroyed a small tractor and a helicopter. It destroyed one of our C-130's, nearly destroyed the one we were in, and basically eats anything that uses electricity. There are no vehicles at all running out here, no buses, trains or cars, period. There is no electrical power at all. That Green Ghost simply attacks and eats the generators of any engine. I don't know how long we'll maintain this connection."

"Anything that uses electricity or just generates electricity?"

"Good question, General. We think it attacks anything that generates an appreciable amount of electricity."

"How about humans?"

"I checked with our scientists, and they believe that the human body generates too little electricity to attract this Green Ghost."

"How do we fight this force, this what did you call it, the Green Ghost?"

"That's what the natives called it because when you can see it, it has a green transparent film. We don't know of any way to stop this force, Sir," Colonel Devonshirk said heavily, despair in his voice. "Our scientists, perhaps two of the leading people in the world, reported that they had no idea on how to stop it."

A sudden, violent wave of static penetrated their conversation.

"I thought this hookup was secure from interference," General Spencer demanded from someone.

"This proves our point, General," Joseph Robinson said, bluntly.

A sudden silence filled both rooms, one in California and one in Washington, D.C., as the magnitude of the Green Ghost sank in.

An involuntarily uttered "Jesus" was heard.

"Suggestions, Mr. Robinson or Colonel?" General Spencer broke the heavy silence.

"I have our scientists checking with Los Alamos Research Center and the Center up in Livermore, but that will take time. Frankly, Sir, I don't expect any favorable answers, if we could get any answers at all!" Joseph said.

Colonel Devonshirk looked at Joseph Robinson. The thought crossed his mind: *"Well, I'm not going to make any friends anyway and don't expect to get promoted soon."*

"I would respectfully suggest, Sir, that you do several things: Number one: place all of the armed forces on emergency full alert; Number two: get our ships into safe harbor before they are attacked; and Number three: immediately ground every airborne plane, military and civilian, until we find some way to fight this Green Ghost," Colonel Devonshirk responded heavily. "Someone out here was smart enough to close down John Wayne Airport where their pilot crash landed the C-130. All the lights are off including the tower."

"I would add, General," Joseph interrupted, "That you notify the nuclear power plants and the big hydroelectric dams to hit their emergency shutdowns. We just don't know what the Green Ghost will do with those facilities, but it wouldn't be nice."

"Oh My God," whispered a voice from the background in Washington, D.C.

"I also suggest, General," Joseph said, "that you activate all of the National Guard units because if the United States, hell, the world loses its electricity, the consequences will be catastrophic and our military will be the only authority in command."

"Do you know what you're suggesting? Those orders must come from the President," said an unknown voice. "We need to get him out of here and to his plane to escape!"

Joseph took a deep breath, "Then get the orders, dam it! We don't have much time! Also, don't, don't put the President on a plane! The Green Ghost will eat that poor plane alive. We lost one of our C-130s; our own plane crash-landed while being eaten by the Ghost!"

"We'll get back to you!" And the connection was abruptly severed.

The 0800 meeting in Joseph's office was postponed. The next afternoon, after meeting with his Colonel and his two scientists, Joseph

Robinson found a worried Sergeant Dean Morris and said, "Get our people together and meet me in my office."

At about eighteen hundred hours, with the shadows lengthening, approximately twenty-three people met in the musty downstairs conference room of Joseph's building. Windows were pried open for air circulation. Joseph's men lounged in their chairs leaning on the walls of the room, their Colt M-16's or FN Herstal M4A1s and 9 mm. weapons in plain sight.

Major Jane Ostmark, sitting close to Sergeant Dean Morris, and her co-pilot Paul Weaver were present and about a half dozen wives and girlfriends.

"Attn. Hut!" barked Sergeant Dean Morris.

The room snapped to attention, a few wives and girlfriends looked on curiously.

Colonel Devonshirk, wearing his full Class-A uniform, marched into the room surprising his subordinates who had never seen him in full uniform.

As whisper was heard, "Jesus, he's got more medals than the last general I saw in Washington, D.C."

"As you were," he ordered. He looked around and spotted Joseph Robinson.

"Mr. Robinson, you want to take over and handle this?" he asked.

"Thank you, Sir," Joseph said. "Everyone, let me tell you what I know and we'll go from there. Then, we'll need to make some decisions. (Little did Joseph Robinson realize that his statement was what endeared him to the military personal under him. He sought their advice before making major decisions.) As you know, there has been no electricity in Southern California for the last few days."

Joseph moved to the front of his desk and sat on it. "We have reports from Southern California Edison, our electric company, that almost all of the electrical power plants and electrical substations have been either destroyed or burnt. They see a green transparent substance flying through the air attacking their substations and anything using electricity."

The silence in the room was absolute.

Joseph paused for a moment trying not to show fear to his men, it took an extraordinary amount of control to stop his hands from shaking. "We had received word of an enormous explosion in the ocean between Korea and Japan just before our own electrical system went out. We think one of our nuclear submarines was attacked and it exploded. The last word we received was that our country, our United States, hell, the whole dam world has basically shut down."

Joseph paused for a moment, the silence deafening, his tanned face lean and drawn. "Our scientists also think that at this time, we, the human race, have no way to fight that force. Our scientists believe that that Green Ghost has been around since the beginning of the universe, since The Big Bang. That Green Ghost simply pierces through anything to get to electricity. I know all of you walked here because the engines in any vehicles have been destroyed if the engine is turned on. And if you look around the city, there are wrecks and burnt vehicles everywhere."

Joseph met the fear-filled eyes of the people crowded in the room. "Plus, I need to give you something straight. A bigger problem is that soon, very soon, this entire Southern California, and all the big cities for that matter, will run out of food. It was estimated that the average family has about seven days of food in their home. I frankly don't want to be around here when people start searching for food. If you've paid attention to conditions in our city here, people are already starting to worry because their electricity has been off for a couple of days. You know we don't have any water or gas either because it takes electricity to run those pumps. And it will get worse!"

An approximate 5-foot, 8-inch, skinny woman with short bleached blond hair and a narrow face with bright red lipstick (Sergeant Dean Morris thought it looked like a weasel, he had never seen her before.) standing in the corner spoke with a voice that felt like fingernails scratching on a whiteboard.

"Well, what's Washington doing about this; we pay their huge salaries," the voice screeched. "All they do is sit around, scratching their big fat butts trying to figure out how to run our country!"

"The same thing we're trying to come up with are some suggestions against this Green Ghost," exclaimed Ron Johnson who disliked her on sight. "And we don't have big fat butts to scratch, anyway."

"Nobody scratches my butt!" she flared.

"Oh, don't worry, I don't want to scratch your butt either," growled a deep voice from the crowd.

"All right! Enough!" Commanded Sergeant Dean Morris, fighting to stop an involuntary smile.

Joseph Robinson thought, through the tension and fear, with a sense of pride, *"These are my men, they don't suffer fools gladly."*

"Well, what are you doing about this?" The screecher screeched to Joseph Robinson. "You are the boss, so do something rather than just stand there!"

At that, Mrs. Rosa Maria Munoz Gonzalez, all of 4 feet, 11 inches tall, weighing a skinny 85 pounds, sitting in front of the screecher stood, turned to face the woman, and with a vicious hardened right hand, slapped the screecher on the left side of her face. The screecher's right side of her face slammed against the wall!

She started to collapse.

Rosa grabbed the woman by the front of her blouse, shook her, and snarled, "Don't you ever talk that way to that man again. He has done more for all of us than you'll ever know!" Little Rosa then savagely shoved and bounced the woman against the wall.

"Understand?!

Rosa raised her callused right hand to slap the woman again, demanding, "Apologize to him, now!"

The woman started whimpering "I'm sorry, I'm sorry!"

Rosa ordered, "Sit down. Now!"

The woman sat!

Rosa too sat and looked around as if nothing happened.

Jose Gonzalez and Joseph Robinson both fought to not show their approval and pride in Rosa. And Joseph's grim smile and nod told her of his support and appreciation!

"Do you have any kind of time frame for this lasting?" Sergeant Morris asked, getting back to the subject in question.

The silence grew!

And grew!

And grew!

And didn't stop!

Joseph slowly shook his head, his mouth dry, his eyes meeting Sergeant Morris's.

Off to the side, Joseph heard a muffled sobbing.

"What can we do, Sir?" asked a voice.

"Colonel?" Joseph turned to Colonel Devonshirk. "Would you tell them of our last communication with The Pentagon?"

Colonel Devonshirk stood up. His impressive six rows of ribbons on his left chest (with a Silver Star, a Bronze Star and a Purple Heart) and his silver eagles gleaming from his shoulders with several assignments on his shoulders and right chest simply buttressed his command appearance. "I am operating from orders from Headquarters, United States Army," he began formally. "I was ordered to try to find some way to fight the Green Ghost. I was also ordered to do whatever is necessary, in my best judgment, for the safety of you people. My last communication, both wireless and landline, was abruptly cut off and then, . . . everything shut down."

He paused for a moment, "Mr. Robinson, I understand you have an idea."

"I need to explain something so what I'm about to say makes sense." Joseph Robinson said, "In the early 1800s, a scientist named Michael Faraday discovered that if you move a magnet or a similar magnetic object inside a coil of wire, electricity is generated."

"Dean, out in the hallway is a large piece of cardboard, would you get it for me, please?"

He put the cardboard on his desk and drew what looked like a coil of wire. He then drew a rod with an arrow directed to the inside of the coil. He pointed, "If you take this coil, put this magnetic rod inside of it and turn it, you will generate some tiny bit of electricity."

He paused, "Understand?"

Upon receiving nods, "Now, this coil can be of nearly any size including the rod. You drain the electricity off by wires."

He drew wires leading off the coil. "You can use any form of power to turn this rod: from water power, stream power, nuclear power, coal and oil or natural gas power, man-power, battery power, horse or oxen power or whatever. That, ladies and gentleman, is generally where the overwhelming amount of our electricity comes-came from."

He stepped back, "Every alternator, and/or generator on your car, train, plane and boat has some, much newer, variation of this drawing.

"Now, why do we care?" He paused and drew a filled in circle around the coil. "All of our engines were defenseless against the Green Ghost or Force or Power; there are ladies present, I couldn't say what I wanted to call it." He drew arrows piercing the coil.

Joseph turned to their Coronel, "Now Sir. I have one faint glimmer of hope. I met with our two scientists this afternoon. They seem to think that maybe, just a huge long shot maybe, there might be a shield against that force, that Green Ghost."

Joseph drew a heavy shield around the coil with arrows bouncing off it.

Our scientists think that since that force has been around since the beginning of the universe, and since nature doesn't do anything in a vacuum, if we could find a virgin meteorite and melt it down into sheets of metal, maybe, and that is a large maybe, that metal might, just might have properties that would act as a shield or buffer against the force."

Anticipation, hope, suddenly increased in the room.

Sergeant Dean Morris sputtered, "But, but, where in hell are you going to get a virgin meteorite? The only thing virgin in Southern California is. . . is an ugly fourteen-year old!"

The silence was suddenly broken with hysterical laughter, the rigid tension slowly dissipating into quiet snickers.

After quiet was restored, Joseph said, "Well, the only place I can think of that would have an accessible meteorite that hasn't been fully dug up is in the meteor crater in Arizona. We would have to climb down into the crater and dig out part of that meteor."

"Assuming that, Sir, where would you melt it down?" Sergeant Morris asked. "And a better question is how are we going to get that stuff to the forge?"

"Dammed if I know," Joseph admitted.

He didn't realize that it was because of his honesty toward his men they would follow him almost anywhere. They felt he would give them the straight information, unlike other so-called leaders they had. And he had never asked them to do anything he wasn't willing to do too.

"Anyone have any ideas?"

Shoulders shrugged around the room.

"Well, Sir, how about Illinois or Indiana?" Sergeant Ronald Heightsky asked. "That whole area around the southern part of Lake Michigan is full of forges from those old steel mills. I went to the University of Chicago for a semester before I joined the Army and I think they had a small forge there for research purposes."

Suddenly, memories of his closest friend, Dan Peterson, came flooding back to Joseph and that Dan had gone to the University of Chicago. He remembered some of the vivid "war stores" of Dan Peterson and the healthy Illinois or Wisconsin girls. He never figured out how much was true and how much wishful thinking.

"Do you think any of those forges or any forge could handle melting a couple of hundred pounds of metal?" Joseph asked.

"Sure, or at least I think so. The university used to melt different metals for some of their more esoteric research. If I remember correctly, they had something to do with the Manhattan Project during World War II. That's the project that created the first atomic bomb. If need be, I'm sure we could find someone who knew how to run one of the larger forges around East Illinois or Indiana."

"There you have it," Joseph Robinson said to the whole room.

Joseph took a deep breath. "Colonel, with your permission, I'd like to try. I don't have anything keeping me here, and if I can get some volunteers, I'd like to give it a shot."

Colonel Devonshirk thought for a moment. "In my final conversation with my opposite number in Washington D.C., he said that they were going to try to keep Camp McCoy up in Wisconsin open. You men may know that's where much of your supplies came from. They used McCoy during Desert Storm and a couple of other operations for supplying and staffing purposes and it had tons of materials for almost any operation."

Colonel Devonshirk paused, took a deep breath, and said, "What

I am going to do is issue two orders: the first is to you Mr. Joseph Robinson. Mr. Robinson, you are ordered to find a way to fight that Green Ghost. You and I have discussed this. Pursuant to said orders, I will give you written orders signed by me under General Fox's letterhead. I hope that will be sufficient for you to utilize any necessary military base anywhere in the United States for supplies and anything else you might need. You are to use your best judgment to accomplish that task."

Joseph Robinson stood, nodded, and said, "Yes Sir."

Colonel Devonshirk looked around. "The second order concerns the rest of you. Mr. Robinson will only accept volunteers for his mission. And I emphasize the word volunteer and that applies to single personal only. Those of you who cannot volunteer or who will not volunteer, for whatever reason, may stay here with me. Those of you with families here are encouraged to stay with me. You must understand that Mr. Robinson's mission may be only one way with no return."

Colonel Devonshirk stopped and looked around at his men. "I will try to maintain this unit down at Camp Pendleton, just north of San Diego, and we'll try to survive this coming catastrophe. I've got enough rank to get us and our families at least some quarters and supplies. I'll meet here at ten hundred hours tomorrow for planning purposes with those who want to stay with me. Those who want to volunteer to go with Mr. Robinson meet here in an hour. Again, he will only accept volunteers and his decisions on who will go with him will be final. Mr. Robinson, are you able to discuss your mission as I have given it to you?"

"Yes Sir."

"One other thing needs to be said. All of you are not here willingly. But, this is important, while each of you were here with me for at least a year, Mr. Robinson and Sergeant Morris were cleaning your personal records and jackets. Each record and jacket have been removed of really adverse contents such as projected summary or general court proceedings, Article 15s, written warnings and so on. In each jacket, there are notations of good and valuable service to the Army. Mr. Robinson and Sergeant Morris totally agree with me. In other words, because of your service to me, you no longer have those charges hanging over you. I personally want to thank each of you for your duty to me, to the Army, and to our country. Thank You for a job and jobs well done!"

Colonel Devonshirk stood at attention, "All right, listen up: Squad, Attn. Hut!"

The room came to attention.

"Dismissed! And God have mercy on us all."

About an hour later, after candles were lit in the conference room, Joseph's original squad crowded in minus the friends and relatives.

"Sir, we've been talking," Sergeant Morris began, his men nodding. "Sir, we know that we could stay here or even go our separate ways, but you have always been square with us and we'd all like to follow you. If we have a chance to fight that force, we want to be in on it. Plus, only one of us has ever been in Chicago."

For some reason, Joseph's eyes start to water and he turned away.

After a moment, taking a deep breath, Joseph turned to his squad, his voice husky. "All right, our Colonel said we'll only take those without families. Three reasons for this: we probably will have to fight our way across the United States, and I don't want any wives or kids getting hurt, second, I need only those people who can carry their own weight. And third, this probably will be a one-way trip."

He looked around, "Wilson, Geriers, Rodriguez, Gonzalez, you four have wives and kids here. I thank you from the bottom of my heart, but I'm not going to take you, period. Your families need you more than I do. Plus, you know our Colonel, he knows you and trusts you, and he'll need all the help he can get obtaining housing and supplies. Anyone else, if you have a "friend" you're involved with and want to make that relationship permanent, you've got about a day to make a decision. As the Colonel said, this may be a one-way trip. Everyone else, any suggestions on how we accomplish our mission?"

This was an interesting question. They were accustomed to flying anywhere in the world at a moment's notice and getting whatever equipment and supplies they needed, but now, those options no longer existed. Joseph remembered with interest that an incredible amount of equipment was "lost in combat," but that much equipment seemed to somehow magically appear in his unit's barracks.

"Joe, a long time ago, Private Thomas Trinko here used to drive a stagecoach either at Knott's Berry Amusement Park or Disneyland, "Sergeant Morris said. "He knows horses and I think that is the only way we're going to cross this country."

"I think you're right. Anyone know where we can get a bunch of horses?"

"Well," Sergeant Dean Morris drawled, "These guys are the greatest bunch of scroungers around. Give us a couple of days to get to Knott's Berry Amusement Park or Disneyland and we'll borrow a couple of their horses with a rubber-tired wagon for them to pull. We can keep our supplies and so on it. Oh, by the way, men, be sure to pack your personal items and a uniform or two, but keep it limited. We wouldn't have much room."

"Good thinking. How about two separate teams with two wagons with extra horses as a back-up? Think you could do that?"

"Sure."

It seemed strange that once his men had something physical to do, to plan for, the terrible fear in the room seemed to lose its strength.

Sergeant Morris looked around for Corporal David Musinski, "David, about five or ten miles directly west of here in Huntington Beach are a bunch of horse stables. You know where they are, don't you?"

"Yes Sarge. Those stables are next to that new retirement center for Huntington Beach. Plus, I know the woman that runs, or used to manage those stables. She gives the appearance of a hard-nosed manager, but underneath, she's a wonderful, warm person. I understand that they have about 400 actual stables with about a quarter or so housing riding horses. The people who own or rent those stables probably wouldn't be able to get to them to feed or care for their horses. We might be doing her and them a great favor by taking the horses."

"See what you can 'borrow'. Take Sam and three other men with you. Sam, you used to live on a horse ranch and you know how to ride, don't you?"

"Well, us Texans were all born to ride," Corporal Samuel Kleighorn's full Texan accent drawled. "Plus, my grandpop, may he rest in peace, raised me on a real horse ranch down there. The only way we got around was to ride. You guys that are getting supplies from Knott's or Disneyland or wherever be sure to get horseshoe sets-at least twelve, either barium or hard rubber and nails and a hammer or two. Get extra horseshoes, we'll need them for such a long journey. Also, when you're picking out horses, try not to get one that looks old or needs medication."

"How far can we travel in a day's time?" someone asked.

"Well, normally, a horse and rider can travel about twenty to forty miles a day for long periods of time. Be sure to remember that we'll have two horses pulling a wagon. I suggest we have six pulling horses for the wagons, the fifth and sixth horses will be used to relieve the others. But remember, we'll have a long distance to travel and we don't want to wear them down. Rubber tires will ease their load."

"How far is it to Chicago?"

"About 2000 miles, give or take a couple. Why?"

"So, if we average 20 miles a day, it will take us about six months to get to Chicago, is that right?"

"No! Probably close to four to four and a half months depending on travel conditions, our horses, and so on. Why?"

"Do you mean to say that I'm going to have to sit on a horse for 2000 miles?" asked one man.

"Sounds about right."

"My rear end wouldn't take sitting on a horse for one day, much less 2000 miles," came the complaint.

"Judging from the size of your rear end, it could use a few weeks sitting on a horse!"

After the laughter died down, Sergeant Dean Morris said, "OK, people. Go fully armed. We'll need about a dozen or more decent riding horses and their full gear. I would suggest that you release the rest of the animals over there so they don't starve."

"Anything else, Sir?" Sergeant Morris looked at Joseph.

"Yes. Two things: first, put a couple of people as guards on this place. We'll use the building next door as a headquarters until we leave and I don't want civilians wondering around in there. There's a grassy park with that small lake out back where you can keep the horses. Second, let's expedite getting the wagons. Once we have the wagons, send them over to some of the military warehouses and obtain all the food and other supplies you can find. A wagon load of MREs (Meals Ready to Eat) may be tiresome, but get them, understand? Oh yes, don't forget the very basic necessities such as soap, matches, maybe a fuel-driven lantern or two, and medical and dental supplies such as tooth paste and brushes. Forget about flashlights, they use electricity."

"Oh yes, Dean. Would you get together with a couple of our people and make a list of everything, and I mean everything that you can think of, and what we'll need on our trip and where we can find such. Keep in mind that if we have a critical need of whatever for something, no matter what, and we don't have it, the lack could have dire consequences. Don't forget wrenches for the wagon wheels."

Private Thomas Trinko locked eyes with his buddy, Private Eugene Harrison. The thought crossed their minds, it used to be fun to sneak into forbidden places and "examine or borrow" anything that wasn't nailed down, but this is seriously grim.

"Anyone have anything else?" Joseph asked.

"Uh, Sir," Private Thomas Trinko raised his hand.

"What, Thomas? (Joseph had learned long ago to never call Thomas Trinko 'T.T.!')"

"Sir, it's just a thought, but if we could find some bicycles, it would make it faster for us to get around until we get our horses."

"Excellent suggestion! When you're on your way, look for bicycle shops. Check the yellow pages-there were a few old ones in the office downstairs. for addresses, and again, I don't care how, but you get this stuff. Hang onto the bicycles though, we'll use them later. There used to be one or two large bicycle shops up on Warner Avenue near the 405 Freeway that have great reputations; be sure to get whatever parts and wrenches including tires you can carry. Try to get the same size bikes and tires. If something goes wrong with a bike, we can "cannibalize" it. The bikes might have trailers with them, too."

Joseph looked around. "All right, let's get started."

A few minutes later, Major Jane Ostmark, after a frantic whispered conversation with Captain Paul Weaver and their crew chief, approached Joseph and Sergeant Dean Morris. "Sir, do you have a minute?"

"Sure, and the name is Joseph or Joe, not Sir. I think I have an assimilated rank of Major, but I never use it."

"Well, Sir or Joseph," Major Jane Ostmark began. "We are somewhat of a fifth wheel around here. All we do is drive airplanes. If you're headed toward Arizona and Chicago, can we travel with you until we're near our home, Kirkland Air Force Base, in Albuquerque, New Mexico? And is there anything we can do to help?"

Sergeant Dean Morris looked at Joseph. "Joe, we can use them as guards here and maybe later, relief guards and so on." After glancing at Major Ostmark, Sergeant Morris seemed unusually interested in his reply.

"Well," Joseph thought furiously, "Well, sure. Most of my people have been together for quite a while and know what they're doing, even if I don't want to know. . . .. But if you could relieve the guards on this building, I've got other things for them to do. Further, once we start traveling, you can act as relief guards, or help cook or take care of the horses, and so on."

Upon receiving Major Jane Ostmark's relieved nod, Joseph went on, "I don't think it needs to be said that you and your crew will have to carry your own weight on the trip. I expect it will be tough going."

"Well, it's a little-known secret that my co-pilot, Captain Paul Weaver here, is a very accomplished chef and that he was planning on opening his own restaurant when his tour of duty was up. He'll be glad to help or do the cooking. In addition, my crew chief wants to go with your Coronel because he has relatives in San Diego."

"Great! I had expected to get tired of MRE's (Meals, Ready to Eat) and Captain Weaver here will be a wonderful addition to us. Be sure to send him with our guys on their supply missions. We will need whatever pots and pans you'll use for cooking including knives, forks and that kind of stuff. I think we'll have cooking for about sixteen people, breakfast, maybe lunch and dinner. Remember, we'll probably be out in the middle of nowhere with no restaurants and/or grocery stores; if we don't have it, tough."

"Captain, you'll be a welcome addition to my bunch! Don't forget that we'll need something to cook on, but it can't be very heavy."

Joseph paused, "Oh yes, one thing must be clear: if you want to come with us, the chain of command is me, then Sergeant Morris here with you near the bottom. I know you are officers and therefore outrank my men, but they know what they're doing without heavy supervision. I don't want to referee any squabbles between my people and you people. Any problems with that?"

"Not at all, Sir... Joseph. We'll be glad to help anyway we can." Major Ostmark's glance lingered on Dean Morris' face. "While flying, it was by the book, but on the ground, things were always informal between us."

Late that night, sitting on an outside step, nursing a cup of coffee, Joseph thought, *"Dear Lord, I've got to lead this bunch to do something that nobody ever prepared for or even thought of. I have no idea how we're going to accomplish this assignment. The only good thing is that I've got Dean Morris and a loyal group of men who can and will do anything. You know I'm not very religious, but I would appreciate any help you could give us. Our nation, probably the whole world, needs my men and they need me. I can't promise anything, but I believe we will need your help. Thanks for listening. Sir!"*

"Dam, I'm tired," Joseph mumbled to himself as he slightly staggered off to a lonely bed.

About a day and a half later around 4:00 A.M., Joseph Robinson was in an exhausted sleep in a cot in his office. A soft knock at the door aroused him.

"Sir, it's Sergeant Morris. Are you awake?"

"I am now," Joseph's drowsy voice mumbled back. "What's up, Dean?"

"Joe, could you come with me? I think you'll like to see this."

After a body wrenching yawn and stretch, Joseph pulled on his combat boots, like everyone else, he slept with his clothes on. He opened the door and gestured for Sergeant Morris to lead the way.

Sergeant Morris, holding a candle in his hand, led the way down the scruffy carpeted stairs to the rear and then the outside of the building. Joseph heard the soft snicker of horses and the rattle of chains and straps. He looked and saw in the star-lighted night, two large canvas covered, somewhat Conestoga type, rubber-tired wagons with two teams of horses. To the rear of one wagon was attached two other horses. Sitting in the seat of the front wagon was Private Eugene Harrison, in the back wagon was Private Thomas Trinko. Both looked extraordinarily pleased with themselves.

"Well, well, well! Good job, guys," Joseph exclaimed. "How are the horses?"

"They're in great shape," Private Trinko said. "Plus, we've got a wagon load of grain, hay and spare rubber horseshoes and supplies for them. Knott's Berry Farm took good care of their animals."

"*Maybe, just maybe, that will give us a chance!*" crossed Joseph's mind. He then uttered that thought to his men.

"O.K.," Sergeant Morris said. "Leave the loaded wagon here and head on over to that military supply area with the other wagon to obtain supplies. Thomas, take Eugene and I'll get you two other men to help."

"Hold on," Joseph said. "Take three men, armed, and Captain Weaver with you; the point is that we need those supplies, no matter what. Guys, Captain Weaver is going to be our main cook and we want to make sure he has everything he needs. Oh yes, we found a heavy-duty bolt cutter and a crowbar in the leasing office downstairs. Take that with you."

"Dean, see if the men can find a hand-driven water pump or two. We're going back to before the 1900s, before electricity, and people used something to pull up water from wells. Also, water purifying tablets might be worth their weight in gold. Check with Captain Weaver on what he needs to cook stuff. He'll be cooking for around sixteen people and whatever he needs, including stoves and/or ovens, must be lightweight and portable. Oh yes, see if your guys can find a couple of spare inner-tubes for the tires on the wagons. Along with the tubes, we'll need some way to pump them up and a couple of heavy adjustable wrenches."

Captain Paul Weaver interrupted, "Men, since I'm going be your cook, I don't know where you could get it, but a hundred-pound sack of pure flour and another hundred pounds of salt would sure be nice. I'll make sourdough bread, but I need to make a starter. Also, I will need a large glass jar, one gallon or larger and several large pots. Also, we'll need some sort of large cooking grates, perhaps four-feet by four-feet or two three by three grates to cook pots on for sixteen people."

"Captain, Paul, go with our guys to the warehouses and see what else you need. Thanks for volunteering."

Joseph paused for a moment, "Just think everyone, if we're out in the middle of nowhere and when, not if, something breaks, we need basic equipment to fix it."

"Anyone, you heard the boss, any ideas on where we can find those things?" asked Sergeant Dean Morris.

"Aw, don't worry Sarge," came a voice out of the darkness, "Give us a couple of days and if that stuff is somewhere around here, it's ours!"

Late that morning, an exhausted Private Thomas Trinko, his team of horses pulling their wagon, returned to their headquarters. Attached to the rear of the wagon was a two wheeled smaller wagon; both were stacked seven high with cardboard and metal boxes. Fashioned to the sides of their wagon were six large dark blue plastic water barrels. Private Trinko, weaving back and forth from fatigue, reported to Sergeant Morris, "Sarge, I don't know why, but someone left a couple of the warehouses unlocked down there."

Sergeant Morris just shook his head on how someone could do such a thing.

"We couldn't carry any more, but I'd like to go back down there with an empty wagon to get more stuff," Private Trinko said. "We've got the most important food supplies here. Fortunately, we don't need any more ammo or weapons, but we could use a couple of small tents and sleeping bags for everyone"

"Good thinking. But first you guys get some rest. There's a full moon tonight and I think if you leave around midnight, it'll be bright enough for you to see and you'll have less people to contend with. And see if you can find any medical supplies. Take Corporal Jefferson with you and have him figure out what we might need."

Late that afternoon, Corporal David Musinski, Corporal Sam Kleighorn and three others reported in with fourteen horses, each carrying a full saddle and gear with four each carrying a bicycle.

"Good job, people," Sergeant Morris exclaimed.

"Sarge, we picked out the best we could find and released the rest. Some of the horses we released were in bad shape, they hadn't been fed or watered in days," Corporal Musinski said. "Usually, that whole organization takes great care of their horses, but now, most people can't get to them. There was a grassy park and a lake for them just across the street, so they'll be ok now. For our horses here, we'll keep them in the park behind our building, but I'm going to post guards. I don't want any of the locals getting ideas."

The next afternoon, Colonel Devonshirk, Joseph Robinson, Sergeant Dean Morris and Major Jane Ostmark met in Joseph's office.

"What are your plans, Joseph?" Colonel Devonshirk asked.

"Well, we've got actually three wagons loaded with supplies and gear. In addition, we've got, let's see," Joseph counted in his mind, "About twenty horses, six of which will be used to pull the wagons. We'll rotate those daily. There's eleven total of my people and Major Ostmark and her co-pilot makes thirteen all together. Her crew master will stay with you because he has family in San Diego. I'm going to take the scientists with me and they will ride in the wagons. I've had to restrict the number of books they wanted to take otherwise that would have half-filled one of the wagons."

"Very well. When do you plan on leaving?"

"I think day after tomorrow early in the morning. We've heard frequent gunshots and there are a few big fires burning to the west of the Harbor Freeway. They will not be able to stop them! The rest of today and tomorrow is set for getting used to the horses, how to saddle them, and so on. Also, to make sure we have everything we need."

"Things are coming apart, Colonel! They wouldn't be able to stop those fires unless it rains here," Sergeant Morris declared. "Sir, it just doesn't look good!"

"All right. Here are your printed orders. I've made them as strong and as vague as possible. I hope they help," Colonel Devonshirk said. "What about uniforms? Do you plan on having your men in uniforms or civilian clothes?"

"Dean?" Joseph looked at Sergeant Morris.

"Well, since most of the clothes my people have are uniforms except the stuff we wore on our assignments, I think we'll continue wearing whatever they have. I don't plan on getting excited about someone being out of uniform."

"I have a suggestion," Colonel Devonshirk said. "Joseph, I have a spare officer's uniform that should fit you. It was left here by one of the men you took over from. I'm going to put a Major's insignia on it for you to wear when you get near a military base or post. That might carry more weight than acting as a mere civilian."

"Good thinking, Colonel," Sergeant Morris said, his face twitching. "But when that happens, do I really have to salute him and call him 'Sir' and treat him with great respect?"

"Sergeant Morris, you have never truly, really, saluted any officer and your 'Sirs' have always left much to be desired," Colonel Devonshirk replied with a smile.

"Sir, Present Company Excepted, Sir!" Sergeant Morris snapped.

There was more respect in that single statement then either Joseph or Colonel Devonshirk had ever heard from Sergeant Dean Morris.

"Sir, Permission To Withdraw, Sir," barked Sergeant Morris, standing at rigid attention.

"Permission granted."

The salute rendered by Sergeant Morris was parade ground perfect, Joseph almost heard the crack of Dean Morris' arm as his rigid right hand touched his right eyebrow. The about-face turn was also parade ground perfect as he marched out of the office.

After a moment, Colonel Devonshirk, his eyes misty, his voice husky, turned and said, "Joseph, between you and us, I am humbled beyond words to have led that man."

The leaving, after the preparation, was anticlimactic, the morning sun just peaking over the eastern horizon.

Joseph, sitting on a fidgety sorrel horse, said, "Anybody got anything they want to say?"

"All right. Jonesy, you and Flannery to the point, about a hundred yards ahead of us. You know the route to the freeway."

Joseph, feeling foolish, waived his arm in the air and yelled, "Move em out!"

Colonel Devonshirk, standing beside the street, came to attention, his right arm touching the brim of his hat in one final salute. Each solder riding past respectfully returned the salute, knowing probably this was the last time they would see their Colonel.

Joseph, the last to ride past, stopped, dismounted, and shook his Colonel's hand. "Take care of yourself, Sir. It has been a pleasure, an honor working for you."

"You too, Joe. We've come a long way and accomplished much for our county. Goodbye and God speed!"

Both men looked at each other for a long second, knowing that this might be the last time they ever see each other, and in an extraordinary gesture, reached out and quickly hugged the other.

"Take care, my friend," came a mumbled request!

They quickly turned away, neither wanted the other to see the sudden water in their eyes.

Later, Joseph galloped his horse alongside of Sergeant Dean Morris. "Where's Trinko? We need to find out how fast these horses can travel and how much rest and food they need. Also, we need the rest of our bunch to learn how to handle the horses, hooking them up, saddling them and so on."

"I've handled that, Joe," Dean Morris said. "Trinko is in charge of the horses and when he says stop, we stop. I think it'll take a week or so for us humans to become acclimated to riding. Tonight, we'll work on the men repeating how to saddle and unsaddle the horses. My butt and legs are starting to feel it already."

"Aw, you're just plain soft. I thought an old, grizzled veteran like you could ride forever." Truth was Joseph's legs and rear were also feeling a little sore.

"Oh, I forgot to tell you," Trinko approached, "While we're on the road, if possible, we'll have the horses walking on the dirt side of the freeway or field or whatever we're on. The dirt will be easier on their feet."

"Good, well done!" Joseph complemented. "Something else we need to think about, not right now, but soon is our guards. I expect that once it dawns on people that there are no more police, the gangs and general anarchy will take over. Since it will be apparent that we have food and horses, starving people will need do anything for food. You remember our little jaunt to South Africa and the terrible conditions there except for that little village?"

"Yeah, you're right," Dean Morris said, remembering a "black" operation to get an allegedly starving tribe's medicine man out of the jungle. "Did you ever figure out why the CIA wanted that guy?"

"Well, maybe, but we can talk about that much later. He wouldn't even talk to regular people. But he sure understood English. In our long flight back to that air base outside of Las Vegas, he slept, but he mumbled in his sleep almost like nightmares. And he was no stranger to airplanes, he was no local native and he knew what MRE's were. But he sure looked mean. That whole operation was strange."

"Anyway, I'll set up a rotating guard when we camp this afternoon," Dean Morris said. "I want to keep Jonesy and Flannery as the point. They can smell trouble. Oh yes, do I include Major Ostmark and Captain Weaver in that guard rotation?"

"Oh Yes. Include me too," Joseph said.

Sergeant Dean Morris, United States Army, said nothing, but he thought a true leader would not ask his men to do anything he wouldn't do. Joseph Robinson, only a civilian for crying out loud, more than met the definition of a true leader. Dean Morris knew that their dangerous journey, their search was just beginning and that they would need all the leadership they could get.

CHAPTER THREE

"Where the hell is this Meteor Crater?" asked Sergeant Dean Morris.

"Well, let's see what the map says," said Joseph Robinson.

He rode his horse to the side of a wagon, jumped into it and rummaged through a cardboard box. Looking into the wagon, all Dean could see that the box contained was maps.

"Good thinking, boss, I never thought of getting maps."

"That's why you're a lowly Sergeant and I'm a great exulted leader," responded Joseph Robinson.

"Excuse me, great exulted leader, but my horse has to make some droppings."

They grinned at each other.

"Here, that Meteor Crater is almost thirty some miles east of Flagstaff and about six miles south of Interstate 40," Joseph pointed on their map.

"That's in the middle of nowhere," observed Dean.

"Yes, but maybe, if we're very lucky, that hole in the ground may save us all," said Joseph Robinson.

"How deep is that thing?" asked Dean Morris.

"I don't know, but we've got about eight hundred feet of rope with a couple of pulleys to help us pull up whatever we dig up. Plus, I made sure that we had a couple of shovels, heavy duty picks and a sling to lift that meteor to the top. We've got enough men to dig and enough horses to pull up the whole meteorite if necessary. I know that scientists have been down in the middle of the Crater, so there must be some way for them to get there."

"How large or heavy is that meteor or parts of that meteor?"

"Technically, it is a meteorite; this object was called a meteor before it lands on earth."

"Ok, whatever it is called, how big or heavy is it?"

"I don't know for sure, but my limited research showed that when it impacted that plateau, it broke up into a number of pieces. I'm hoping for a couple of small pieces, but we'll take whatever we can find. I don't want anything more than four or five hundred pounds. That way, they would be easier to handle and easier to melt down. We shall see, I guess."

"I meant to tell you, Dean, that if we are successful with this meteorite project, there was a huge meteor nicknamed Allende that landed in northern Mexico in February of 1969. About two tons of this meteorite were recovered and examined."

"So?" asked Dean Morris.

"The reason it is interesting is that part of this object was over four and a half billion years old, thirty million years older than our earth, and somewhere around two hundred and fifty million years older than any rock on earth. Maybe, just maybe it might be usable if our search is successful."

The days and miles passed. After the first week, sore muscles and legs from unaccustomed horseback riding toughened and the time in the saddles lengthened. To the side, they could see heavily burnt electrical enclosures with an occasional green mist flowing over them. Frequently, they saw burning transformers on electrical poles having been attacked by the Green Ghost.

Even more depressing, off to the side of the freeway, they saw burned houses and in a few small towns, whole streets were burnt and destroyed while the Green Ghost circled violently overhead. Fire trucks were useless because they were ruined by the Green Ghost while fire hydrants had no water pressure!

Soon after they left Orange County in Southern California, Joseph Robinson and Sergeant Dean Morris required each person to carry a sidearm. If one was riding his horse, each saddle had either a M—14 or a M—16 in a saddle holster.

"Sam?" Joseph called Sam Kleighorn.

"Yes Sir," said Sam when he rode up.

"I forgot to mention your thinking of and finding the saddle holsters was a good move. That way, all our guards can go fully armed. Well done!"

"Aw, thank you Sir," said Sam, fighting a smile.

Dean Morris held an informal meeting, "People, when we are riding through any towns, I want three men as point about two to three hundred yards ahead of us. Keep yourself in a combat spread. Whoever is in the rear is not to be a hero. Everyone understand?"

After receiving nods, Sergeant Dean Morris went on, "The rear person will return to us if something goes down. Any questions?"

Seeing the question in Major Ostmark's eyes, he explained, "I gather you remember what 'combat spread' means: it means that the point people will be separated from each other by no less than thirty yards. I'd like that to be about fifty yards apart. Further, we'll have one driver and at least one armed passenger riding shotgun on each wagon. The doctors will ride in the wagons in towns, but don't depend on them for anything, they'll probably get in the way if something goes down. The rest of us will spread around the wagons as guards."

"I agree," Joseph said. "Our greatest danger will be when we're passing through any built-up area; be alert for any ambushes because desperate or starving people will do anything for food. We're a good-sized group, but. . . "

Little did they know that they were following in the tracks of Daniel Peterson and his family as they too fled Southern California. The Riverside Freeway was followed to the Interstate 15 Freeway, and they turned north. Their ride to the Cajon Summit at 4268 feet elevation was slow.

Trinko ordered, "We'll make it easy on the horses. I don't want to wear them down this early."

The town of Victorville, California, was passed.

On the outskirts of Victorville, they were forced off the freeway.

Apparently, a huge gas truck containing about 12,000 gallons of fuel had been struck by the Green Ghost and blew up under an overpass. In doing so, because of the extreme high heat from the truck, the overpass collapsed, blocking the freeway.

At the high desert town of Barstow, California, they planned to turn eastbound, following generally Interstate 40.

On the outskirts of Barstow city limits, Sergeant Dean Morris rode up to Joseph Robinson, worried, "We're going to need water soon. We're down to about a half barrel and we need that for the animals."

"I know. We'll have to wait until we hit downtown Barstow itself and get water there, I hope."

After camping about a mile inside the wide city limits of Barstow, Joseph Robinson asked a group of men sitting in front of an empty and ransacked 7-11 store, "Anyone know where we can get water for our horses?"

After some conversation, Joseph was told, "About three quarters of a mile past the MacDonald restaurant ahead of you, a couple of men broke into a city owned deep water well and somehow build a pump to pull up water. I've got to warn you, they are not nice people.".

"Why?" asked Dean Morris.

"Because they'll charge you for the water. The charges are whatever you've got and what they want," responded one of the men disgustedly. "And they enforce those charges with a bunch of guns, including shotguns and an AK-47."

"What does the building look like?" asked Joseph.

"It was, correction, is a small concrete building on a side street; you can't miss it. I think their general headquarters is a house just across the street."

"Ok, thanks, men," said Joseph.

"Dean, there's a vacant lot behind us, have our people set up there. You and I will see if we can get some water."

When Joseph and Dean Morris rode up to the water building, they were met by four men casually sitting on lawn chairs holding weapons by their sides.

Joseph asked, "Howdy, we need some water for our animals. What does it take for that?"

"Let's see, we can use a horse or two and maybe some guns and ammo in exchange for a few gallons of water," replied a short, squat silver-haired man. "That sounds like a fair trade for all the work we've done."

"Well, we'll need our horses and weapons," Sergeant Morris said. "So?"

Dean Morris and Joseph eyes briefly met. "We'll think about it. Will you be here tomorrow afternoon?"

"We'll be here as long as the water holds out. Don't wait too long, the price may go up," came a snickered response.

Joseph and Dean rode away. "We really need that water, Joe," Sergeant Morris said quietly. "We've got all of those horses and we can't cross the desert without it."

"Oh, I know that! Tonight, after midnight, we'll take them down. That building has only one entrance and they'll have to post guards. Think you can do that without destroying the neighborhood?"

"Gee, I don't know sir," said Sergeant Dean Morris, knowing full well that if they traveled nearly twelve thousand miles to a jungle in Africa, struggle several miles through a dense jungle, retrieve a medicine man from a not very cooperative tribe, and get that medicine man to Nellis Air Force Base in Nevada, this shouldn't be much of a problem.

"Don't forget that we blew up a bunch of houses in Northern Mexico and Southern California and even hit Arizona. I remember one of the first was just outside of Henderson, Nevada, replied Joseph."

"You know," Sergeant Morris said remembering their African jaunt, "I never did figure out what that medicine man we got out of the jungle had. He refused to say a word to us, but he knew English well and he was no stranger to airplanes. He even knew how to work the microwave on the plane. Strange."

"I remember that project, one of several such projects," replied Joseph Robinson. "What was even stranger about him was the people he met outside of Las Vegas. They knew each other."

They forgot a different operation in East Tijuana where they had to sneak into Mexico rather than the other way around. When Joseph's team was planning the operation, he mentioned dryly, "Heavens, no one ever tries to sneak *into* Tijuana!"

The local Mexican authorities never figured out how a large house simply blew up early one morning destroying several tons of high-grade cocaine plus enough weapons to equip a small army. The armed guards were found tied up about a block away. The nice part of that explosion was that it blew up nearly a half million U.S. Dollars and spread the wealth over the neighborhood. About fifty thousand dollars of that money was confiscated by Joseph and used to purchase the now useless high-tech computer equipment that his group were planning on using. There were other similar "tasks."

Joseph forgot, but Dean Morris and his men never forgot, that the reward money for their first "assignment" went to pay some heavy personal debts and helped considerably a few poor (because their breadwinner was in trouble and couldn't earn any salary) members of the group.

Dean Morris and Joseph grimly smiled at each other.

Upon their return, Joseph Robinson briefed his troops. "The problem is that we need water, they have it and they want too much for it. So, we're going to get it."

Joseph glanced at Sergeant Dean Morris standing, as usual, next to Major Jane Ostmark, "Dean, do you want to plan this?"

"No. You go ahead."

"All right. There is one entrance to this building on the west side facing the street and facing the building across the street."

In the light of their campfire, he drew a diagram in the dirt and pointed, "I didn't see any windows in the water shed, but the two-story house just across the street seemed to be a headquarters. I saw only about a half dozen people wondering around those two buildings. We'll probably find some of the guards in the headquarters, but I would expect that they'll have at least two guards on the target building."

Sergeant Morris said, "We should use two squads, one to take the well building itself and one to control the headquarters building across the street."

What neither Joseph Robinson nor Dean Morris realized that because of experience and trust, their minds meshed on nearly every point. When one hesitated, the other simply jumped in.

"Yes," Joseph Robinson said. "This will be a little different from our usual get in, get it, set explosives, leave as quietly as possible, and blow it up. We'll have to hold that building until we fill our water barrels and every empty container we have. Coordination of our squads and timing the attack will be a problem because we don't have radios anymore."

"I don't think so, Sir," Sergeant Morris said. He had learned to support Joseph Robinson's tactical plans because his ideas worked, and Joseph listened to and respected his suggestions. More than once he blessed the day Joseph Robinson had been assigned to his squads. Before him, so-called leaders Dean Morris had suffered through in his career had found innovative ways to screw up any assignment.

Sergeant Morris continued, "I'd like to have each squad handle its own assignment. What makes this approach work is that each building is on the opposite side of the street. Each squad will be responsible for its building and our men will not cross the street. As a matter of fact, anyone crossing the street is fair game until we secure the buildings."

"Sounds good to me," Joseph Robinson said. "I would not like any fatalities if at all possible. Let's make the attack at about oh dark hundred because whatever guards there will be sleepy then. Dean, you take the headquarters side. You've got a couple of guys who could sneak into a king's palace and steal the bras off his princesses," he said casually.

"Why would we want to do that, Sir?" asked one of Dean Morris' solders. "They would give it to us willingly!"

"Probably, but we would have to show you what to do after they removed their bras which is the real problem," Sergeant Morris said dryly.

"OK, OK," Joseph Robinson said before the snickers died down. "We're about two miles from the buildings which means we'll go on foot. Dean, have your A squad neutralize the house as quietly as possible. I'll take B squad and we'll hit the water building. It's getting close to evening, have two of your guys stake out the place. Take a good pair of binoculars and see if they can get a count on bodies in the house and the water building, and keep an eye out for dogs; we don't want to wake up the neighborhood."

Major Jane Ostmark had to ask, 'I've heard the phrase, but what does oh dark hundred mean?"

Sergeant Dean Morris patiently explained, "That time means somewhere between 0300 and 0500 hours."

"Oh."

Joseph wondered why the Major, a West Point graduate, didn't know what oh dark hundred meant. Then he realized that the answer, of course, came from his Sergeant.

Uh huh!

Around three in the morning, Sergeant Dean Morris came to Joseph Robinson, "Sir, we're ready. I've had two men sitting on the house and water building. One is here now."

"Ok, let's hear his report."

"Well, Sir," Private Wilfred St. Clare said, "They build a large fire in front of the house. That fire has burnt down quite a bit. We saw six people go into the house and they're still there. We counted four guards on the water building, one inside and three on the outside. I think they locked the door and I believe I saw the relief pound on the door three times before it was opened."

"Did you see the outside guards 'walking a post?'"

Private St. Clare knew that walking a post meant walking and being responsible for a designated area. "No Sir. They just seemed to occasionally walk around and then sit down and play cards or something."

"Any dogs?"

"No Sir."

"Arms?"

"The only weapons we could see were shotguns. I couldn't tell for sure, but the guards on the water building may have handguns. We didn't want to get too close to find out."

"Did you or could you see any tin cans attached to each other hanging from a tree or bush around the building?"

"No sir. Sir, why the question?"

"Simple, if someone is sneaking around the building in the dark, they might bump into or shake the tin cans which would rattle or clang together and alert the suspects that someone is sneaking up on them. It's the poor-man's alarm system. The military in Vietnam, at night, used them for protection from the Vietcong crawling around the outskirts of their camp."

"OK, good job guys. When we were there, two of the water building guards had shotguns and automatics on their right side, the third had a Winchester 30-30 and the fourth had a Mac-10 in a cross-draw holster on his left side when we were there," Joseph said. "I didn't see any AK-47s."

One of the men asked, "Sir, what's the difference between a Mac-10 and an Uzi?"

"Well, they look somewhat alike, and both shoot pistol type cartridges. A Mac frequently uses a 45-caliber round while an Uzi can use a variety of rounds but can also fire a 45. The Uzi was manufactured in Israel while the Mac was made here in the U.S. Both are military weapons; the Mac has an effective range of about a hundred yards while the Uzi is about double that. The difficulty is hitting a target/ bad guy beyond that range. Both will burn through dozens of rounds in a few seconds. Not very accurate; they want to climb because of the recoil. Essentially a cross between our handguns and a rifle. Very nasty weapons!"

He paused, thinking, "They are useful only in a short-range heavy combat, usually jungle, and when you have unlimited ammo. If we retrieve those weapons, we will destroy them. I do not intend for us to get into that kind of situation."

Sergeant Morris glanced at Joseph, impressed. He had not seen that many weapons. "Did you see anyone walking around the house?"

"No, Sarge."

"All right. We'll hit the two buildings at the same time," Joseph Robinson said. "Ideally, we can do this before anyone wakes up and tries to become a hero. The horses will remain here and I want us do this on foot. My group will circle around and hit the water building from the rear coming around the sides toward the front." He drew arrows in the dirt showing the direction of each of his men.

Joseph gestured to Major Jane Ostmark, "Major, would you and your crew stay here with our scientists and guard the camp? We've got enough men to handle this and they know what they're doing."

While the request was in the form of a question, there was no doubt that it was an order.

"Of course," replied Major Ostmark. A thought crossed her mind, *"Dam, I almost called him Sir!"*

Major Ostmark, accustomed to a regular heavily starched uniform of highly polished and shiny insignia, buttons, and shoes, looked at Joseph and Dean. They were dressed in black as were all the men. Each had black camouflage paint on their faces and hands. Each person was wearing a black stocking cap. Kevlar vests under their shirts bulked up the upper part of their bodies. Side arms were encased in Velcro holsters with K-Bar knives strapped to a leg. Each man had a blackened approximate twelve-inch steel rod in a holster over a hip. She'd seen shadows that were more visible.

She walked to Dean Morris, reached out and unnecessarily smeared some camouflage paint over his face. "You be careful now. Hear?" she said quietly.

He nodded, not trusting himself to speak while his eyes looked deep into hers.

Joseph coughed and growled, "All right, let's get moving. We can walk down the main highway until we get close."

The night was moonless, but the light from the stars was bright enough to nearly read a magazine. About an hour later, the two teams separated.

"Give us some time, we've got to circle around a block or so to the rear of the water building," whispered Joseph. The only sound was off in the distance where a lowly dog barked.

Joseph's team, after moving quietly from house to house, filtered to the back of the water building. They stopped about a hundred yards away.

He gestured: one half to the right and the other half to the left. He pointed to his holstered weapon, shaking his head, "No shooting if at all possible!" After receiving nods, the men separated without further orders. They had done this before, and Joseph knew they needed little or no supervision.

Step by quiet little step.

Hearts beating faster, a little louder.

Breathing a little deeper.

One foot placed gently toes first on the ground in front and then the other foot noiselessly followed, black shadows filtering from one tree or bush to another.

Jefferson Parker Stansbury, age 55, weighing 240 pounds on his 5-foot, 9-inch frame, with two felony convictions and wanted in San Jose, California, for murder, was guarding the front of the water building. He leaned back from his lawn chair. God, he had to urinate. It was all that coffee he drank to stay awake. "I've got to piss," he announced to the other two sleepy guards.

Stansbury tilted his chair forward, picked up his shotgun, yawned, and strolled around to the south side of the building to find a place to pee.

When he turned the corner, he came face to face with a black shadow that had clear, hard eyes. Before he could even open his mouth to yell, a twelve-inch steel rod driven by rock-hard hands impacted his solar plexus explosively forcing the air out of his lungs. He could not even grunt when hands grabbed the shotgun and his body before it collapsed. His body was gently and quietly laid down on the concrete. He could not struggle as tape was slapped over his mouth. His hands and arms were twisted behind him and more tape was wrapped around his wrists. Total elapsed time: 4.8 seconds!

One shadow put his knee on his chest, shoved a 9.mm Glock semi-automatic handgun up under his nose and placed his finger in front of his lips in a universally accepted signal.

Stansbury, trying to breathe, his eyes wide, was silent.

A large stain on the front of his pants said he didn't have to worry any longer about urinating.

Meanwhile four men crept around to the front of the water building, two on each side, their shadows blending into the building. The first man on each side carried a 9.mm Glock semi-automatic handgun in which was closest to the wall. His partner, on his outside, carried strips of duct tape. The two remaining guards, nearly asleep, awoke when handguns were jammed in their ears. They too made no sound when tape was immediately slapped over their mouths. They were jerked forward and dumped, not gently, on the ground. More tape was wrapped around their arms and hands behind their backs.

Joseph looked at the men on the ground and by signal asked "Anymore?"

Upon receiving a shake of their heads, Joseph pounded three times on the door.

"What?" came a sleepy reply.

"I need to get in," he growled.

"Jesus Christ, don't you ever sleep? Just a dam minute!"

Locks squeaked open.

"What the hell do you w...?" as two hard bodies tackled him and then a third jumped in.

A thud was heard and a groan, then two more thuds. Then silence.

Joseph waited a moment. "Secure?" he whispered.

"Yes sir!" came a quiet reply. "This guy didn't want to go down and I sprained my wrist. But he's not going anywhere."

"Good job, guys!" Joseph whispered. "Take these three to the south side of the building and post a guard on all four of them. Be sure to search them for weapons or knives. If one so much as belches, quiet him! We'll wait until Sergeant Morris's team neutralizes that building across the street. On second thought, three of you make like guards in the front; think you can sit on the chairs and look guardian like?"

Grins were flashed. There had always been friendly competition between the squads and this one had finished their goal first. Before the Green Ghost, the loser had to buy the beer; now, however, the winners would figure out something.

Three of Joseph's men sat in the recently vacated chairs and leaned back against the wall. The night's dark shadows hid who they were but left enough starlight to see there were bodies there.

Minutes passed, nothing happened at the house across the street. The whole area was silent.

"See anybody?" whispered one guard to another.

"No. But the Sarge is better than that. He'll probably try to go in the back way."

It was quiet, almost too quiet.

"Think we should help them, Sir?" whispered one of Joseph's men.

"No! Anyone crossing the street now is fair game."

They waited.

Suddenly, the front door of the house flew open with a crash. A shirt-less half-naked figure ran out shouting and shooting back into the house.

Joseph grabbed his M—16 hanging from his shoulder, flicked the safety lever downward one notch, aimed and fired a single shot.

The figure, about ten feet in front of the house and approximately thirty yards from Joseph went down as if he had been hit by a baseball bat, his weapon flying. Joseph's shot had hit him in the right knee.

"I didn't want to kill him," Joseph grumbled. "I just wanted him to stop all that racket."

"Good shooting, Boss! Should we go across?"

"No! Wait."

After a minute which seemed much longer, they heard a voice, "Joe?"

"Secure here, Dean, the water is ours. Is the house secure?"

"It is now. That clown in the front was walking out the door when we scared the hell out of him. Outside of him shooting up half of the house, he missed everything else."

"Well, he succeeded in waking up the neighborhood. We'll have people crawling out of the woodwork before too long. Get your medic over to look at the man on the front lawn. He has only a leg wound, but he might bleed to death unless someone looks at him quickly. How many people did you have in the house?"

"We found seven total, one lookout was asleep on the back porch, three were asleep downstairs and two were sleeping upstairs plus the guy out front. I still don't know where he came from."

"Good job! Make sure everyone is tied up. We should send a couple of guys back to get the wagons and horses. On second thought, Dean, you go back for the wagons, and I'll organize a guard detail for the prisoners and the water building."

"Consider it done. Jonesy, come with me."

A short time later, Private Jones and Sergeant Morris were walking back to their original camp.

"Halt! Who goes there?" barked a voice from the darkness.

They froze.

"Sergeant Morris and Private Jones. Good job, we didn't even see you."

Captain Weaver walked out from around the bush he had been hiding behind, a M—16 carried casually in his arms as if he was duck hunting, "I never thought I'd ever use those words again."

Dean Morris walked up to the wagons. A shadow disengaged itself from a wheel and quickly walked to him. This shadow had long blond hair.

"Are you ok?" asked a soft worried voice as a hand reached out to tenderly touch his face.

"We're fine. We have a bunch of prisoners, but we have the water we need," Dean said as his hand touched her shoulder.

"I was so worried! We heard the gunshots, then a single M—16 gunshot and then nothing."

She looked around and whispered, "If we weren't in front of the men, I'd, I'd hug you!"

"I consider that an order, Major. I'll take you up on that later."

That morning, after the water barrels, canteens and empty jars had been filled and the horses watered, they were approached by a group of men and women.

"Hello, I'm Tom Storman. I'm the mayor of Barstow. Can we ask what your plans are?"

"Sure," Joseph said. "We're planning on leaving almost immediately. If you're the mayor, I would suggest that you organize a system and a committee where the whole town can use this water."

He pointed at the trussed up former guards who didn't look very happy, "We'll leave them in your hands, but you should make sure that this doesn't happen again. We'll turn them and this building over to you when we leave."

"You can be sure that we'll handle them. Do you know what happened to the electricity? A number of our townspeople were killed when that stuff attacked their cars and our local power stations. And we've been without electricity for quite a while now. We have no radio, no telephone, no communication at all with the rest of the world."

Joseph spent about ten minutes telling the mayor of the Green Ghost, thinking that the classification of "Secret" was useless now.

Strained faces greeted his explanation. Finally, the mayor said, "Well, thank you for telling us. Are you saying that we can't expect any assistance from anyone or any government for the foreseeable future?"

Joseph nodded. "You'll need to revamp your thinking to go back to the 1800's, before there was any electricity, any cars, trucks, and so on. You have an advantage out here because you have water, and you can grow your own food. The big cities will shortly face starvation and soon, people will roam the countryside looking for food. You should plan to protect yourselves."

He shrugged his shoulders, "Beyond that, there isn't much I can tell you."

"Well, we'll make do," the mayor replied sadly, "It doesn't look like we have much of a choice. Our people here are small-town folks with most of them either farmers or doing something related to farming. Best of luck to you."

"Where are you headed? The mayor asked.

Joseph told the mayor where they were traveling through and their ultimate destination.

The mayor thought for a second. "Do you have a map?"

Joseph unfolded their map, and the mayor pointed, "You'll need water for yourselves and horses." He pointed to two tiny towns on the road the first about a three-four-day ride, "My brother owns that gas station, and they'll have water, he spent a small fortune drilling for water."

He pointed to another gas station about three days' ride further, "My wife's family owns that gas station. Mention my name and, Julia, my wife's name. Tell them where you are going and why; they'll fill you up with water, too."

"Thank you very much," exclaimed Joseph shaking the mayor's hand. "I was worried about the desert."

They left, the two-point guards leading the way onto Interstate 40. Joseph noticed that more and more, his Sergeant Dean Morris and Major Jane Ostmark were spending time together, either as guards, simply sitting with each other during meals, or just relaxing together.

The thought crossed his mind, *"It's pretty obvious what they feel for each other even if they refuse to acknowledge such emotions. If the Major decides to leave us in New Mexico as she planned, what will Dean's reaction be? Will he stay with me or her?"* He could not afford to lose his Sergeant, but what could he do?

Somewhat the same thoughts were flowing through Sergeant Dean Morris' mind. During his years in the army, he had met and served under numerous officers. And he was hardly a virgin. However, there were only a very few officers he respected, and now, he couldn't believe that he was falling for an officer. *"But she is the most beautiful person, inside and out, I've ever known, and those eyes, I get lost in them,"* he argued deep within himself.

One night, Joseph, while on guard duty with the horses and sleeping group, watched a brilliant yellow full moon creep over the eastern horizon.

A soft harmonica from his fellow guard playing what sounded like a Patsy Cline lonely love song echoed faintly among the horses and group.

A sudden wave of loneliness swept over him. He knew and admired the relationship between his Sergeant and Major; perhaps some slight envy was a better description. As much as he valued the judgment and assistance of his sergeant, he didn't expect the solitude suffered by other leaders of dangerous, slightly possible, and totally unforeseen but unequivocally necessary operations for the preservation of his country and its way of life. While his one-night stands were occasional, there was no one, no one, with he could share his deepest feelings and thoughts. After a few moments of creeping self-pity, he shook his head, conquering the thoughts while his attention turned to his sergeant and major.

A few days after leaving Barstow, Dean and Jane (it was no longer Sergeant and Major, it was now Dean and Jane) were riding together as point guard on a vacant road.

"Jane?"

She looked around, saw no one else near them and replied, "What, Dean?"

"I've got to ask, what are your plans after we get to your home in New Mexico?"

"Well, I plan on riding up to my home and greet my mother and father: 'Hello Mother, Hello Father....'" she sang the old song.

"That's not what I meant!"

"I know." She smiled.

Dean paused for a moment, "I think Joe would be willing to spend a day or so at your parents' place, but what are your plans after that?" The answer was vitally important to him.

Jane Ostmark, Major, United States Army, looked at "her" sergeant, her bright blue eyes deep in her face. She too had been thinking about her future after they arrived in New Mexico. There was little or nothing for her there. It had been years since she spent any appreciable amount of time at her "home," and her sisters would take care of and probably had been taking care of her parents.

Most importantly, her feelings for this hard-nosed sergeant were distorting her logical mind, a mind honed by four stressful years at West Point with later training for flying the big C-130s.

From the first time she became an officer, it had been driven into her: "There will be no relationships between officers and enlisted personal. Your duty, your job, is to lead, direct and order subordinates to accomplish the mission, period!"

In several of her command lectures, it was pointed out that it was impossible to lead, direct or order friends into lethal or fatal danger. She remembered the huge controversy that happened when an Air Force B-52 female pilot lieutenant had an affair with an enlisted man. It simply wasn't accepted by the upper echelon of the services. Of course, their escapades were never published!

Never-the-less, from the first second she laid eyes on "her" sergeant, something thumped heavily in her heart. And the subsequent mild flirting, especially when they were alone, simply reinforced her feelings for him. When he touched her shoulder or arm, the sudden weakness in her stomach was unexpected and almost overwhelming. His eyes, so fierce with his men, so gentle when he looked at her, were in her dreams at night.

"*What would his arms around me feel like?*" was the surprised dream.

She shook her head, bringing her back to the present with Dean Morris. "Well, 'home' was just someplace to write to my parents. I haven't spent much time there since I went into the Army. My home truly has been the many Army bases and my airplane."

They rode in silence for a few moments, the silent and cool desert air on their faces unfelt as they struggled to not say too much to the other.

"Dean, you know that Joseph needs you?"

"I know, Jane, and we were given our own mission, that to try to fight the Green Ghost." He paused and then blurted out, "I, I simply can't leave him."

"Oh, I know that!"

Just then, their relief rode up, "There's food back in the wagons if you two are hungry."

Dean and Jane glanced at each other both knowing that their relationship had somehow changed, but they didn't understand how or what yet.

CHAPTER FOUR

In the late afternoon, on the outskirts of Two Gun, Arizona, a large black bear suddenly charged out of a bunch of trees, scaring the horses, and about half the group. It probably was looking for lunch!

Guards, on horseback, waving their hats and shooting a few rounds near the bear without hitting it, chased the bear back into the forest.

After things quieted down and the horses calmed, three miles further east, they turned south, the constant clop, clop, clop of the horses' hooves was no longer consciously heard. As they approached the Meteor Crater, they could see that the immediate area appeared higher than the surrounding desert.

Joseph Robinson pointed to the rising ground, "This ground was thrown up when the impact occurred. You can see that we're climbing to the top of this so-called hill. We'll park around those buildings."

The buildings sitting on top of the miles wide mound of dirt appeared ransacked.

"Sir, look at the horses. They're skittish," said Private "Tex" Trinko. "They looked that way when we ran into that bear."

"All right, Tex. Grab a couple of guys. Take the horses back to that little hollow we passed. We wouldn't need them tonight and we can keep them in that abandoned corral that was back there," Joseph Robinson said. "Do you think we should post guards to protect them from bears or other wild critters?"

"I don't think so, Sir, but I'll volunteer to watch them tonight."

"Thank you, Tex. Dean, get a couple of guys to relieve Tex. Two at a time should be enough, but I hope the horses will tell us if any wild things are around."

After sending the horses back, Joseph and the rest of the group walked to the edge of the crater.

"Boy, that's a long way down."

"Yes,' said Joseph Robinson. "However, look across to the other side, there seems to be a path down to the bottom. There seems to be boarded path down from here, too."

"Sure, but I don't think we ought to take the horses down there," said Dean Morris.

"You're right, Sergeant," said Corporal David Musinski. "For some reason, they don't like being here."

"Well, let's set up camp back at that old corral and tomorrow morning, we'll go down there. Jonesy, you, and David get the ropes, shovels and picks ready and we'll either walk or rappel down. We'll set up a pulley and rope and we'll use the horses to pull up what we've uncovered."

"Sarge, there's a couple of pieces of that meteor inside these buildings. Could we use them instead?" asked P.F.C Ion Flannery.

"I don't know. Dr. Samualson, could we use them instead?"

The shaggy haired doctor shook his head. "I don't think so. We might try to bring them along with us to Chicago, but I don't know how long they have been up here exposed to the gamma, cosmic or x or other rays from space or even if they were thrown out from the original impact. We think that unexposed material has the best chance of having the properties to fight that Green Ghost. Sorry."

"Nice try, Ion." said Sergeant Dean Morris, smiling. "Always trying to get out of some decent labor."

"Aw, Sarge."

"Dr. Samualson, you need to go down there," said Joseph. "The men will do the digging, but you need to show them what and where."

Dr. Samualson shook his head, his eyes wide behind his coke bottle glasses. It finally dawned on Joseph that Dr. Samualson never approached the edge of the crater and that he stayed by or inside of the buildings.

"You've got this problem with heights?" Joseph, with sudden insight, asked quietly.

Dr. Samualson just looked at Joseph, beads of sweat on his forehead, his hands trembling.

"How the hell did you fly?"

"If I don't have to look down, if I don't have to see where I'm standing, I can control it for a period of time. My mind gets lost in some of its equations. It's only when I can see below me is when I, I,..." he stumbled over his words, ". . I have problems."

"Dam, now what?" Joseph mumbled to himself. "All this way and we can't get him to go down there."

"Well, there's a diagram of the bottom of that crater in the building. Can you show us where to dig?"

Dr. Samualson nodded eagerly, the relief evident on his face, "Yes, Yes, of course."

Ion called from the building, "Everyone, come here and look at this. These rocks feel warm."

They hurried to the inside of the building and looked at what was once a part of the meteor. It originally had been placed on a pedestal, but now, it lay in pieces on the floor.

"Here, feel this."

Dr. Samualson felt the pieces and they were warm! His excitement lit up his seamed face, his white hair standing, "Yes, yes! This supports our theory that there is some type of adverse reaction between the Green Ghost and the meteor. Maybe, just maybe..."

"Great!" said Joseph Robinson. "Ok, we'll go down in the crater in the morning and try to find some original part of the meteor."

The next morning, after rigging an overhanging brace with 4x4 pieces of lumber found near one of the buildings and attaching a set of pulleys to it, ropes were attached to one wagon. Two men at a time, including Sergeant Dean Morris, were lowered to the bottom of the crater.

"Be sure to take your canteens, men, I don't think there's water down there."

Sergeant Dean Morris spread out a hand-drawn map copied from a diagram inside one of the tourist buildings by Dr. Samualson. Around them at the bottom they could see holes where previous scientists or miners had dug to retrieve pieces of the meteor. On the far side wall of the crater, they could see old mining equipment and tailings where others had dug looking for minerals. Close to the buildings was a walkway from the upper edge to the bottom part of the crater.

Sergeant Morris carefully examined his map and then paced, his thirty-inch pace giving him a closely approximate location according to his map.

"Here, I think we'll dig here," he pointed. We'll need to remove a couple of feet of topsoil to get to the remains of the meteor itself. Dr. Samualson said that we can't use the pieces lying on top here."

After the usual grumbling and what Sergeant Morris called their B.M.G. (Bitch, Moan, and Groan) session, his men got to work. He was pleased; unless his men were complaining about something, they weren't happy doing whatever needed to be done. What his men really liked was they were very good at: breaking into restricted or secret places and blowing them to pieces!

A day and a half later, after a huge hole had been dug, Private Spenser Gerry, four feet down at the bottom, struck something. "Sarge, I think I hit something. It feels like a huge rock."

"Good. Just dig around it to see what we have. Alvin, send them up on top a note to send us a couple of empty pails. We'll fill up the pails with the little pieces around the meteor and those little pieces will be easier to melt down."

A few hours later, Joseph Robinson and Sergeant Dean Morris looked down into a hole with a large broken piece of the meteor sitting in it.

"That looks like it got burnt," said Dean Morris.

"It was," replied Joseph Robinson. "It was heated when it came through the atmosphere at about 22,000 miles per hour. Most small pieces of rock burn up when they hit our atmosphere."

Joseph Robinson jumped down into the hole and brushed off the burnt meteor. "We got lucky guys. If we can force that meteor apart, we can haul it up to the top in pieces."

After much swearing with more shoveling, they could see that nature had helped them by providing a split meteor, each of about twenty pieces weighing about a thousand pounds total.

"Anyone got any ideas on how we can get those pieces out of this hole?" asked Sergeant Morris.

"Well, we could tie a cradled bowline around each piece and pull them out," suggested Major Jane Ostmark who had come down into the Crater to bring water and lunch prepared by Captain Weaver.

"Huh?"

"Sure, I used to be a Girl Scout and I learned to tie all kinds of knots for one of my merit badges. Here, toss me that rope and a shovel," she said as she slid down into the hole.

Ion looked at her, "I'm impressed. Here, Sergeant Morris thought that you were just a pretty face."

The glares from Dean Morris and Jane Ostmark would have gone intentionally unnoticed except for the snickers by the men.

An hour or so later, a piece of the meteor was securely fashioned into a cradle like knot. Jane pointed, "Somebody run over to that old mine and grab a couple of pieces of wood. We'll make a sled to drag these rocks to the lift so they can pull them up to the top."

Soon, sets of pieces of meteor, each weighing approximately five hundred pounds, was slowly making its way to the top, two horses pulling a wagon onto which the rope had been attached.

"Get out of the way, people," said Sergeant Morris looking up at the swinging pieces of meteor on their way to the top. "If one of those knots comes loose, we don't want to be near the bottom."

"Why Sergeant Morris," Jane Ostmark asked, "How could you doubt my knot tying ability?"

Ion Flannery had to ask innocently, "Yeah, Sergeant? Don't you know that Majors are supposed to be able to tie anything, particularly certain sergeants, into knots?"

More red-faced glares from both Major Jane Ostmark and Sergeant Dean Morris could not stop the laughter.

Once the heavy pieces had been pulled to the top, the ropes were lowered to pull the people up to the top. Sergeant Morris and Major Ostmark were the last.

"Maybe we should leave them down there tonight," suggested Ion Flannery. "The way they look at each other, they'd never notice that we're not there."

"Sure, Ion," said Tex. "I'll let you tell Sergeant Morris that you left them down there intentionally. But we've got a long way to go to get to Chicago. I would not want him mad at me for the next couple of months. He is still our sergeant!"

"Yeah, I'm just kidding," said Flannery, quietly. "I think that the major is the best thing that happened to our sergeant, even if he refuses to admit it. I am worried about when we get to her air base. What are they going to do then?"

"I don't know either."

"Ok, men, as soon as we get those two up here, I want to load those meteorites on one of the wagons. Also, I'm curious: the horses are either afraid of or skittish toward this whole area. I wonder what their reaction will be toward the meteorites," ordered Joseph.

Later the heavy meteorites were dragged to the back of one of the wagons. Tex was struggling with two of the horses.

"Sir, the horses are ok until they get about seven or eight feet from those meteorites," said Tex. "Then, they simply wouldn't come any closer. That's strange."

"I kind of thought that might happen. When we rode up here, they were nervous," Joseph replied.

"Joe, I think if we keep those meteorites in the last wagon, the horses should be all right pulling them," suggested Dean Morris. "The wagons are about ten feet or so long. The relief horses can be tied to the front wagon."

"All right, let's see what happens."

After much grunting and groaning, the meteorites were lifted and unceremoniously dumped into the back of the last wagon. When the horses were hitched to the front of the wagon, they seemed calm.

"Looks ok to me," said Tex.

"We've got a couple of pails of small pieces; put those in the back too. We probably got over a thousand pounds total of that stuff, but our horses can pull that easily on the rubber tires," Joseph directed.

Back on the road, Joseph met with his two doctors.

"What do you make of the fact that our horses seemed to be afraid of the meteorites?"

"Well," said Doctor Samualson, "The horses seem to be able to sense the force, and if so, the fact that they can sense something about our meteorites gives me hope."

"What do you mean, hope?"

"Well, there seems to be a connection between the meteorites and the Green Ghost. That connection gives weight to our thinking that maybe, just maybe our theory has possibilities."

"For whatever its worth, I thought so too," said Joseph Robinson. "But how do we tell when that force is really around?"

"That, my friend, is the big question. While it seems that domesticated animals such as our horses have acute senses, I would think that an animal in the wild, or a tame wild animal if such a thing exists would have even more sensitive senses and therefore be able to give us a greater warning on the presence of the Green Ghost," said Dr. Samualson.

"Well, I have no idea who would have a tame wild animal," replied Joseph.

Joseph placed that question on the back burner for the time being was starting to worry about his Sergeant Dean Morris and Major Jane Ostmark.

The thoughts of "*What was his Sergeant going to do?*"

It was clear that the relationship between the two was serious. The last word he received from Major Jane Ostmark was that her home was in Albuquerque and that she was looking forward to seeing her family. He could not afford to lose his Sergeant and friend because he was a natural leader of the men.

Little did he realize that his sergeant had similar thoughts.

Days later, they camped at a man-made lake fueled by a deep drilled artisan well. The few houses and buildings around the lake were vacant.

Late that night, Sergeant Dean Morris retrieved a towel and soap and walked to the far end of the lake for a bath. The night was warm, dark, and moonless. The stars of the Milky Way, gave enough light to see where he was walking.

Major Jane Ostmark quietly watched Sergeant Dean Morris walk out of the camp and disappear into the quiet night. With a feeling deep inside, she too grabbed a towel and a bar of soap and quietly slipped out of the camp.

The path where her sergeant had walked was paved around the entire lake. Her tennis shoes were nearly silent on the path while she listened for any noise.

There!

Up ahead, she heard the splash of water as if someone made a running dive into the lake.

Quietly, quietly she crept up to a pile of clothes.

Her heart thumping deep in her chest, her clothes joined the pile.

Quietly, she walked to the edge of the water and took a tentative step. It was warm, almost like bath water. God, it had been too long since she had a bath; there never was enough water on the trail.

One quiet step brought the water to her knees, another to her waist and then another step caused her to sink into six feet of water. She surfaced, blowing water out of her nose and mouth.

"Who's there?" came an alarmed whispered voice close by.

"Who do you think?"

"Jane? Jane! What are you doing here?"

"I needed a bath too! Where are you, it's so dark out here?"

A voice next to her whispered, "I'm right here."

Her hand touched a bare chest. "Come here Dean," came a throatily command.

His reaching hand found a waist and then both hands grabbed her naked shoulders. At the same time, her hands pulled him to her.

"Don't talk, my sergeant, just hold me!"

He felt lightheaded as her naked body pressed against him. "Oh my God, Jane!"

"Shhhh," she said as her lips sought his. Their lips touched, then crushed together.

"So long I've wanted to do this," she whispered, her breath hot in his ear, her kisses burning on his face and neck.

His hands swept around her naked back and cupped her breasts, a thumb caressing a needy nipple.

Her teeth chattered as she felt him hard against her abdomen. She clasped her hands around his neck and pulled herself up, so her legs grasped his hips. She could feel him against her.

He bent in the water raising her breasts to his seeking lips, the dark nipples standing out like statutes waiting for his tongue, his lips on her. The shock on her was like nothing she had ever experienced before. While not a virgin, his lips pulling and sucking on her nipples shook her to her very soul.

The rest of the world ceased to exist for them. She pulled herself higher against him, reached down and grasped his erection. He was so huge! She guided him gently into her, the feeling was like a hot poker sliding easily and wonderfully into soft butter. He abandoned her breasts and grasped her buttocks, slowly moved her up and down on him.

Their lips sought and found each other, their heavy breathing deep in each other's mouths. Again and again, he moved inside of her. She felt her body, her mind, her entire self being driven to unknown heights. Suddenly, she shuttered as her climax cascaded in waves through her, her teeth involuntarily clasping his neck, his shoulder, her voice moaning against his damp skin. Again, and again, her climaxes pounded through her as he drove his erection deeper and deeper into her.

Suddenly, she felt him knowing that now he would climax. She weakly pushed herself up and down on him faster until he exploded into her, crying her name against her neck.

His knees collapsed, he staggered backward into shallow water with her still wrapped around him. He fell backward and roughly sat on the sandy bottom with the water around his chest, but her legs were still wrapped around him. He was still in her!

Their breathing slowed, she reached for and found his lips, murmuring "Oh! Oh! My Darling, My Darling!"

Later that night, they washed each other and after drying each other in the starlight, they again found each other to love and to cherish.

The next morning, Joseph Robinson walked up to Dean while they were preparing to break camp. "Dean, I need to talk to you for a minute."

"Sure, Boss, what's up?"

"Dr. Samualson asked how close we're going to be to Durango, Colorado. He knows a physics professor there at Fort Lewis College in Durango that might have some ideas on "The Green Ghost.""

"Oh? What kind of ideas?"

"Well, according to both Doctor Samualson and Doctor Isaacson, this physics scientist has an I.Q. equal to Einstein and the great Steven Hawking and is just as learned, but he is so reclusive that he can only teach one class. He refuses to fly and abhors any publicity. Both of our doctors have some calculations that they would like to discuss with him or at least let him review these documents."

"What kind of documents?" asked Dean Morris.

"They showed me about fifty pages full of calculations and notes all involving their theories on the Green Ghost. I could only understand about the first sentence."

Dean looked at his boss with affection, knowing that if his boss didn't know what the scientists were talking about, he sure as hell had no clue. Joe had once spent two hours with him discussing the Lorenz-Fitzgerald Contraction's effect on Einstein's Theory of Relativity. Dean remembered looking at his boss and casually asking "Do you think that the speed of light and the curvature of space and time and Lorenz whatever his name was is going to change the muzzle velocity of my M-16 when I'm trying to blow away some bad guy?"

Joseph Robinson's mouth had dropped open for a second until he saw the twitch of Dean's mouth. Joseph just shook his head and walked away.

Joseph Robinson pulled a map from a wagon. "Look, Durango is northeast of us, but it would be about a ten-day ride up there, maybe a couple of days there, and another ten-day ride to get back on our trail here. I don't really want to take that kind of time out of our schedule. Any suggestions?"

After looking at the map, Dean said, "Well, why do all of us have to go up there? One man riding up there could make better time and he could meet us in either Gallop or Albuquerque. I got a better idea. He-you could take one of the bikes that we've got attached to the wagons and make better time than on a horse."

"Sure, that makes sense."

After a moment of thought, Joseph said, "Dean, I think that I'm the one who needs to go. I know what our scientists need and want, and I speak a little of their language. Plus, if you remember, my friend Dan Peterson might be up in that area. He was looking for his little daughter."

Dean nodded at his boss for a second, "I think so too, Joe. I hate to say this, but I think you should probably travel alone. You can't take our scientists with you, they couldn't last two days without us, and they would slow you down."

"Ok, I'll leave tomorrow morning. Have someone check one of the bikes. I'll need food and water for about a week or more. You'll have the helm until I get back. How about I meet you in Albuquerque in, say not less than two weeks. Let's meet at Jane's military base, Kirtland Air Force Base, or her home, ok?"

"Sounds good to me, it shouldn't be too hard to find us, I don't think there are too many white canvases covered wagons there. I'll get your supplies ready."

"Oh, by the way, you ought to start wearing high collar shirts," Joseph remarked casually when Major Jane Ostmark, as usual, was standing nearby.

"What? What the hell are you talking about?"

"Well, there some bad sunburn going around and maybe Jane has some sunburn lotion to put on it."

"What are you talking about?"

"Well, it looks to me that you have a bad case of sunburn on your neck," Joseph remarked casually as he turned and walked away barely able to hide his grin.

Sergeant Dean Morris looked at Jane. Her hands were in front of her mouth stifling her giggling, her face bright red.

"What?"

"You have the world's biggest hickey on your neck," she whispered through her hands. "I must have done it last night. I had to stop myself from screaming, you were so good."

"Aw!"

What he really wanted to do was let out a Tarzan yell, pound his chest, and prance around yelling, "Boys, did I have a night!" but he couldn't!

"Jones, come here." Sergeant Dean Morris barked and gave instructions to have a bike checked and to have ten days of food and water ready for Joseph in the morning. "Also, get his weapons and clean them, will you?"

The next morning dawned bright and cloudless. Joseph's bike was examined, and his food and water stuffed into a large backpack. Attached to the bottom of the backpack was a lightweight sleeping bag. "Can you handle that?" asked Sergeant Morris.

"Yes."

"Are you ready?"

"Sure. I've got our scientists' documents, enough food and water, my weapons, and I think I'm ready.

"All right."

Sergeant Dean Morris raised his voice: "Squad, Fall In."

Under instructions, the men, including Major Jane Ostmark, lined up on the road leading to Durango.

"Squad, Atten-Hut".

"Dress Right: Dress!"

"Recover."

"Squad, Present Arms!"

"Sir," Sergeant Dean Morris said, first quietly, "Via Con Dios, my friend," and then, "See you in a couple of weeks."

Joseph Robinson, his eyes leaking water, rode past his men and headed for Durango, Colorado.

"Order Arms! Fall out." came the command from Sergeant Morris. "All right, let's get this show on the road."

CHAPTER FIVE

Before leaving, Joseph Robinson met with Sergeant Dean Morris. Dean Morris sketched out his supervisor's route, "You should go to Gallup, New Mexico, turn North on Highway 491 to Cortez, Colorado, and then East to Durango on whatever highway takes you there. I think it'll take you about two days, give or take a little."

While Joseph Robinson was leaving, Major Jane Ostmark said to Dean Morris, "Dean, as you know, my parents live in Albuquerque, and I'm concerned about them and my sisters too. They knew I was taking an emergency flight to Orange County, but I didn't tell them anything else. There was no way for them to know if I survived or what I'm doing."

"I understand," replied Dean Morris. "We'll push as hard as we can, but I can't break up my men or this bunch."

"Oh, I know that! I'm just asking that maybe we can push it a little faster. I can't get there alone, and I refuse to leave you!"

Dean Morris nodded and later briefed his troops asking them to expedite their journey.

Days later, after turning south off Highway 40 on to the Pan American Highway (aka Interstate 25) they exited onto Gibson.

"Jane, lead us to your parent's house," directed Dean.

After a few blocks, Jane pointed "To the south is Kirkland Air Force Base where I'm stationed. Maybe we can go out there tomorrow?"

Later, she led them into a housing track and slowly approached a nice, two-story house surrounded by trees. Her breath came faster, the worry in her heart nearly consumed her.

Suddenly, a young girl came out of the house, stopped, and stared at Jane and the group.

She screamed, "Mom, Dad, Come Here!"

She ran to Jane and pulled her off her horse, "Oh my God, we didn't know what happened to you" as she grabbed Jane, tears drenching them. At that second, an elderly man and woman ran out of the house to Jane. All four hugged, tears and words flinging about, both parents pushed her away just to see their daughter, then clutched her again, and cried together.

"How, how did you get here?" gasped her dad, tears streaming down his lined face.

After things quieted a little, Jane turned to her interested group, "People, this is my kid sister Julie and my father and mother. My dad was a Master Sergeant when he retired from Kirkland."

She introduced each person, paying special attention to Sergeant Dean Morris. "I'll explain what we're doing and everything. I'm just so glad that you are all right," she said to her family. "Oh, where's Jessica?"

"She's with her boyfriend at Kirkland getting some supplies. She will be glad to see you, too." said Jane's parents.

Sergeant Dean Morris was nearly correct. Riding through the northern part of New Mexico showed Joseph Robinson he was in the middle of nowhere! About halfway there, he came upon a large gulch that had washed out the road. Little did he realize this very spot had nearly killed his friend, Dan Peterson, and his family. Huge, majestic pillars of stone dotted the barren and desolate area.

It would be interesting to see what's on top of those buttes, he thought. *"Maybe sometime in the future, just maybe. . ."*

After riding into Durango in the early evening, he asked directions to the police station and was directed to East 2nd Avenue between 9th and 10th Streets, thinking they would know where Fort Lewis College was. If he was lucky, they might know something about his friend, Dan Peterson. He found horses and a few bicycles tied up in front of the police station.

Upon entering the police station, the female officer at the front desk viewed him with considerable suspicion, her hand hovering over her sidearm. He was wearing a 9 .mm Glock in a shoulder holster and an M-16 strapped on his back with his backpack.

"Can I help you?" Patrol Officer Sandy McPherson, her four-foot, eleven-inch stocky body wearing a Class B uniform, but hanging a worn 45 cal. revolver on her waist, asked cautiously.

"Yes officer. My name is Joseph Robinson and I've come from California looking for a professor at Fort Lewis College. Would you give me directions on how to get there?"

"Lieutenant!"

A moment later, one of Durango's finest strolled out of one of the back offices. His six-foot one inch slim, but muscled body was dressed in the dark blue uniform of the Durango Police Department, a badge glistened on his left chest and first lieutenant's silver bars gleamed from his shoulders. His dark hair was cut in a short military crew cut.

"Sir, he's from California and he's looking for someone at Fort Lewis College."

"Hello, I'm Lieutenant Woodston." He shook hands with Joseph, strong hands met strong hands, keen eyes meeting keen eyes.

"Hello, I'm Joseph Robinson from Southern California. I'm trying to locate an instructor at your local college. I have some documents for him."

Lieutenant Woodston's sharp blue eyes looked at Joseph with the calm, critical and analyzing scrutiny of a typical law enforcement officer and figured him out in a second. This was a good guy!

He turned to the female officer, "You know, Sandy, he is the second person we had from California that's gone through here

"Yes, you're right! I forgot about him and his family." She turned to Joseph, "Does the name Dan Peterson ring a bell?"

"Oh! My Lord, yes! He's my friend from Orange County, California. Is he here?"

"No, I'm afraid not. They left several weeks ago to get to his home in Wisconsin."

"They?"

"Yes, he, his family, his little girl that they retrieved from some ding-a-ling religious commune up in our mountains, and one of our most popular people, Lorraine Fairly." Sandy McPherson said. "I know her very well. He and his son rescued her from a gang rape by a couple of escaped convicts from Arizona or New Mexico." She smiled, "Lorraine and your friend have a love story you only find in books."

She turned to Lieutenant Woodston, "Do you know where La Plata County Deputy Sheriff Hank Rinokowski lives?"

"Sure, his ranch is out past the Fairly place."

"Deputy 'Hank' knows the whole story. I suggest you see him while you're here. He should know where they went."

"Tell you what, Mr. Robinson," Lt. Woodston said, "It's too late to find anyone at the College or to get out to Hank's place tonight. I've got an extra bedroom at my place over one of our downtown stores. Feel like spending the night, I'll feed you, we can swap war stories, and tomorrow morning we'll find your instructor and then we'll go out to Deputy Hank's place, ok?"

Lt. Woodston paused for a second, thinking, *"I think I know who you really are."*

They shook hands again. "I accept. Thank you very much, and the name is Joe."

"Tim."

"Mr. Robinson, "Sandy said, smiling at her Lieutenant, "Keep your door locked. He has more females wondering in and out of his apartment than the big department stores downtown. I've heard that they meander into his department store and somehow stroll up to his place."

"And there's something wrong with that?" Joseph asked Sandy, his face twitching.

Sandy giggled.

"Lies, all lies, and the photographs are of someone else! You're just jealous that I've never invited you up to my bordello, or excuse me, my dignified apartments," Tim Woodson proclaimed.

They grinned at each other.

That night after dinner furnished by Lt. Tim Woodson, Tim said casually, "I have a friend, a Captain at Kirkland Air Force Base, who was inspecting a C-130 that was full of bullet holes and burnt-out J-pods. He told me to forget seeing that airplane, but I recognize AK-47 and M-16 bullet holes when I see them. I glanced inside the rear and saw a large pile of empty M-16 shells."

Tim paused for a second, "My informants here and in La Plata County are telling me that the heavy narcotics are much more difficult to obtain than ever before. They hear rumors of supply houses and drug cartels blowing up and everyone is blaming their competition."

Joe shrugged his shoulders, "I don't know much about that, but marijuana is now big in California. I heard your government earned a ton of money on marijuana. True?"

"Yes, but little of that money filtered down to my level."

A thought crossed Joe's mind, *"This officer knows much more than he is telling me. I need to be a little careful."* And the conversations went to other subjects.

The next morning, Joseph and Tim rode up the hill to the Fort Lewis College.

"What was the name of the physics professor you were looking for? They've got a bunch of instructors over there that I don't know. My degrees are in criminal justice, and I stayed away from the egghead classes."

"Let's see, his name was Dr. Theodious Bell."

"We probably shouldn't ask anyone if his name rings. . ." Tim Woodson remarked quietly. Joe couldn't help but smile at him.

After finding the admissions office and being directed to the human resources office, they finally found a male clerk in one of the mostly empty back offices.

"Can I help you?' came a snippy voice from behind a pink and blue ornate sign stating that its owner was Mr. R. Lucston Sleck. Mr. Sleck was around five feet, three inches in height and weighted about a hundred and ninety-five pounds. He had dyed blond hair (with very dark roots), wore a bright blue shirt with tiny flowers on it and his tight green pants looked like he was poured into them.

"Yes, I'm Lt. Woodston, Durango Police Department, and I need the home address of Dr. Theodious Bell."

"Well, we can't give out that kind of information. Do you have a warrant? What do you want him for?"

Joseph interrupted, "I have some documents to show him. OK?"

"Well, what kind of documents? I need to see them first."

"If we had wanted you to see the documents, we would have showed them to you." Tim growled, already fed up with Mr. Sleck's prissy attitude. He quoted a famous movie scrip's "'I don't need no stinking warrant!' Now, what is his home address?"

"I don't think I can give it to you."

Lt. Tim Woodston leaned over Sleck's desk, and growled at him- "Listen, Mr. Slop, er, Sleck, you have two choices: one, give me the address- now!" Tim shoved aside a very neat and organized stack of papers and pointed to the desk. "Choice number two: this man and I are going to go through each one of your files until we find it. When we get done, your nice, cute, little, sweet, office will look like a tornado hit it. We don't find it here, we'll start with the rest of this place, and you're responsible. You have one minute!"

Lt. Woodston looked at his watch.

"Forty-five seconds."

"Thirty seconds."

"Fifteen seconds."

"You wouldn't dare?"

"Watch us. I am the police, remember. Who are you going to complain to? Ten seconds."

"Nine."

"Eight."

"Five seconds."

"Oh. All Right!"

Mr. R. Lucston Sleck's five-foot three-inch, 195 pound body

flounced out of his chair and waddled to a file cabinet. After some search, he obtained a large personnel file and threw it on the desk.

"Here!"

"I don't think you understood me. I don't want his personnel file. All I wanted was his home address. Just tell me his home address."

With hate tinged with fear, Mr. Sleck finally gave Tim the address.

Joseph and Tim left without another word.

"I don't understand why he doesn't like you, you seem like such a reasonable person," remarked Joseph.

Now Tim smiled, "Oh I am. But I arrested him for drunk driving a few years ago and I had to get him out of the general population inmate cells. A couple of the good-old-boys were taking a liking to his soft 195-pound body. He probably remembers me."

Just on the outskirts of Durango, they peddled up to a traditional log cabin surrounded by huge pine trees. Someone had planted flowers along the brick walkway to the front door.

Lt. Woodston knocked on the heavy wooden door of the cabin.

After a few moments, it was opened by a small, white-haired elderly man wearing the traditional plaid shirt and well-worn blue jeans. He was puffing on a pipe that smelt like burnt rhubarb.

"Yes?"

"Dr. Bell?" asked Joseph.

"Yes."

"Sir, my name is Joseph Robinson and I've come from California to see you. Does the names Dr. Samualson and Dr. Isaacson mean anything?" (Joseph wanted to say "ring a bell?" but quickly thought better.)

"Why yes. We corresponded frequently, but since that force came . . . nothing."

"Sir, they've given me some documents and calculations that they want you to look at. They have some ideas that might help me to fight that Green Ghost. I have a group of people dragging about a thousand pounds of virgin meteorite across the county to Chicago for melting. Doctors Samualson and Isaacson think that if we can melt that meteorite, it might provide protection against the Green Ghost. They'll meet me down in Albuquerque in about a week or so."

"I see. Oh yes, come in, I'm not used to many visitors."

The interior of the cabin smelled like burnt rhubarb. Burnt alfalfa or burnt anything would have been an improvement but this was Dr. Bell's home and pipe!

Joseph handed the package of documents to Dr. Bell. He opened it and quickly scanned the contents. "Hmmm, it will take me a little time to go through this. How much time do you have?"

"How much time do you need?"

"Well, since I don't have a class, about two days. Is that all right? But preliminarily, it seems that their main problem is to determine when that force is around. A wild animal would probably be suitable because a domesticated animal has lost its acute senses."

"I'll keep that in mind. I'll come back in two days for your final thoughts. Thank you, Dr. Bell."

Tim and Joseph looked at each other. Dr. Bell had heard nothing that Joseph said after looking at the documents. Tim nodded to the door, and they left themselves out gently closing it after them.

"I remember him now" Tim told Joe. "Someone told me that he had a fear of, what was it, flying, traveling, open spaces, something like that. Students respected him as a teacher, but he was so engrossed in his research that he could hardly do anything else. I've heard that the students loved him like a brilliant grandfather, and I would guess some are taking care of him here."

"Let's go find your Deputy Hank."

After leading Joe Robinson to the outskirts of Durango and on a dirt road, Lt. Tim Woodston pointed out a frequently modified log cabin, "That was where Lorraine Fairly lived. Her parents died some time ago. I think she was born there and nearly everyone around here knew her. I believe she was a runner-up for Miss Colorado's beauty pageant or something like that. Deputy Hank's place is up a short distance on this road."

As they rode up to a large farmhouse surrounded by evergreen trees, a small barn with several horses in a corral on the side, a brown-haired man wearing a leather vest and what appeared to be a .357 Colt Trooper in a high-rise holster on his right hip came to the door.

"Well, well, Lt. Woodston, Durango P.D. A little out of your jurisdiction, aren't you? What brings you out this way, Tim?"

"Hello, Hank, how are you? It's been some time, hasn't it?"

Roughened hands met roughened hands.

"Sure, it's good to see you, and who's your friend?"

"Hank, this is Joe Robinson from Southern California. He had some documents for Professor Bell at the college. He's also looking for Dan Peterson and I heard you know him."

"Oh my Lord yes, I would say I know him! Oh, I'm sorry, I keep forgetting my manners. Please come in; we have coffee on the stove."

Over a steaming cup of coffee, Joseph Robinson explained who he was and what he was trying to accomplish. He found it interesting that both officers, while holding steaming coffee cups in their hands, their eyes were continually scanning over their cups.

Old habits never die!

"Tim, did you know that Lorraine was my daughter?"

"No!"

"Yes. She had that pet cougar and her half-wild German Sheppard dog that she raised together. She found the cougar when it was just a few days old, and her dog was just a puppy. She somehow could get them to do what she wanted, almost without saying a word. Both slept together in her barn and sometimes when it was very cold, they slept in her house. They were her pets and went with them to Wisconsin."

"Tim," hope flaring in Joseph Robinson's chest, "Didn't Dr. Bell say that we needed a wild animal to determine when the Green Ghost was around?"

"Why yes, he did."

"Great! Deputy Hank, can your daughter somehow control her cougar?"

"Sure, it is kind of strange, they seem to have an almost E.S.P. communication. They look at each other and I swear that that cougar nods its head and does whatever she wants."

Deputy Hank paused for a moment, lost in memories. "When we

rescued his little red headed daughter, Dan Peterson had gotten into a bad knife fight with a Charlie Manson look-alike who was the leader of one of our religious communes we have up in the mountains. I came on Dan just after the fight and I understand that cougar saved Dan's life. I'll never forget the sight of that cougar crouching over Dan's body, guarding him from some suspects and snarling with that wide-open tooth-laden mouth. The only way that could have happened is that Lorraine sent her cougar to protect Dan. So, the answer to your question is yes."

"Wait a second!" Lt. Woodson exclaimed, "Around a year ago, we had a peeping Tom running around out near here looking into bathrooms or bedrooms at night, but we never could catch him. I got a call from the Durango Hospital E.R. one night. A guy staggered in looking like he had a fight with a barbed wire fence, and lost! They gave him over a hundred stitches mostly over his back and buttocks. Those cuts could have been from a cougar. The victim/possible suspect refused to talk to us."

Lt. Woodson laughed, "However, we had no more complaints from someone looking into bedroom windows."

The two officers smiled at each other. Deputy Hanks opinion, "That was one way to solve a crime problem. We need more four-legged cougars; this being a tourist town, we have plenty of two legged ones!"

More smiles! Joseph had to join in watching two experienced police officers swapping war stories!

"Do you know where your Lorraine Fairly is or where she is going?" asked Joseph Robinson.

"Yes, she's going with her 'husband' Dan Peterson to his home near Manitowoc, I think I'm pronouncing that correctly, or Two Rivers, Wisconsin. Peterson, his family, and another couple left several weeks ago riding their bikes. They told me about where his family lives which is near a small town named after some Indian tribe or Chief. Are you planning on seeing him?"

"Absolutely. Maybe she'll be able to solve one of my problems of knowing when the Green Ghost is immediately around."

"Ok, I'll give you what directions I have and before you go, would you be so kind as to carry a letter from me, from my family?"

"Of course. I'll see Dr. Bell tomorrow afternoon and I'll leave as soon as possible to meet up with my men in Albuquerque. Would your letters be ready by then?"

"Oh sure. I can't pay you for that, but I really appreciate it. Maybe, if you're successful, I'll see her again sometime," Hank said, heavy emotion apparent in his voice. "I have plenty of food here or at least enough to get you past Albuquerque. So when you stop by here, we'll load you up."

The next afternoon, over a cup of coffee at Professor Bell's home with two of his students hoovering over him, Lt. Woodston and Joseph Robinson looked curiously at the professor as he finished writing a letter to Joseph Robinson's scientists.

"They have got a great idea, "Professor Bell said, "and here are a couple of thoughts that might help them. They may not necessarily need a complete meteorite; it may be that the inside of the meteorite is sufficient. I was impressed that a part of the Arizona meteorite did in fact break up when the force thing, the Green Ghost, arrived and that there was some form of physical and chemical reaction."

After a moment, Professor Bell continued, "A major problem is to determine precisely when that force is around so that humans don't get hurt. A wild animal would probably be best."

"How about a cougar?" asked Joseph Robinson, hope tight in his body.

"Cougar? A wild animal? Oh, yes, I would think so."

Joseph Robinson locked eyes with Lt. Woodston after a deep breath, "Maybe, Tim, just maybe my journey is not in vain. Now, all I must do is find a tame cougar! I guess I'll be going to Wisconsin."

"Tim, thank you for your help. I sincerely appreciate it. I'm going out to Deputy Hank's place, get directions to my friend Dan Peterson's home, and I'm on my way. I had planned on leaving tomorrow, but now I really want to get to my team in Albuquerque."

As they shook hands, Tim murmured softly, "I said before that I thought I know who you were, but I don't want any response from you. The reason is because now I'm convinced who or more likely what you were. Whatever it was you did, I just want to say 'Thanks for your service!' You may not be aware that there is a sort of underground of upper-level narcotics officers who meet occasionally and swap ideas, theories, and results for fighting the entire field of narcotics. We looked interestingly at strange houses (with whatever police reports there were) blowing up all over the southwest part of our country including northern Mexico. We had information on some of those houses or empty business buildings, but most D.A.s and/or police agencies needed good probable cause to take any action. Then, suddenly, to our truthful surprise, an interesting number of those places either burnt down or blew up. And, somehow every single one of those places had huge amounts of narcotics! My fellow officers did not know how, or who, or what was giving the drug cartels such hell, but we blessed those people, or group or whatever they were!"

Tim continued emotionally, "Our meeting here will stay with me, but I'm proud to have met you. *Vaya con Dios, my friend!*"

Joe said nothing, but simply shook Tim's hand.

After receiving a plastic wrapped package from Deputy Hank Rinokowski and his family, together with additional food and a fresh baked loaf of bread and a small jar of jam, Joseph Robinson left, thinking he could make about fifty miles before dark.

Deputy Hank told him, "You can pick up Highway 550 not far from here and that'll take you to Interstate 25, South, and that will take you into Albuquerque. It's about 210 miles. The only problem you'll have is that you are going over the Continental Divide."

The next afternoon, after riding over the Continental Divide and into and through Albuquerque's downtown, an exhausted Joseph Robinson exited on Gibson Boulevard and turned east.

He followed Major Jane Ostmark's instructions to her parent's house on the outskirts of Kirkland Air Force Base. As he turned the corner, about half-way up the block a startled soldier handling horses looked, and then scooted into a two-story house, yelling "He's back, he's back."

Sergeant Dean Morris, Major Jane Ostmark, and the rest of Joseph

Robinson's crew scurried out and crowded around, Jane Ostmark hugging him with a "Welcome Back!"

After the welcomes quieted, Sergeant Dean Morris looked at Joseph and said "Well?"

Joseph smiled at Dean Morris, "I've got some good news." And Joseph told the rest of what he found in Durango and affirmation of his scientists' thinking on fighting the Green Ghost. "Now it looks like we're going to Wisconsin to find a pet cougar."

"How long have you been here?" Joseph asked.

Dean Morris replied, "We pulled in here two and a half days ago. Yesterday, Jane, a couple of our guys and I rode out to see a General Fencior at Kirkland. They gave us a decent welcome, but he really wanted to see you. I don't know how, but he knew of your conversation with Washington D.C. when you told the CIA and the Chief of Staff of The Green Ghost. He had no communication with anyone since then and he was, of course, concerned about the future of Kirkland, and this city."

"OK, we'll go out there tomorrow. I need to take a little rest; I've been pushing it from Durango and am exhausted. In any event, out mission has now solidified: we'll go to Wisconsin, somehow get that pet cougar, and then probably fight our way to the University of Chicago to melt down some meteorites and see what happens." Joseph, shaking his fist, exclaimed, "We'll get there, people, we'll get there! Things are getting better!"

Dean Morris looked at his leader with fondness, Joseph's enthusiasm and drive was exciting even him.

That evening, after dinner, Sergeant Dean Morris went for a quiet walk with Jane Ostmark's parents.

"As you are aware," Dean Morris started, "We don't know what's going to happen to our country, our society, but I must tell you that I've met the most incredible person I've ever known in my life: she is your daughter." He paused for a moment, "I don't know how this works, but I believe she feels the same way about me." He took a deep breath, "I would like for your permission to ask for her hand in marriage."

Mr. and Mrs. Ostmark had noted and talked about the relationship between their daughter and this man. More importantly, Mr. Ostmark, as a former Master Sergeant and thereby a long-time supervisor of men and women, saw the respect given Dean Morris as a leader, and importantly what his subordinates thought of him as a man. They rightly concluded this man, this person who had asked them for their daughter's hand in marriage, was a good man.

Mother Ostmark's eyes leaking water and Father Ostmark's quivering "stiff upper lip" was answer enough. A few moments later, after receiving something from Mother Ostmark, they returned to the house.

Later, Dean asked Joseph for a little walk.

"Joe, I've got a favor to ask."

"Of course, I agree and will do so."

"You don't even know what I'm going to ask you!"

"Well, I would be honored to be your best man."

Stunned, "How...how the hell did you figure that out?"

"You may not know that I've had two 'best-friends' in my life. You are one and Dan Peterson, who you might meet, is the second. As such, I should know you quite well, and Jane too. I certainly approve of your future together. It was clear from the date you shook hands with her on that runaway in Orange County, California."

Joseph happily shook his friend's hand and hugged him.

That evening at Major Ostmark's parent's house, after venison steaks generously supplied by a friendly Kirkland mess-hall Sergeant, Major Ostmark took "her" Sergeant Dean Morris to the front porch of the house.

"Dean," Jane Ostmark started, "No, don't say anything, let me finish. When I landed my C-130 at John Wayne Airport in Orange County, California, I never, ever in my wildest dreams, ever thought I'd be here under these circumstances with someone like you or you. I've been talking to my sisters who are taking care of our parents and they are doing all right. The Air Force takes care of its own. What I'm trying to say is that I'm not really needed here. "

Jane Ostmark paused for a moment and took a deep breath, "My Sergeant, what I do know is that you need to be with your Joseph

Robinson, you need to fight this Green Ghost, and you need to finish your mission. And since I met you and especially since that night at the lake, I, I need to be with you, to follow you wherever you go. That is, if, if, you'll have me?" she asked with quivering lips, tears hovering in her eyes.

The response from Dean Morris was a surprising immediate, "Come With Me!"

Startling and scaring her, he grabbed her hand and led her back into her parent's house. His crew, his leader, Joseph Robinson, and her parents with her sisters and a few neighbors were lounging in the big living room. A huge roaring fireplace and several lanterns furnished light.

Dean took a chair from the kitchen and placed it in the middle of the living room. The room fell silent.

Dean pointed at the chair and said, "Please sit!"

"What?"

"Sit!"

She sat.

Sergeant Dean Morris, mentally and physically tough, hard-nosed survivor and leader of more than a few enormously hazardous combat and secret missions looked around the room. He was about to do something he had never, even in his wildest dreams, thought he would or could do.

He took a deep breath, and shaking, knelt on one knee in front of Jane Ostmark.

"Oh my God," came a whispered voice from a sister. The silence in the room was absolute.

"Jane, I don't know what they have for marriages now, but will you marry me, Jane Fern Ostmark? To have and hold me and in return, just all my love, my admiration, my respect forever? Will you?"

Dean held in his shaking hand a small well-worn small diamond ring, his heart pounding.

Tears flooded Jane Fern Ostmark's cheeks, her hands clasped to her face as she felt faint, she reached down to hold "her" Sergeant to her was all the answer he needed. She tried to stand but couldn't, she felt light-headed, her knees wobbly.

Jane held out her hand and he placed the ring on her finger. She looked at it through wet eyes; wait, she'd seen this before, but where? Then suddenly she looked at her mother and knew that it was her mother's engagement ring, which meant that her parents fully approved of Dean Morris.

Cheers of approval by Dean's men could be heard for a block!

The next day, Joseph Robinson, Dean Morris and Jane Ostmark, and the rest of Joseph's crew rode out to see Brigadier General Fencior, base commander of Kirkland Air Force Base. Surprising Joseph, both Major Ostmark, Sergeant Morris and his soldiers wore what they could of their Class A uniforms. On the flight line, they could see rows of C-130s and numerous other now useless planes, parked, collecting dust and birds.

As they entered the large Headquarters building for the base, they were met by Captain James Wisnicki, aide to General Fencior. He said, "Just a minute, please, I'll check if the General can see you."

"General, Major Ostmark and her party are here, do you want them in?"

"Oh yes, and see if you can scrounge up some coffee, Jim."

Major Jane Ostmark looked at "her" squad of enlisted men, "Ok, let's do this by the book, Ok?"

"Detail, Att-hut! Forward, March."

Major Jane Ostmark marched in with Sergeant Morris at her side, the rest of the enlisted men following. "Detail, Halt." She ordered.

She saluted, "Sir, Major Ostmark, Jane, and detail reporting as ordered, Sir." Her salute would have made any military Academy instructor proud.

"At ease, all!" ordered General Fencior, his stocky six-foot, one-inch frame returned Major Ostmark's salute. His Class A uniform looked like it had more medals than Colon Powell.

"Let's all move to my conference room next door. My aide is bringing coffee for us. Please sit."

As they walked to the general's conference room, General Fencior stopped Joseph Robinson. "You must be the famous Joseph Robinson?"

"Err-Yes Sir?"

"Good to see you, I've been looking forward to meeting you for some time."

Questions were glanced to Dean Morris and Jane Ostmark by Joseph Robinson, with shrugs of shoulders the only reply.

After everyone was seated with General Fencior at the head of the table, "How is my friend, Colonel Devonshirk III, as far as I know, the only one-legged Colonel in the U.S. Army?"

Surprised, Joseph replied, "He's fine Sir. He and the rest of my crew were going to Camp Pendleton, down in Oceanside, California, to wait this thing out. Sir, how do you know of him?"

"Well, you know that usually Army and Air Force people don't easily mix, but his wife, may she rest in peace, was my sister. We met at their wedding and have remained friends ever since. I knew a lot of what you, and your people, did, for instance, in East Tijuana when that house of cocaine blew up, and a little escapade in Africa; where do you think the plane that took you there and brought you and that medicine man back came from? You should know that even I don't know the whole story behind that."

Joseph glanced at his sergeant, Dean Morris with the same thought *"What the hell? Those missions were top secret; nobody was supposed to know about them."*

"Sir, with respect," Sergeant Dean Morris leaned forward, "this may be academic, but are you, were you, cleared for that information? They all had different code titles and secret funding and we were ordered to never discuss them, ever, with anyone, Sir."

General Fencior smiled as he noted the almost unconscious squirming of a few of Sergeant Morris' enlisted men. "Relax, men, that information and missions stay here, they go no further. I'm just trying to tell you that I know more about you and your men, what you men did, why you did it, and what it took to keep your successes secret from anyone else. While your orders, or more precisely requests, came from Washington D.C., where do you think the funding and equipment came from? "

General Fencior continued smiling, "Did you know your paychecks came through my office? If all of you remember, you got paid. That funding and your personal records are here, but my aide is so incompetent that he somehow can't find them. Right, Jim? If anyone, including the left-wing liberals in Congress, the ACLU, or anyone started asking questions about any of you, or more importantly, any of the project's you men accomplished, your personal jackets would always turn up missing and we've never heard of you. I've got, or had, about 53,000 acres of base here with around 30,000 plus or minus civilians and just over 4000 military personal; it was quite easy to absorb a small unit like yours and my aide, Captain, who should have been Major Wisnicki, is great at losing paperwork. If a question would come up from some governmental or congressional agency, somehow, the projects never crossed our desks, and we had no idea what they were talking about."

General Fencior paused for a moment, debating whether he should share certain information, and decided, *"The hell with it, these guys may save our nation yet."*

"This is Top Secret and above, gentlemen and you too, Major Ostmark, with a couple of subclassifications. By the way, this conversation never took place, I and my staff never heard of you

and we have no idea what anyone is talking about." He hesitated for another moment.

Understand?"

Upon receiving nods from everyone in the conference room, General Fencior continued, "All of you should know is that for many years, certain senior members of the Armed Forces recognized that the United States needed a unit, generally removed from visible, active service that had the ability to sneak into forbidden areas and cause destruction without any bad guys knowing who destroyed their contraband or disrupted their operations. Without ever mentioning any names or identifying anyone, some of you were facing general court-marshals for the stuff you had done, but we found a purpose for each one of your, let us say," he grinned, "unique talents. Plus, that kept several of you from going to prison, and most importantly, you did a service for our country."

With effort, he refrained from more smiling at the squirming of a few more of Sergeant Dean Morris' men.

He continued, "Sergeant Dean Morris under Colonel Devonshirk in Orange County, California, after a long search, was selected to lead you. A much bigger problem was finding a civilian to head your unit because while the military can't do a lot of things, a unit led by a civilian, was in all legal terms, a civilian unit and not subject to the Uniform Code of Military Justice, nor subject to the military command and control, and thus, able to perform the number of questionable operations you men admirably completed."

He looked at Joseph, "As you know, Mr. Joseph Robinson was chosen. You gentlemen know that you were quite successful. As a matter of fact, you were successful beyond our original planning and expectations. There are only three people in the United States that know the entire story of you men. It was planned that not even these three people could know who you men are, where you are, or who is leading you and, in all cases, are told nothing of what you are doing."

"I do have one question, however. About six months before this Green Ghost thing, we were tasked to send one of my 130s, pick up you people, and do a modified touch and go maneuver just outside of Panama City in Panama on some dark deserted road. My people were supposed to recover you four days later upon receipt of a radio message. After picking you people up, my plane came back with dozens of bullet holes, one shot-up engine and used JATO units. My pilot and co-pilot both reported that immediately after they performed another quick landing for your recovery, a series of enormous explosions rocked their plane. They said they took off in a nasty rainstorm while in the middle of a running gunfight between you people and some very irate bad guys. Can you satisfy my curiosity?"

Sergeant Dean Morris glanced at Joseph Robinson who slightly nodded his head.

"Sir, we had received word, outside of official channels, from DEA or someone, that sixty or more tons of cocaine and about an equal amount of marijuana were being funneled through Panama in eight huge long-distance trucks. These were very well escorted by about ten heavily armed thugs for each truck. They had the regular AK-47s, some M-16s and a few even had grenades and all of them had various side arms. We thought about maybe ambushing them, but there were way too many of them. We also thought about dumping a bunch of mortars on them, but we didn't have enough to do a good job."

"Jesus," *Captain* James Wisnicki interrupted, "That's, that's about 54,000 kilos of coke at about, street value, $30,000 a kilo, equals, I can't count that high, but that's a huge amount of dope and money."

Sergeant Morris turned to Joseph Robinson, "Sir, you can finish the story."

"Ok, after excluding the options that Sergeant Morris told you about, it dawned on me that I have a couple of men who would put Comanche Indians to shame. As I'm sure you know, they were great on getting into places where they weren't supposed to be. So, why not use them."

Joseph looked fondly at two of his men. He continued, "Before we landed, we put together a plan to attach timed explosives underneath the front and rear of each truck. Each explosive package contained about a half-pound white phosphorus which was intended to burn anything around it. The plan was to use about ten pounds of C-4 on each end with a remote trigger. We landed four days before they were to arrive and were told where they would stop for fuel and food. I don't know where DEA or CIA or whatever got that information, but it was truly accurate."

He paused for a moment, remembering. "We got lucky. When they stopped, the rain started in buckets. You couldn't see two feet in front of you. My guys crawled in and attached the explosives and got out without anyone seeing them. We then radioed your plane to come and get us. I think now that someone saw us because we were about a quarter mile away from them and our pick-up point was about two or three miles away."

"Whoever saw us knew we weren't friendly and raised an alarm. Some of the thugs started chasing us, firing as they came on. We ran and as your plane landed, I triggered the explosives. I believe now that at least some of the trucks carried either arms or regular explosives. When the trucks went off, there were a series of huge sympathetic explosions indicating that not only did our explosives detonate the regular dope trucks, a whole bunch of other stuff also blew up. The great part was whatever wasn't blown up, because of the rain, the phosphorus ate. "

Joseph grinned at his guys, "Good job, people." He glanced at General Fencior, "Sorry about your plane, General. I know your crew wasn't injured and they were ordered to not, repeat, not to discuss where they were or what they saw."

General Fencior said "I heard from a few military people in the Canal Zone that they heard and felt a huge rumbling, but they didn't know where it came from."

He looked at Joseph, "Did you take part in that operation?"

"Yes Sir, of course. But my guys and Sergeant Morris here needed little supervision; they knew what had to be done and did it. If credit is to be given, they truly deserve it!"

"Sir, with respect, I can't let that comment stand on its own." Sergeant Dean Morris rose "Sir, Sergeant Morris, Dean, request permission to speak, Sir."

"Of course, permission granted!"

Sergeant Dean Morris pointed at Joseph. "The true story is that Joseph here was the last one on the plane. He was exchanging covering fire with the suspects as we piled onto the plane. We pulled him onto the back part of the plane, still firing, as we were taking off. He is a true leader of our bunch!"

General Fencior saw and heard rumblings of approval from Joseph's men. They agreed with their Sergeant's statements. He looked at Joseph and gave a nod of respect thinking *"My Coronel in Orange County was absolutely right!"*

General Fencior took a deep breath, "Which leads me to your Joseph Robinson here. Just as a side issue, I have two airmen here who were, are, true computer geeks that had the ability to hack into nearly every computer system in the world, including yours. When their personal misdeeds were brought to my attention, I gave them a choice, work only for me, and do what I tell them to do, or face a military general court trial with very probable time in prison with a dishonorable discharge. Mr. Robinson, when you sent your report to Washington, D.C. on the Green Ghost, we knew about it. We listened in on your conversation with Washington and that gave us some advance notice to prepare for the Green Ghost."

He took a deep breath, "I've got to tell you that that was one of the scariest conversations I ever heard. But it did give us some warning."

He leaned forward, "So, what can we do for you?"

Joseph Robinson paused for a moment, "Well, General, this is what we have planned." He described his conversation with Dr. Bell and the two scientists, the pieces of meteorite he and his group was dragging across the country, his plan to contact his friend in Wisconsin whose girl friend had a tame cougar, and their ultimate destination at the University of Chicago."

Joseph paused for a moment, "We plan on stopping for supplies at Camp or Fort McCoy in Southeastern Wisconsin and going on from there."

He stopped for a second, then his voice low and intense, "General, my last orders were to try to fight that Green Ghost. Sir, I think we have a chance with my guys, just a chance that we might be successful and I'm going to do everything in my power to follow my last order!"

"I thought so. Jim, where are you from?" asked General Fencior to Captain James Wisnicki.

"Sir, from near a tiny town just north of Madison, Wisconsin."

"How do you feel about going home with Mr. Robinson?"

"Sir, I would love to, but I thought you needed me more here."

"I probably shouldn't say this, but you are one of the finest aides I've ever had. I think, however, that you can do a great service for maybe all of us, for our country. Do you know a Major General Gus Klinger who's overall in charge of McCoy and a few other bases? There's another Major General named Douglass that has some influence there."

"Yes Sir. Gus Klinger just made Major General, and he was in and out of my last Base. I know him quite well. However, there is a Colonel Blossitt who is in charge of the largest unit at McCoy. He is *de facto* in charge of the entire base; I knew him when he was a Major, then a light bird and now with eagles, he is a good guy. And I do know Wisconsin quite well, too."

"Mr. Robinson, how do you feel about having him along with you to sort of pave the way to obtain whatever you need? You should know that my Jim is a recognized explosive expert and that might come in handy if you must fight your way into Chicago."

"Yes Sir, thank you, he would be welcome, but" Joseph Robinson hesitated, "I want to clear up what might be a little problem. Our chain of command is me, then Sergeant Dean Morris, then probably Major Ostmark and then you."

Mr. Robinson turned to Captain Jim Wisnicki. "Can you live with that? That has worked well for the time my group has been together and I'm not inclined to change that arrangement."

"Yes sir, that's no problem." Captain Wisnicki glanced at General Fencior, "After working for the General, I can do and have done anything and everything!" They smiled at each other.

Captain Paul Weaver stood, "Sir, my assignment is here at Kirkland, but I've been acting as the chief cook for this group from Orange County. I am simply a co-pilot with Major Ostmark. I request permission to continue with Mr. Robinson and his group to wherever they go. They need someone to cook and I'm the most qualified to do so. Sir."

"Mr. Robinson?"

"Oh yes, we need him. We'd starve if he wasn't with us. I speak for the rest of my bunch in that we really appreciate him." The murmurs from Joseph's group simply echoed his comments.

"So Ordered! Jim, prepare a transfer of yourself and Captain Weaver to McCoy in Wisconsin; let them figure out what to do with you after you get there."

Major Ostmark, who had remained quiet during the meeting, finally blurted out, "General, I must tell you that I feel I must resign my commission before we go too much further. I will be, correction, I am in violation of U.C.M.J. Section, I believe it's 133.

General Fencior glared at his Major Ostmark, surprise clearly visible on his face.

One of Sergeant Dean Morris' men whispered to his buddy, "What the hell is Section 133?

"It says that an officer cannot have a relationship with an enlisted man, like our Major with our Sergeant."

Hearing the explanation of Section 133, Corporal Samuel Kleighorn, stood, came to attention, and said formally in his Texas drawl, "General, Corporal Kleighorn, Samuel, requests permission to speak, Sir?"

"Permission granted."

"Sir, I know I speak for all my men, and I'm sure for Mr. Robinson when I state unequivocally that none of us have ever, ever, seen at any time or anywhere any untoward and/or illegal and/or unethical action by and between Major Jane Ostmark and Sergeant Dean Morris. Sir, their conduct has always been in accordance with the highest legal and ethical standards that we were taught by the Army, Sir!"

A rumbling murmur from Joseph's group expressed agreement!

Sergeant Dean Morris found that something was in his eyes and could not speak; Major Jane Ostmark simply had tears starting to flow down her down her cheeks.

General Fencior took a deep breath, glanced at Sergeant Morris and Major Ostmark, took a lengthy thoughtful sip of his coffee, and finally stated, "Major Ostmark, you have been one of my best C-130 pilots, calm, cool under tough circumstances and probably would have been a Lt. Colonel soon. As you may know, I have this occasional hearing problem and I missed what you tried to tell me. And I don't want to revisit this issue again. Is that clear?"

Seldom seen tears running down her face, Major Jane Fern Ostmark could only nod.

"Sir, may I have a moment of your time, privately?" Captain James Wisnicki asked. "In your office! Now, Sir?"

Surprised, "Ok."

The general, upon entered his private office, demanded, "What?"

"General," Captain Wisnicki said, unintimidated, "I know you didn't hear what Major Ostmark said, but I have a staffing problem and a solution thereof. Sir, we're in a battlefield-combat situation. Hell, our whole nation is in a combat zone. If so, to benefit the Air Force and Army and if the situation demands it, you have the authority to issue battlefield-combat promotions. It seems to me that a promotion to Second Lieutenant for Sergeant Morris, and a one or two-level promotion for each of his men are completely warranted. They have fought all the way here. If they can't win this battle, I don't know what else our nation can do. We need them, Sir! In addition, since Major Ostmark is overdue for a promotion, her promotion to Lt. Coronel is necessary, subject to eventual approval by the U.S. Government, and/or the Senate, if or when that ever happens. Let's include Captain Paul Weaver in that promotion concept, too. One final point, Sir, my understanding of the regulations is that if the promotions are not changed within thirty to forty-five days, they become permanent."

After a very few seconds, General Fencior looked at his Captain, "Dam, that is positively brilliant, Jim, I was trying to figure out some way to reward these men, and Major Ostmark too, for what they did and are about to do."

He said emotionally, "I'm really going to miss you! How long would it take for you to do the paperwork?"

"Sir, it is now 1000 hours; my staff hung with me through this tragedy, and we should have it done by 1400 hours. Since we couldn't use the computers, I found a couple of old typewriters and we've been using them. I'll also have someone find stripes for the men and second lieutenant's bars and whatever I can find for an officer's uniform for Sergeant Morris.

After a moment, General Fencior and Captain Wisnicki returned to the conference room.

"All right, we're going to continue this conference. You and each of you, including you Mr. Robinson and Major Ostmark are ordered back here at 1400 hours," commanded General Fencior. "So, Mr. Robinson what can I do for you until that time?"

Joseph Robinson turned to Sergeant Dean Morris, "Dean, are we ready to leave?"

"Yes Sir. The supply sergeant gave us everything we need, the horses are rested and well fed; we could leave first thing in the morning."

Joseph Robinson turned to Captain Wisnicki, "Jim, can I call you

Jim? I was planning on leaving tomorrow morning, but if we delay this for a day, can you arrange a quick wedding by your base chaplain tomorrow? I've got two people who really want to be married."

Captain James Wisnicki smiled widely, "Consider it done! General, we'll meet back here after the chaplain talks with the bride and groom and her family and get this organized. I guess that'll be the last official duty I can do for you?"

Captain James Wisnicki turned to Joseph, "I know it isn't for you, but does the couple have a ring or rings?"

"Dammed if I know, Dean, Jane?

"Does your PX or BX here have any jewelry or rings?" asked Dean after looking at Jane.

"I think so. After you leave here and talk to the chaplain, our BX is open and they might have what you need. Do you have any cash because that's all they will accept" He paused for a second, "If you run a little short on cash, send someone to see me. I've got extra for special purposes."

"We've got cash," chimed in Dean's group. "That will be our gift for our Sergeant and Major."

Surprised, both Dean Morris and Jane Ostmark looked at their group of hard-nosed, rough, battle-hardened, tough men. A soft, heart filled "Thank You," came from both Dean and Jane.

Captain James Wisnicki stood, came to a rigid attention: "Sir, request permission to speak, Sir."

General Fencior looked at his Captain with surprise and after a second said, "Permission Granted."

"Sir, it has been my great honor and privilege to have served and work for you. You are the most incredible leader and man I have ever known. You taught me what true duty for our country, and our nation should be, and I am eternally grateful! Thank you, Sir."

His salute was Air Force Academy perfect, "Permission to withdraw, Sir?"

Something seemed to be in General Fencior's eyes as he huskily responded, "Granted."

"All right, everyone dismissed. Mr. Robinson, could I have a moment of your time?"

Once out of the conference room, Major Jane Ostmark turned to Corporal Kleighorn, grabbed him and hugged him with tears flowing down her cheeks. "Sam, you didn't have to say that."

"Oh yes I did! You are part of our squad and importantly, we've never seen our Sergeant as happy since he met you. You two belong together, period, Sir, er Mam."

Meanwhile, General Fencior turned to Joseph Robinson, "Well, Mr. Robinson, I must tell you that when we developed your squad, we never, ever conceived the situation we're in now. And that telephone call you made to the Chiefs- that scared the hell out of us! I was forced to make plans and arrangements for this base to survive as if we were back in the 1800's with no electricity or electrical assistance. But you gave us whatever notice you could. Now! Now, you come riding in with a possible solution to the Green Ghost."

From deep inside of himself, General Fencior said, "I thank you personally, and on behalf of a grateful nation, I thank you and God be with you."

"Thank you, sir. When I took this job, I too never conceived the Green Ghost, but I've got a great bunch of people. We'll do our best."

As they shook hands, Joseph Robinson asked "I'll see you at the wedding tomorrow?"

"You couldn't keep me away. Oh, at 1400 hours, your men are in for a great and deserved surprise, but don't say anything to them before."

Outside, Captain Wisnicki pointed the group: "Down that street is the base chaplains' office, I'll meet you there, but tell him that this wedding is to be done tomorrow afternoon around 1300 hours. He may complain a little but tell him that I said so. I've got to give my staff some orders."

General Fencior approached Captain Wisnicki, "Jim, we have that General Officer's cottage over by housing that is empty. Let's get that cleaned up a little and have our new Colonel and new Lieutenant spend their first night there? But don't tell them until they are married."

"Great idea, Sir!"

As soon as Captain Wisnicki left, General Fencior walked to the captain's staff and issued a few additional orders. One was to prepare for Joseph's men an immediate single level promotion with a second promotion in thirty days only because regulations required at least thirty days between promotions. The promotions were necessary due to combat conditions, and that the general personally would sign them. He instructed them to not say anything about the second order.

At 1400 hours (2:00 P.M.), Captain Wisnicki told Major Ostmark, Sergeant Morris, his men, and Joseph Robinson to report to the General in the now enlarged conference room.

As Major Ostmark and her group reported to General Fencior, she saw out of her side vision that the room was crowded with her parents, her sisters, relatives, neighbors, and friends.

"*What's going on?*" came the thought. She was not given the command to be "at ease."

General Fencior, in his Class A uniform, stood and cleared his throat, "Remain at attention!"

He addressed the audience, "As all of you know, our nation is in a terrible situation. That horrible problem, commonly called The Green Ghost, has attacked our nation, our people, and the entire world. We, all of us, are in a terrible fight, it is a battle for our lives, our survival, our nation, our way of living. As commander in charge of our area, I have authority to and do hereby make certain battlefield promotions. Unless revoked within, I believe, thirty days, they become permanent. I understand that my aide, Captain Wisnicki, has found an old camera that doesn't use electricity, and eventually we'll have the film developed. He also has stacks of paper for signatures."

General Fencior commanded, "Major Jane Fern Ostmark, Front and Center."

Surprised, she took the required steps and stood at attention in front of the General.

"Sir!"

"Major Ostmark, by the authority invested in me, I hereby promote you to the position of Lieutenant Coronel, United States Air Force. Captain Wisnicki, may I have the appropriate insignia of that rank? And would you take a photograph of me pinning the Lt. Coronel's insignia on her shoulders? Please include her parents too. Master Sergeant Ostmark and Mrs. Ostmark, front and center, please! Ladies and gentlemen, this sergeant, her father, was one of my best Sergeants."

General Fencior removed the Major's gold leaf insignia and replaced them with a silver leaf, assisted by her parents, on a bemused Major, now Lt. Coronal, Jane Fern Ostmark.

He said, "Congratulations. Well deserved, Coronel!" She shook his offered hand, not quite believing what just happened to her.

"Return to your position."

"Sergeant Dean Morris, Front and Center!"

A surprised Sergeant Dean Morris reported, "Sir."

"Ladies and Gentlemen, Sergeant Dean Morris has led his men through incredibly difficult, harsh, and highly classified missions, some involving personal combat, none of which will be discussed with anyone, ever. Sergeant, I would like to ask a personal favor of you?"

"Yes Sir," stammered the reply.

"Sergeant Dean Morris, I would like for you to resign from the Non-Commissioned Officers Corps of the United States Army."

"*What?*" stammered Sergeant Dean Morris, so surprised that he omitted an ingrained "Sir."

"Instead, I would like you to sign the papers that Captain Wisnicki has on that table," he pointed.

"I would personally like for you to accept the appointment of an officer of the United States Army, that of a Second Lieutenant. Would you do that for me?"

Sergeant Dean Morris numbly and suddenly light-headed simply nodded his head.

"I need to swear you in. Please raise your right hand." General Fencior ordered: "Please repeat after me: I, state your name-- having been appointed as a Second Lieutenant, an officer in the Army of the United States--do solemnly swear that I will support and defend the Constitution of the United States against all enemies, foreign and domestic--that I will bear true faith and allegiance to the same; that I take this obligation freely, without any mental reservations or purpose of evasion-- and that I will well and faithfully discharge the duties of the office upon which I am about to enter-- So help me God."

Stunned and shaking, Lt. Dean Morris, mumbled "I do!"

Photographs were taken of the new Lieutenant receiving his gold bar from General Fencior with the assistance of Master Sergeant and Mrs. Ostmark.

"Captain Paul Weaver, front and center."

"Sir?"

"Ladies and Gentlemen, Captain Weaver has been one of my great co-pilots who is overdue for a promotion, but he rose above his general duties in his support of Mr. Robinson's group. Without him, Mr. Robinson's group could not have succeeded in where they are, and his assistance is sorely needed in their future. By the powers invested in me, he is hereby promoted to the rank of Major, United States Air Force. There is no one here to celebrate his promotion, but the photographer will take photos of me fastening his rank on him. We hope of some future date, such photos will be available."

A few minutes later, General Fencior turned and addressed the visitors, "Ladies and Gentlemen, it gives me great pleasure and honor to introduce brand new officers of our United States military: Lt. Coronel Ostmark and Second Lieutenant Dean Morris. Lieutenant Morris, Captain Wisnicki has a new uniform jacket for you. You'll notice that your metals, all three and a half rows transfer over with your promotion."

A wave of shouting and clapping burst forth.

"Dam, I didn't know the Sarge had all those metals," whispered one of the privates.

"Dummy, it is no longer Sergeant, it's now Lieutenant!"

General Fencior glared at the private, "Now, for each of you enlisted men, there is a two-level promotion for each one of you. This will be a two-step process, the first takes place immediately, the second in 30 days. Captain Wisnicki has the additional stripes for you, but you'll have to sew them on yourself."

At this time, it dawned on Lt. Coronel Ostmark that "her" man was now an officer and she didn't need to worry about section 133 or anything like it. She could get married! The front of her uniform suddenly was damp from the water leaking, unofficer-like, from her eyes.

"I have one further matter. Captain Wisnicki, front and center!"

Shaken, Captain Wisnicki, who had been standing on the side during the prior ceremony, reported, "Sir?"

"Ladies and gentlemen, fellow members of the armed forces of these United States, Captain James Wisnicki has been my aide for the past two plus years. His loyal service to me has been outstanding in every way. I will miss him! Because of the prior mentioned combat conditions, you are hereby promoted to the rank of Major, United States Air Force, effective immediately. Photographer, I would like a photograph of me pining his new rank on now Major James Wisnicki."

General Fencior grinned at the shocked expression on his new Major's face, "You didn't know about that, did you. I've finally done something you didn't know about. It is the least I can do for you, Jim! Good luck and God speed."

"I think that's it. Be sure to sign the promotion documents. I'll see everyone at the wedding tomorrow's afternoon to which you are all invited. Dismissed!"

Cheers and yells could be heard several blocks away.

CHAPTER SIX

After the wedding and subsequent raucous party, two days late, they started Eastbound on Interstate 40, all very hung-over.

Privates, now Corporals, J. J. Jones and Ronald Flannery had been generally assigned as lead, both because they enjoyed being the front of the group and more importantly, they spotted potential problems with desperate people and developed avoidance routes.

"Boy, that was one helliva a party last night," Jones mumbled to his partner. "My head feels like someone jumped up and down on it. I don't remember anything after the singing."

"Well, when I saw you crawling through the base parking lot holding a half a bottle of cheap wine, I figured you might need some help," snickered his buddy Flannery. "Don't you remember I dragged you to the barracks and finally dumped you on the floor because you kept falling off the bed?"

"No, but I'm grateful to the Major. She made me drink some rotgut coffee this morning and that's the only reason I can stay on this stupid horse. I thought I was going to die when I woke up. But it sure was great that the Major and our Sarge finally got married."

"It just proves my point, you're still drunk!" Ron Flannery snorted, attempting to not laugh at his buddy's pain. "Don't you remember our Serge is no longer a Sergeant, and our Major is no longer a Major? That general at Kirkland seemed to know all about us and the stuff we did and still promoted us. "

"Aw hell. Whatever he is, he was and will always be 'Our Sarge!'"

"By the way, our new Captain, however you pronounce his name, brought along a few very heavy boxes. Know what was in them?"

"I haven't a clue, but if it was ok with Joe and our new Lt., it's ok with me."

The days passed, New Mexico faded into the past. At Tucumcari, New Mexico, passing the Dinosaur Park, they picked up Highway 54 going Northeast eventually to Wichita, Kansas.

Several days later past Tucumcari, J.J. Jones and Ron Flannery were, as usual, "on point." They were about a half mile ahead of the others. A hundred yards off to the side of a deserted stretch of road, they could see what looked like an abandoned once-white two-story house. About half of the windows appeared to be blown out. Parked in the driveway was an old rusty V.W. bus with bullet holes seeming to hold the rust together. Next to it was a burnt new Cadillac on four flat tires, also with bullet holes in it.

However, standing near the main highway were two children, a little girl of about three in a faded and dirty multi-colored dress and a boy of about two wearing only a dirty shirt and a diaper. Both looked starved, thirsty and a long way from a washcloth and a bath.

J. J. Jones said to Flannery, "Ride back and get the Major up here as fast as possible. I'll try to take care of the kids."

J. J. dismounted, grabbed his canteen, approached the children, and knelt. "Hi kids, my name is J.J. Would you like a drink?"

He held out his canteen to the little girl. Streaks of tears stained the dirt on her face and her long dark very uncombed hair looked caked with dirt and several unknown substances. She held the canteen for a moment. J. J. then realized that she didn't know how to unscrew the top. He did so and held it out again. Her big dark eyes looked at him for a moment and then took the canteen and helped her younger brother drink first and then herself. They both sat down and drank again.

Major Jane Ostmark galloped up on Flannery's horse. "Did you see any parents, J.J.?"

"Nothing, Major. (In his mind, she would always be their "Major.") They were just standing out here when we rode up. Do we have some food we can give them?"

"Of course, J.J., any idea of where their parents are?"

"Well, the kids are so small, they couldn't have gone far; they probably belong in that house over there," he gestured to the apparently deserted house.

The rest of the group galloped up. "What do we have?" asked Joseph Robinson.

After J. J. Jones explained what they saw, Joseph Robinson turned and said "J.J., you, Ron Flannery, Conners, and Dean, check out that house. Be careful, something is not right, and I don't think we're going to like whatever you find."

Dean Morris took over his squad, "Combat spread, men! Leave the horses, we'll go on foot. Conners, to the far left, Flannery, to the far right. J.J., you and I will approach the front. Weapons out!"

Slowly, the squad approached the house, the whisper of weapons being pulled from their holsters and the quiet cocking of the weapons was the only sound.

Dean Morris yelled, "Hello The House! Anybody Home?"

J.J. jumped at the yell, it was so unexpected.

Silence, only the sound of a lonely wind blowing through shattered windows broke the stillness.

Nothing.

No response.

No movement.

"Ok, J.J. let's do this." Dean Morris quietly ordered. They signaled to the other two they were going in.

Dean Morris and J. J. Jones quietly snuck up to the front door which was swinging open from the wind blowing through the house.

They peered in. The inside looked like the scene of a battle zone. Pieces of severely broken lamps containing footprints, overturned furniture and bullet holes littered the left side of the room.

They slowly entered; the only sound was their feet crunching on broken glass and parts of shot-up furniture. Dean Morris mouthed to J.J. "It looks like either a nasty gunfight or a war zone." He motioned to J.J. to examine the downstairs rooms while he acted as backup.

J.J. nodded and glided to examine the first-floor room on their right.

Bullet holes decorated the walls and ceiling. Spent rifle and handgun shells were scattered over the floor. But no one there. Toward a back room, he glanced in and then waved Dean Morris over, his face pale while his stomach tried to lurch somewhere.

Inside were four obviously dead bodies, three covered with flies, all repeated shot, mostly in the back with their hands tied behind them. They looked like they were kneeling before they were killed, execution style. The rest of the room looked like a high school lab.

Dean Morris whispered, "A meth lab gone bad. Let's check out the rest of the house including the upstairs, but I doubt there's anyone alive here. Be sure to check under any beds and in the closets."

Later, Dean Morris reported, "Joe, there's four dead bodies in that house. It looks like a meth lab and the inside looks like a nasty gun fight went down. There are bullet holes all over and the bodies were shot, execution style, multiple times. I'd say the three males and one female were dead for two to three or four days; rigor mortis was absent and that lasts only about 24 hours post-death. Probably, it was the last time these kids were fed. There's a small closet in a children's room on the second floor in a back corner where the kids apparently were hiding during the shootings. That's why they lived through the gunfight."

After listening to Dean Morris, Major (actually now Lt. Colonel) Ostmark asked, "Joe, what do we do with these kids? We can't leave them here. They need different clothes and diapers and food, and eventually a good bath."

She locked deep and somber eyes with her new husband, Dean Morris, with a sudden epiphany that shook him, *Jesus, she loves and wants a kid! I never ever thought of children. The mothering instinct comes out!"*

"Yeah, I agree." Joseph replied. "Dean, if you would, take a couple of extra men and search that house and try to find some kid's clothes that they need. Also, see if their parents had any kid's food and if so, grab it. Priority right now is to get these little ones fed. Conners, Flannery, J.J., everyone also search the house for any forms of identification. Be sure to check out the vehicles. Look especially for any birth certificates or something with the kids' names on it. We'll try to find someone who either knows them and/or is willing to take them in. Any questions, anyone?"

Jane Ostmark/Morris said, "Oh hell, I'll go. I know what the little ones need, the little boy desperately needs a diaper change. Look for a little portable toilet for the kids; there's bound to be one there."

Dean Morris had another thought: *How the hell does she know what the little ones need? And she's swearing; she never swears! Those little kids got to her! There's a lot that I don't know about this woman, my wife."*

"You guys back her up, OK?" said Joseph. "That's a two-story house with a window facing the road. Dean, put someone in that window with binoculars. We want to know if someone is coming up or down the road."

Upon receiving no questions, "Ok, let's get this done, quickly! Leave the bodies. We'll try to notify the local authorities if there are any. There's a town up ahead in a few miles and there might be someone who knows these kids."

An hour later, they returned dragging four large suitcases and several boxes filled with clothing, diapers, wipes, blankets, and such. One suitcase contained whatever identification they could find including about $10,000 in cash and various kinds of jewelry and precious stones.

J.J. Jones hand-carried an armful of toys for the children.

"I found the jewelry and stones hidden in a closet," Ron Flannery told Joseph Robinson. "We also took whatever weapons, and ammunition we could find. We can either use or trade them."

"Good thinking, guys."

Conners reported, "I had to search those dead bodies and that was tough. I got as much of the identification as I could find and grabbed their guns and ammo. But please, don't ask me to do that again."

"Well done, men," complemented Joseph. "I don't know what good the money and stones will do, but maybe eventually, they might be worth something. And if we have the guns and ammo, somebody else wouldn't get them. The most important point is that we'll give them to whoever takes the kids. And by the way, these kids have names?"

"According to their birth certificates, the little girl's name is Cassie Fern Clisper and the boy's name is Douglas Runion Clisper. She answers to CeCe and I think he answers to whoever has food for him," Jane smiled.

"Jane," Joseph Robinson correctly interpreted the look between her and Dean Morris, "We can't take them with us all the way to Wisconsin and Chicago. I hope you understand."

"Oh, I know, Joe," Jane responded with emotion, "but my heart, and I think all of our hearts go out to and for these little ones."

"I agree," Sergeant, now Second Lieutenant, Dean Morris said. "It's the little ones who always suffer. I don't care about the adults; in this case, they got what was coming to them, only I wish it was worse than a simple shooting."

"We agree," was the mumbled reply from the entire group. Joseph recalled how enthusiastically his squad went after cocaine and narcotic dealers both in Panama, Tijuana, and several southwestern U.S. cities. They always made sure that there were no children in the houses they destroyed or blew up. Other times and other places caught fire and then blew up, their guards deposited at the local sheriffs' or police station, heavily duct taped. It was merely coincidental that most had various felony warrants.

"Jane, do we have enough water to give them a light bath tonight?" asked Joseph Robinson.

Yes, and we'll make a place for them in one of the wagons to sleep after they had something to eat and were bathed."

"Ok, Ron, you're our medic, take a look at the kids and see if they need any specific medical attention,"

"Ok. Let's hit the road. I don't want to spend any more time around here," Joseph Robinson ordered. "Remember, somebody shot those suspects, and the killers may come back. I'd rather not get into a gunfight although they may have done the locals a favor. Dean, for the next few days, I want to double the night guard, include me in that. J.J, and Ron, I want a third body with you in a full combat spread as our lead. Also, for the next couple of days, the leads should wear our Kevlar vests. I know that you guys don't like to wear them, but you saw what happened here."

"Any questions, anyone?"

"Remember, the locals had to have known of this house and the shooting, and I don't want to be in the middle of a retaliation or gang war. We find someone to take care of the children and we're gone, OK?"

Later that night, after the children were fed, bathed and asleep, Dean Morris and his new wife, Jane, approached Joseph. "Joe, as you suggested, we tried to avoid towns and cities, but there is a small town a few miles ahead and I think we should go through the town to find someone for the kids. I think as well armed as we are, and if we show that, we shouldn't have any trouble."

Jane somberly looked at Joseph and asked quietly, "And if we can't find someone?"

Joseph, startled, could see where this was going, and was surprised that he was internally surprised; he correctly could see Jane's natural maternal side coming out to protect the little ones and for once, he was at a loss for a solution. The worst-case scenario would have been that his newly married C-130 pilot now wanted to keep the children and he would be stuck hauling the children across the United States.

"Well," he delayed, "Let's cross that bridge if we come to it. We need not make any decisions until if, and that's a big if, we can't find someone to take care of the kids. Agreed?" He asked Jane.

Reluctantly, she nodded.

Later that day, Dean Morris quietly asked his wife, "Jane, you're a pilot, how do you know so much about kids?"

She laughed, "During my off-duty hours, I helped at the Kirkland Base hospital with pediatrics, in other words, helping our newly married airman and their wives on how to care for babies. It was surprising how little the wives knew about raising kids, particularly newborns. That was a labor of love for the tiny ones."

As she was talking, she was changing the little boy, exchanging with wipes a very dirty diaper with a new one. The men crowed around, fascinated with the change.

Someone said surprised, "Well, he's just like us."

"Dummy, what did you expect, he's a boy."

Someone else said, "Yeah, just like our Sarge; it's amazing."

"What are you talking about?"

"It's the same size, too!"

Jane Ostmark's head turned violently, thinking to chastise, to reprimand the person making the remark about her lover and new husband, but listening to the hardy laughter, realized that she too was now part of this group.

"Aw, come on guys. You've been looking at too many mirrors!"

More laughter.

The next day, about noon, they rode to what normally would be called a tiny village with a population of about 200. A few homes extended to each side of the main highway, with the center of the town the crossroads between the main highway and a smaller county highway. There was a single closed gas station and a closed small strip mall.

They were met by three men on horses. The apparent leader wore the requisite white Stetson and was well dressed, but a sheriff's badge flashed from his left chest. His two "deputies," both wearing unpolished badges and dirty jeans with Pendleton shirts surrounded the sheriff. There was not a single person in the streets; most of the houses all appeared to be barricaded or vacant.

Dean Morris silently moved his hands. His squad, without further instruction or order, moved to a simplified combat spread which meant that each man quietly moved out about ten yards apart to the right and left away from the wagons; each had a straight shot at the so-called officers. The horses were guided to keep their sides to the sheriff so he couldn't see M-16s being drawn from their holsters.

"Howdy folks." said Sheriff John Johnson, looking at the armed group. "I'm the Sheriff around here. We don't see many strangers through here. What can we do for you?"

"Hello Sheriff, I'm Joseph Robinson, that's Lieutenant Dean Morris, United States Army, Major James Wisnicki, U.S Air Force, Lt. Colonel Jane Morris, and the rest of my group are all enlisted men. We're from California and on our way to Wisconsin and ultimately Chicago. We can use your help. About twenty miles behind us, we came upon these two kids standing on the side of the road." Joseph pointed at the two kids sitting in a wagon.

Joseph continued, "They apparently came from a family named

Clisper. We found four people shot to death in what appeared to be a meth lab. No one else was alive when we got there, and they had been dead for about three or four days."

At Joseph's comments, one deputy snickered. Dean Morris and his men shared quick glances. They understood that snicker.

Joseph continued, "The kids were starving, and we fed and bathed them. They are about three and two years old and we need someone to take care of them."

Sheriff Johnson looked at them and at the children. He shook his head, "We know about the Clisper bunch. They are just part of the meth and narcotic bunch infecting my town and this area. However, I have some bad news. I don't know of anyone here that would be willing to take the kids off your hands. We're a small office and pretty much just attempt to keep outsiders from invading our town. If the kids were older and could work and help, they'd be welcome, but I will tell you that no one here either wants or can take the kids. As you know, we no longer have electricity or anything using electricity and so, everything is done manually."

He shrugged, "No work, no food, is the basic rule here."

"Well," Joseph argued, "We recovered a bunch of money and jewels that might help support the children."

"Nope," replied Sheriff Johnson. "No work, no staying, period."

"And," Sheriff Johnson continued, "I suggest that you leave, now."

At that- he and his deputies reached for their guns.

Mistake!

The unmistakable sound of at least eight M-16's receivers clanging into place sounded throughout the area, the loud whisper of .223 cartridges sliding into place. At the same time, Joseph's right hand was a blur as he reached for and pulled his 9 .mm Glock and fired one shot, hitting the peak of the sheriff's white Stetson hat, and knocking it off his bald head. The hat was no longer white with a bullet hole in it.

"Hold your fire!" commanded Joseph Robinson raising his smoking gun. "Sheriff, I suggest that you and your deputies slowly remove your hands from your guns. My men are all expert shots and you'd be dead before you even 'cleared leather,'" Joseph's cold, cold eyes locked on the Sheriff.

"NOW! Sheriff!" commanded Joseph Robinson.

Hands were slowly raised, but the glares from angry beady eyes were deadly.

"Now, Sheriff, if you don't want us and to help us, and refuse to help those poor little kids, that's your problem. You can tell us if we must fight our way through your town, and if we must, we'll do so, but a whole lot of people, including you and your deputies, will be dead because my men are very good. However, is there a way around your domain? You will want to remember what Teddy Roosevelt said."

Sheriff Johnson glared at Joseph Robinson, but the outnumbered Sheriff slowly took his hand away from his gun. He refused to admit that he had no idea what Teddy Roosevelt said.

He pointed to a dirt side-street to the north of the town and fumed, "That road goes around the town, and you can get back on the main highway on the other side, but," he couldn't resist a final threat, "Don't let sundown see you around here."

"OK, guys, you heard the man." Joseph Robinson pointed, "That way and let's get out of here, quickly. J.J. and Ron, front lead and close combat, Dean and Conners, cover our back and keep an eye on the Sheriff. The rest of you circle the wagons. Rifles in your hands, and in sight, but no shooting unless fired upon, you guys know the drill. Keep the kids and our scientists in the wagons but sitting down inside. Move!"

Several hours later and about perhaps ten or fifteen miles later, they camped. "All right let's eat and then we'll have a meeting," ordered Joseph. "I think that sheriff knew more about those dead bodies then they would admit, and I just don't trust them."

Dean Morris and his new wife, Jane, shared concerned looks; they knew the subject of the meeting.

As a bright sun lowered itself behind them in a beautiful red and white sunset, they gathered around the campfire after dinner, the little ones clinging to Jane Morris.

Joseph Robinson stood up, "All right, you all heard the lovely reception we had in the last town. Any questions about what happened?"

J.J. Jones had to ask, "All right, I give up, what did Teddy Roosevelt say?"

Joseph could not help a large smile, "He said, and I quote 'Walk softly and carry a big stick.'"

J.J. Jones chuckled, "Well, that's sure as hell us."

"Is there any question that those so-called sheriffs shot and executed the Clispers?"

"No." Ron Johnstone asked, "But, I have a question: why shoot the hat off that cowboy's head? By the way, I've never seen a draw of a weapon that fast and such good shooting."

"Thank you! That nitwit recognized only strength and power. I have a bunch of people I'm responsible for including two little tykes and I wanted to have absolute control over the situation. That we accomplished! I hope he must go home to change his pants," Joseph said, without a smile.

"Yeah!" was the unanimous agreement.

"OK, now, what are we going to do with the kids?" Joseph asked. "I really had never ever planned to haul some children across the U.S., but frankly, now, I'm at a loss. I was certain that someone in that town would take them. Suggestions anyone?"

Joseph Robinson never realized that the reason he was so respected by his team was just that: he asked for suggestions and acted on them!

Before dinner, Joseph had watched his men and their relationship with the children. Nearly every man had found an excuse to give the little ones something, sometimes just a gentle rub on the head with a smile, but some reason to say little words of affection or encouragement. They were eventually rewarded with a smile or a little giggle.

Joseph thought, *"My men have answered the problem for me, but I'm going to let them tell me. Hell, I don't know what else to do with the children."*

Dean Morris stood, "Joe, would you take a little walk please? I want to talk to our men, and my wife."

Joseph took a little walk.

"Well, men, what do you want to do?" Lt. Dean Morris asked.

J.J. responded, "Well, hell, Sarge..." he was loudly interrupted, "He's not a Sergeant anymore, he's an officer!"

"Ok, Ok, Sir. I see what the rest of us want to do with the little ones. Both CeCe and Doug need someone to protect them and care for them. We surely can do the best job of that, and we have a built-in Mom, the Major, err the Colonel, for those things that we can't do. I say we keep the kids at least until we get to Wisconsin and see how everything works out."

Jane Morris asked, her eyes brimming, "Are you guys sure you want to do this?"

"Yes!" came the resounding answer. "They are like my little sister and brother that I never had," from an unknown gruff voice.

A deep male voice with unexpected emotion exclaimed "Cassie gave me a hug a little while ago. We can't let them go!"

Another voice commented, "Yeah, well, wait until she grows up and learns what you really are."

After the laughter, Dean Morris called "Joe?"

"Well, what's the answer?" asked Joseph, knowing full well what the "answer" would be.

"Joe, we think we should try to keep the kids until we get to Wisconsin or finish our mission."

"Yeah, I figured that would be your decision and I fully agree. OK, what then? Jane, I guess they're your responsibility now. Let us know what kind of food and any specific clothes they need. We'll stop and either trade for that, or this bunch of mine will "acquire" whatever you need. Ron Jefferson, you help her in keeping the kids healthy. They'll probably need some medication and stuff. I don't know much if anything, about children, but I guess we'll all learn."

"You're not the only one," thought Dean Morris as he shared a deep, soul searching look with his new wife, Jane.

As the days passed, Joseph noted that the kids frequently rode with one or another of his men. He ordered however, that no kids were on the leaders' horses; outriders around the wagons were ok, but the leaders' jobs were too important for distractions.

Wichita was passed riding toward Kansas City, Missouri.

About four days outside of Kansas City, Captain, now Major Jim Wisnicki, their recruit from Kirkland Air Force Base, approached Joseph Robinson. "Joe," he had learned to call Joseph Robinson "Joe" as everyone else did, "We're getting a little low on supplies. I have a friend, a Colonel Jerry Windson, who oversees base supply at Whiteman Air Force Base. We could stop there and get ourselves whatever we need."

Jane Ostmark/Morris rode up, "I agree, Joseph, plus in addition, they have a pretty good hospital there and maybe we can get our kids checked and hopefully get whatever shots they need."

Dean Morris rode up "I also agree, Joe. Maybe we can get something other than the MREs that we've been dining up for the last several days." Joseph smiled recalling that the GIs who normally had to eat the MREs in combat called them "Meals Rejected by Ethiopians!" While they were not bad, they got monotonous no matter what Major Weaver did with them.

"OK." Joseph stopped at one of the wagons and hauled out his trusty road map. "Jim, where is this base and how do we get there."

Major Jim Wisnicki pointed on the map, "Whiteman is between Warrensburg and Sedalia. Warrensburg is about 58 or so miles from Kansas City. I suggest that we bypass the entire Kansas City proper and pick up Route 50 east of K.C. That runs just north of Whiteman and is a main highway through there. Then, from there is pretty much a straight shot north to Wisconsin."

"Dean, Jane, any comments?" Joseph asked.

"Jim, where's Ferguson? Joseph asked, "How far is it from Kansas City to Ferguson?

"I'd guess about 230 miles, give, or take 10 or 20 miles. Why?"

"We don't go through it, do we?"

"No, it's way East of us, close to St. Louis. Again, why?

"About a week or so before we started the Green Ghost journey, I had a Los Angeles County Deputy Sheriff-Sergeant a friend, gave me an analysis of the big riots that occurred in Ferguson back around August of 2014.

"That's right, I had forgotten about that."

"The investigation I read was about 174 or so pages, and discussed the 17 days of disorder, destruction, burning, looting, and general loss of control over that poor city. It all started with a shooting of a black male by a white officer and things went downhill after that."

Dean Morris interjected, "Yeah, in one of my supervision classes long before I met you, we discussed the lack of leadership by the local chief of police and just about everyone else."

"You are right. The interesting part was that while there were four major police agencies and about 10 or 20 other agencies responding to the riot, no one knew who was in control until much control was lost. There is a mandatory system called NIMS which is short for National Incident Management System which is required for most states and cities. If you want federal money, you must plan for and use it. There is a similar system in California which handles all the catastrophic fires, earthquakes, and so on."

"What's that got to do with us?" asked one of the men.

"Here's the point, the military, that's you,' Joseph gestured to his men, "always know who is running the situation. It's called the chain of command. Somebody must make the hard decisions on what to do. Ferguson didn't and now, you heard the consequences. A riot is a great way to get rid of your hated neighbor or enemy.

I do not remember what the total loss of life or the financial losses were due to the burning and ransacking. Los Angeles, in their Watt's riots, and the Rodney King riots, and the East L.A. riots didn't suffer from lack of leadership, but it took time to control the rioters and looters and burnings."

Joseph paused for a moment, "Other factors entered the situation: Ferguson's population was around 75 percent, or more, black and of the 77 members of Ferguson P.D., only one or two were black. In addition, the local police would issue traffic citations to only blacks, who were so poor, they could not pay the fines. So, the citations went to warrant, and the next time, the defendant/suspect was stopped, he had warrants which meant he was arrested and lost his car. There was no question that the locals hated the police. No Community Policing or community involvement at all. Somebody described the city as a cauldron just waiting to erupt, but the local officials including the chief of police either were blind to the situation, were too afraid to make any waves, or lacked the education or training to solve the problems. "

"Interesting, but Sir, but I don't understand why you're discussing this with us." One of the men said, "All we did was blow up a bunch of houses and buildings and did away with a whole lot of truly bad guys. We all know who our leader is; we couldn't have got this far without our Major bossing us and frequently whipping and beating us with a stick."

After the laughter died down, Joseph continued, "If you have been paying attention, as much as possible, we always avoided the large cites or towns. In many of the small towns we went through, I stopped and talked to the local authorities, who sometimes were all Mexican, or black, or something else whomever was living in the towns. While a true majority was in charge, there were many other races represented in the political and criminal justice systems."

Joseph paused for a moment and took a deep breath, "That, my people, means that true democracy is spreading across our nation. If you living in a total Mexican town, guess what the chief, mayor, and others, are? No more of the Ferguson problem. The general public will suffer with less and less fools, and not allowing said fools to run the place.

When, not if, we are successful in our fight against the Green Ghost, we, our nation will have changed, I believe for the better. California's legislature, and Washington's federal legislature are a good example: no more laws favoring who paid you the most last; no more laws being passed by senators and congresspersons who have NEVER gone hungry or lost their homes or children. We, each one of you, could have never done what we did unless the system was corrupt and wasteful. The United States spent billions of dollars fighting the drug problem and had little or nothing to show for all that money. But someone got that money! Maybe now, we'll have a chance to really help our people, our country. Our military, you men, will be the only organization capable of fighting that dam Green Ghost and not allowing the corrupt political system to rise its ugly head ever again. Those who are left love our country, just like each of you. Several times, the people buried those who did not care for or respect our country."

He paused, taking a deep breath knowing that he had the undivided attention of his men.

Joseph continued, "That's why I discussed Ferguson with you, it was the representation of everything that was immoral, indeed, criminal about our political system. The small towns now understand the need for the change"

"We see," murmured J.J. Jones and several of Joseph's men. "We know we did a lot of good, but now, thanks, boss, for putting it into some perspective."

"You're very welcome. Keep in mind that our society, such as it might be, is still full of corruption, but that system is now essentially gone. People want people who help them, not just the elected clowns who promise everything, but accomplish nothing! And said clowns always got paid and went on expensive vacations. California was a great example, answer me this, what good did the senators and assembly persons and governor in Sacramento do that was worthwhile. They voted for a high-speed rail that was fraudulent from the start, very poorly planned and supervised, and never went anywhere, but someone got tons of money. Worse, the legislature in Sacramento refused to cancel the high-speed rail! Someone was getting the money. And the so-called rail was only going from one small town to another, not from L.A. to San Francisco. And so on! Now we have a chance to change that corrupt system. And you will be in the vanguard of that change."

"Any questions?"

Upon receiving a somber negative shake of their heads, he said, "OK, Jim, you know this area more than any of us, lead off!"

A day or two later, Dean Morris asked Major Jim Wisnicki, "Jim, is there anything I should know about Whiteman?"

"Not that I'm aware of, Dean. I think Whiteman is smaller than Kirkland; it is the home of the Air Force's B-2 Spirits, a squadron of A-10 Thunderbolt IIs, a couple of T-38 trainers and a whole bunch of AH-64 Apache attack helicopters. They're part of the Air Combat Command which is part of the Air Force Global Strike Command. Of course, because of the Green Ghost, much of that is simply history."

"They do have a medical facility there?" asked Dean Morris. "For shots and stuff for kids?"

"I don't know for sure, but Jane thought there was a substantial hospital facility there and in addition, there are many permanent personal and civilians stationed there with their families. I'm sure that includes pediatricians for our kids, so don't worry."

Jim Wisnicki grinned at the stocky former sergeant, now Second Lieutenant, "You're starting to talk like a father."

"Aw, nuts."

"Jim, I've got a question. Your general said that he and you knew about our quote "assignments" unquote. If you remember, we flew to Africa and got that so-called medicine man out and dropped him at Nellis Air Force Base. He said not one word to us, but he knew planes and what was in them. In addition, the people that picked him up simply disappeared when we turned around. What was that entire thing all about?"

"Dam, I knew this issue would come up. These people are too smart," thought Major Jim Wisnicki. He took a deep breath, "Well, here's what I do know. Keep in mind that this is so highly classified that even the name is classified. The CIA had received rumors that a tribe in the area you were sent was unreasonably healthy. No AIDS, no TB, no diseases, no dental problems, no anything. There were a few rumors that there weren't even any unhealthy old people. And interestingly, there were a few, three I think, who always wore turbans and I mean always."

Jim paused for a moment, "What the CIA did was recruit a couple of people who could pass for the local natives, and they even found a few who could speak the language. They sent your guy in about three or four villages away from your village with a history of a traveling witch doctor. It took him about three months to work his way into your village. He carried with him a camera disguised as part of an elephant tusk. He also had on his backpack several sunken heads that when pressed a certain way, triggered a signal to satellite telling us to get him out immediately. What he did find was frightening and alarming."

Jim paused for a moment.

"Well, what the hell did he find?" demanded 2nd Lt. Dean Morris.

"You must remember that this entire assignment was so highly classified that even my general did not know the entire story; he just knew to send you people there. I knew and organized the entire process so that no one else, including my general, had any idea of what was necessary and what did happen. After all, no one in Congress or higher levels listens to a lowly Captain!"

"Well, crap. I knew that! Most of the stuff we did was so clandestine and so underground that very few people knew that we even existed. But what the hell did our guy find?"

"He got a picture of one of the natives with no turban on his head while he was asleep. He looked quite normal except. . . ." he paused.

"Except what?"

"He had a third eye in his forehead that was covered by the turban."

"What? Holy Cripes, you're kidding?!" His horse lurched sideways!

"Not only that, but your witch doctor also managed to take a sample of some of the food prepared by the so-called natives and he brought that out with him. If you remember, he had a package that he never let anyone touch it."

"What, what the hell were these so-called natives?" grunted Dean as he fought to quiet his horse.

"We think, with absolutely no foundation for that thinking, that some kind of spaceship probably crashed in that area and these whatever they are survived. Their medicine is probably years ahead of us. However, from what I surmise, the people you dropped your guy off with knew more. But they too didn't want any word getting out. Now, however, you and Joe show up and the Ultra Top-Secret classification means nothing. Maybe in some way, they can help us fight the Green Ghost. And that my friend, is all I know. Can they help us? Will they help us? If you and Joe are successful, maybe we can contact them and establish a friendly relationship. I bet that the Green Ghost affects them too. But that is quite a bit in the future."

They rode in silence for a few moments.

Lt. Dean Morris was stunned. "We knew something was strange, but never this."

"The reality was that we, the general and others, knew that we could trust you and your men. We had a huge ax over your men's heads because of what they faced, and we knew you would keep quiet about something like this. I'm asking you to remain quiet about this until and that's a big until, we are successful in fighting the Ghost."

"Oh, don't worry. They wouldn't believe me anyway. But thanks for telling me."

CHAPTER SEVEN

About two days ride south of Kansas City, while bypassing that city, J.J. Jones and Ron Flannery were "on point." The area and road had the usual hills and valleys. J.J. and Ron were about three-quarters of a mile ahead of their group. They were in a valley and approached the top of a hill and could see ahead of them. About a half mile away, the entire road was barricaded. A few destroyed tractors, what looked like four wrecked cars, and a decrepit looking green combine were spread out to make a large V of the road forcing anyone on the road to the point.

Immediately, J.J. Jones raised his closed right fist, indicating a possible enemy ahead to those behind him.

"Everyone, circle the wagons, keep the kids in the wagons and be prepared for anything. Dean, come with me," ordered Joe Robinson. He reached into the back of one of the wagons, "But, put this on first." He tossed a new top-of-the-line bulletproof vest to Dean.

Joseph Robinson and Dean Morris galloped up to where Jones and Flannery had stopped. "What do you have, guys?"

When being shown the barricade, he said, "I've been expecting something like this. Ron, ride back to the wagons, tell them what we have, and you and two guys spread out very, very quietly into those trees over there. I want at least one guy on each side of the road, fully armed with extra ammo. Hurry, Dean and I are going to meet whoever is there."

He looked through a set of 10 x 50 Bushnell binoculars, "There are several people there, all armed, and a few working in the fields behind them. What looks like a command post is right in the middle of the road. I see a small shed about a hundred feet or so south of the rest of the barricade."

"Let's give our guys a few more minutes to get into place and we'll just saunter over there."

After about ten minutes, Joseph jumped off his horse, ran to a small tree and cut a long branch, attached a white t-shirt to it and climb back onto his horse.

"Good thinking, Joe."

They rode over the top of the hill and slowly approached the V of the blockade. They were met by two men on foot, both heavily armed with weapons on their waist and M-16s on their backs.

One, an unshaved, approximately 25 years old, wearing dirty jeans and totally unwashed shirt with a "W" cap and wild looking eyes, demanded, "Drop your weapons!"

"In case you didn't notice, we come under a flag of truce, not intending to fight you." Joseph said quietly. "Bring your leader up here so we can talk."

The other man, similarly dressed, laughed, "Man, you just don't understand, we control this area, you do what we tell you to do."

Joseph again said quietly, "We came under the universally recognized flag of truce. We should not be harmed. Bring your leader here so we can talk."

"I told you we control this area; that means you." At that, he raised his rifle, cocked it, and pointed it at Joseph.

Joseph in a stronger voice, "We are leaving, I hope you don't do anything stupid. This flag means something." He pulled his horse around and Dean and he slowly moved away.

They were about a hundred yards before the top of the hill when one of the men fired a single shot at Joseph.

He felt a sharp blow to his back nearly knocking him off his horse. What saved his life was his top-of-the-line bullet-proof vest. Upon arriving back at the wagons suffering from the blow, he nearly fell off his horse. Many hands helped him down.

Joseph's shirt and vest were carefully taken off by Jane Ostmark/

Morris and helping hands. Then, Joe was examined by their medic, Ron Johnson. With no X-Rays, it looked like Joe only suffered a large bruise on his upper middle back. With no vest, he would be dead!

Meanwhile, LeRoy Johnstone, one of the men hiding in the nearby woods and a designed sharpshooter in the Army, seeing the shot at his leader, took a deep breath, let it nearly out, and squeezed the trigger of his silenced M-16. Its .223 bullet, traveling approximately 3000 feet per second blasted out of his rifle. At about 300 yards distance, the bullet dropped 10 inches and impacted the shooter in his left eye and bounced around the interior of his skull. He was dead before he hit the ground.

"Nice shot," complemented one of his buddies. "Thank you," LeRoy Johnstone said, "But nobody shoots at Mr. Robinson and gets away with it. I hope he is all right; I knew he had a good vest on."

"Are you OK?" a worried squad asked. After examining Joseph Robinson, Medic Ron Johnson felt that while there was a severe bruise, there seemed to be nothing broken. "I'll give you 600 mgs. of ibuprofen to stop the swelling and help with the pain. I'll give you more tonight." He looked around and said "In one of the wagons, we have a few pieces of steel. Bring them here. Jane, can you compress his bruise for about fifteen minutes time off and on to help reduce the swelling?"

"That vest saved my life, now you see why I require some of you to wear it," grunted Joseph Robinson.

"Thank heavens," exclaimed Jane Ostmark/Morris. She was surprised at her reaction to the shooting; while she unconditionally loved and respected her husband, Joseph Robinson earned her deep and high respect.

"Ok, now what?" asked Dean Morris.

Joseph, squirming because of the pain in his back, said "We need information. Dean, get two of our guys to carefully scout out the area to the south of us and get two more to do the same for the north of us. We must get past those clowns, but I would rather try to evade them rather than get into a full-fledged firefight. That, I think, should be as a last resort. Remember, we have the two scientists and two kids."

Two hours later, the men returned. To the south was a nearly impassable swamp. To the north was a large lake surrounded also by a swamp. The gang enforcing the blockade had chosen well, there were two choices, go back or go through. Their map showed there would be about at least a two-week delay in going around.

Joseph gathered his entire group around him and explained the options. "Suggestions anyone?"

He was surprised when Major Jim Wisnicki spoke: "Sir, I might have some assistance, if you remember I loaded a few very heavy boxes when we left Kirkland and I thought they might come in handy."

At that, he got up, and went to one of the wagons. From his right shoe, he pulled out an interesting switch blade knife with Mexican symbols on its highly polished silver handle. Upon pressing the handle, and with a loud snap, the seven-inch, very sharp, double-edged blade sprang out.

"Very nice!" exclaimed Ion. "Where did you get that?"

"Compliments of Tijuana, Mexico. They are all over that city! With a little money, they'll make it how you want it."

Jim cut open the tape sealing a box, removed an object and showed it to the group.

"I'll be dammed," exclaimed Robert Jones, one of the enlisted men "That's a G-dammed mortar. What kind of range does those have?"

"Absolutely right, and it has an approximate distance of about a half mile, which seems what we need right now," smiled Major Jim Wisnicki. "I have an even dozen which should be enough. Technically, these are part of what is called the M224A1s. Originally, the entire system weighted about 47 pounds, but now the foundation plate is much lighter. These mortars are High Explosive (HE). They should flatten anything within about forty yards. Plus, during training, I was pretty accurate with these; I can hit whatever you designate, Sir. I would need two men to help me set it up."

"Good thinking, Jim," exclaimed Joe and Dean together.

"We need more intelligence about them. Dean, have two or three of our guys try to sneak into their camp tonight and find out what they have. No heroes, men, if it is too heavily guarded or if they have dogs, come back. Wait until midnight, but return before sunrise, here are my binoculars. Find out if they have guards and when and where they are. You know, it would be nice to capture somebody who could tell us all we needed to plan. Keep that in mind, but take some duct-tape with you."

After a moment's thought, Joe said "We need to move back about a mile; there's two hills between us and I would like to be a little safer there. Also, I want two or three guards at the 'military crest' to make sure they don't scout us."

"My God, I haven't heard that term since the academy," thought Jane.

"Dean, while we're doing that, do you remember in the ditch alongside of the road and about halfway to the camp, there was a large thicket of shrubs?"

"Sure, why?"

"Sometime tonight, I want a couple of guys to sneak into that thicket and leave a hat or two and maybe an old gun or two that we found in CeCe's house. I want these items to be readily visible by the camp people. In addition, I would like a string attached to some of the bushes and this string could be pulled at sunup. Of course, it must be maybe hundred yards at an angle from the bushes. At sunup, we shake the bushes as if someone was there. I want to see if the camp people are peaceable or if, as I think they will, blow the heck out of the bushes and then, only then, investigate it. That, my good people, will determine their fate!"

"Good thinking, Sir," replied one of the men. "How about if we take an old shirt or two and make it look like there are people there?"

"Great idea. Let's make it happen."

Time passed, night came, and double guards were posted around the camp. Dean sent two of his best men to scout the blockade. They reported back late that night. Unexpectedly, they brought a prisoner back with them. He was duct-taped around his mouth, his hands behind his back, and a little the worse for wear. The bruises around his face, a bloody nose, and remnants of his torn shirt showed he was not happy.

"We found him at the outskirts sound asleep. We went by him and looked the place over," explained Sergeant Alvin Swanson. "I thought he would give us the intelligence we needed."

"Great job, men!" exclaimed Joseph Robinson. "Take him to the far outside of the wagons and tie him to a wheel. I'll talk to him there. Light a small fire in front of him and start heating a small piece of iron, oh, about three feet long or so. I want it nice and red at one end. See if anyone has any heavy gloves or wrap some clothing around the other end."

After about thirty or forty minutes, Joseph sat down in front of the prisoner.

Looking at the prisoner and while continually heating the iron rod, he said casually, "You should be aware of several things: one, if you give me your word you will not call for help or scream, we'll remove the tape from your mouth and give you something to drink. Do you agree? Nod if yes. If you do not agree, well..."

Joseph continued to stroke the iron rod.

The prisoner, eyeing the heating iron rod starting to radiate red at its end, violently nodded his head.

"All right, take the tape off," Joseph ordered. "Give him something to drink."

"Research has shown that prisoners subjected to considerable fear are always thirsty," Joseph told his curious staff.

"Feel a little better now?" Joseph asked after the prisoner received a drink of water.

"Thank you, sir, but you don't know who you are fucking with. We have twice as many men as you have, and we have more ammunition then you could believe. They don't negotiate, they just take whatever anyone has and sometimes let them loose. They think they control this whole area and road, and they believe they have enough guns and people to enforce that."

"Any prisoners?"

"Oh sure, we have about a dozen women, some of them are pretty, too."

Joseph did not need to look at Jane when he heard this; he knew her thoughts and what she would want to do.

"Let me tell you what's going to happen in the next few hours," wincing from the pain in his back, Joseph said quietly and calmly to the prisoner. "We are going through your camp, period. It is up to you if a bunch of your fellow men die or worse. We will release the women since they are innocent of anything, so, tell me where they are housed. Second, if you cooperate with us, we'll take you along and release you down the road. No one will know what you told us. If you refuse, we'll tie you to a tree over there and leave. You will not be able to call for help. You may survive for a few days unless someone comes along, but I think that's unlikely. Oh, by-the-way, I've heard there are wolves around here."

Joseph casually shrugged his shoulders, "Your choice!"

Joseph got up, leaving the iron bar in the fire, and walked to his people who were fascinated by the conversation between Joseph and the prisoner.

"Dam, you're good!" exclaimed Ion.

"Let him think for a few minutes while I have a cup of coffee, then we'll see if he tells us what we want to know."

"If he doesn't want to tell us what we want, we'll take all his clothes off and resume our questions. Research has shown that being naked, particularly in front of a woman, will get the point across."

"Come with me," Joseph said to the group. "If anyone has any questions, please ask."

Carrying his cup of hot coffee, Joseph sat down and said, "All right, now, how many men are there and where are they housed?"

All the time Joseph was speaking, he was admiring the glowing red tip on the iron bar. "Isn't that nice?" he asked Dean Morris.

Dean took a little water from his cup and sprinkled it on the red tip. It sizzled! "Man, that would hurt!" He exclaimed!

The prisoner, whose name they never asked, his eyes locked on the iron bar, exclaimed, "Ok, ok, if you take me with you, they are ruthless and I'm dead meat if they find out. There are about thirty of us, all armed with M-16s and AK-47s. Most have side-arms of whatever they could steal." He went to say that the women prisoners were locked in a wooden shed to the left or far north of the camp; their male companions were either killed or chased away. There is a bunch of graves next to the ammo shed. They had controlled this area since the Green Ghost came.

"Do they have explosives?" asked Jim Wisnicki.

"Oh hell Yes! That little shed to the right or south of the road has a bunch of C-4 or C-5 or whatever the hell it is called. They broke into a National Guard Armory and stole a bunch of stuff including a huge amount of ammunition."

"Target one, Jim," said Joseph.

"Ok, now, at sunrise, where is everyone sleeping? Do you have a mess hall or someplace everyone gets fed?"

The prisoner, fixated on the glowing iron rod that Joseph was smiling and stroking, admitted where everyone slept; he also said that they were a gang that got chased out of the South Kansas City area.

Private Spenser Gerry, now Corporal, and Private First Class, Alvin Swanson, now Sergeant, drew a diagram in the dirt near their fire. "We couldn't get inside the camp; they had armed guards all over the place," reported Spenser. "But, just to the south of the road is a large tent which seems to be the command post. You could get through the camp only be going past the command post. They had living quarters way to the north of the road, what looks like a mess hall next to the living quarters."

Alvin Swanson said "There is a small building south of the camp, almost by itself in a field next a wrecked John Deere tractor. I think it is their storage building for explosives and stuff. There were no children, but there were women essentially working in the fields to the north and east of the camp. They seemed to be prisoners because each group of women had armed escorts. Also, in the field next to the storage building appeared to be several graves. I got the impression that these were unlucky travelers. I don't know what they did with the guy Johnstone shot. I also listened to some of the guards talking with each other. They were discussing which women they were going to get from the chief. So, in essence, the women were slaves/prisoners."

"Are they dangerous?" asked Joseph Robinson.

"Oh, my heavens yes!" exclaimed Spenser Gerry. "These guys will kill their mothers to make a point. Judging from the conversations, they are ruthless, no compromise, nothing but their way!"

"I think so too," agreed Alvin Swanson. "These people will never give up."

"Ok, Dean, is the bush thing set up?"

"Yes, at sunup, we'll shake the bushes and see what happens. I anticipate that they will shoot the hell out of that bush."

"Jim, how accurate are you with the mortars? What I would like to do is after they shoot up the bush, drop a mortar on that building south of the road, and then, drop a series of them in a row, essentially giving them a chance to run. If any start firing at us, take them out."

"Sir, with respect, they attempted to kill you, our leader, the best person we've ever had; they get no mercy from us!" exclaimed LeRoy.

"We agree!" Every single man in Joe's group stated flatly. "They tried to kill you; they have killed probably many before; they get no "giving up" from us!"

Something was in Joe's eyes for a moment.

"Thank you, men! Every one of you, make sure your silencers are on and be certain of your cover."

"Jim?"

"I can place a mortar anywhere you want it," replied Jim Wisnicki. "I practiced with duds which were easy since I didn't blow anything up. I will put one each on the tractors and that combine; that will make pieces of metal flying everywhere and what doesn't get them by the mortar, the metal will. You never knew this, but I wanted to go with you on some of your assignments, but my general flatly refused. Who do you want to go with me, I need two men."

"Robert, you and Ion help Jim," ordered Dean Morris.

Before the actual sunrise, but while it was getting light, Jim Wisnicki, two men and Jane Ostmark/Morris, who volunteered to go along stating that she was a good judge of distances, crawled to the crest of the hill before the barricade.

Jim whispered to Robert Jones, "How many yards is it from here to that shed? Think football fields. Did you play football, Robert?"

"Sure, I was the quarterback for my high school team before I . . . got caught."

"Caught at what?" asked Jane Ostmark/Morris.

"Aw, well, I got caught making love to a girl."

"Really? So what? People get caught doing that all the time."

"Well, Major (she would always be known as their Major), the girl was the coach's daughter and we, well, we didn't have any clothes on. He gave me two choices, face criminal charges, or quit school and join the Army."

Robert smiled at the memory, "What her father never knew was that she had a uniform fetish, in other words, she liked to take off her and my clothes, all of them, a piece at a time as she was disrobing, and I had had my football uniform on. That included my jockstrap!"

"Did you use condoms?" asked Jane trying very hard not to smile.

"Major, there weren't enough condoms in the entire city of Detroit for what we did to each other!"

Robert Jones heard some rustling of grass below him and looked around. He saw both Jim and Jane laying on the ground, tears in their eyes, holding their sides and struggling not to howl or make noise with hysterical laughter.

Later, Jane whispered to Jim, "Every time I will hear the word Detroit, I will remember Robert and this time!"

After some moments, they crawled back to the top of the hill, trying very hard not to snicker, and agreed on Jim's distances. They went back to the bottom and set up the mortar system which consisted of a large pipe, a tripod with measurement adjustments and a base plate. Jim crawled back to the top and marked with branches the exact directions of the first mortar and the second mortar.

They sat back and waited for Joseph Robinson's signal. Jim explained how each mortar was to be handled which was simple: the mortar was simply dropped down the tube, bottom first.

Sunrise started. Dean Morris' men crawled to their positions to pull the string on the bush. They waited until they saw movement in the blockade and pulled on the string. In the blockade someone pointed to the bushes, several men huddled for a moment and then four men using AK-47s and M-16s fired at the shaking bushes and hats.

"Jesus, they shot the crap out of that bush," exclaimed Ion.

Joseph Robinson signaled down to Major Jim Wisnicki, fire one finger, then a delay of eight to ten seconds, target number two. They had targeted the mess tent as target number three.

Behind Joseph and his men on the hillside, they heard the thump of a mortar firing, then the whistling as it soared overhead.

Then quiet.

Suddenly, a huge dual explosion resulted from the impact of the mortar striking the explosive shed. Dirt, pieces of wood and parts of a wrecked tractor flew everywhere. The ground shook and everything within a two-hundred-foot radius was flattened and destroyed. Surrounding the two-hundred-foot center sounds of exploding rifle, shotgun, and handgun shells echoed off the trees.

Almost immediately, six gangsters started firing their rifles in the general direction of the road. Bullets whistled through the trees surrounding Joe's group. That lasted about two seconds when deadly silenced M-16 rifles spoke from behind trees and under logs; there were six less suspects/gang members.

About ten seconds later, a second mortar handled by Ion landed in a combine which was to the entrance of the command tent. Small pieces, pulleys, pipes, and green colored tin of a demolished John Deere green combine sliced everywhere.

Robert exclaimed, "I bet that's a use for an old John Deere combine that they wouldn't find in the Yellow Pages."

In about five more seconds, a third mortar impacted in what was the dining/lunchroom, destroying it and the fifteen or more gang members in it. Just to the north of the now bombed out barricade, they could see men running away through the fields, a few were dragging wounded men.

Sergeant Dean Morris ordered, "Those running away, if you can make the shot, take them! They would have done that to us!"

A volley of M-16s, at 3000 feet per second, swept through the fields eliminating five but missing three. These three turned and fired their AK-47s back at the camp which was a huge mistake. A second volley resolved that problem!

Prior to the attack, Joseph had ordered the horses held

in the group's camp, about three-quarters of a mile away. So, Joseph and three of his men advanced on foot to examine the bombed out southern part of the enemy camp. Three others covered them from the safety of trees. He sent two of his men to the north part where allegedly the slave women were held. Joseph's men, checking the meeting area found little in original pieces, including parts of 15 bodies that clearly were no longer a threat.

Joseph's two men returned bringing eleven women, some young and some middle aged, many looked beaten. "Sir, all the men fled leaving these women. We took them out! Then we shot out the lock and freed them. What do we do with them?"

"Well, we can't take them with us, but let me talk with them," replied Joseph.

"Is there someone somewhat in charge among you?" Joseph asked the huddled women.

"Well, I guess I'm the one," replied Dorothy Willison, an older, stout, motherly looking woman whose white hair and body hadn't seen a bath in weeks. "That gang captured us while we and our men were on the road, they killed my husband and our men and enslaved us. We were forced to work in the fields for food for the gang, and at night, one or two of us were raped."

She hugged a crying young girl, "It is ok now, we're free, honey." Dorothy looked at Joseph, "I can't express how thankful we are, but now we're free, and we'll grab some of the guns, we'll be all right. Don't worry about the men who fled, if they came back, we'll take nice and good care of them!"

The look in her eyes was terrifying!

Joseph Robinson spent a little time telling the women what had happened to the world and what they could expect for the near future, which unfortunately wasn't much, but at least now they know enough to plan to survive.

Joseph turned to Dean Morris, "Dean, get the wagons up here and we're gone. Mam," he turned to face Dorothy, "You should be able to find some food and other supplies left, but I would be careful to make sure no one is left alive. We found no one, but our search was quick."

"Someone make sure the little ones can't see out of the wagons; they don't need to see all this." Joseph ordered.

After skirting the debris and holes left by the mortar, they continued to Whiteman Air Force Base. They released the prisoner about ten miles past the location. That night, they camped about fifteen miles past the barricade.

Joseph gathered everyone: "Anyone have any questions about what we did to get through that shall we say, obstacle? I must say that I am very proud of all of you. Jim, your mortars were great and precisely on target. Well done! The rest of you, you did exactly what was necessary. You must remember that gang deserved absolutely no mercy. That older woman said that they were slaves and that the gang had killed their men and took turns raping the women; I would not want to be captured by those women. Did you see her eyes?"

He paused and looked each member in the eye: "You and each of you worked as part of a team without needing to be told what to do. Again, great job, guys! I'm a little surprised that we haven't run into similar situations before. We've all seen the starvation and desperation in our travels and the lack of government organization. It's been a lesson in anarchy more than anything else. I firmly believe that we may be the only hope for our world; now, you understand what we are fighting for."

CHAPTER EIGHT

WHITEMAN AIR FORCE BASE

Before approaching the Base, Joseph Robinson suggested, "I think we should put on whatever uniforms we have. We will be more easily accepted because we obviously are one of them."

As they went through Sprit Gate and returned salutes by the guards, they were directed to the base headquarters. On the way, they passed the requisite inactive fighter airplanes and a B-29 bomber that was in great condition. It looked like it was ready to take off and drop bombs on something.

After talking to General Wilson Craig, the base commander, and obtaining his approval, they were directed to the base hospital. General Craig suggested, "When you get situated, come back here; I have a couple of barbers that, looking at your men, they need desperately."

Lt. Colonel Jane Ostmark/Morris (she still hadn't gotten used to her rank and new last name) had explained to the base commander and now the medical staff who they were, what they were doing and that their two little children needed shots.

They were met with the hospital medical staff, all very curious on how they acquired Cassie and Douglas. Joseph Robinson explained briefly that they were orphans. Jane Morris showed them what shot records they could find of the kids stating, "This is all we could find. I hope that these are satisfactory."

A Physician's Assistant, 1st Lt. Roberta Peterson, young, slim, about five-three, shoulder length brown hair, wearing the requisite white smocks, Robbie to her friends, was helping Doctor Adolph Reseses, the base pediatrician, getting ready to give Cassie and Douglas their needed shots.

She casually asked Joe, "Where are you folks from and where are you headed from here?"

After explaining where they came from, Joe continued, "We are headed for Fort McCoy or Camp McCoy or whatever it's called up in Wisconsin."

"I'm from Wisconsin and I know where McCoy is," exclaimed Robbie Peterson. "What are you going to do up there?" She was carrying a tray full of medical utensils; the doctor was going to give the kids a regular examination.

"Well, from there, I'm going to look for my friend Dan Peterson up around Manitowoc/Two Rivers area. He, his wife, and three kids are supposed to be there."

Crash!

She dropped her tray, utensils flying everywhere!

"He, he," she stuttered through sudden tears, "He's my brother; wh... why do you want him?"

She collapsed to her knees, her hands to her face, her eyes leaking, her body shaking, "I, I thought he was dead out in California. After this green thing came, there was no word from anyone."

She shook her head, "I couldn't even get to my parents, to see if even they were still alive. How, how do you know about him?"

She felt faint, her body started to collapse, "Who, who are you!?"

Doctor Reseses took charge and grabbed her, "Nurse, get a chair for her, Robbie, put your head between your knees, take deep breaths; somebody sweep this mess up!" He held her for a few moments.

Cassie and Douglas started crying, afraid. After a few minutes, calm was restored. Jane Morris and several of Joe's men hugged and soothed the kids telling them that everything was ok, that it was a happy time.

"H ...H...How do you know my brother?" sobbed Robbie Peterson.

"Well, Robbie, your brother Dan was/is my best friend from college.

Lieutenant Dean Morris is also my best friend. Your brother Dan got me out of some trouble I was in, and now, we think he and his, I guess for lack of a better definition, wife, have an ability to help us fight the Green Ghost. She has a pet cougar that we need. This is a long story."

"Wait a second! I, I know you!" She grasped, almost unable to breathe. "We talked on the phone a long, long time ago. Oh my God!"

Joe turned to Doctor Reseses, "Doctor, can we get our kids taken care of and if you have some coffee, we can explain who and what we are, OK?"

"Done, who is first, the little girl or boy?"

After an examination of the little ones, Dr. Reseses pronounced them surprisingly fit. "They have the appropriate weight, are well cared for, and their lungs are clear," he smiled at Jane, "And they are well loved. All they need are shots and they are getting them now. I must be careful because the Lord knows when we'll get any more medication. Is one of you their parent?"

His question was met with hoots of laughter. He looked puzzled, "What?"

Joe responded, "Jane, why don't you tell our doctor how we become parents?"

While Jane Morris was explaining how they obtained Cassie and Douglas, Joe was talking with Robbie Peterson,

"After the Green Ghost came and we had received orders to fight it, we left California with two brilliant scientists and my group of men. I was, much later, told that your brother, Dan, and his two older kids were on the way to Wisconsin and stopped in Durango, Colorado, to try to find their youngest sister. I had to see a teacher-scientist in Durango that had some additional ideas for us to fight the Ghost. There, I was told that Dan's second wife had run off to a commune in Colorado with their daughter. In essence, Dan, his son Tom, a woman named Lorraine, and two men retrieved their little one from the commune. They are unquestioned heroes in Durango, Colorado."

He paused, smiling, "Several weeks before I got there, they had left and were making their way to his, err, your parent's house in Wisconsin. His girl/wife has a pet cougar that we want to be able to use when we get to Chicago. We need to ascertain if the Green Ghost is around us and her cougar should be able to tell us that. We think we have something to fight the Green Ghost."

Joe paused, "Would it be presumptuous to say that you know where your parents live?"

"Oh-my Lord-yes!"

Joe Robinson asked, "Dr. Reseses, how do you feel about Robbie coming with us?"

"I would and do feel badly about losing her! She is one of, if not the best, Physician's Assistant I have, but it seems you need her more than I do. Robbie, I'm going to miss you; you are quite bright and have a great bedside manner. I hope you get a chance to go to medical school. If so, find me and I'll give you the best recommendation I can."

Dr. Reseses paused for a moment thinking, "I have a suggestion, let's make this legal. Since you," he nodded at Robbie Peterson, "are going up to Wisconsin, what do you think of me transferring you to Fort McCoy, essentially leaving it open as your reporting date? That way, you can spend whatever time you want with your parents and family, and eventually report in. That way, we'll keep everyone happy. OK?"

Robbie Peterson, still wobbly on her feet, reached and hugged Dr. Reseses, "Thank you, thank you so much!"

She turned to Joe, "When do you-we leave?"

"Jim, did you see your friend? Dean, how soon can be ready?"

"Does anyone know Colonel Jerry Winsome? I haven't had a chance to see him yet. I understand he runs Base Supply."

Laughter filled the emergency room. "Well, I would think that every nurse here knows Colonel Winsome," Dr. Reseses said dryly. "He is relatively young, good looking, single, and apparently quite friendly." He pointed at a large building near the flight-line, "His office is down there."

"I'll ride over there. Dean, can you come along and let him know what we need?" Major Jim Wisnicki said.

"See if you can get about 30 or 40 pounds of coffee, preferable ground, because that is worth its weight in gold for trade," Joe said.

Paul, their chef, interrupted, "If possible, get a large sack of regular flour and a fifty-pound sack of salt. As you know, I need that for our sourdough bread. Oh heck, I'll go with you and see what else we could use."

"Joe, how about leaving tomorrow afternoon?" Jane Ostmark/ Morris asked. "Remember, the base commander gave us the vacant BOQ building; he said there was a constant running water source for the showers, and I think we all could use one. We could give Cassie and Douglas decent baths, too."

"Great! Maybe we can all take showers, and our guys can get their haircuts. We'll wash our clothes; they need that badly, they can stand by themselves," responded Dean Morris.

"OK, Robbie, we don't have much room, maybe a duffle bag plus whatever medical stuff you think we could use. Check with our medic to see what he needs," Joseph Robinson said,

"Oh, do you have a working bicycle because if so, Ion, help her attach it to one of our wagons. I hope you can ride a horse because that's how we get around. How do you feel about guard duty? All of us perform that, including me and our Lt. Colonel, whatever is necessary to accomplish whatever needs doing."

She grinned through shaking tears, "No problem, Sir, I'll do whatever I'm asked. Just think, I can't believe it, I may get to see my sister, brother, and parents! Oh-My Lord. Thank you so much."

Hugs again!

Joseph continued, "One final thing, I see that you are an officer. We don't follow rank much, if at all. Actually, the Chain of Command is me, formerly Sergeant and now 2nd Lt. Dean Morris, and everyone else is below that. Dean and Jane, over there, just got married. We usually agree on what needs to be done and it gets done. Everything from guard duty, caring for the horses, helping Captain, now Major, Weaver, our chief cook, and now watching the kids is included."

Joe met Jane Morris' eyes, she nodded approval. It would be nice to have another female with this bunch of rough men.

They, however, left the second day. There was a quick, wild, going-away party for Robbie given by the employees of the hospital. And Jane demanded time to hang their clothes, including Cassie and Douglas's and everyone else's, to dry on makeshift drying lines between the BOQ buildings. Also, short haircuts of all the men were necessary-according to the base commander. Joe wasn't about to argue with the commander! Jane had to look twice of some of the men, how different they looked without long hair and beards.

Just before they left, Dean and Joe examined their maps, trying to determine the quickest route to Camp/Fort McCoy (or whatever it was called). The route was nearly straight North, however when Dean closely examined the map, he pointed, "Joe, we have a little problem; according to these maps, apparently, there is no direct route into McCoy. Either we come in quite a few miles West of there or miles East of there."

"Ok, Dean, then what?" asked Joe. "I've been thinking about Wisconsin and our search for Dan Peterson. Let me run something past you. On horse-back it would take about four or five days to ride from McCoy to Manitowoc or Two Rivers and about an equal amount of time back. If we took bikes, we could do it in maybe two days. The second idea I had is this: I originally thought about taking our scientists, but there is no need of them; so, if I, and how about you, Robbie and one or two men, went on bikes? Third, sequential idea, is this: Jim and Jane can handle the meeting in McCoy because they have the ranks, and we could give them instructions on what we want. There is no real need for us to go first to McCoy and then to Manitowoc/Two Rivers and then return to McCoy. In fact, they could take the wagon train and we would leave them somewhere in Southern Wisconsin. It would save us time. What do you think?"

Dean looked at his leader and with a straight face said, "I think you have been thinking way, way too much about thinking about what I'm thinking you're thinking I've been thinking!"

"What?"

Jane and Robbie giggled. Jane whispered, "See, what I have to put up with!"

Then Joe looked at his friend, Dean, and discovered a sneaky smile.

"Seriously Joe, I think that is brilliant planning and makes a lot of sense. We have four bikes attached to the wagons, and Robbie's make five. That would work, and I trust Jim and Jane to do the right thing. Let's run this past the gang and see what they say?"

That night, they discussed the plan with their "gang," as usual. The only difference was tonight, it included Roberta Peterson.

Joe explained to Roberta, "This is the way we operate. I trust my bunch, and everyone knows what must be done, when and who does whatever."

Roberta Peterson pointed out, "We will miss Chicago by quite a margin. If we split up in or around Madison, Wisconsin, it is about 140 miles, give or take, to Manitowoc and my parents live about 12 or 13 miles north of that. For us, unless we really start training on the bikes, it would be about a two-day ride. I've attached a small trailer to one of the bikes, and if we use it, it will slow us down a little."

She glanced at Dean and Joe, "With respect, Sirs, even if we only had backpacks, that is an additional weight which will also slow us; I don't think either of you, or anyone in this group has ridden their bikes much and there are different muscles between riding some horse and a bike."

"Hay guys, she's telling us that we're out of shape," laughed Jane.

"Well, we probably are," replied Joe. "Ok, here's what I suggest: Robbie, Dean, I, and two volunteers will go the Peterson's home. I believe that Robbie's trip is one way, right?"

"Yes Sir, at least that's my plan now. I'm impressed with your medic, he is good, in fact very good. However, I've had nearly two year's considerable experience in the emergency room and from what I understand, we don't know if you might have to fight to get through the gangs in Chicago. Also, we don't know what we'll find at my parent's place. I can only hope and pray that they're ok."

"From what the Deputy Sheriff told me in Durango, Dan and his family had an AR-15, several handguns including a 9 mm., at least a 357 or 45 caliber handgun, two power bows, and his oldest little girl of about eight or nine, also had a small 22 semi-automatic. Plus that cougar, and I forgot, they'll have a dog too. I would think they'll be all right." Joe said.

"All right, unless somebody has any objections, here's what we'll do.

All bike riders will spend a minimum of two hours of day on a bike per day until we hit Madison. I think it would be beneficial for all of us to ride as much as we can. Dean, figure out which two get to go with us and make sure they, you and I get our more than two hours in. I've checked with our horse people and if we average about 20 miles a day, it should take us less than a month to Wisconsin. Our guys know that we're traveling through farms and we'll keep our horses well fed and well hydrated. I don't want to waste any more time."

Somebody grumbled, "I don't think my rear end could handle that much time on a bike."

Someone else responded, "Well, judging from the size of your rear end, it would take at least several months of riding just to reduce it to normal size. And I pity the poor bike!"

Both Jane and Robbie tried to stop laughing, "Now you see what these guys are like." Jane loudly whispered to Robbie.

CHAPTER NINE

About a week north of Whiteman, Dean Morris motioned to Joseph Robinson, "Is it my imagination or in the last few days, and today, is it warmer and more humid? I'm sweating more like when we were in Africa or Panama."

Joseph Robinson turned on his horse and looked toward the south and southwest. "You're right! Look at those high cumulonimbus clouds; the turbulent bottoms are turning dark, black, and green. You can see them moving. That means very probable heavy rain and worse, maybe even tornados. If you watch them, they're growing larger!"

Joseph looked down the road, pointed and shouted, "Everyone, about a mile ahead of us is that large six-lane overpass. That's the best protection around here from that storm. Hurry up, people, we may not have much time!"

Once under the overpass, Joseph ordered, "Everyone, help with the horses, we're going the get heavy rain and wind, lightening, and nasty thunder, probably a tornado and I want to keep them as calm as possible. Be sure to block the wagons' wheels; it may get very windy through here. Also, please start playing the harmonica to calm the horses.'"

About an hour or two later, flashes of lightening striking the ground two or three miles away lit the underside of the overpass. Eight seconds later, the crash of thunder startled the horses. However, each person except the two little ones were holding on and soothing a horse. Wind driven heavy rain poured down on the road, but Joseph had been right, they were protected.

Hours later, through frequent lightening, bursts of wind, rain, occasional hail, and once a squall that sounded like a freight train, their cover held up.

Two days were lost when they huddled under a concrete overpass while tornado laden thunder and lightning rainstorms pounded around them.

As they emerged from under the cover, what was left of a near-by destroyed barn and silo were visible and a bunch of trees transformed into kindling thanks to a freight train sounding tornado.

After letting the horses eat at a local alfalfa field, they continued north to Wisconsin. To the sides of the road, they could see flattened barns and houses. Cattle were wondering around loose. Joseph observed, "I hate to say this, but we can't stop to help. We could not do much to help them and we're running out of time before winter."

Joe's men, while truly wanting to help the storm's victims, understood that they could spend weeks which would really interfere with their critical mission.

Crossing the Wisconsin border and the shot-up Wisconsin sign, Joseph asked, "OK, Robbie, we're here just south of Madison. How do we get to your parent's place?"

"It's easy, we'll just ride up Highway 155 past Fond du Lac, turn right on, I think Wisconsin 23, to Sheboygan, and pick up 43. That is an Interstate highway, and it runs from Milwaukee to Green Bay. Once past Manitowoc, we'll pick up Highway 10 which runs East and West to County Highway Q which runs north and south. Then, we will be close to home!" she said with tears in her eyes. She reached over and hugged Joseph; he just touched her shoulder; he understood.

Joseph asked Robbie about the populations of Manitowoc/ Two Rivers

"They are separate cities. Manitowoc has a population of approximately 34,500 and Two Rivers has a population of around 11,300, both give or take a few thousand. That's hoping that most of the people could survive."

Joseph asked, "Are you closer to one or the other?"

"The answer is neither, about twelve miles from Manitowoc and about ten miles from Two Rivers. We will be closer to Manitowoc in our route."

Joseph turned to Jane, "Just a little reminder, when you get to McCoy and check in with Coronel Blossitt in charge and get some place to sleep, you'll have time to rest the horses. I would really like someone who is familiar with Chicago and the Chicago gangs to join us. I fear that we might have to fight through their territory to get to the University of Chicago. See if anyone went to the University and if they have any maps. Try to talk the Coronel into giving us maybe a half dozen or more men and heavy weapons; additional people might be useful. Remember to get food for everyone. Also, see if he has anyone who knows something about blast furnaces."

He turned to Jim Wisnicki, "Jim, your mortars were lifesavers. Figure out what we might need to fight through some gangs. I think more mortars, grenades and so on might be needed. Also, for all of you, if possible, try to get some time on a firing range with both handguns and our rifles. Oh yes, Jim, since your family lives around here, as soon as you get that organized, head on your home which if I recall, is just north of Madison, I think we'll be at McCoy about ten days to two weeks and then, off to Chicago. Can you be back to McCoy by then?"

"Sure thing, Sir. My family will be glad to see me. Thank you very much."

Joe turned back to Jane, "Two additional points: one, emphasize to Coronel Blossitt that if, if we are successful, the point of the nation's recovery might very well be through him. Second, please be thinking of Cassie and Douglas. What will we do with them? We are their family now and I mean that in every sense of the word."

"All right, listen up everyone, Jane is in charge while I'm gone."

"Oh noooo. More whipping and beating!" exclaimed a male voice.

After the laughter died down, Joe continued, "I really don't need to tell you we've been together for a long time, and you all know what needs to be done. Jim, Jane, do you have your route mapped out?"

"Yes, we're leaving as soon as you."

"Robbie, I see you will be towing your trailer. If you get tired, we'll swap. Dean, our two volunteers, and me are wearing backpacks; we also have our weapons and ammo. Hopefully, we wouldn't need them. All right, let's hit the road!"

It was interesting that before Joe and his group left, they had to hug and kiss the two little ones telling them they would be back soon. After all, they were family!

Highway 151 was followed Wisconsin 23 to Wisconsin 43. As they passed though the outskirts of Sheboygan, Wisconsin, it was turning dark.

"I don't think we can make it to my home today. I suggest that we spend the night anywhere around here, and in the morning, we'll be at my house," suggested Robbie Peterson.

Later that night, after nearly everyone was asleep, Robbie, unable to sleep, sat looking into the campfire, her arms folded to her body.

"Can't sleep, huh?" asked Joseph quietly.

"Joe, I owe you more than I could ever repay, but I'm worried about my family, my brother, my sister, and most importantly, my parents," she whispered. "I had no way to contact them, and my base couldn't afford to release both me and a couple of guards to protect me."

"Well, if it makes you feel a little better, I would put long odds on your brother making it. He, his kids, a girl named Lorraine Fairly, her big cougar and a German Sheppard dog, and another couple were all quite well armed. I think the animals would be great sentries. And everyone was riding bicycles."

Joseph reached out to touch her shoulder, "Try to get some rest. Tomorrow will be a long day."

The Peterson Farm

One bright sun-shining day shortly after breakfast, at the Peterson farm about a half mile from the main road, the temperature was nearly in the sixties and Sarah, Daniel Peterson's sister, visited early that morning. Tom Peterson's dog barked and growled. He was standing in the front yard, looking up toward the highway.

Daniel Peterson, stretched his nearly six-foot body and strolled to the front door. He could see a group of riders on bicycles up on the highway.

The riders stopped and one pointed to the Peterson's buildings. They slowly rode down the muddy one lane road. Dan didn't like what he was seeing.

(Unknown to Dan Peterson, Robbie Peterson, up on the main highway, pointed to the farm buildings, tears flowing down her cheeks, "That's my home, and someone is there! There's smoke coming out of the chimney!")

"Tom, Geoff, get out here quick," Dan Peterson called.

"What, Dad?" asked Tom breathlessly from running down the steps to the outside of the house.

"Quickly everyone! We've got five people on bikes coming in here! I don't know who they are or what they want. Geoff, you get your gun in the kitchen, and climb up in the granary. Keep yourself hidden; you can see out that upstairs window."

"Tom, you take the AR-15 and cover them from the upstairs bedroom window of the house. You know how to use that weapon. I'll wear the 38 revolver. Don't show yourself, boys, but keep them covered," ordered Dan.

"Lor, take Sue and Ginger with one of the power bows and your .357 that you got from your Dad and hide in the barn. You've got your big cat to help, too. If they are looking for anyone, the barn is the last place they will look."

Lorraine Fairly, worried, grabbed one of the power bows, her precious .357 Colt Python, and strapped it on. "Come on kids, lets hurry into the barn."

"Dad, Mom, Sarah, you stay in the house and keep me covered. Dad, you have my 9.mm; you've fired it before. I'll meet them in the yard, OK?" asked Dan. "Keep an eye on the back of the house toward the woods. Everyone, if I raise both, understand both, of my hands above my head and kneel, we're in deep trouble, I strongly suggest that you shoot them and maybe, we'll ask questions later. If I take my cap off, it's all right. Understand?"

Everyone nodded their understanding and ran to their places. They knew the possible hazards strangers could be.

Dan waited in the middle of the yard, Tom's dog growling by his side. Dan reached down and rubbed the dogs head, "Good boy."

The group stopped on the road leading to the farm buildings.

"Hello the house!" called a voice.

Dan thought, *"Dam! That voice sounds familiar."*

"Come on in!"

The party, five in number, slowly rode past the huge lilac bushes planted by Dan's mother and into the front yard, their hands in plain sight.

"Joe, that's my brother, Dan!" exclaimed Robbie, barely able to breathe.

"Dan, it's me, Robbie," she shouted.

Dan Peterson, shocked, uttered "Robbie? Robbie, is that you? Oh my God!"

She jumped off her bike and ran to Dan, clutching him, "I didn't know if you were even alive," she cried.

Water poured from their faces while they clasped each other.

"Where, where did you come from?" Dan managed to ask.

In the house, Mother Peterson screamed, "That's Robbie, Oh my Lord, that's our Robbie!"

Both ran out of the house, Father Peterson slightly behind while he jammed a 9 mm. weapon into its holster.

Robbie saw her parents come out of the house at that second.

They saw her, sprinted to their daughter, and joined the family, tears flying, each pushing back to look at faces and again clutching each other, unintelligent words flinging about!

A few seconds later, Sarah, Dan and Robbie's sister, flew out of the house and joined the family- more tears and hugs!

After a few long moments, things quieted down and they turned to the other riders.

The fourth man, obviously in charge, looked at Dan from beneath a battered felt hat. He peered out through mirrored sunglasses, a dark laced Lincolnesque beard lining his face and chin.

Dan thought, *"My God, he looks familiar."*

Dan exclaimed, "Wait a second, don't I know you?"

"You should, Dan."

"Oh my God!" Dan said, stunned. "I, I don't believe it, Joe, Joe Robinson!"

Dan just stood there, dazed, shaking his head. "How, how in the hell did you get here? What are you doing here?

Then after a second, Dan said, "Get off those bikes and come on in."

"Is it all right?" asked Joe Robinson with a smile on his face. "I see you have someone covering us from that upstairs window, and there is someone in that shed or granary, and you probably have someone covering us from the barn."

"Oh sure," said Dan. He took off his cap and waved it around.

"We come in peace," Joe said. He added cryptically, "We also need your help."

"Lor, Tom, Geoff, it's ok." Dan called. "It's Joe Robinson from California."

Slowly, Lorraine, Dan's son Tom, and his friend Geoff came out of their hiding places and approached the four men.

Dan and Joe Robinson ran to each other, grabbed each other's hands and then hugged each other, pounding each other on the back.

"What on earth are you doing here?" repeated Dan.

"Well, as I said, I need your help. We can talk about that in a minute."

Tom and Geoff approached the men. "Joe, you might remember my son, Tom, and this is his friend, Geoff. Boys, this is Joe Robinson, my friend from California."

"Joe, please introduce your men."

Joe pointed out his Lt. and Sergeants while Dan's entire family approached. "Joe, this is my father and mother and my sister, Sarah. This is Joe Robinson, who if you remember was my roommate in college back in California."

"I'm pleased to finally meet you in person, Mr., Mrs. Peterson. We've talked several times on the telephone a long time ago," Joe said as they shook hands.

"Hello, so you are Sarah," said Joe warmly as he shook hands with Dan's sister, Sarah, their eyes meeting. "There must be a mistake. You don't look at all like how he described you."

"How did my beloved brother describe me?" smiled Sarah as their hands remained clasped several seconds longer, her eyes sparkling.

"Well, he said that you were short, fat, ugly and on top of that, frumpy looking. And he didn't even say that you had a nice personality," as their hands reluctantly separated.

"I did too say that she had a nice personality!"

"I'll get you for that, brother of mine."

Lorraine Fairly walked out of the barn, carrying one of the power bows with her left hand, the.357 Colt Python strapped to her right-side waist. Holding onto her were Dan's younger children, Sue, and Ginger, all three with worried looks on their faces.

Lorraine whispered to the children, "I think Dad knows them, but what do they want here? I don't think I like it."

Lorraine, Sue, and Ginger walked over to Dan, the two children hanging onto her.

"Joe, this is the rest of my family: Lor, Sue, and Ginger. Hon, this is Joe Robinson, my friend from California."

"Good to meet you, Joe. Dan has told me so much about you," Lor said as they shook hands.

"So, you are the Lorraine that has made a happy man out of my friend," Joe said. "I've heard good, great things about him and you."

Questions occurred to both Lor and Dan. They glanced at each other puzzled. "What are you doing here, Joe? The last time we saw each other, you said you were going someplace to try to wait this force thing out."

"Just give me a couple of minutes, I'll explain as much as I can why I'm here."

He turned to Lor, "You are Lorraine Fairly, aren't you?"

Lor nodded, stunned-shocked, "Y-Yes! How, how do you know that?"

"Do you know a Henry Rinokowski?"

"Henry Rinokowski? Oh my Lord, yes!" she exclaimed, her hands to her face. She turned to Dan, "That's La Plata Sheriff's Deputy Hank from back in Colorado. You know him! My real father. W-why?"

"I have a letter from him to you," Joe said as he reached into one of his saddlebags, retrieved a heavy plastic wrapped manila envelope simply marked "Lorraine Fairly, Wisconsin" and handed it to her.

"Why are you here?" asked Dan again.

"That's a long story, and one of the reasons we're here."

"Would you men like to come in for some coffee?" asked Dan's mother, interrupting politely.

"Thank you, Mrs. Peterson, we'll accept your kind offer, but we'll supply the coffee."

Joe turned, "Dean, we've got enough coffee to supply an army; do you think we can spare a couple of pounds for Mrs. Peterson here?"

"Sure thing, Sir, gladly!"

While Dean was retrieving a ten-pound bag of ground coffee from his saddle bags, Dan asked, "How did you find us, Joe? It's not like we left messages all over where we were going."

Dan's father interrupted, convinced that these men meant his family no harm, "We can talk inside." He pointed to the side of the house, "Do you want to park your bikes over there?"

They all trooped into the Peterson kitchen. Due to the mud in the yard, each had to take their shoes and boots off and leave them in the porch.

Both Sergeant David Musinski and Corporal Roger Sampson looked embarrassed when they revealed large holes in their socks. Mrs. Peterson took one look at the holes and smiled, "If you will stay around here for a day or so, I'll fix those socks right up."

They nodded their thanks.

"How. . . how did you get this?" stammered Lorrain Fairly, her body shaking, holding the manila envelope as if it was a precious heirloom. She looked around for someplace to sit while she opened the package.

Mrs. Peterson looked at her, "Lor, let's go sit in the living room where you can open that package in peace; here, sit down and I'll get you a cup of coffee. I, I still can't believe it, I have my two daughters and my son here with me, finally." Sobs, water escaped from her face again.

Lorraine hugged Mother Peterson, "I, I can't believe that they found us."

Lorraine sat on a sofa that clearly had seen better days, the rips in the fabric had been carefully sewed together. A painted brown two by four piece of wood took the place of a broken leg.

Lorraine Fairly carefully opened the package. It contained two layers, the outer layer was the yellow wrapping paper, inside was a waterproof plastic liner protecting the interior contents. She slowly removed about a dozen photographs, one, an old photograph of a couple with their arms around each other, the black and white photograph so old it was faded brown around the edges. Also enclosed were two letters. She glanced at the photographs and with trembling hands opened the first letter addressed simply "Lorraine Fairly."

She could hear her real father's voice:

"My Dearest Darling Daughter,

At last - at last, I can call you my beloved daughter! I cannot tell you how many times I've wanted to say those words to you. Now you know! (Tears flowed down her checks as she read on.)

Your mother and I made a promise to each other that no one else would ever know the truth. We both believed that any marriage between us would have destroyed our families; we <u>never</u> could have lived in peace! Your mother's parents and my parents hated each other with a malicious passion that was restrained somewhat only by a greater fear of the police and prison!

From what your mother and I could determine much later (after your "other" father died and after all of our parents had passed away) was that the hostility started in the old country in Europe. We thought that because my grandparents and great grandparents were poor and *uneducated farmers on the one hand, and that your mother's grandparents and great grandparents had royal blood on the other hand equated to two different and irreconcilable classes of people. Apparently, your great, great grand uncle (or some similar relative) was a duke or a baron or something which meant that they <u>owned</u> people like my forefathers. While all of this may have been accurate, <u>your</u> true grandparents and great grandparents forgot one single vital fact: your mother and I fell in love in America, not Europe!*

I don't know if your man, Dan Peterson, (I guess that makes you <u>Mrs</u>. Dan Peterson!) told you he knew of the true relationship between us. I told him the whole story that first time we went looking for his daughter; I felt it was important for him to understand why I was helping him find <u>his</u> daughter. After all, he saved <u>my</u> daughter's life! He is a good man, Lorraine; the rest is up to you.

Enclosed are a number of photographs. Some are individual photos of your (new) brothers and sisters taken when we still had a regular school, some are of Betty, my beloved wife with our bunch. (She knows of you now, but you have not affected our marriage. I never asked, but your mother may have told her because they were close friends for years.) Betty is also a wonderful and cherished woman! There is a letter from her to you in this package, too.

The most important photograph is one I forgot even existed. Betty found it a long time ago and kept it for me. It is the only photograph in existence of your mother and me together! I think you should have it. I asked Betty why she kept it for me and she said, "Lorraine is a part of you, and by the time I met and fell in love with you, the thing between you and her mother had been over for a long time.

That entire affair made you the deeper, stronger, and more responsible man that I love!"

See, Lorraine, how unbelievably lucky I have been: I have had the love of three wonderful women.

My Darling Daughter! How wonderful to be able to say those cherished words after all these years. (More tears!)

I hope this letter gets to you. Joe Robinson came through here looking for Dan about a month after you left. He and his scientists have an idea that may resist that Green Ghost thing. Once they discovered you and your animals, those scientists became excited because your animals can sense when that force or energy is present. Apparently, they could not determine when that force was nearby unless electricity was being utilized, and then it was too late. I couldn't speak the same language (even in English) that Joe said his scientists spoke, but apparently, your animals will give them the ability to test whether their idea works or not. It has something to do with that thousand pounds of meteorite they are dragging across the country. I pray that they are successful. Their science is way above me (remember, I'm just a simple cop!), but if you get this letter, they may be able to fill you in on the details.

We are well here. Smiley comes by occasionally and sends his regards. He said to tell you he had "a blast!" Tell Tom that some very good-looking girl named Cindy says "Hi!" (with a blush) and if he gets back here, to come and see her.

So much for now, My Darling Daughter!

I love you, Lorraine,
Dad

Tears stained the front of her blouse as she clutched the letter to her breast. With shaking hands, she carefully examined each photograph and shared them with Dan's mother, Sarah and Robbie.

"I remember now that he always called me 'Lorraine,' never Lor as most of my friends did."

Lor handed the letter to Dan's mother, "Here, read this. It explains a little of my life."

"So those are your real parents," Dan's mother murmured as she looked at a faded photograph of a young couple, their arms around each other, clearly in love. "Just a minute," she said as she rose and rummaged in a closet under the stairs to the second floor. "Ah, yes, I thought we had this here."

She left the closet and went into the kitchen, coming back with a towel dusting off a small object. She handed it to Lorraine.

"Here, your photograph will fit quite nicely in this silver picture frame. Someone gave it to us a long time ago and I've been waiting for a special photograph to place in it. If your photograph isn't special, I don't know what is!"

Eyes brimming, Lor reached over and hugged Dan's mother, then gently removed the back and carefully placed the faded photograph in the frame. In a few seconds the photograph was safe and secure.

"Here, we'll keep it up here on the living room shelf where our family's photographs are kept; I think it belongs there too."

Over a fresh pot of coffee in the now crowded kitchen, Joe introduced his men.

Second Lieutenant Dean Morris, Sergeant David Musinski and Corporal Roger Sampson were from the U.S. Army, and assigned to Joe's detail. Dan thought that one of them looked vaguely familiar as one guard outside of the building where he had last seen Joe.

"All right, Joe, what are you doing here?" asked Dan.

"Let me explain," said Joe Robinson. "Dan, you may remember that I was in charge of a task force funded through the National Security Agency to investigate that life force or energy thing. I told you that in California." (*The thought crossed his mind that it was unnecessary to discuss their real task.*)"

Dan nodded, "Our last conversation with each other was impossible to forget."

Joe refilled his coffee cup; he had the undivided attention of the entire Peterson family. He paused for a moment to think and then continued.

"We have two scientists, now at Camp McCoy, who think that the Green Ghost--Sarah was surprised at the venom in Joseph's voice at the mention of the Green Ghost-- was around since the beginning of the universe. They think that if we could melt down a meteorite into sheets of metal, that metal might, just might serve as a shield against that force."

Joseph took a contemplative sip of his coffee, "We dug up about a thousand pounds or so of what we think was a virgin meteorite out of the Meteor Crater in Arizona and we're dragging that to Chicago to try to melt it down."

"Why a virgin meteorite?" asked Tom Peterson.

"Good question, Tom. It's Tom, right?

"Yes Sir," replied Tom Peterson. It seemed to him that the appropriate response was "Sir."

Joe nodded, "We don't even know if our theory will work, but if it does work, according to my scientists, virgin meteorites have the best chance of having whatever that substance is that might shield the force. They think that if a meteorite was on the surface of the earth or unprotected, cosmic rays might have an effect on it. Remember, this is all theory, but it's the only theory in town."

Joseph paused and then changed the subject, "Right before we left the Orange County, California area, I had stopped and talked to your secretary, Joyce. She told us where you were going and why."

Dan interrupted, "How is she? She was with me for a long time."

"Well, we left her in Victorville, California, with her husband, apparently doing all right. They came with us a little way; I guess you had told them what I told you and they accepted our offer of help," replied Joe.

"Thank heavens," said Dan. "I was worried about her, but there was nothing I could do about it."

"Do you remember an old couple by the name of Gunnerson?"

"Sure," interjected Tom, "They were that nice old couple on the Colorado River. We stayed at their place for a couple of days."

"Well, they are doing fine. They told us more where you were headed and what you were looking for. I wanted to find you, Dan. I knew that you had some knowledge of the Chicago area, and we were early for the meeting in Chicago. Right before everything shut down, a number of researchers and scientists agreed to meet in at the University of Chicago if they could make it there about in October or November. Most importantly, my two scientists referred me to a third brilliant scientist, a teacher named Dr. Bell in Durango, Colorado."

"Wait a second, was this Dr. Bell's first initial T with some unpronounceable first name?" asked Lorraine Fairly. "I think I had one of his classes in physics."

"The one and the same," smiled Joseph Robinson.

"You are right," exclaimed Lorraine Fairly. "He was the most intelligent person I've ever met, and really a sweet old man."

Joseph continued, "Apparently Dr. Bell had/has a Steven Hawking/ Einstein intellect and he verified the theory I'm working with. Anyway, to make a long story short, when I was in Durango and asked a few questions if anyone had seen you."

Joe Robinson looked at Tom Peterson over his coffee, "A better question, Tom, would have been if there was anyone in Durango, Colorado that did not know of you!"

"Us? Why?" asked Tom, surprised.

"Well, it seems that your Lorraine Fairly there was a local heroine. She was Miss Durango for a while and just about everyone knew her or of her. And when you, Tom, and your Dad saved her life, that made you famous!"

"You never told us that you were Miss Durango!"

"I couldn't accomplish much and it never came up between us."

"Well, you were-are still beautiful. No wonder we- my Dad- fell for you!"

At that, Tom reached over and hugged a blushing Lorraine.

"You see, what my friend Dan and his son did by saving you,

Lorraine, and then what you all did in recovering your little girl is what legends are made of. Is that her?" He smiled at a bright redheaded little girl. She smiled back at him. "When I identified myself to your "Deputy Hank", he told me the whole true story."

"Here, let me refill your cups." interrupted Dan's mother, carrying the coffee pot.

"Thank you, Mum." said Dan. "Joe, this is French Roast coffee, where did you guys get it?"

"We stopped at Whiteman Air Force Base and they supplied it."

"Anyway, as I was saying, in these sad times, to hear stories like yours makes people think that there still a chance; that the human race will somehow overcome that force thing."

After a moment, Joe continued, "In order for you to understand what we're doing here, I have to tell you a little story."

He slowly filled his cup his cup with fresh French Roast coffee, the aroma of fresh brewed coffee drifting up into his face. He smiled down at the floor, the two girls sitting there, one with bright red hair, smiled back at him. His gaze went off into the distance, almost as if he was recalling a memory:

"About fifty thousand years or so ago, give or take a century or two, long before humans walked on North America, a mother saber tooth cat was laying in the shade of a tree growing out of the edge of an arroyo. The arroyo was located in the northern continent, a few miles east of what was eventually to become a town by the name of Flagstaff, Arizona, United States of America."

He paused and looked at the oldest girl, "Do you know where that is?"

"Sure, we went through Flagstaff on our way to Lor's house."

"Very good. Getting back to our saber tooth cat, she was about the size of a modern day lion weighing about four hundred pounds with a spotted tawny coloring on her short fur. Her broad forehead sloped back to two dark round ears. Two seven-inch long yellowish tusks protruded from her upper jaw. She had two little six-week old cubs playing near her, their tusks just starting to grow below their mouth.

The day was warm; she idly scratched a wayward flea with a two-inch nail on her right rear foot. She had killed the night before and was half asleep, digesting the food. The two cubs wondered over to her belly meowing for milk. She rolled on her side and they greedily fed, pulling on a full nipple for more milk."

"Suddenly," he waived his hands eastward, "Far to the east, a bright flash fell from the clear blue sky. A few seconds later, a brighter flash swept the land, turning shadows into brightness. The mother saber tooth cat snarled at the brightness and it quickly disappeared into regular daylight.

Moments later, the earth violently shook, throwing the big cat several feet into the air. She narrowly missed landing on her cubs, the shock was so great! The earth was as if a giant hand had taken hold of the ground and shook it. It was like someone spreading a sheet over a bed, snapping it so it would lie in place. The shock wave continued for hundreds, perhaps thousands of miles, churning ancient rocks into dust and leveling sharp edges.

The huge tree under which the big cat had been resting toppled over into the arroyo, its deep roots severed by jagged rocks sliding back and forth.

Why this story? Because some think that this big cat was a remote cousin to Lorraine's big cat. That's one of the reasons we're here. But, let me continue my story on the meteor.

Slowly the dust settled, the sheer deep thundering noise of the earth displacement quieted. The big cat's approximate human fist size brain never related the shock to the next winter's severe cold; she never appreciated the magnificent sunsets for weeks after the shock.

The thunder and shock wave had been caused by an incoming part-iron meteorite traveling at about fifteen kilometers per second at the time of impact with the ground. This partial iron or more accurately bolide meteorite struck the layered rock on what was to be named the Colorado Plateau. The impact pulverized or destroyed about three tenths of a cubic kilometer of plain old Arizona dirt! Later scientists estimated that the original meteorite had a mass of about 63,000 metric tons and that it was larger than twenty-five meters in diameter. However, remember that figure was only an educated guess.

"How fast was that meteorite traveling in miles per hour? Tom, Geoff?"

Tom's face went blank for about ten seconds, "I'd guess maybe somewhere 29,000 to 40,000 miles per hour. If I had a computer, I could tell you more precisely."

"Very good!" Joseph said, impressed. "No, wrong word: outstanding young man!"

"Do you see what we're fighting for, Dean?" With deep emotion, Joe looked at the rest of the family stating, "We're for kids like him getting a chance to attend college, and families like these. We must win, we need to win, Dean!"

Joseph Robinson stopped, took a deep breath, and then continued his discussion on the meteorite.

"Now we know that at impact point zero, the shock pressure was more than 18,000 pounds per square inch and it blew out a crater nearly a mile wide. The pressure, almost equivalent to the center of a small atomic bomb, caused a momentary liquefying of the rock below it."

Joe continued his story after replenishing his coffee, "We've known for some time that such impact craters show slight to strong negative gravity anomalies because of brachiation and the creation of other small cavities. We found such a crater off the east coast of Mexico, in the Gulf of Mexico, up in Hudson Bay and in this crater in Arizona."

Joe continued, "Our scientists think that the object that landed in Arizona, and the other places, were remnants of the big bang. They believe that for some reason, they just were never absorbed by planets, suns, and so on."

"KISS, Joe," Dan said quietly.

Joe quickly became aware that eyes were glazing over; he was clearly losing his audience. "Oh, I'm sorry. Forget all of that stuff," he smiled at the girls. "I had to learn it to be able to talk to our scientists."

"This is important because they believe that some of these Type I carbonaceous chondrites might be the key to fighting the "Green Ghost!"

"We repelled down into the Arizona crater and retrieved about a thousand pounds of the meteorite itself. We tried to melt or smelt some of the meteorite to perform a few experiments, but we didn't have the equipment to do it."

We did notice one thing, though," he paused for a moment. "We discovered that our horses did not like being near that stuff. We tried to get one of the larger horses to carry at least part of that meteorite with us, however, the horse refused to allow that meteorite on its back by bucking and fighting with us."

"We hauled that stuff across the county by pulling it in a small wagon; apparently, if the horses are about five to seven feet away from the meteorite, it doesn't affect them. The rest of our group is sort of guarding it south of here at Camp McCoy. We'll pick them up on our way to Chicago."

"What are you doing here, Joe?" Lor asked, a sinking feeling inside of her.

"Well, we are here for two reasons. We've determined that certain wild animals can sense that force, that 'Green Ghost!' Your friends in Durango and your father told us that you have a special way with animals. I know you have your dog, but do you still have that big cougar with you?"

"Sure, we still have 'Baby'" Tom said.

"Baby?"

"Are you talking about 'Baby?" Ginger asked. Dan took a second or two to realize that "Baby" was the name the kids gave to the big cougar.

"Oh, that's our cat's name."

"I see," Joe said. "Some baby. Lorraine, I understand that you can control those animals. Is that true?"

"No. That's wrong!" Lor stated, flatly. "Yes, I can somewhat communicate with my babies, but I can't control them; they are both very independent and intelligent, too. I've never made them do something that they didn't want to do; actually, I don't think I've ever tried to do so."

"But, yes, Honey," Lor smiled gently at Ginger. "'Baby' and Tom's dog, too, can sense when that force is around."

"Well, Lorraine, as you know, that force attacks anything that uses electricity. What our scientists have in mind is to try to refine some of that metal we recovered from the meteorite. They are hoping that a chemical or nuclear property in that metal may shield an electrical source from the energy."

"You mean Joe, that there's a chance that we may be able to fight that 'Green Ghost'?" Dan exclaimed, hope flaming inside of him.

"We think so, but we needed some way to prove that that force is around, right then, right there! Your animals," Joe nodded at Lor, "will tell us that."

Upon seeing the look on Lor's face and on the children's faces, Joe hastened to add, "Oh don't worry! Your animals wouldn't come to any harm. We just need to have them close to us and stay with us to tell if the force is nearby."

"I see," Lor said slowly, her hand clutching Dan's in a vice like grip. "And what is the second reason you're here?"

"The second reason, Lorraine, is your man, here," he nodded at Dan. "You see, I, and the rest of my group, don't know the Chicago area at all. My only connection with Chicago was passing through O'Hara airport. I know that Dan spent a considerable amount of time there, and if any of his war stories are true, he knows Chicago quite well. I lost my guy who knew Chicago when he was wounded on the east side of New Mexico in a small gunfight we had. I would like Dan to come along with us to the University of Chicago while we try to fight that force."

"What we have in mind is to find or build a forge to melt some of that metal we carried across the country. We've been told there are or at least were forges in and around Chicago. And Chicago is somewhat in the center of the United States. Then we want to try to shape it into a shield of some kind to put over or around a generator or motor that is generating electricity. If, and this is a big if," he paused for a second and then continued with deep passion that was felt throughout the room, "if we can protect that engine or motor from The Green Ghost, our civilization, our country, our world, will have a chance to claw itself back on its feet! And we, the people, will have a new opportunity to fix the terrible mistakes that were made in our history. We might have a chance, we must do whatever is necessary to make a new, a better start!"

After listening to Joseph, Sarah was impressed, she felt she too wanted to somehow fight that Green Ghost. This man had depth!

Lt. Morris interrupted the long silence, "We were lucky in choosing Chicago because that city has many museums which contain meteorites and similar displays; if our experiment works, we'll have a ready source of material. And I understand there is a decent museum of these meteorites in Green Bay, too."

"Plus, Dan's my friend," Joe Robinson quietly commented, glancing quickly over at Sarah, "I owe him more than I could say."

"Joe, we don't need to go into that," Dan murmured.

A long contemplative expression flowed from Sarah to Joe and her brother; it was clear in her own mind that the subject would be vigorously explored at some later time.

CHAPTER TEN

That afternoon, Sarah said, "Dan, I need to get back to my farm to do some milking. You know the cows need to milked twice a day."

"Do you need some help?" Joe asked.

"Well, I've only got a few head of cattle, but do you know how to milk a cow?"

"No. But I'm always willing to learn," Joe smiled. "How far is your place?"

"About two and a half miles from here."

"Do you know how to ride a bike?"

"Sure, it's been a long time, but I'm no circus rider. You must remember that I'm only a lowly Wisconsin farm girl."

"Watch it, Joe," Dan said. "If you're not careful, she'll make you milk all of the cows and clean out her barn to boot."

"A little hard work wouldn't hurt him," Dean Morris interrupted, his face twitching. "All he does is ride around all day."

Joe shook his head, "You see what I had to put up with, it's impossible to get any respectful help anywhere these days."

"Sarah, you can borrow my bike," Dean Morris said. "And I would like a report on exactly how many cows he does, in fact, milk."

They left soon after. Sarah told Dan they would be back before sunset after they traded their milk for some vegetables with one of the neighbors.

At Sarah's farm, she was surprised at the firm gentleness Joe had with her animals. Even more surprised was Joe when he discovered he really enjoyed handling her cows and the young calves. He scratched the head of a scruffy and friendly brown and white three-month old calf, "How you doing, pal?"

Sarah showed him how to milk a cow and direct a warm stream of milk into a waiting cat's mouth. He wasted more milk then he saved, but there were two well-filled cats with round bellies sleeping off a full meal. Laughter filled the barn when a stream of warm milk somehow found its way across the center aisle to narrowly miss a grinning face.

Late that afternoon, when the sun was slowly sinking into the west, vivid reds flooded the sky casting a serene and peaceful glow over the lonely Wisconsin road. Sarah and Joe rode slowly back to the Peterson farm after stopping at a neighbor to exchange milk for vegetables.

"Joe, tell me, how do you know my brother?" she asked, deeply wanting to know the story.

"Well, he was my friend in college out in California and we roomed together. I met this girl and to make a shorter story out of a very quick courtship, we got married. I was terribly in love, Sarah! Now, I realize I was in love with lust; she was the most incredible thing in bed I've had, before or since."

He paused, lost in memories. A pang of jealousy or perhaps envy flamed briefly in Sarah's breast.

"What happened, Joe?"

"Well, one day I came home early from work and found her stark naked in bed with another man."

"Oh no!"

"Oh yes! I went a little crazy and dam near killed them both. Heck, I went more than just a little crazy. Anyway, I got arrested for Assault with a Deadly Weapon and so on. In desperation, Sarah, I called your brother. I have no family and he was the only person I could turn to. He visited me at the county jail, paid for a bail bondsman, and got me released. He later found me a heavy-duty criminal defense attorney and we, in essence, beat the case."

He paused for a second. "I pled guilty to a disturbing the peace charge, got time served and paid a small fine. It turns out that the other so-called victim was also married and the last thing he wanted was to have this affair publicized. The point is if it hadn't been for your brother, there is no doubt that I would be in prison. I owe him more than I could ever repay!"

"Oh."

"You see, my folks were killed in a traffic accident when I was 12 and my uncle and aunt essentially raised me. There was a court ordered settlement from the accident which financially helped my uncle and aunt. They were quite elderly, but they took care of me as well as they could until I graduated from high school. They passed away soon after I graduated. I had a trust fund from my parents' accident and after a couple of different jobs, I started college. That's when I met Dan. I didn't have anyone to turn to when I was arrested except your brother. He's essentially all the family I have. He is the best friend I ever had."

They continued slowly riding. After a moment or two, Sarah murmured, "Dan never told us or me what had happened. He wrote and talked of you often. He only mentioned that you had a little bit of trouble, but that everything had worked out fine."

"I don't know what he told you. It wasn't something I was proud of, but later on, I was surprised."

"Surprised?"

"Yes. Before I was sent to apply for my present job with this security service via the U.S. Army, they did a complete background check on me. I had expected that the incident with my ex-wife would have kept me out of any meaningful employment. After I was hired as a civilian, my immediate supervisor, an old highly decorated Colonel, told me that that was only a small part of their evaluation of me. They said they understood what had happened and they were more interested in my future and leadership skills then that single episode."

"Ex-wife!?"

"Oh sure. I've never seen her since that afternoon and the divorce was handled by my attorney. Good riddance even though it hurt like hell for a while. I finally realized that the only thing we had in common was in bed. That's all behind me now."

His brown eyes held hers for a second, seeming to tug at something deep inside of her.

"I'm sorry, Joe." Sarah managed to hide the feeling of relief that flowed through her.

"What about you, Sarah? I think your mother said that you were married."

"I was, Joe. But it was a marriage in name only. He was killed by your Green Ghost."

"It's not MY Green Ghost; don't say that!" came the angry reply.

Sarah was startled by the anger in Joe's voice. "Well, I'm sorry. I, I didn't mean "your" Green Ghost."

"I've seen what that thing did to our country." Joe said bitterly. "My last orders were to try to find some way to fight, to conquer that life force. Humanity took about 50,000 years to crawl out of a cave, and that force took less than a month to dam near put us back into it. Now, I have a chance, just a chance to fight that force. That's why I came to see your brother, or more precisely, his Lorraine and her animals."

He touched her arm. "I'm sorry. I've seen the terrible effect that force has upon our country. It is astonishing the devastation a lack of electricity has upon our country and our society. Our major cities are half vacant and essentially useless. The cemeteries are full when people can even get their dead to them. We were lucky in a way. The Green Ghost came in spring and our country therefore had time during the spring and summer to plant crops and plan for the winter to help prevent starvation. I simply don't know what other countries are doing, but I bet only the strong will survive," he said bitterly.

She shivered inside of her heavy sheepskin coat even though the temperature wasn't cold. "I knew things were in bad shape before Dan came home. And when he arrived, he told us what you had told him and what he experienced in their long ride home. I understand though he and his family tried to stay out of the big cities, and they didn't want to talk much about what they had seen anyway."

"We used the military bases, both Air Force and Army to help replenish our supplies in our ride from Southern California. The military, what was left of them, kept us apprised of their surrounding conditions. I learned more then I even wanted to know about starvation and desperate people."

With effort, Joe changed the subject: "You said your husband was killed by the Green Ghost, but that you had a bad marriage. Can I ask what happened?" For some reason, the answers were important.

"Sure. It wasn't until after we were married that I found out that he was an alcoholic. And when he was drinking, he got mean! He used to hit me and slap me until the neighbors called the police. They never did anything to stop him. Finally, my Dad stepped in with his shotgun and threatened to blow his privates off if he hit me again."

She paused for a second, unpleasant memories flooding over her. "After that, it wasn't any kind of a marriage. He was incredibly good looking with a great body, but I didn't care anymore. Anyway, one evening after the Green Ghost came, it was clear that it attacked anything using electricity. Several of our neighbors lost their lives driving their cars or farm machinery when the force attacked their engines."

She signed, "He started drinking that afternoon and ran out of booze by about seven in the evening. He said he was going to drive to the local tavern. I told him not to drive because people were getting killed. He ignored me, as usual, got into our car and that was the last time I saw him alive. The next afternoon, one of the neighbors came over and said they found his car and his body. His car had been attacked and burnt by the force and it crashed into a concrete embankment on a bridge, killing him."

She shook herself, "We buried him the next day on a hillside overlooking the river. Only his sister showed up for the burial. We didn't even have any facilities for a regular funeral, nor did we have transportation to get him to a cemetery."

"I'm sorry to hear that," Joe said. "Yours was just one of thousands of similar stories across the country."

His somber brown eyes met hers, "How are you doing now?"

Something changed!

Something flowed between them!

Something touched each other!

Their eyes, their *being*, their *souls,* meshed for a seemingly endless moment while the world around them ceased to exist!

For that unknown instant of time, they were one!

The seemingly endless search through loneliness ceased to exist! Defenses hardened by constant struggles against unwanted solitude lay shattered for that one measureless infinity in time.

They never knew what it was, or even if "it" had a name, but they knew the overwhelming effect it had on them!

With considerable effort, both broke away from the heart to heart, the soul-to-soul search for completeness.

They continued their ride to the Peterson's home in silence, their existence shaken to its core by the encounter of that single exchange.

Their bikes moved together. Almost by itself, Joe's hand, trembling, reached out and was met by Sarah's seeking hand.

Again, deep somber eyes met deep troubled eyes, both searching, both hoping and finding an end to terrible loneliness.

And for that unexpected one moment in time, both found a surprising completeness, a togetherness that shook them to their very depth.

"I, I never expected something like this," Joe stumbled over his words.

"Don't, don't say anything," Sarah said, her voice quiet and trembling.

As they approached the Peterson farm, they released their hands, their eyes promising much more.

Lt. Dean Morris, Dan Peterson and his father were walking from the barn to the house after caring for Sarah's cow. As Sarah and Joseph rode in, Dean took one look at Joseph and murmured to Dan, "Oh! Oh. What has your sister done to my boss?"

"What are you talking about?"

"I've known Joe through some tough times and I've never seen that look on his face before." Dean paused thoughtfully, "We were planning on leaving tomorrow or the day after. I'll give you ten to one that somehow we're going to have to stay for a couple of days more."

"Well, we're glad to have you, but I think you're out of your mind."

"Nope. Just wait," Dean Morris said. "Tell you what; let's bet, ten push-ups to one push-up? Deal?"

"I still think you're out of your mind. Ok, it's a deal."

Later that evening after dinner, Joseph Robinson casually mentioned to his men, the Petersons and Sarah, "You know, we've been traveling hard for the last couple of months, I think I'd like to rest for a few more days before we try to get back down to Camp McCoy and to Chicago."

He could not understand the grunt of laughter from Dean Morris.

And when Dan Peterson got up, extended himself on the floor and did a push-up, his family looked at him with astonishment.

"Right, boss," said Dean Morris. "I sure do agree that we need more rest." He paused and then drawled, "I guess it doesn't make any difference that the way Sarah and you look at each other, it looks like you're both in the Garden of Eden and you both are trying to figure out what to do about the fig leaf problem."

Howls of laughter filled the room. Sarah covered her crimson face with her hands. Her mother, looking at her daughter with wise eyes, said, "Oh my!"

Joseph, at a loss for words, sputtered, "Well. . ." and finally shut up knowing that anything he said would be adding fuel to the fire.

Later that night, Sarah said to her parents, "I've got to get back to my farm. Those cows need to be fed and milked in the morning.

"Take my bike," Dean Morris said.

"Thank you," Sarah said.

"Boss, why don't you escort her home," Dean Morris said, "There's a lot of wild critters out there and she needs some protection."

Joseph Robinson glared at Dean Morris.

"Do you want my cat or Tom's dog to go along with you?" asked Lor, innocently.

"I don't think they need that kind of protection," Dean Morris drawled to more laughter.

Sarah, her face bright red, hugged her mom and dad, "I'll see you guys tomorrow morning."

Later that night, after showing Joe her house and pointing out her guest room for him, she said, "I'm going to make some coffee, Ok? By the way, thanks for the coffee."

"Sounds good to me," he said after pulling out a chair at her kitchen table and sitting down. The two oil lamps cast a soft yellow light over the remarkably clean and organized kitchen.

As he watched her slim figure busy with making the coffee over the wood stove, the thought came *"What the hell am I doing? I never saw this woman before and now, every time I look into her eyes, I can hardly breathe. Those eyes, oh my God, they get deeper and deeper, those eyes!"*

"And she's my best friend's sister. What am I doing?"

As she poured the streaming hot coffee into two well used cups, one with a big green and gold GB on it, the other with a large M on it, she refused to look at him. She placed a small container of cream and sugar on the table in front of him and sat down somewhat next to him. She took a small sip, her hands shaking slightly.

The silence was overwhelming, even the crickets were silent.

Joe opened his mouth to say something when her farm-roughened hand on his lips stopped him. "Don't, don't say anything," she said, quietly.

Her eyes flashed onto his. He could feel himself being drawn into her eyes, her mind, her soul. She whispered, almost to herself, "I don't know what this is, but, but, whatever you are, *whoever* you are, whatever this is, I've, I've got to give it time."

"Sarah, you are my best friend's sister! I never thought something like this would happen. I never even conceived that whatever this is, that this, this, *this,* could happen." As he stumbled over his words, he took a deep breath, "We don't even know each other."

She put her hand on his. "Oh yes we do!" she exclaimed. The thought came unbidden to her: *"I can't tell him that I feel we've been searching for each other forever. I knew, just knew THAT the first second I touched his hand! Oh My God! I, I'm so scared."*

"We've got time, . . . Joseph," she said quietly. She thought to herself, *"My God, I almost said 'My Joseph!'"*

Both picked up their cups of coffee and together took sips of coffee and looked at each other over the cups. Joseph smiled and Sarah smiled back. "What are we smiling about?" asked Joseph.

"I haven't the faintest idea, but I can't stop," said Sarah.

The tension broken, they talked of tomorrow and many tomorrows.

Finally, Sarah said, "Joe, I've got to get up early tomorrow to milk my cows, and I'm tired. This has been a long day, no, wrong definition, a great day, a day that I'll never forget. You know where the guest room is."

She looked at him and then blurted in a whisper, "I'm not going to kiss you, not now, not tonight because if I started, I, I could not stop!"

Grabbing one of the lamps, she fled the kitchen to her bedroom.

After a while, Joe's hand stopped shaking! He washed his coffee cup and took the remaining lamp to the guest bedroom.

Sleep was a long time coming in that old Wisconsin farmhouse. It didn't seem quite so lonely this one night!

The next morning, after Joe helping to milk Sarah's cows and feeding them and one scruffy calf, she scrambled eggs, captured from her complaining hens, and bacon for breakfast.

Joe thought *"This feels like I've just come home."* Her touch on his shoulder as she placed food on the table was shocking, but she refused to look at him. They ate quietly, each afraid to say anything.

Over his coffee, Joseph eyes captured Sarah's and he quietly said, "You know I've got to go to Chicago and try to melt our meteorites to fight the Green Ghost. I didn't have any firm plans after that, but I've got to ask: I never ever thought I would ask this: will you wait" he stuttered, "wait for me?"

Her heart pounding, her eyes brimming, Sarah murmured "Oh my God, I, I think I've waited my whole life. I, I can't kiss you now, I couldn't stop!"

Their hands clasped, promising much more.

"I must get back to Dan's place and get going. It'll take us over two weeks to get to Chicago and I don't know how long to get that stuff melted. Hopefully, our theories will work," Joseph said. "It will probably take at least a month before we will know anything."

"I know," she said, grabbing a thermos bottle of milk for Dan's children.

They left shortly after, their hands again clasped together.

After arrival at Dan Peterson's farm, Joseph called everyone together. "As much as I would like to stay, we must get our show on the road. I really need to find out if our theories work in Chicago. Lorraine," he looked at Lorraine Fairly, "We really need your cougar to tell us when the Green Ghost is around. I never received an answer from you or Dan, but are you willing to either send the big cat alone with us, or better yet, are you willing to come with us? Dan, we'll need you too."

Dan Peterson and Loraine Fairly looked at each other and together nodded, "We talked about this, we'll go with you." She said, "While my big cat will usually do what I ask, I don't think he or Tom's dog either would really obey anyone else."

Dan turned to his father and mother, "Would you take care of the kids while we're gone?" The answer was "Of course!"

Tom Peterson interrupted, "Count me in too! You may need all the help you can get. But, Sir, may I ask a question?"

Dan Peterson looked like he would object to his son, Tom, coming along, but then said, "Son, you've earned a right to participate in whatever was going to happen."

"What's on your mind, Tom?"

"Sir, I've heard of Camp McCoy or Fort McCoy, but what is it, what's there that would help you, us?"

"Well, Tom, Fort McCoy is the only U.S. Army installation in Wisconsin with facilities dealing with providing total war fighting training. During Operations Desert Shield/Storm, over 9000 soldiers from about 70 separate units and their equipment were deployed and redeployed at Fort McCoy. They have or had a huge staff and reservoir of supplies and equipment, some of which we need. They have about 50,000 to 60,000 acres they normally use and, probably, agreements with Monroe and Jacksons Counties, to use more for training.

Joseph hesitated, "I am not sure of how difficult it will be getting through central Chicago to the University of Chicago and protecting ourselves while we do our research. Some reports, admittedly sketchy at best, said that gangs control and run Chicago today. I will not negotiate with them to get what we want and need and therefore, we might need some of the heavy supplies at McCoy."

He paused, "Heavy means big caliber guns, mortars, grenades, and so on. I hope it doesn't come to that, but my experience with gangs means dealing from strength and power. McCoy can supply that and probably several additional men. I frankly would like more people to protect not only my core people, but as importantly, you people and your animals."

Joseph added, "In addition, assuming we are successful, I will need the Army's men and organization at McCoy to, in essence, get our country back. Plus, now, I have a different commitment." He locked eyes with Sarah.

"When did you want to leave?" Dan Peterson asked Joseph.

"As soon as we can," was the answer. "I don't want to spend the winter without some resolution of our search."

After thinking for a moment, Dan said "I would suggest that you leave now, and we'll meet you in McCoy. It's about 150 miles to McCoy and it will take us about two to three days to get there since we'll be towing trailers. We can be ready and leave tomorrow morning and either meet you on the road to McCoy or at McCoy itself."

"OK, Dean, let's get ready to move."

"Mr. Peterson, Mrs. Peterson, I want to thank you from the bottom of my heart for your courtesy in having us. I hope to repay you sometime."

"No problem having you and your men, you'll always have a home here." Mrs. Peterson replied, hugging Joe with tears in her eyes. "You brought my family together!"

Joseph nodded to Sarah, and they walked off a short distance by the lilacs to talk alone. "You come back now, please, My Joseph!" Sarah said through quivering lips, eyes brimming.

"I will be back. . ." he said, nearly saying "*my love*!" Then he uttered: "My love! I don't know how soon, but it will be as soon as possible!" After more goodbyes, they returned to the Peterson group.

"Ready, Dean, men? Let's go!"

As they rode out, Joseph turned and saw taller Sarah with her arm around her shorter mother, arms waving, tears flowing.

He waved.

It was a scene he would never forget.

CHAPTER ELEVEN

Two days later, after hard paddling, Joseph Robinson, Lt. Dean Morris and their two men arrived at Fort McCoy. As they rode up the white stoned Main Gate with the name U.S. Army, Fort McCoy, on it, they were met by two armed guards-military policemen. After being saluted, Lt. Morris asked for directions to Garrison Headquarters.

"Sir, you are very welcome here," replied one of the M. P.s, a two striper. "Your men are housed in one of the empty barracks," he pointed. "It's not hard to find, they have the only covered wagons on the road. Sir, I've also received orders to send you straight to Headquarters," he pointed.

"Thank you, soldier," responded Dean Morris. "Oh, by the way, in about a day or so, several civilian people will come here on bikes. The leader is Dan Peterson. They will be pulling trailers, but what is important is that they will have two different animals with them: one is a dog and the second is a mountain lion or as it is called in California and Colorado, a cougar. Send them to where my men are housed. Any questions?"

"No Sir."

"Would one of you do me a favor? We have a Lt. Coronel and a Major with our group who are here. We're going to Headquarters, would one of you run over there and ask them to meet us at your Coronel's office?"

"I'll do it, Sir." responded the one striper.

"Thank you, I appreciate it."

They rode past a black helicopter up on a pedestal, various tanks, and military trucks, all uniformly covered in desert tan. Off in the distance were the red roofed and white painted barracks. Joe noticed that many burnt vehicles and equipment stopped on the roads after being hit by the Green Ghost. They rode up to the red roofed, white painted two-story Garrison Headquarters.

"I'm really glad to see the American flag still flying," Joe Robinson murmured to Dean Morris.

"Yes, me too. It means that a sense of order still exists."

"It is important for another, perhaps greater, reason. Know what I'm talking about?"

"Knowing you, that 'reason' is probably three steps above me. You must remember that all I am is a lowly Ser…, crap, I'm no longer a Sergeant, but a lofty Lieutenant. In any event, I still don't know what the hell you are talking about half the time."

Joe Robinson grinned at his friend, "Just think, if we're successful in Chicago, our unit and this Fort will be the Vanguard of our country, and ultimately the entire world, fighting our way back to civilization."

Joe muttered, almost to himself, "I've been carrying that vision, that goal, that duty, that onus, since we landed in Orange County, California, and we're getting closer every day. I, for one, will be glad when our quest is over in Chicago, one way or another. Plus, now I have someone to come back to."

"Oh! I see. Dan Peterson's sister really got to you, didn't she?"

"My friend, I see what you and Jane have, and I'm proud to say that I was there in the beginning. You two have something special!"

Joe paused and then said with deep emotion, "Most men don't talk about these issues, but from the first second I touched her hand, I *knew, I knew* she was someone incredibly special." The memory of that single touch resonated in his mind, his being. "The good Lord knows I've been with a bunch of women, but never, ever, someone like her."

Dean Morris grasped his shoulder and smiled at his leader, his friend; he knew what Joe was talking about!

About that time, Lt. Colonel Jane Morris and Major Wisnicki galloped up.

Both swung off their horses, Jane Morris rushed to her husband

Dean and enveloped him, crying "You made it, you're here! Oh my God, I can't believe how I've missed you."

Joe Robinson and Major Jim Wisnicki looked at the two with amusement, it didn't look like Dean was contesting her affections very much, if at all. Jim said to Joe, "Ya think there is a pail of cold water we could throw on them to cool them a little?"

"Dean Morris released his wife, "I heard that." He said sheepishly.

"Did you check in here?" asked Joe Robinson.

"Yes, we did," replied Jane Morris, "Colonel Blossitt is in charge, he seems quite receptive, but there is a Lt. Colonel Harquick who is giving us problems. He is one of those "by the book" and only by the book inflexible asses."

Dean looked at his wife with surprise. She simply doesn't swear.

"Ok, let's go meet Coronel Blossitt," said Joe.

Full bird Coronel James Blossitt turned out to be the traditional crew-cut, trim, just under six-foot, military officer, but his blood-shot eyes showed stress and worry. His eagles flashed from his shoulders. His return salute was casual while his handshake was strong.

"Welcome to Fort McCoy gentlemen. Coronel Morris and Major Wisnicki gave us a very limited brief of who you are and what all of you are doing."

"Thank you, sir," replied Joseph Robinson. He fished out of his backpack the letter he had received from Coronel Devonshirk in California under General Fox's letterhead with a copy to a General Douglas. "This should tell you my authority to be here. I'll fill you in on what we are doing, what we need and where we are going. By the way, I have several citizens due here in the next day or so. They are carrying a German Shepard and a tame cougar which we may need in Chicago. They need housing too."

Lt. Colonel Ducett Harquick, his uniform was parade-ground perfect with every single metal and award awarded to him hanging on it, his narrow fully shaved face glaring at Joseph, was standing to the side of Coronel Blossitt's desk, interrupted snippily, "Well, whoever you are, you don't have the authority to enter on this base and in addition, you certainly don't have the authority to have and/or house citizens on this base. The Coronel," he said referring to Coronel Blossitt, "did your people a great favor, even if it was in violation of the regulations under humanitarian purposes. I want to see what regulation gives you the right to even be here. Oh yes, I want to see your license and permission to carry a wild animal cougar." He struck out his narrow face, "And in addition, we need permission from higher authority to give you anything!"

He turned to Coronel Blossitt, "Did you know, Sir, that they have two little kids with them! There's nothing that permits that."

Joseph Robinson turned slowly and faced the Lt. Coronel.

Dean Morris was alarmed; he had never seen such cold, hard, hatred on his leader/friend's face.

Joseph took a deep breath, "Listen Harddick, I and my men have traveled over two thousand hard and dangerous miles to get here. We, in essence, fought all the way while you sat here on your narrow ass doing nothing but reading regulations! Our country, our world has gone to shit! We have a chance, just a chance to fight the Green Ghost and MY last orders were to fight that G-D dam thing! If you don't like it, take it up with the General, did you hear that, Hardbrick, GENERAL, not me!"

Neither Dean nor Jane Morris had ever heard Joseph use a swear word!

Joseph Robinson continued, his eyes ice and hard, "I intend to follow my last order, period! Now, Hardlick, you can assist me or get the hell out of my way."

His hand casually caressed, then rested on the 9-mm handgun at his waist, and the click and snap of the retainer strap holding his weapon in its holster echoed throughout the office.

"And I will do whatever it takes to obey that order. Do you understand, Limpnick?"

Lt. Colonel Harquick sputtered, "You... you..."

Coronel Blossitt yelled "At Ease!"

Lt. Colonel Harquick stammered, "But, but..." He pointed at Joseph Robinson

Coronel Blossitt ordered in an I Will Be Obeyed Voice: "Just because your uncle is the Commanding General does NOT give you the right to order people around in my office. Clear? Remain At Ease!"

"Let's take a ten-minute break for coffee in my conference room. Colonel, you are excused. You may leave- now!" Colonel Blossitt ordered.

A few minutes later, Colonel Blossitt told Joseph Robinson, over coffee, "I was told privately by my Commanding General that I was probably the only full bird Coronel that could handle and control Harquick. We need people like him in the military, but he can be a royal pain in the lower part of my body. He can't understand the need for flexibility and/or reason." He grinned at Joseph, "Good job in handling him. But you people forget about him. What can I do for you?"

"Oh yes," he looked at Lt. Coronel Jane Morris, "Do you really have two little kids with you? How did that happen?"

"Sir," replied Jane, and she told the story of how they, meaning Joe's entire group, become the adopted parents of CeCe and Douglas. "We stopped at Whiteman Air Force Base and got them shots and other things. Now, they ride with us on the horses and our men treat them as their little brother and sister. Plus, there is no one else to take them." She smiled, "When CeCe gives one of our big burley men a hug, he just melts."

"Are you planning on taking them to Chicago?" asked Colonel Blossitt.

Joseph replied, "Dammed if I know. We are just doing what we have to do to accomplish our mission. I think realistically it brings home to my bunch exactly what we are fighting for!" He grinned at Jane, "But you would have extreme difficulty in separating them from us."

"OK, what can I do for you?"

"Thank you. First, we need to plan our route to the University of Chicago. Second, we have been told that gangs now control the whole city, so we need intelligence on the gangs, how strong are they and so on. Judging by what we experienced getting here, they will be very reluctant to give up passage through their territory and if so, we'll probably have to fight. In other words, we need to plan to do whatever it takes to get to the University. I would like maybe ten or so volunteers with plenty of firepower such as grenades, maybe a bazooka or two, mortars, the usual rifles, and handguns and plenty of ammunition. Finally, your men must arrange their own transportation, either horses and/or bicycles, and food." He smiled, "That's all, Sir."

He asked the Coronel. "Oh, if anyone in your Command knows anything about blast furnaces or melting metals, or the Univ. of Chicago. we would really need that person."

"Well, let's see what we can do for you," said Coronel Blossitt as he walked to the conference room main door.

"Sergeant Major," he yelled.

Sergeant Major Samuel Herring, African American, bald headed, just over six-foot with a very trim 175 pounds, came running, "Here Sir."

"Sergeant Major Sam Herring, meet Joseph Robinson from California."

As they shook hands, Sergeant Major Herring said, "I heard you were coming. It's good to meet you. And I like your kids, too."

"You knew about the children?" asked Colonel Blossitt.

"Of course, Sir. Don't you know that Sergeant Majors know everything?"

"You see what I have to put up with," Coronel Blossitt grinned at Joseph and the Sergeant Major.

Coronel Blossitt then impressed Lt. Dean Morris when he repeated, nearly word for word, Joseph Robinson's requests, and finally said, "What do you think, horses or bicycles?"

"I think bicycles, Sir. When that Green Ghost came, I contacted our local police departments and obtained about a hundred and fifty stolen, recovered, and unclaimed bicycles. They were glad to get rid of them. I'll get my men working on finding someone who knows about blast furnaces. I'll get a briefing set up on the Chicago gangs; we've got a about a half-dozen experts on the subject."

Sergeant Major Herring turned to Joseph Robinson, "Sir, it will take about two days to get everything ready. Will that work for you?"

Coronel Blossitt interrupted, "See what I have, Mr. Robinson? I know I have here the best dam Sergeant Major in the whole Army. If Sam can't help you, no one can."

Without speaking, surprised, Sergeant Major Sam Herring stood a little taller, fighting to suppress a smile.

"Sure" Joseph responded to the Sergeant Major, "and can my men use your chow hall? I understand that they are temporarily housed in one of your vacant barracks. Is that all right? You know about the kids."

"No problem. I've seen the children. They're cute as hell. We're putting two little cribs for them in barracks 12, but I can't figure out who the parents are."

Both Dean and Jane Morris laughed, "I guess our whole bunch is the kid's parents. Their parents were shot and killed in a drug raid, and we sort of adopted them. No one else wanted them. And they have been with us for over a month or two now."

"Oh, I almost forgot, we have at least three civilians, Dan Peterson, his wife Lorraine, and Dan's son Tom, a dog and a cougar meeting us here in the next few days." Joe said, "The cougar is quite tame, but he will feed himself."

"Cougar? I think we call them mountain lions, but what on earth is he for?"

"I'll explain later, Sam; why don't you get started," suggested Coronel Blossitt.

Three days later, after Dan Peterson, surprisingly his sister, Robbie Peterson, his son Tom, and Lorraine Fairly arrived. Lorraine's cougar and German Shepard were introduced, and shaggy heads were rubbed.

"What are you doing here?" Joe asked Robbie Peterson.

"Our parents are doing fine, and the kids are ok. The neighbors will keep an eye on them and Sarah, our sister, is also there. I needed to report in here, and in addition, I believed that if you had to fight your way through the gangs, you could use an experienced hand in dealing with combat injuries and so on. That was my medical training, and you might need me. So, I volunteered!"

"Well, I hope to not use you, but if it is necessary, welcome!"

Dan Peterson handed a thick letter to Joseph Robinson. "This is from my sister. She said to give it to you and for you to read it in private. She had tears in her eyes; what the heck did you do to her?"

"Oh no, it's the other way around, Dan, she is the most incredible woman I've ever met. I haven't told anyone yet, but when we finish in Chicago, I have to return to her."

Dan Peterson grinned at his friend and grasping his shoulder, "I never thought I'd say this, but my sister will be waiting for you! And you impressed the heck out of my parents. You know you'll always be welcome there."

That night, in his private room in one of the barracks, near a lighted gas lantern, with a cup of hot coffee from the mess hall, Joseph Robinson fondled the thick envelope, almost afraid to open it. He brought it to his face and could sense a faint, very pleasant perfume.

He carefully opened the envelope and removed a small photograph. *Oh my God, she is so beautiful!* He gently unfolded the enclosed letter.

He could hear her voice:

"My Dearest Joseph,

I don't know who you are, what you are or even where you are, but, I will wait for you! For some reason, Joseph had difficulty in seeing for a moment or two. After wiping his face, he finally read on:

Maybe it was fate, or something more. I had not planned on being at my parent's house the day you arrived since I was there with milk for the kids the day before, but something pulled me home that incredible day.

I could not tell you that first night we were together, but it was so right. I felt I had been <u>looking for you forever</u>. I was, I am so scared. It seemed to me that I was, we were at a level, a higher empathy, an intimate communication I never even knew existed. But your gentle touch on my hand was magic, it was burning my soul. I could not sleep, knowing you were in my home that first time.

I must tell you I hunger for your arms around me! It hurt

too much to see you leave. Oh, don't worry, I know you have your orders and purpose which must come first, but my Darling, can I call you that (?), My Darling, I will wait for you! I will pray for your success.

Please hurry to <u>your</u> home!
Sarah

Joseph Robinson gently placed the letter down on his desk and attempted to pick up his coffee. His eyes were wet. He looked at his hands, they were shaking so much that if he held the hot coffee cup, it would spill. The fear of this woman, the fear for this woman and the fear with this woman shook him to his intentionally hardened soul.

The fear should not have been surprising because of the loneliness of the daunting, arduous, and dangerous leadership of not only his original duties, but this present search against the Green Ghost. He had to maintain a façade of knowing leadership to accomplish his mission, but now, win and find a method to control or fight the Green Ghost or be unsuccessful in his mission (which he could not allow his subordinates to consider); in either event, he had an unforeseen, an unknowing future, but a future of incredible promise, Oh My God, a future of completeness, of hope and joy.

He laid back on his bed, Sarah's letter on his chest, a rare smile on his face as he fell asleep.

Early the fourth day, shortly after Major Jim Wisnicki reported in from visiting his family near Madison, Dan Peterson reintroduced his sister, Robbie Peterson to him, he saw both quietly talking, both oblivious to the rest of the world. Apparently, Robbie Peterson did not know Jim before Whiteman, but went to college with his sister. The thought ran through Dan Peterson's mind, *"What the hell, am I going to lose both of my sisters because of this Green Ghost? Well, in my mind, both men are really good guys."*

Around noon, Coronel Blossitt sent word there would be a briefing at 1300 hours for all personal involved in Joe's party. The meeting was held in Fort McCoy's main mess hall wherein very strong coffee was provided. Jane Morris exclaimed "I really like the dark green painted tables. Each mess hall is different and I've seen a bunch. And everything is so neat and orderly. Tom, you would like this."

Dan Peterson's boy, Tom, was wide-eyed: "So this was what the military was like. They had breakfast in the mess hall that morning and the food was great; he had his first experience with the famous military food called SOS."

Joe and his entire crew attended. Sergeant Major Samuel Herring took charge.

"We're working on the blast furnaces area. I've got a ton of volunteers, but I've picked fifteen men, some are combat vets, and all are extremely good shooters. I understand you have two boxes of mortars, and we'll replenish the ones you used. I'll have two of the men carrying grenade launchers, both with the M320s with 40 mm fragmentation grenades. All will carry M-16s with some ammo, but if it is all right with you, one of your wagons will carry four boxes of M-16 ammo weighing about 120 pounds. Can your wagons handle that additional weight?

"Sure, no problem," said 2n Lt. Dean Morris.

"OK, next issue: food. I've got tons of MREs (meals ready to eat), but we have various informal agreements with the locals, sometimes we'll get part of a deer or an unneeded cow or something like that. How long will my men be gone?"

"Honestly, we don't know."

Joseph Robinson said, "It depends on if we can get our meteorites melted and then, shaped in some form around an electrical generator. If all goes well, that melted meteorite may provide protection to a electrical generator which could be anything from an actual generator running a home or building to a vehicle and so on.

We are about 260 miles to the University and about 45 miles south to South Chicago. Our horses/trailers would take about fifteen days to the University and then, if necessary, about two more days for South Chicago. Then, maybe a week or two to find a furnace or forge and a week or ten days to get that running and another three or four days to test the results. So, about a month or more to see results and then, whatever time it takes to return here or wherever."

Joseph turned to Dean Morris, "What do you think, Dean?"

"I agree that time estimate sounds about right. As far as food is concerned, we also used MREs, but many times, simply lived off the land, finding vegetables or fruit in the fields, a couple of times, we shot a deer, and so on. I think we can do the same here. Each MRE weights about 20 or so ounces, our only issue is size, but I think we could get a good sized bunch in one of our wagons. We did that out of California, New Mexico, and Whiteman, remember?"

A nerdy looking corporal with glasses, a shallow skinny face, about five-three and weighing about a hundred and twenty pounds, entered the conference room holding a handful of papers, some of which looked like they were torn out of a telephone book.

"What do you have, Stanley?" asked Sergeant Major Samuel Herring fondly of his Corporal Stanley Silverstein.

"Well, Sir, I was thinking about the blast furnaces and did whatever research I could without the Internet. As far as we can determine, most, if not all blast furnaces in Chicago are closed. There seems to be several major blast furnaces South of Chicago around East Chicago, Burns Harbor, Indiana, and a few others about 45 or maybe 50 miles from Chicago."

He turned to Joseph, "Sir, with respect, it seems to me that at least one of these companies may be able to melt down your meteorites without any electricity. They should have the necessary materials, such as coke, etc., to get the furnace up to about 1600 degrees, which is about what you need. The only question is do they have or can they make hand mechanical blowers to force air through the furnace."

"Well done, Corporal." Joseph said, impressed with the relationship between a high-level Sergeant Major and a lower Corporal. "May I call you Stanley?"

"Certainly Sir, Thank you Sir." Stanley beamed.

"Coronel, Dean, Jim, Jane, what do you think of taking all fifteen men, breaking them into four groups of three and having each group assigned a specific company? We would keep three with us as additional manpower, err, excuse me, person power?"

Coronel Blossitt cleared this throat, "I don't like the idea of just three men going into that potential war zone. How about we keep two separate groups, each containing seven men and a sergeant and assign each group two areas. Each group, on bicycles, would be heavily armed suitable to convince any gang leader to at least leave them alone or maybe even help. We can instruct each group on what to look for, and if possible, ask anyone still working there if they can do what you need."

"Dean?" asked Joseph.

Coronel Blossitt looked startled. He was unaccustomed to having a mere second Lieutenant approve his ideas. Joseph, on the other hand, knew "his" second Lieutenant and further knew that whatever answer he received, it would be what Dean thought, not necessarily the Coronel's ideas (which usually were interpreted in the form of orders to subordinate officers). In other words, were the Coronel's ideas workable?

After seven or eight seconds thought, it seemed much longer to the Coronel, Dean responded, "I think the Coronel is right. It would be much more difficult to overcome seven verses a mere three. Let's take that idea a step further. Since we're following the groups with the wagons at a much slower pace, how about we send the groups ahead of us because they will be much faster, and they can do their looking and meet us somewhere along the route. We could stop at your university for a day or two, and then, continue to south of Chicago to meet up with the troops if necessary."

"Jim, Jane?" asked Joseph.

"Yes, it makes sense to us."

Joseph seeing the surprised expression on Coronel Blossitt's face, explained, "Sir, this is the way I run my group. We've traveled over 2000 miles and before the Green Ghost came, we were involved in a number of super-secret assignments, none of which we are at liberty to discuss. This works!"

"Jesus!" Coronel Blossitt exclaimed. "I should have known! Does the name Devonshirk ring a bell?"

Surprised, Joseph Robinson blurted, "Sir, if you know the name, you know who we are."

"Dam! Oh My Lord! I have too many Sergeants, Lieutenants, and various units to keep track of, but I should have remembered you,

Major Jim Wisnicki; you were a Captain the last time I knew of you. We've met before."

He shook his head, "I never ever thought I'd see you again, Jim, because of your high-level secret work. Mr. Robinson, some of your supplies, ammo, weapons, explosives and so on were funneled through us and through Jim. Mr. Robinson and Sergeant, now Lieutenant Morris, well deserved by the way, it is my honor, it is my privilege, to work with you and your group," he said emotionally.

"Whatever you need and if we got it, you can have it! Thank you for what you did and what you are doing!" He reached over and shook Joseph's and Dean's hands.

A bemused and flattered Joseph responded, "Coronal, that is unnecessary." He gestured to his men, "I have a great bunch of people with me. Thank them!"

A very interested Robbie Peterson closely watched Jim Wisnicki's expression. He would have a lot of explaining to her because he told her he was only a general's aide and didn't do much.

"Ok, Jane, what should we do with the kids?"

"Well, we will need all of our group. If so, I don't want to leave the kids here because they'll feel abandoned again, and I don't want to subject them to that. All of us are their family and a day or two might be all right, but not a month or more. So, I think we need to take them with us, Sir."

Both the Coronel and his Sergeant Major were quietly impressed that a Lt. Coronel and a Second Lieutenant called this civilian "Sir!" They noticed that Joseph didn't Order, Command, or Demand anything but everything got done! Of course, they didn't know the results of the considerable assignments in the West Coast, but they did know of the difficulties and hardships in their two-thousand-mile trip to get here!

"Sergeant Major, how soon could your men be ready to move out?" asked Joseph.

"Sir, they will be ready the day after tomorrow with rations for fifteen days. They'll need to be briefed on what to look for, who to talk to, whatever information we can supply them and so on. They will have to make decisions on whether the specific company could perform what you needed. I've got Sergeant Matt Rourque and Sergeant Lou Graham who will lead each group. We will attempt to narrow the search. I've got four men who are knowledgeable about the gangs in and around Chicago and about 1430 hours, they will brief all of us on what could be expected."

He turned to Corporal Silverstein, "Prepare a full briefing on whatever you can find on blast furnaces. It seems that you have become our resident expert on such furnaces. Can you have that ready about 1600 hours?"

"Yes, Sarge."

Corporal Juan Lopez took the lead at 1430 hours: "Chicago has a population of around 2.7 million. First, there are around 57 to 70 known separate gangs in Chicago with about 740 or so factions, depending on who you ask and around 2400 subsets. The total membership may be anywhere from 60,000 to 150,000 with a best guess of 100,000. More than half are in three gangs: The Gangster Disciples, Latin Kings, and Black P Stones. These percentages are very approximate but there is around 40 per cent Black and about 30 per cent Hispanic. There is a white group, but that is mostly white radicals and similar to the old Italian Mafia."

He showed a map of Chicago. One of Joe's men exclaimed, "That looks like a map of Mexico's drug cartels."

Corporal Juan Lopez replied, "Oh, we think the Sinaloa drug cartel is the major source of the narcotics in our area.

The problem is that credible information changed almost on a daily basis as one gang joined with another to fight/kill, etc., a third or fourth gang because of an alleged slur or trespassing on controlled territory, and who, out of necessity, joined with a fifth, and you get the idea. Police, who are overwhelmed with the murders and who have little, if any, political support, think that about 80 percent of the homicides in Chicago are gang related."

"Do you know who or what we could expect when we travel through the city?" asked Lt. Dean Morris.

The 1600 briefing, attended by the fifteen volunteers and all of Joseph's group, was not encouraging.

"A better question is what do we know today? Sir, because of the lack of electricity or any regular form of communication, the answer is: we truly don't know. All we can do is make guesses or assumptions."

A frustrated Dean Morris questioned, "Do you have any names for these?"

"Oh yes," said Corporal Lopez, "Much depends on location or race. We simply don't know if these names are current or not. Our information is at least a year old. We understand that about one-half of the gangsters belong to three separate gangs: Gangster Disciples, Latin Kings is obvious, and Black P Stones make up the that one-half. For the African Americans, probably the largest is the Gangster Disciples which generally breaks down into two warring sets: one called People Nation with about 9 or 10 subsets; and two, Folk Nation which also has about the same number of subsets. They are throughout the entire Chicago area. There may be some relationships with your Bloods and Crips from L.A. area. The Latin Kings run the East side while the Lobos still run the South side. We simply don't know if this information is accurate or not. In addition, like you have in California, Chinatown, Little Saigon and so on, are enclaves developed for mutual protection."

James A. Roosevelt, a very black Corporal, joined in the conversation, "We," he included his three other experts, "we think that because of the total lack of transportation and communication, these gangs will entrench in their areas trying to survive. The bigger warehouses and stores are looted, and wiser chiefs of these gangs are rigidly controlling the proceeds to survive. Remember that simply because one is a gang member does not mean he is stupid or dumb. Many of the higher-level bosses, for lack of a better word, are intelligent and, as of necessity, very shrewd. They must be to run a large organization. Finally, Sirs, remember their main concern now is food and preparation for the winter."

Corporal Roosevelt paused for a moment, "Sirs, if I could make a suggestion, when you meet them, and you <u>will</u> meet them, you should point out that it is to their benefit to assist you. The clear reason is that if you are successful, they may be able to have heat for the cold winter. For those of you from sunny California, Chicago is also known as the windy city with an average January/February low temperature of around 17 degrees. I was told by a friend that just came out of Chicago that the freeways/tollways/expressways are free passage, but if you step off into a street, look out!"

"How about a white flag of truce? Will they honor that?" asked Coronal Blossitt.

"Sir, great question. I simply don't know, but it is certainly worth a try," responded Corporal Roosevelt.

"All right," Coronel Blossitt ordered, "My men are divided into A-Squad and B-Squad. Mr. Robinson, please brief my men on what you need and when you are finished, we'll have at least some information on who and what they need to find and if the company can help us."

Two days later, Joseph stood in the enlisted mess hall containing everyone except two little kids, "OK, as a little review, we have about a thousand pounds of a virgin meteorite broken down into a bunch of pieces. What we need is a forge to melt that down and pour it into thin flat sheets. Keep in mind that blast furnaces have been around since about the 14th century. That was a long time before electricity, so melting our meteorite is doable without electricity. Try to find people that worked at your company and explain what we need. They will need to somehow get their furnace working without power. Make sure that they have adequate supplies of coke, limestone and if possible, oxygen. See if they can manufacture bellows. I think much of the process will be quite labor intensive. The meteorite must be melted into flat sheets that are bendable when cool. Consider getting the local gangs to help you. Their benefit is, assuming our theories work, that they will have heat for the winter. Any questions so far?"

Joseph waited for a moment for the note takers to catch up. "Sergeants, if you make the decision that your company is workable, we need some way to communicate with us and the other groups. If you have an ideal company, there's no sense in everyone looking elsewhere. Keep in mind that at all times, everyone must know about where all others are. Suggestions anyone?"

After some discussion, each sergeant agreed to designate two men to act as "runners," one to contact the other group and one to contact Joseph.

Joseph continued: "Once that meteorite cools, we'll cut it into pieces and wrap it around an electrical generating engine or machine, start the engine, and see if the sheet protects against the Green Ghost."

He paused and then standing on a chair, (surprising everyone except Dean Morris), with deep emotion, his body rigid, his fists clenched, "Ladies and gentlemen, that is why we are here! If we are successful, we not only can, we absolutely will start our county, our civilization, our way of life, Our Right To Live, back to where we belong. We Must, We Must Win, We Have To Win! This may be our last chance as humans to fight that dam Green Ghost! We can do this, people, We Can Do This!"

Joseph Robinson did not understand the sudden standing and cheering in the entire mess hall, hugs by Jane and Dean Morris. "That's why we're here, boss!" whispered Dean. "You are our leader, thank Heaven."

"All right, all right," Joseph quieted the crowd, "For you sixteen men going ahead of us on bikes, you have received your assigned areas. You must ascertain if a company has a good supply of coke, not necessarily coal, a means to light that coke and the means to drain the melted liquid meteorite into flat sheets. They/you will need hand-held blowers to force air, preferably straight oxygen, into the bottom of the forge, and preferably someone who works there and knows how to do that."

He continued, "I also would like several different engines, such as anything with a small open engine such as a self-propelled lawn mower, a larger tractor and later, a helicopter engine. I think all of you have met Lorraine's cougar and a German Shepard which will simply be used to determine if our melted meteorite will, in fact, protect against the Green Ghost. Our scientists think that it will, and if so, the second question is how much meteorite is necessary. My hope, my idea is that if only a little part of the meteorite is necessary, we can organize retrieving more meteorites and get them melted down. If we're successful, we could get the gangs to find more material. Then, with a little bit of luck, we can send a fleet of helicopters to Camp McCoy which will organize notifying the rest of our country."

"Any questions so far?"

"OK, you men on bicycles will be ahead of us. We have two and a half wagons pulled by horses and it will take about ten days for us to reach Chicago itself. We'll have the meteorites, ammunition, and enough food supplies for over a month. Each of you will have your own weapons, ammo, and food for about fifteen or twenty days. While you could hit Chicago in about two days, we'll be about twelve days behind you. Our original plan was to meet at the University of Chicago, but with that change of blast furnaces south of us, we'll only stop there for a day or two and then continue to your areas. Lt. Morris has maps showing our route: all major freeways, and directions you could take to your assignments. Take those with you showing about where everyone will be."

"Ok, our route in relatively simple, 21 East to 94 South to 90 South. Everything is close to that Interstate," explained Dean Morris.

Joseph paused while Squads A and B examined the maps. Sergeant Matt Rouque pointed, "Sir, our companies are close together in the Southside of Chicago and over into Indiana. We'll stay together on the expressway until we reach that area and use the same exit. I kind of doubt that there are any gangs in that area because there are no residents living around that location. You are looking at about fifteen days to get your people down there. By then, we should know something."

"I agree," said Sergeant Lou Graham.

"Good! How soon can you leave?" Joseph asked.

Both Sergeants replied, "How about tomorrow morning, Sir?"

"Dean, Jane, are we ready?"

Dean replied, "All we must do is pack the wagons with food, which we'll do as soon as we break here. Our weapons are ready. The horses are well fed and rested. We too can leave tomorrow morning. I'll get our group ready and loaded."

"For you sergeants, when you meet the gangs and their leaders, be sure to emphasize that they will have problems for the coming winter with lack of heat and food. Do your best to get them to understand that if our quest, our job, our search is successful, they can have and will have a decent future; a future that is in their best interest to help us," advised Joseph Robinson.

"Coronel? Any thoughts/questions?" asked Joseph.

"I think you've covered everything. You've got two of my best Sergeants who are both experienced, respected, and well-liked by their men. My aide, Captain Hunsiker, made sure that they had everything they needed regardless of the requisition forms demanded by a certain superior officer. I'll run interference on that nonsense."

Joseph and Dean understood who he was referring to and they smiled at the Coronel. "Oh yes, one last thing, my mess sergeant will prepare as big a breakfast as he can to feed all of you right before you leave.

"Ok, listen up everyone: we leave tomorrow morning-early. Let's plan on leaving at around 0800 and breakfast at 0630. Jane, can you have the kids ready at that time?"

Upon receiving a nod, Joseph said to all, "Unless someone has a question, we're finished."

CHAPTER TWELVE

The leaving next morning was routine. Both A and B units decided to travel together until they reached the routes to their assignments. Dan Peterson and Lorraine Fairly rode their bikes pulling their heavy-duty trailers for the cougar and dog to ride on. Their personal supplies were stored in Joseph's wagons lightening the bicycle loads. Dean Morris thought it interesting that Dan Peterson carried an A-R 15 on his back and a 9 mm in a shoulder holster while Lorraine Fairly had a nasty looking 357 Colt Python on her waist. After Lorraine introduced Cassie and Douglas to her cougar and dog, the four were nearly inseparable.

Three days later, both Lt. Robbie Peterson and Major Jim Wisnicki were riding their bicycles as outside guards. They were armed with 9mms. She asked, "Jim, would you tell me why the Coronal thanked Joseph Robinson, Lt. Morris, and you? What was that all about?"

"Dam, she saw what she wasn't supposed to see. I can't lie to this woman, this incredible woman!" Thoughts ran through his mind.

"Robbie, listen to me. You're in the military. What I'm going to tell you was, is, and will continue to be classified way beyond simply Top Secret. This stays between you and me; you don't discuss this with Joe Robinson, Lt. Morris or any of their men or even let them know what I'm about to tell you. Can you live with that? If not, that's ok too."

"Geese, what did you guys do, declare war on Canada or Mexico?" Jim was silent.

She looked at him and he remained silent.

She looked again, his deep eyes blinking slowly, seeming to look into her heart.

The thoughts ran through her mind, *"Good Heavens, I want to know about this man, this extraordinary person who is like no one else I've ever met."*

"I agree!"

"Robbie, about four years ago, a number of high-ranking military officers, after deep thinking and secret communication, decided that the U.S. military was unable to fight all of American conflicts or wars. More specifically, the military was ill-suited to fight a single pressing social problem. Narcotics was infecting our society and the military. Also, there was a need for a team that was outside the Uniformed Code of Military Justice, or in other words, some kind of civilian group not answerable to anyone. As you know, our military floats on paper, paper for everything from a B-2 bomber to toilet paper. What developed beyond our expectations was the group you see around you. Each of the enlisted men were facing some heavy criminal charges because of being in the wrong place, doing the wrong, illegal things, and so on. You will never know the true background of our group. Suffice it to say that they could and did sneak into places that you never dreamed of and perform unique, for lack of better words: conduct or requirements."

She had noticed that Joseph's men were unusually not very talkative about where they were from, what they did and where they served. All military people she had known were freely sharing their backgrounds, but not Joseph's group. She also noticed that their eyes were hard, not unfriendly but untrusting. They simply stopped talking when she or others walked in on them.

"How did you get involved in that?"

"Easy. There were cut-outs put in place. Joseph and his men were stationed in California and from there they blew up houses of full of dope, truckloads of narcotics, probably killed a bunch of bad guys, and an interesting number of other assignments. There was a Coronel somewhat in charge in California, but the entire group was led by Joseph Robinson, who you know as a civilian, which legally, made this entire squad a civilian operation. He, with Sergeant Dean Morris, now Lieutenant, had the ultimate decision on three issues: one, did the squad want to perform the assignment; second, could they do so; and third, when and how it was to be done. Their decision was final."

"Where did you come in?"

"Each member of Joseph's squad was sworn to secrecy, on pain of death. And that secrecy was precisely that. Their personal records were kept by me at Kirkland Air Force Base which were always lost or non-existent. In addition, with the blessing of my general, much of their supplies, weapons, ammunition, and so on was funneled from Fort McCoy through me to a location in Southern California. Their pay was directed through me and mailed to Joseph Robinson. The reason I was doing this is that no one pays any attention to a Captain; they always expect at least a Coronel or a General to be doing whatever anyone might have thought was going on."

"I don't understand, Jim," Robbie asked. "It sounds like they were doing a good deed, why so secret?"

"The reason is that while yes, many of the things they accomplished come under the classification of a 'good deed," the problem is how they achieved their assignment. With absolutely no publicity or recognition, the way they did things was usually illegal, violation of some bad guys' constitutional rights and usually sneaky. The ACLU would have slobbered all over themselves to hear about Joseph's crew. Let me give you an example. About half a year ago, around 4:00 a.m., a house on the outskirts of Tucson, Arizona, suddenly blew up and burnt, destroying it completely and spreading it and its contents over a two-block area. There were about a dozen guards surrounding the house and they were found duct taped, blind-folded and handcuffed with Mexican handcuffs about two blocks away. By the way, most had felony warrants in the U.S. I was told that it wasn't necessary to kill them. The house contained somewhere between seven and ten tons of cocaine and a couple of tons of marijuana including some meth. The Coronel out there had to send two 'black' (totally unmarked) helicopters to get Joseph's men out of the area before the local police and/or the local drug cartel spotted them."

Jim smiled, "He, we, just happened to have them ready. . . I understand that the helicopters were on the ground for about seven to eight seconds!"

"Their assignments, note not orders and more like requests, came through or from a General in Washington D.C who shall remain nameless and absolutely unidentified, or most frequently me. I would pass on whatever intelligence and information I had and a request to Joseph and/or Dean Morris to let me know what they needed in the way of supplies, equipment, and explosives. Let me tell you, they went through a lot of supplies and explosives. We would load a UPS semi with whatever they needed, and UPS would deliver the stuff, if possible, to a military base near where they would be working."

Jim paused remembering, "I had three groups of carefully selected men at Kirkland, group one would put the supplies into large wooden and locked boxes needing forklifts to handle, group two, totally separate from group one, would mark the boxes with their contents such as clothing, shoes, and so on. The third totally separate group would load the boxes on the UPS trucks, not knowing where they were going. The UPS driver was given an invoice containing his trip tickets and stuff including an inventory of what was in the sealed boxes, which was sufficient to get him past whatever inspection occurred on the state borders. Of course, the driver had no clue what was in the trailer he was hauling. Sometimes those shipments went out several times a month and others not so frequently."

"My God, how many assignments did they handle?"

"A lot, but I don't know and don't want to know. The idea was not to let the right hand know what the left was doing. And both hands were discouraged to ask questions."

"And that, my dear, is all you're going to know or get from me. By the way, this conversation never took place, and I will deny it if it is ever mentioned."

"Oh, don't worry, it stays with me."

She looked at Jim, "But I do have a question: why did you want to tell me?"

After stuttering for a second or two, Jim admitted, while looking into her eyes, "Robbie, I, I can't tell you how I feel right now, but it was important that you knew something about me."

Her heart pounding, she reached out and touched his hand, that gesture and look promised much more.

About three days later, they camped near the Wisconsin-Illinois border. As usual, that night, Lor sent her "babies" out to protect the group. Around 'O-dark hundred', Lor very quietly woke Joseph, telling him, "My animals are telling me we are getting surrounded by unknown people, just to the southeast of us."

"Any idea how many?"

"No, they are not that sophisticated, but that people are moving to there."

"Thanks."

Very quietly, Joseph shook Dean: "Dean, wake up! We will have visitors."

"Huh? Ok," Dean crawled quietly to Jim Wisnicki, "Jim, wake up, we need a mortar or two. Did you get the flares I told you about?"

"Oh yes. I've been expecting something like this. I have our M301A3s with their Mt. M-84 fuses. Give me a minute and we'll be set up."

Ninety second later, Jim asked Dean or Joe, "What direction and how far?"

Lor whispered, "My babies tell me about 200 to maybe 300 yards down that street and they were very quiet."

Joseph whispered to Jim, "Can you light them up and then, drop a regular mortar about halfway between us and off the right, just to show we don't want to kill them, but just to leave us alone?"

Jim quickly made an adjustment to his mortar tube and said, "Here goes-don't look at the flare, it will blind you. Just look at the ground."

At that, the thump of a mortar hitting the bottom of its tube with the second sound of a mortar reaching its height of approximately 750 feet with an initial flash of exploding mortar and about a one and one-half minute of slowly descending bright light. On the street below of descending light, Joseph, Dean, Jim, and the rest of the group could see approximately 30 or more people, most appeared to be armed, but starting to retreat.

At that moment, the second mortar went off! That resulted in headlong flight by the whole crowd on the street.

Joseph turned to Lor, "You and your animals deserve a great thank-you from us! I am trying to avoid unnecessary bloodshed; you and your animals saved us and again, many thanks! On our way here, we avoided cities and towns as much as possible, but now, here, we have no choice. We'll put on four-person guards, but our best guards are here," as he rubbed the heads of both animals. Dean could have sworn the big cat and the smaller dog both smiled.

About eight days later, Jones and Flannery were, as usual, on front detail. About a mile ahead, they came upon an overpass where Interstate 90 went under a series of railroad tracks. The highway was blocked with wrecked cars and trucks. Sitting in front of the blockage were about a half-dozen men, all heavily armed. Bicycles were parked on the side of the highway. Both Jones and Flannery quickly turned and galloped back to Joseph. They reported what they had seen, Jones explaining, "They picked well, this is about a four mile stretch with no exits."

"Did you see any sniper lookouts?" asked Dean Morris.

"Sir, I wasn't looking, they saw us, and we retreated," admitted Flannery. "I did see that there was a combination of black and brown men."

"That's ok, guys, you did well," said Joseph.

"Question: how did our scouts get through this blockade?" asked Joseph. His question was met with shrugs, obviously, no one knew.

"Ok, Dean, you and I will approach under a white flag. Have eight of your sharpshooters at the military crest of the nearest hill covering us. There must have been some way our scouts got through. I'm a little worried that two of the gangs may have joined forces."

"We have any grey clothing or cloth?" Joseph asked the group.

"I have some E.R. gowns that might work," responded Robbie Peterson. "But, what on earth why?"

"Simple, this concrete is grey and if our guys are looking over a military crest, their weapons and heads might stand out. If so, grey clothing covering each weapon, and grey clothing covering the heads of our shooters should help make them more imperceptible. I like them at our back! You shooters: if Dean or I raise both of our arms, fire!'

"Don't worry boss, we've got you covered!" came the reply.

Second Lt. Dean Morris ordered, "Men, combat spread! From left to right by the numbers. #1 start on the left side and everyone count off by your target. Sound off, now so we don't miss anyone."

"1. I got the Mexican dude with a green shirt."

"2. I got the #2 black dude, with a red shirt."

"3. I got the third dark-skinned whatever he is holding what looks like an AK-47," . . . And so on, eight for seven. . .

"Good job, men, everyone has a target and are they all accounted for?" asked Dean Morris.

"We said we have your back, boss. Don't worry!" growled a grimly voice.

Tom Peterson exclaimed to his father, "Dad, did you see the organization of those men? That's incredible!"

Joseph and Dean, after putting on their bullet-proof vests, mounted up and slowly rode to the blockade. It was piled with wrecked cars and trucks, and it was difficult to see how anyone could pass through. It was protected by seven men of mixed Black and Hispanic races.

Dean Morris whispered, "Joe, don't look down now, but there are blood trails under our horses' feet. That tells us what we're dealing with."

Joseph, carrying a white flag, "Howdy, we're just passing through to the University of Chicago and eventually to South Eastern Chicago/Illinois. I am part of a group trying to fight the Green Ghost. I assume you know what that is."

Dean Morris continued, "Who is your leader or boss? We need to talk to him. Oh, did you see a platoon of Army men through here about a week or so ago?"

Jose Rudolpho Gamaz-Lopez, his prison and gang tattoos decorating his arms and neck snarled, "You don't tell us who you want to see and no, we ain't seen any stinking Army people through here."

"We were told that the freeways or tollways were free passage while we stayed on the highway. Was that not true?"

"We control this area and any honkeys traveling through our safe area has to pay for that privilege," growled Allen Decker Washington, a tall, skinny Black fondling a 12-gage pump shotgun. "How much food do you have?"

"We came under a flag of truce; do you honor that?" asked Joseph.

There came a simultaneous sound of weapons being cocked by the remaining men under the overpass. Someone yelled, "That's your flag of truce! Put your hands up and get off the horses!"

Joseph looked at Dean, "Think we should raise our hands?"

"On a count of two. One, Two!" Joseph and Dean together raised their hands in the air.

The crashing sound of eight M-16s firing simultaneously echoed off the surrounding buildings while eight separate .223 bullets traveling approximately 3000 feet a second found their targets, also known as gangster heads.

A second volley, while unnecessary, also found their intended targets while they were falling. Empty .223 cartridges after being ejected from the right side of the M-16s, clanged together on the concrete road.

A third volley ricocheted off and around the wrecked cars and trucks to insure there were no other suspects around. Sergeant Leroy Johnson yelled "Cease Fire!"

Joseph turned to Dean and smiled, "Don't you just love it when a plan works?"

Dean returned the smile and waived to his men, "Come up and let's grab their weapons; if we have them, someone else wouldn't be able to use them."

As his eight men ran up, "Great shooting, guys!" exclaimed Dean. "Search them and the area for weapons.

"Well, we were almost ready to shoot anyway, two of that bunch had raised their rifles as if to fire at you. We couldn't have that," responded Sergeant Leroy Johnson.

"OK, now what? We can't get through that barricade, I guess we'll have to go around on surface streets. Let's get back to the rest of our people and figure out some side streets."

"Dad, did you see that? Those guys know precisely what they're doing. Incredible!" Tom Peterson exclaimed to Dan Peterson.

"Now you see what control, training, practice, and leadership accomplishes," replied Dan Peterson.

After telling the rest of his group what happened at the barricade, and after looking at street maps, Joseph asked Loraine Fairly, "Can your animals tell us if someone is hiding in buildings along this route?"

"I think so, Joe, much depends on which way the wind is blowing; in our face, easy, behind us, probably not."

"I'd really like to know how the Army got around the barricade," said Joseph. All he received was shrugs.

"Anyone remember what moon is out tonight?" asked Dean Morris.

"It's been quite dark the last couple of nights, I think we're due for a full moon," responded Jamie Robinson.

"OK, unless someone has a better idea, with a full moon, we'll bypass this area and sneak past whoever is still alive. We'll go back to the nearest exit and start there. I think if we quietly go about three blocks away from this freeway, and then turn south on a handy street, we might be safe", said Joseph.

He turned to Dan Peterson and Lorraine Fairly, "Lorraine, how do you feel about becoming our leading scout with your pets? My plan is to have the scouts about a block or two ahead of us. Do you think they'll be able to sense people ahead of us?"

Lorraine looked at Dan and then Joseph, "I think so, providing the wind is against us. Baby will warn me easily by quietly growling, but I must make sure my dog doesn't bark. I don't want to warn anyone ahead of us."

"I've got an idea," Sergeant Leroy Johnson suggested, "The horses make considerable noise on concrete; see if we can find a blacktop street, that should be quieter."

"Excellent point," exclaimed Dean, "We may have to travel further to find one, but it's worth it for less noise."

"Great! Dean, I would like four fully armed scouts, in a combat spread, supporting them, but only a very little behind them. Everyone will be on bikes because they are quieter. Any questions or suggestions anyone?" Joseph didn't realize that the reason his men would follow him anywhere was because he asked for suggestions, not simply gave orders.

Later that night, as a huge orange moon peaked over the horizon and Lake Michigan, they moved out. In the distance, a few high-rise buildings continued smoking, several had collapsed. Six blocks later, they found a blacktopped street and turned south. Hours, quiet hours later, as a benevolent full moon smiled down on them, the 90's Turnpike had turned in their direction. As they made camp under the 90's overpass, Joseph Robinson walked to his group, "I must tell you that I've very proud of each of you. This was very difficult, and I was sure that there would be people awake, but we made it. Great work everyone!"

The next days to the University of Chicago were uneventful. Joseph ordered everyone not in the wagons to openly carry weapons including any M-16s, and on trailers, a bazooka, and the mortar tube. In addition, any hand weapons were to be carried on the outside of clothing.

Major Jim Wisnicki murmured to Robbie Peterson "I like the thinking. It looks like we're spoiling for a gun fight which will make anybody think twice before attempting to stop or interfere with us."

They spent two days at the University of Chicago. While the horses feasted on the green grasses of the college lawns, Joseph, Dean and Jim met with most professors and many of the approximately 5700 students who remained to attempt continuation of classes. Joseph explained the Green Ghost and what they were attempting to do. The two professors who traveled with Joseph from California met with their counterparts; soon hope radiated throughout the extensive campus. Two professors who specialized in Metallurgy and knew something of blast furnaces joined them to their trip south.

CHAPTER THIRTEEN

As they exited the University, they were met by two Army Corporals, part of the advance party. Corporal Billings told Joseph, attempting to not appear excited, "Sir, we think we've found what you are looking for. There is a large company just off Highways 90-94. They also have a small blast furnace and the men who run it are working on getting it ready for you. They said they use it for research and test purposes. They seem to know what they're doing. Sir, I think it is what you are looking for!"

Corporal Tresert chimed in "Sir, it is about 50-60 miles, a two-day ride for you. We made it in a half day. We'll lead you to it."

"Great job, guys. Thank you. We're on our way now."

"Maybe, just maybe!" Joseph whispered to his friends, Dan Peterson, and Dean Morris. His excitement was contagious.

Two and a half days later.

Corporals Billings and Tresert led them on an exit off I/S 94 and down a well-worn street. Off to the left side they could see a large jumble of now silent conveyors, belts, pipes and scaffolding leading from about ten railroad cars to two huge domes with tops of a maze of large and small pipes, overhead cranes, and four Manitowoc crawler cranes near heavily discolored smokestacks. The bottoms of the domes consisted of more cranes and troughs running in different directions.

At a much smaller version of the domes, Joseph and his crew were met by Sergeants Matt Rorque and Lou Graham with a group of six men.

"All right, Matt, Lou, what do we have?"

Matt waived at one of the men to come, "Sir, this is Steven Kakowoski, the foreman of this business. Would you explain what you/we need; I think he can help us."

Joseph shook hands with Steven Kakowoski, a six-foot, two-inch, 230-pound man, all muscle. His arms looked like a Chicago Bear's linebacker's legs with hands that were larger than most people's feet. "It's good to meet you, Mr. Kakowoski, am I saying that correctly?"

A voice rumbled from deep within Steven Kakowoski's chest, "That's ok, Sir, most everyone calls me KaKo. I understand that you need this furnace running again. Would you tell me specifically what you need and why?"

"I'm glad to." Joseph explained who they were, what they had and why they needed it done. He finished "I must tell you that if we are successful, you will be busy for a long time. This is so important that this material, and others like it, may be the only way we, as a county, as a planet, can fight that Green Ghost."

"I think we can help you. It takes between four to five days to get our puppy here to over 1600 degrees." He gestured to the small dome. "We used this for research purposes to experiment with different mixtures of material. You have about a ton of material, and she can easily handle that. We'll have to use simple manual labor to feed her and manually work out a blower to help increase the temperature. Our flow troughs need to be adjusted to let the very hot liquid cool. Everything has to be done by hand. But, we can do it!"

A spontaneous cheer arose from Joseph's men. After traveling over 2000 miles, mostly on horseback and through some hazardous situations, a possible and positive end was in sight.

Joseph Robinson again shook KaKo's hand, nearly hugging him. Both Jane and Dean Morris however, grabbed Joseph and hugged him, Jane crying, "You did it! Against all odds, you got us here. Whatever happens, you are our hero!"

Embarrassed, Joseph shook them off, "You and everyone here helped too. It's not over."

He turned to KaKo, "Ok, tell us what you need us to do."

Amused, KaKo pointed across the street, "There is a nice grassy park with a small lake. You can keep your horses there, but I suggest you keep heavy guards on them."

He turned and spotted Lorraine Fairly's big cat. "What the hell are you doing with that?"

Laughing, Lorraine said, "We'll use him after you get that stuff melted and put over an electrical source. We need him to sense if the Green Ghost is nearby. Don't worry, he's tame and will tell me if someone is here that shouldn't be. I need to introduce you and your men to him. He will leave you alone. The horses are used to him."

Lorraine rubbed KaKo's hands and called the big cat to her; she rubbed the face of the big cat and then, the cat casually strolled to KaKo with little girl Cassie hanging on him.

"Scratch him behind his ears," she said. "He likes that."

KaKo, afraid of no man, very cautiously reached out and rubbed the big cat's head. "I've never seen an animal like this so close and so tame."

He looked at little Cassie and shook his head, "Hello, little girl. Now, now, I've seen everything!"

After Lorraine introduced KaKo's men to the big cat, they unhooked the wagon containing the meteorite pieces. "Just leave it here and we'll unload the material in a few days when we get our temperature up. You might as well make yourselves at home over in the park," KaKo said, "My men know what they're doing,

and we'll also use your people for the manual labor."

He looked at Joseph and pointed at about twenty or thirty large green cylinders about two hundred yards away, "Sir, could you get your men to bring those O2 bottles over here? We'll need the oxygen to increase the heat."

"Consider it done, show us where you want them," Joseph responded.

They solved the problem by finding several large rubber-tired carts and simply stacked the 150-pound cylinders on them and pushing and pulling the carts to where KaKo needed them. KaKO and his men them hooked several bottles to a confusing array of pipes and valves. "There's a lot of oxygen in each and it will be used to push the heat once we get a good level of coke and stuff burning. She's pretty loaded right now because we were just getting started to do some research when the

Green Ghost shut us down. We'll haul a bunch of coke and limestone here to continue enforce the burn once it gets started."

Joseph Robinson met with Sergeants Matt Rorque and Lou Graham, "Men, I have an idea. Would you assign some of your men to ride out and meet with the local gang leaders? What I would like is for the gang leaders to search out the museums and similar place that have meteorites and haul those meteorites here. Your men would explain what we're doing and why. If our process works, we will have a supply for the furnace to make and we're on the way. The leaders and their followers also may have heat for the winter, too. What do you think?"

Sergeant Matt Rorque said, "Good thinking, Sir. I would like to send two teams of three. Could we use the horses to haul the rocks if they find a good supply?"

"Of course. Keep me posted. I would suggest that our guys report back here in three or four days to see how successful they've been."

"Consider it done," exclaimed both Sergeants.

"KaKo, how long will it take for the furnace to melt our meteorite?" asked Dean Morris.

"Well," KaKo said, "It will take about six to eight hours to melt your material. That's the small stuff, the small pieces. It will take about twice as long to melt the big piece because we have no way to break it into smaller pieces."

"Excuse me for a minute," KaKo called his men to him, "I almost forgot, the material from the melted meteorite must be in thin sheets. We have no rollers to flatten the material, so we need to design our receiving troughs to drain a sixteen of an inch to no more than an eighth inch thickness. Joseph Robinson wants to fold the sheets. Can we do that?"

His men huddled for a minute and then one responded, "I think so, KaKo, but we'll need that material a little hotter so it will run more freely. We've got enough help here to change the troughs.

Four days later, after three days of heavy labor modifying three flow troughs with three overflow channels including overhead-sprinklers and listening to KaKo explain what and why they were doing, which almost all was incomprehensible to Joseph's men, he was satisfied.

Finally, KaKo said, "Ok, we need a decent supply of water. Guys, in the next block is a 500-gallon water wagon. We'll need that to supply the sprinkler water cooling systems."

"All right, let's use the horses. Hook them up to the wagon and pull it over the pond. Dean, send a couple of guys to find pails and we'll fill it. Count me in that group. KaKo, can your guys hook it up?" Joseph asked.

"Not a problem."

Early the next morning, KaKo woke Joseph. "Our temperature is a little above 1600 degrees, maybe close to 1700. We just dumped in more coke and limestone and we're ready for your stuff."

Joseph woke everyone and they hurried to the wagon containing the meteorite pieces. Pails of pieces were man-handled to the top of KaKo's "baby" and dumped in on an extended 45 degree overhead trough. The pieces were fed into the "baby" while the largest piece weighing over 500 pounds was carried by five men and dumped in.

Lorraine Fairly yelled to Dean Morris, "Dean, help me hold my animals. They know the Green Ghost is here! Look!"

She pointed about a hundred yards above KaKo's baby; they could see shades of green flowing violently back and forth. The big cat snarled as the dog furiously growled at the alien substance.

Doctor Isabel Samualson, one of the scientists who had traveled with Joseph since California, ran to Joseph, and grasped his arm, "Look, Look! The Green Ghost has penetrated everything we had including engines, but now, look, look," he excitedly shook Joseph's arm. "It hasn't pierced or breached the blast furnace. Our theory is valid, the substance in the meteorite is keeping it away. Oh My God, thank you!"

Jane Morris grabbed her husband, Dean Morris, and exclaimed with tears running down her face, "It works, my Darling, O.M.G. it works." Joseph's men gathered around them, mutually back-slapping and hugging.

Joseph Robinson stood a little apart from the celebration.

After things quieted down, he spoke with tears in his eyes, "Congratulations people, we fought the battle to get here against overwhelming odds and obstacles. I can't tell you how proud I am of each of you."

He paused, "But our job isn't done. Now, we need to find out how to use our material. KiKo tells me that the metal will cool enough tomorrow for us to cut it into small pieces. He has several heavy sledgehammers and chisels. He has a small lawn mower engine which we'll start tomorrow. We'll figure out how much substance we need to use to determine how far we can keep the Green Ghost away from it. Assuming that works, next, we'll turn on a truck's engine with the same test. With some luck, maybe our next transportation will be by truck."

"And," smiling with a rare huge grin, "If all that works, we'll head for whatever airport has helicopters, find some pilots, and we'll return to McCoy and spread the word."

KiKo and his men joined the celebration. "We were here when the Green Ghost shut down our systems here. It scared the hell out of us because we couldn't fight it and we lost three men doing that. Now, there's hope. And if your men come back with more meteorites, we'll have a job again. Absolutely wonderful!"

He turned to Joseph, "You deserve a metal for what you did!"

"Nonsense!" Joseph stated flatly, "The credit goes to my men, they fought all the way and we wouldn't be here if it wasn't for each and every one of them, including the late arrival out of New Mexico."

KiKo said, "Well, you heard what I said. Anyway, as you know, we set up a system of blowers which will have to be done by hand. My men are working the blowers now, but could you men relieve them? That is hard work. In an hour or two, we'll turn on the oxygen to help melt the stuff."

"Done. OK, guys, please line up and relieve KiKo's men. They'll show you want needs to be done. Jane, Robbie, Lorraine, would you make a lunch for the troops?" asked Joseph.

Major Jim Wisnicki found it interesting, while both he and Joseph too, lined up to help, he observed that Joseph found it unnecessary to order anyone to do anything. A simple request was all that was needed. After some thought, Jim realized that Joseph's demeanor and leadership skills were incredible; that is why in California and other places, his group, performing mostly illegal and specifically prohibited assignments were so successful. Jim quietly blessed the Coronel in California who had spotted Joseph and hired him. No one else could have done everything Joseph accomplished.

As busy as they were, they kept a critical eye upwards. Tentacles, vicious green tentacles darted back and forth over their heads, but the Green Ghost remained between a hundred and two hundred yards above the furnace. Lorraine Fairly calmed her big cat and dog; however, both were quietly very alert, watching and softly growling if a tentacle wondered their way.

Close to sunset KiKo approached Joseph, "We're ready to pour. Please keep your people about fifty yards or so away."

KiKo attempted to explain technically what they were doing, but most of the entire group had no idea what he was talking about. What was understood was that a plug would be pulled from the bottom of the furnace which would release melted meteorite material at the temperature of around 1700 or more degrees. He commented to Joseph's group, "Very dangerous indeed. That's way we spent so much time getting the flow troughs just right, because once it starts, there's no stopping the movement until it rests in the troughs."

After watching KiKo's men make incomprehensible moves and adjustments with much shouting and some waving of arms, Robbie Peterson quietly mentioned to Jane Morris, "If I didn't know be better, I'd swear that they are chanting and talking to that big furnace."

Jane nodded, "I've been in some strange places and done some weird things, but I've never seen anything like this. KiKo's guys really know what they're doing."

Suddenly, everyone around the furnace was motionless, KiKo was counting down on his fingers, five, four, three, two, one. One of the men swung a heavy sledgehammer and bright silver light flashed out from the bottom. Immediately, silver flashing material flowed like liquid mercury out of the furnace down chutes into prepared troughs.

Doctor Isabel Samualson shook Joseph's arm, "Look at the Green Ghost, it is much more active."

Joseph looked, the Green Ghost was even more agitated, flowing more rapidly back and forth over the furnace. Joseph pointed, "Look, yes, that force is now higher than it was originally and even more animated. Congratulations, Dr. Samualson, you were right all along. Very good job!"

KiKo walked up to Joseph, "That turned out ok, we have another load in my baby. This is just the small stuff we dumped in first, but the huge rock will take some time. We'll release her tomorrow some time. This pour should cool by tomorrow morning, and we can remove it and then work on cutting it into your various sizes."

He happily lit a cigar; it smelled like the residue of a north end of a south-bound skunk.

The crowd around him quickly dispersed.

"What? You people have no appreciation of a great cigar."

"Wrong! We like the smell of a good cigar, that, that thing your smoking doesn't even qualify as a reject from a horse barn," responded Jane Morris. "What on earth do you have in it?"

"Well, I quit smoking about five years ago, and I've carried this puppy around with me since then. It was intended to remind me not to smoke anymore. But, today, you people, deserve a celebration and this is all I could do."

"So," he waved the smelly old cigar around; people backed further away!

"This is my way of thanking all of you."

Jane Morris looked at her two female companions, "Girls, if he promises to not blow smoke at us, let's hug him."

Giggling, Jane Morris, Robbi Peterson and Lorraine Fairly ran to KiKo and hugged him. For once, KiKo, a leader of rough and tough men in a hard industry, was speechless. Later, Robbie Peterson said laughing, "You must know, girls, that that hug was the strangest and smelliest hug I was ever involved in."

Later that evening, KiKo quietly approached Dean Morris. "I have a question about Joseph Robinson. I noticed that he doesn't yell or argue, but the men just naturally do whatever he asks with no complaints. I don't understand how he does that. What did he do before you and your men were with him?"

"Do you ever read anything by a famous writer named W.E.B. Griffin?"

"Oh yes, I've read everything he has written. I really like his novels, that's whenever I have time. Why""

"In a few of his novels, Griffin talks about a person who is a natural leader whose men would follow into hell. Joe is one of those men whose men, me included, would follow him into hell! He led us through over 2000 miles of tough and sometimes combat conditions, our version of hell, and here we are, with a chance, a good chance to beat that dam Green Ghost. No other man could have done that! He is special, but don't tell him I said so."

It never dawned on KiKo that Dean never answered his question about Joseph's background.

Late that night, actually early morning, Lt. Coronel Jane Morris saw Joseph Robinson on a large rock, alone, away from the wagons, nursing a hot cup of coffee. She walked over to Joseph, "Well, my friend, a penny for your thoughts?"

"Oh, hi Jane," Joseph took a contemplative sip of his coffee. "I couldn't sleep. Just a few thoughts on my mind."

Wise eyes considered this incredible leader, this man who had not only led a different type of men though strange, needed and probably illegal hazards and perils and who drove this entire rag-tag bunch across over 2000 miles of hazardous county, but now, was strangely quiet.

She quietly analyzed what was not bothering her friend. "Well, it's not tomorrow, either this melted meteorite works or in does not. You have done everything humanly possible to bring us here and there is nothing left to do. So, that's not it, right?"

Another sip of coffee, "Jane, can I tell you something that stays with us?"

Surprised, "Of course."

"Dean knows a little. When we were at Dan Peterson's place, I met Dan's sister, Sarah. I spent a night with her at her farm. No, nothing happened, but we, we connected. We never even kissed! But, now, Jane, I can't get her out of my mind. I know it sounds unmanly, but, but I.

. . . I see her face in the clouds. I can still feel the touch of her hand. I wish she was here with me tomorrow."

"Do you know, does she feel the same about you?"

"Here." He retrieved Jane's letter from his chest pocket. "No one else has seen this."

She gently unfolded the letter and quietly walked close to the fire to read it. She read and then refolded it in its envelope.

She silently returned to Joseph and sat next to him.

"Oh, My God! Joe, my friend, I'm humbled beyond words to express thanks for your trust in me."

She took a deep breath, "I want to make two points: first, I've never read a deeper love letter in my life! There is no question that she feels the same about you. Second, I don't know how or what Dean and I will be doing, but you must promise me I will meet this woman! If she so loves the man that I deeply respect, she must be an incredible person."

She paused for a second or two, "Joe, can I share something with you? The first time I met Dean on that lonely airport run- way in Orange County, California, the first time I shook his hand, I knew; something moved deeply in me, but I had a job to do and had to override that feeling." She smiled, "And you know what ultimately happened."

"Yes, especially after the first night at that pond while we were on the road."

Shocked to her core, she stuttered, "What, what do you mean?"

He grinned, "I knew you two were close, but the next morning, after you and Dean snuck back into camp close to sunrise, you and my friend, Dean, had to fight to keep your hands away from each other. Plus, there was the evidence of a huge hickey on Dean's neck. Even though we had two rocket scientists with us, it certainly didn't take one to figure out what had happened."

"I, I didn't think we were that obvious," she said, embarrassed almost beyond words.

"It was interesting that you forgot that my men were highly observant. Many times, in some of the things we accomplished, their very lives depended on being alert. My bunch had known about you two, maybe even before that night; it was clear that they all approved of your, shall we say union."

They smiled at each other, "But that turned out very positively. Thank you, Jane, for everything and for talking to me. As far as tomorrow is concerned, I think we will be successful. Then, if all goes well, we'll plan for KiKo and his men to continue melting meteorites for us. I want to find a helicopter or two, get them working and take us to back to McCoy. Then, I'm done. We'll get the Coronel to start the process of spreading the word. That's what the rest of the military is for; let them handle the getting our country back on its feet."

"Then you're on your way to Sarah?"

"Oh yes, I'm very tired of the constant stress and worry about my guys and our entire team and will be truly happy when this duty, this assignment is completed. It would be something really different, raising cows or whatever she does. But I will be with her!"

Joseph mused to himself, "Now, I've got to find a helicopter pilot or two."

"Well, that's not so hard," Jane Morris smiled at her leader.

"Oh?"

"How could you know? Both Jim and I are rated pilots for most of the helicopters we'll find around here. I spend a lot of free time studying and flying various types of anything that could fly, including the big C-130s and helicopters. My Dad, bless his heart, pushed me to do that, and now, I'm truly grateful for his foresight. I believe that Jim can fly as many as me, our general at Kirkland supported us to broaden ourselves."

The next morning dawned bright and clear.

Most, if not all of Joseph's crew had little or no sleep. The stress, the anticipation, the worry about if their huge quest would actually succeed, was overwhelming. The only exceptions were the two little ones, Cassie and Douglas Crisper, who slept comfortably in "their" wagon.

KiKo and his men dragged a sheet of thin meteorite measuring about four feet by ten feet out of its trough and laid it on concrete. They had several heavy sledgehammers and large chisels.

He addressed Joseph, "OK sir, how do you want this done?"

Standing in front of his group, the tension was overwhelming. "OK, where is the lawn mower and will it run?"

"About a forty yards over in the parking lot, and yes, it should run."

"Ok, KiKo, cut off a square of about five inches by five inches."

While the Green Ghost hovered overhead, a square was easily cut.

Joseph picked up the square and walked to the lawn mower. He placed it on top of the motor. He bent to pull the rope starting the engine.

"STOP!" The command rang out by 2nd Lt. Dean Morris. He shouted "WAIT! How are you going to get away from that if the Ghost attacks?"

"I'm not," Joseph said calmly. "I can't ask anyone else to do this. Lorraine's big cat is telling us that the Ghost is here, but our scientists think this square might keep the Ghost away. I want you people to stay away. Is that clear?"

"NO, Absolutely NOT! If the Green Ghost attacks that mower, you will be severely burnt." Dean Morris thought for a second, "How about this, we'll put a harness on you and if the force comes down, we can pull you out of there?"

He turned to his men, "Hurry, get some ropes, we'll tie him up and if necessary, we can yank him out of there. My God, that's one of the bravest things I've even seen," mumbled Dean Morris.

Soon, a grumbling, but attached to a harness, Joseph Robinson bent and pulled the starting rope. No response.

Again, he pulled the rope and the engine started.

"Look!"

Someone shouted, the Green Ghost swirled and dived toward the lawn mower.

"Pull him out of there," yelled Dean Morris.

A shaken Joseph Robinson was rudely jerked to the ground, landing on his rear, and quickly dragged away from the lawn mower.

The Green Ghost struck down! It violently penetrated the engine, and having no protection against the force, the engine simply ground to a sputtering stop.

Lorraine Fairly yelled for help in holding the big cat and dog. They were fiercely growling and barking at the force as it disappeared back into the clouds.

A stunned and silent group of people stared in shocked disbelief at the destroyed lawn mower.

Everything they had traveled over 2000 hard and difficult miles for-everything they had fought for-everything they had worked for-everything they had sacrificed for-everything they had hoped for-everything they believed in-was in that destroyed lawn mower!

CHAPTER FIFTEEN

Joseph Robinson disentangled himself from the harness after being dragged across the concrete parking lot. Struggling to overcome the disappointment, the blow, the distress, the disbelief felt by him and his people, and the pain in his buttocks from being dragged on concrete, he fought to stand.

He croaked out a response, "All right! Everyone, there must be an explanation. I will not give up. We will not give up! We have come too far to give up! We must find out why this experiment didn't work this time! I will not let you quit. We Will Do This!" he croaked/shouting, waving his arms!

His group, his men and women, almost collectively shook themselves, wiped away tears, hugged each other and turned to Joseph Robinson.

"OK, let's take an hour or two to try to figure out what happened. I need to recover after you guys dragged my butt across that nice soft concrete," he managed a crocked smile. "I think we all need some coffee."

The hour or two turned into several hours. A brief talk with Joseph's scientists revealed no useful information. Shakes of the heads and shrugs of shoulders were spread throughout the group as no one had any suggestions. They too believed in their quest- their search!

Jane and Dean Morris, Jim Wisnicki, Jane Peterson, Dan, and Tom Peterson, Lorraine Fairly, and several of Joseph's men gathered and sat around Joseph as he cradled a third cup of hot coffee.

Also joining them was Cassie and Douglass. Cassie, with tears in her little eyes, clutched onto Jane Morris, asking, "What's wrong, Mom?"

Douglass joined her crying, not understanding what was wrong. Jane hugged the little ones, murmuring, "It's ok, guys, everything will be all right, don't cry now, OK?" Several of Joseph's men also patted the little one's backs whispering that "Everything will be ok, please don't cry."

Joseph demanded, "What did we do wrong, people?"

There was no response to the question. "Well, if we didn't do anything wrong, what did we do right? Correct me if I'm wrong: we hauled that dam meteorite across the country fighting all the way, we know there was a physical reaction to the Green Ghost when we saw a broken part warmed at the crater, we melted it down, that melting should not have affected it if it was around since the Big Bang, it was turned into a sheet by KiKo."

"Wait a second. Just wait a second!"

Joseph called, "KiKo, come here please." There were startled looks on faces.

"What do you need, Sir," KiKo trotted up and sat down, his disappointment on his face.

"KiKo, were you present when the Green Ghost shut down your factory here?"

"Uh, sure, so were my men. That was nasty, I'll tell you. We didn't know what the hell that was, but it didn't take us long to figure out how dangerous it was. It killed three of my men, why?"

"Tell me how the entire factory was shut down."

"It wasn't 'shut down' as you call it. When we lost our electricity, everything simply stopped running. Most of the heavy-duty generators and motors were burnt though, but that was it, again, why?"

"OK, were all of your units running when they were attacked by the Green Ghost?"

Puzzled looks were exchanged by Joseph's group.

"Oh, hell yes, begging your pardon, ladies. We kept everything running, once the furnaces started, we didn't want to stop them because it took several days to get them working again. If they weren't working, we wouldn't have a job. Again, why, what are you getting at?"

"Did that include the one we're trying to use now?"

"Of course."

Then Joseph narrowed his look at KiKo, "Then, there was stuff in this furnace when it stopped running! Is that correct?!"

"Oh, Jesus Christ, you're right!" KiKo excitedly blurted, jumping up, waving his arms.

"Both my men and I forgot about that. The stuff we poured yesterday was an old mineral combination from one of our test programs. That stuff was on the bottom of the furnace."

He pointed his shaking finger at Joseph, "Your stuff is still in there! Oh, My God, yes!"

"Give us about three or four hours. We'll remodify the troughs to receive your stuff and we'll pour before sunset, and it will take about a day to cool. OK, Sir?"

"Go to it. Let us know what we can do to help," beamed Joseph, the relief resounding in his voice.

He turned to his group, astonished to see them crowd around him, tears of happiness, hugs and handshakes smothered him. Cassie and Douglas stopped crying and jumped up and down, not understanding why, but everyone around them was jubilant and therefore, so were they.

"You did it, boss! Great Thinking!" murmured Dean Morris.

"Aw, go away people. But thanks; let's wait until tomorrow to see how successful we really are."

Again, not much sleep that night.

Late the next afternoon, KiKo again cut a five-inch by five- inch square and handed it to Joseph.

Another lawn mower had been found, the spark plug cleaned, and fresh gasoline and oil poured into it

Again, Dean Morris demanded the same harness wrapped around his friend, his leader, Joseph, to Joseph's reluctant agreement.

At that, Joseph bent and pulled the starting rope.

No response.

He pulled a second time, again no response from the engine.

He stopped for a second, took a deep breath and pulled a third time.

The lawn mower engine fired! It ran rough for a few seconds or so, then smoothed and ran normally.

Joseph squatted next to the mower. Lorraine's big cat and her dog snarled, but the Green Ghost stayed above them and two hundred yards away.

After a few minutes, the lawn mower continued to run as it was designed to do. For the first time in many months, the sound of a running gas engine echoed off the neighborhood and continued echoing!

Joseph called, "KiKo, cut a two-inch-by-two-inch piece of metal. Dean, would you and KiKo bring the smaller piece over to me. Then, take this larger piece over to one of KiKo's trucks, get it started and drive it over here."

Joseph stood, never-before-seen tears streaming down his face, "People, I think we've got it! Thanks to you, our idea works."

KiKo, the strongest man Joseph had ever known, whose eyes had not wept since he was a baby, suddenly had moisture running down his cheeks, murmured to Joseph, "Oh My God, you read about these critical and crucial times and situations in books, but to be here and a part of this, this moment in time, thanks to the man above and to you, my friend!"

The celebration of Joseph's people was instantaneous with wild hugs, cheering and handshakes. One could not have inserted a piece of paper between Dean and Jane. Robbie Peterson thought to herself, "Oh hell, I want to do this." She grabbed Jim Wisnicki and was wonderfully surprised that his arms held her as tightly as hers while their faces were buried in each other's neck. Dan and Tom Peterson with Lorraine Fairly joined the jubilee!

After a few moments, Joseph, remaining by the running lawn mower, managed to calm his people down.

"Dean, Dean," he called. "Would you do that?"

Wiping his wet face, Dean Morris could barely mumble, "Sure Joseph, Oh My God, it's just that we fought for so long and so hard, it's great to be here!" He ran to Joseph and hugged him- tears streaking both chests!

"Come on KiKo, let's go get your truck. If that square works for the mower, it will work for your truck."

A few minutes later, a large Mack truck engine was heard echoing throughout the neighborhood for the first time in many months.

KiKo, smiling broadly, happily drove the truck to where Joseph was still standing.

"Sir, I can't tell you how happy this makes me. Oh, my Lord, thank you, thank you!" His huge hand slapped Joseph's back. Joseph felt like he had been hugged by a grizzly bear, he thought, "Dam, the Chicago Bears or Green Bay Packers need someone like him!"

After a few hours, lubricated by a case of whiskey furnished by one of KiKo's men, a raucous celebration attracted the few neighbors still left.

"Let them celebrate, they deserve it," Dean Morris said quietly to Joseph Robinson. Joseph, Dean, and Jane Morris and the Petersons were the only non-drinkers of the entire group, KiKo, and his men included.

"Now what, Joe?" asked Jane Morris.

Fondling his now cold cup of coffee, Joseph responded, "Well, we've got a four-foot by ten-foot sheet of meteorite. How many five-inch by five-inch squares can we get out of that?"

After a few seconds pause, Jane Morris said, "I think right around two hundred and something. Oh, I see, you want to have KiKo cut that up so we can spread it around."

"Dam, that was quick, said Dean, impressed. "This woman I love is not only beautiful, but brilliant as well. I ran out of fingers and toes very quickly on that question."

"Those aren't your best part," Jane Morris uttered. She then buried her face in her hands, mumbling, "Dam, I can't believe I said that!"

For the first time in months, Dean and Jane heard wild, almost hysterical laughter from Joseph as he fell off the rock he was sitting on.

With tears in his eyes, Joseph grabbed and hugged them, "You two are incredibly good for each other, thank you Jane from me and for my friend here."

After Joseph Robinson quieted, even with a few snickers, he offered, "Here's my thinking and it's only that. We'll leave most of the military men here to handle the gangs coming in with meteorites. The Sergeants know what to do with that material."

Joe paused for a moment, thinking. "We need to warn or brief the Sergeants that the gang leaders believe in control, and they might try to take over our process here. I will tell Coronel Blossitt and the Generals up in McCoy to ASAP send reinforcements down here. All of Chicago's Police Department could not handle or stop the gangs, so our military will have to protect this area, obviously with heavy weapons and armed troops. Maybe the leaders could help doing research on how far the effect works in an apartment building, high-rise or even just a house. But I'm going to let others worry about that."

Dean Morris agreed, "Yes, you are right that those leaders could be a hazard or useful. I never thought that this place would be in danger, but I can see some gang leader trying to own Chicago, or the world, by controlling what we've accomplished here."

Joe continued his thinking, "Now, we have trucks! KiKo will cut the material into 5 X 5 squares, and we'll take about one hundred and fifty of them and head back to McCoy. The horses will stay here and the military and KiKo can figure out what to do about them. I was thinking of taking our entire bunch back to McCoy, turning the squares over to the military there and they can work on getting our country back. I was also thinking of leaving it up to each of our men if they want to stay in the military or be honorably discharged and go back to their homes or wherever. Then, Jane, as you know, my assignment and direct order is over; I've got a place to go!"

"That is, my dear friends, my thoughts. Any comments, questions, criticisms, suggestions or whatever?"

"Oh yes, I forgot something. I had originally thought to take a helicopter back to McCoy, but I must admit I forgot about the rest of my bunch and most importantly, the two little ones. I honestly don't have any idea what to do with them. Also, I forgot about Lorraine's big cat and dog. I don't think the animals would like a ride in a helicopter. So the trucks. . . . Anyway, you have the floor."

"Dam, I just haven't thought much ahead," admitted Dean Morris. "I was so wrapped up in just getting us here and not knowing if we would be successful, it was difficult to plan. And someone I never ever dreamed about was this woman, my wife, I'm not embarrassed to say the love of my life; our marriage was the scariest time and the happiest time of my life. But now, thanks to you, my friend," Dean reached forward and placed his hand on Joseph's shoulder, "We have a future! I simply can't thank you enough!"

"I totally and absolutely join in my beloved husband's statements, Joe," Jane Morris emphatically agreed, holding Dean's hand. "If it hadn't been for you leading and driving us and our entire bunch, we never would have been here. I'm still not sure who actually hired you, but I will bless that person until the day I die."

"Aw, come on guys. I couldn't have done it without you, Dean, and you know that. And thank Jim Wisnicki for making you a Lieutenant; he talked the General at Kirkland into the promotion that give you an interesting future if you want it. That goes for our bunch, too. Their records are clean and all criminal charges, Article 15s, planned court appearances, etc., have been removed; when I get back to McCoy, I will draft an evaluation and recommendation for each of them to receive at least The Bronze Star, and maybe The Silver Star, and whatever combat metals the Coronel or General at McCoy can dream up. Oh, by the way, the same goes for you two, except I'll be asking for a Silver Star for each of you. I believe I'll get it, too."

Lieutenant Dean Morris and Lt. Coronal Jane Morris looked at him in astonishment.

"I'm not kidding. I have at least a General and two full Coronals who will support my recommendations. And once the word gets out what my bunch did, they, and you two, will be considered what they and you really and truly are: heroes!"

Joseph Robinson stood, "I'm going to get another cup of coffee and then, get some sleep. How does noon tomorrow sound for a full meeting?" He laughed, "It will take that long for them to sober up. Oh, who's taking care of the kids?"

"I am," Jane Morris whispered, still in stunned surprise at the conversation with Joseph. She shook her head, recovering and said, "Joe, I, I can't thank you enough for what you said. I want a promise from you, however,"

"Sure, what?"

"Whatever Dean's and my futures are, I must, absolutely must, meet your girl up in Wisconsin. She must be one incredible woman."

"Aw sure, we can talk about that tomorrow. Plus, we need to figure out what to do with the two little ones. We'll have a few days to think about all that. Good night, all." He walked away carrying his, now cold, cup of coffee.

After Joseph left, Jane told Dean, "Two points: one, I never realized how lonely he was or is. That girl, Dan Peterson's other sister, I think her name is Sarah, wrote him one of the most incredible letters I've ever read. I don't think he would show it to you; he was quite lonely and down in the dumps the other night and just needed someone to talk to. In that letter, she expressed a love, a sharing, a soulmate concept with him that I thought only you and I have. Wait a second! You know her, you met her! Tell me about her."

Dean Morris took a deep breath, "Do you remember the first time we met on that dark and lonely runway in Orange County, California? I've never told you this, but the first time we shook hands, from that single touch, I knew, I knew, there were something special between us. And you want to know something else, Joe somehow also recognized it, but he never said anything."

Dean paused for a second and then in a stream of consciousness, "I saw the same whatever the heck it is between Joe and Sarah-from the first time they met and shook hands, and when he went to her farm to help milk some cows and they rode back, I could see that there was something, I don't know what it's called, but it was extraordinary between them." He touched his Jane's face, "Just like us!"

With tears running down her face, she grabbed him; the words should remain with them.

The next day, or more precisely, early afternoon, Joseph called for everyone to meet by KiKo's truck. Severely hung-over bodies crawled out of tents or if they were lucky, sleeping bags, and three bodies hadn't made it that far and passed out on the ground. Jane and Lorraine handed each person with horribly blood-shot eyes and pallor skin a cup of true rot-gut Texas coffee (If you stuck a fork in it and the fork remained standing, the coffee was almost ready!) and forced them to drink it. Joseph fought to keep from grinning at the wretched condition of his men.

After his men sobered up somewhat with an additional cup of coffee, their stomachs couldn't handle food yet, he said quietly, in his opinion, they couldn't stand any loud noises yet, "Well, what a helliva of a party! You, and each of you deserve *to celebrate." This statement was met with a weak cheer that sounded more like a glorified moan.*

"We need to talk about what's next. KiKo, we need you and your men to cut that four by ten sheet into five-inch by five-inch sections. Can you do that?"

Upon receiving a nod, Joseph pushed a little, "You have office buildings over there; is there a generator that we could hook up to put a little electricity into an office? I want to use an electric typewriter and a working Xerox machine. I want to make about five hundred or so copies of a letter to everyone we come across in Chicago telling them to check their local museums to find meteorites and have them transported here. You know what to do with them."

"Oh, by the way, Kiko and your men, keep accurate records of what you are doing, pounds melted, or however you keep track of the work you have done and will do, including, if possible, hours. When we get our country back on its feet, I want you and your men to get paid. Keep in mind that if you have any trouble getting paid, the people at Fort McCoy up in Wisconsin will know how to get in touch with me or us."

Dean Morris chimed in, "You will be busy for a long time. You and your men did a great thing here. I know I speak for our country and all of us in saying thank you. But," he said with a grin, "Please no more whiskey for my men, they can't handle that."

That was met with a mutual groan, "Oh, my God, I hurt!"

Giving way to a grin, Joseph continued, "Sergeants, we have talked about this. You and your men will stay here until relieved from McCoy, which should be in a week or ten days. KiKo, as we discussed, I and my people will take two of your big trucks and return to McCoy. I'll leave the horses and wagons here. A few of the bicycles belong to the civilians here and we'll load them on the trucks, the rest will stay here for use around here. Keep in mind that they can be used as trade for things you might need. Any questions so far?"

"When do we leave, Joe?" asked Dan Peterson.

"I would like to leave tomorrow morning, if possible."

"Is everyone ok with that?" asked Lieutenant Dean Morris.

Upon receiving no response, he turned to Joseph, "You've got it, Sir. We'll start transferring our stuff to a truck. KiKo, can we have two trucks?"

KiKo smiled, "I can do you one better. Gus?" he called to one of his men, "About two blocks south of here is a huge parking lot filled with yellow trucks. You know what I mean. Get a larger one, as new as possible. Take two men and two or three of the 'plates" with you. Fill it with whatever fuel it needs, check the oil and stuff and make sure it runs well, put a five gallon can of fuel in it and bring it back here. OK?"

"On the way, boss."

KiKo smiled at the puzzled looks from both Dean Morris and Joseph Robinson. "You'll see. I would suggest that the second truck should be the lead and be open with your men sitting on the sides, weapons in hand and in the clear view. You'll be traveling through some tough areas, and they don't know about us yet. And the only thing they respect is force, superior force. You have a couple of large calibers, high powered rifles. I would suggest that you have cartridges hanging from them and pointed to each side. That should keep our local idiots from being stupid. We did that in Iraq and it helped- a little."

About two hours later, the sound of a diesel engine echoed throughout the area. Around a corner came a 72 passenger-bright yellow school bus, Gus, grinning from ear-to-ear, driving.

"Oh, my God," exclaimed Lorraine Fairly. "I think my cat and dog and your babies will like riding in that."

Early the next morning, after five seats were removed for two beds for the two children, and the back of the bus was filled with duffle bags, bicycles, wagons, and Lorraine's animals (of course, the cougar took a whole three-person seat!), assignments were given for Joseph's men in riding on an open-bed truck, and everyone else piled in.

Somber goodbyes were given to KiKo and his men.

Sergeant LeRoy Johnstone, who was a school bus driver in his earlier life, was driving the big bus. Dean Morris, stating there isn't a truck he couldn't drive, handled the lead truck with his wife Jane as front seat passenger.

What normally might have an approximate seven-hour drive to Fort McCoy turned out to be closer to nine hours. Joseph's caravan, because of the trucks, was stopped several times, not for malevolent purposes, but by excited citizens recognizing that a change was coming and there was a positive future. They were given copies of Joseph's letter explaining what had happened and what they should do.

In route, while maneuvering around a burnt car on the expressway, Dean turned to Jane, "Two?"

"What?"

"Two, you said two points the other night."

She remembered precisely what she said. She was also scared, unsure how this man, her lover, her husband would react to her question.

Lt. Coronal Jane Morris, pilot of huge C-130s in some hazardous situations and usually unshakeable, took a deep trembling breath, remembering the clutch of tiny arms calling her "Mom" and uttered, "Dean, my love, how do you feel about a family?"

Lt. Dean Morris, leader of men in true hazardous situations including vicious gun fights, nearly ran into an abandoned truck that had mated and burnt with a small car on the expressway. That was the last thing he expected. "Are, are," he stuttered, "are you pregnant?"

Jane laughed, "No."

"Then what the hell are you talking about?"

"We've got two little ones in the bus behind us. Remember, they are true orphans and when we get back to McCoy, decisions will have to be made for them. We can't leave them in limbo because our assignment, our duty will be over." She thought, *"I know what I truly want, but I need his full, pleased agreement."*

"Now, that question I didn't expect!" Dean Morris admitted, "My association with Joseph has taught me to think ahead and I too have been thinking about the little ones. I don't know much, change that to anything, about kids, but I really like those two. Their little hugs are incredible."

"Let's see, Robbie Peterson and our Jim are not ready for the kids yet. Dan Peterson and his Lorraine have a couple of kids at home. So, those four are out. The rest of my bunch are totally unqualified to handle the kids, no matter how much mutual attraction there is. I don't think any of them have even changed a diaper."

Dean paused for a moment, and then with sudden understanding, he took a deep breath, "I believe, my darling wife, that my love for you will easily spill over to the little ones. I will try to be the best father I can to them. I truly care for them! Does that answer your number two?"

With tears of joy running down her cheeks, Jane muttered, "Oh yes, my love. That is what I wanted, but I couldn't say it without you. They have really grown since we discovered them and I, I've beginning to treat them as if they were actually mine. It's interesting, Cassie and I have the same middle name: Fern. Thank you, thank you!"

"That brings up a new problem: how do we adopt them, and assuming we can, can we change their name to ours?"

"I don't know either, but that Coronel at McCoy might have a legal staff, and if he doesn't maybe his General does, or we can somehow make it back to Kirkland and my general should know. I just thought of something. Since the little ones are orphans and their parents are probably dead, just maybe our little kids would own that land where the house is or was."

Discussion and opinions flowed back and forth on whether they wanted to stay in the Army or try civilian life. Interestingly, both were happy with the Army and looked forward to the United States clawing its way back to normal.

Close to sunset, Corporal Rufas Maraton and Private David Berling were standing guard at the front entrance to Camp McCoy. It was quiet, a few birds and lonely crickets were the only disturbance. There had been no one passing while they were on duty.

Suddenly, the sound of truck diesel engines echoed faintly down the road. They looked at each other and simultaneously yelled, "They're back, they made it! Oh My God, they made it!"

A big open Mack truck and a large yellow school bus pulled up. The truck contained about a half-dozen or so men, all heavily armed and the bus contained men, three women and two little kids and two animals. The guards ran around to the front of the truck, seeing Lt. Morris and Lt. Coronal Morris, and saluted, barely able to control their excitement.

"Welcome back! Did you do it?" asked Corporal Maraton, forgetting the proper approach to an officer.

Both officers returned the salutes with grins, "Yes, we were successful. We need to see Coronel Blossitt and I'm sure there will be a briefing."

"You remember the way. Hold on, Private Berling will ride with you to headquarters. I'll continue the guard. Come back, David, when they're checked in"

Shortly after, as the vehicles noisily rumbled to a stop in front of the headquarters building, they were surrounded by hundreds, perhaps thousands of Army personnel, all clapping and cheering. They knew that however the truck and bus got here, there was resolution against the Green Ghost.

Coronel James Blossitt ran out of the building. He slowed and received a salute from both Lt. Dean Morris and Lt. Coronel Morris, with Joseph Robinson standing by, all four grinning. "You did it!" exclaimed Coronel Blossitt, shaking hands. "I'm so dam proud of all of you."

Sergeant Major Samuel Herring ran up and saluted. "Sirs, great to see you back. As much as I want to know what you did, let's get your people housed and fed first, and Coronel, then can we have a briefing. I imagine that they're tired of MREs?"

"Mr. Robinson, Lieutenant, Major, Coronel, I have coffee on, let's talk first and then you can brief everyone," Coronel Blossitt said. "Sam, how about we do the briefing for everyone in the large mess hall. There should be enough room for most of our people. In about an hour?"

"My thinking exactly, Coronel." He turned to the Morrises and said, "Sirs, er, Mam, your rooms and places are where you left them, including the cribs. All you need to do is make the beds. Towels and soap are in the regular place. Lanterns are there too."

"Thank you, Sergeant Major, I appreciate your courtesies," said Lt. Coronel Jane Morris. "Your Coronel was right. You are the best Sergeant Major in the Army."

Sergeant Major Samuel Herring stopped, unused to praise. "Thank you, Coronel, it is my deep pleasure to assist you and your men," he paused, "And especially your little ones."

"Let's have the military officers in my office, now," Coronel Blossitt ordered.

A few moments later, Joseph Robinson and the officers crowded into his office. A pot of coffee was passed around and then Coronel Blossitt spoke, "All right, Joseph Robinson, please tell me what happened."

Joseph cleared his throat and spoke for about ten minutes, outlining in detail what he and his crew, including Dean Morris, had encountered, and fought through. He described the men involved with the blast furnace, their first try with the heavy disappointment, and the second highly successful experiment. He downplayed his initial frustration with a lawn mower but described the successful try. He described the distribution of about five hundred copies of the letter to everyone about finding meteorites."

Joseph continued "For you, Coronel, your men will need reinforcements down there. ASAP! When the local gang leaders figure out that the meteorites are potentially valuable, they will demand or attempt to take over what we accomplished there.

I would suggest a considerable degree of military safety plus someone setting up a system of who turned in what from where and some form of compensation. Also, with respect Sir, KiKo and his men need to be compensated because I believe that they will be quite busy in the foreseeable future."

After a moment of silence, Joseph continued, "Coronel, it is my intention to do whatever, whatever, it takes to have the officers present here be awarded the Silver Star. It is also my intention to have my military men who were with us from California receive the same since they fought all way to where we are now. I am also going to be asking that your military men stationed here who went with us be awarded the Bronze Star. They went knowingly into a potential hazardous situation and performed admirably. I left them in South Chicago or wherever that furnace is, to oversee the melting of the meteorites. I told them that we could relive them in about ten days since, now, now, we have trucks! Tomorrow, we'll try helicopters, but I anticipate that our "plates" will also protect them."

There was an awed silence in the room while the Coronel digested everything.

"There are two final items, Coronel."

"OK, what?"

Joseph took a deep breath, he didn't know how this would be received,

"Sir, first. For the benefit of my enlisted men, I would like for them the opportunity to leave the Army. Sir, you know their background, they have repaid whatever minor debt they might have had, their records are clear and as an award of everything they have done, and you know only a little of that, give them that right! Maybe they want to stay in the Army, and if so, they will be great soldiers. You might say they have had training that no other unit, or soldiers, have experienced. I don't know and haven't asked what they want for their future.

However, this is important: I anticipate they, as a unit, may be needed in about six months or a year for another, but perhaps more important very top-secret mission! So, maybe you should find some way to keep them with the Army. Sir, they would be a great asset to any unit.

Second, Sir, my officers. I could not have done this without my friend and second in command, Sergeant, now Lieutenant, Dean Morris and his incredible wife, Jane. They deserve special recognition! I don't know, but I bet they will soon be parents."

At that, Coronel Blossitt's eyes snapped to Jane Morris. "You're pregnant?"

Jane Morris laughed, "Oh no."

"Oh, the two little kids, right?"

"Yes, we're going to adopt them somehow."

Joseph continued, "Sir, if at all possible, at some future time, I would like for all my officers, including Jane Peterson, to have an opportunity to go to whatever the Army has to offer for a command school. If they stay with the Army, they deserve that and will contribute much to our country. And I forgot, each of my men and ladies are due considerable pay and leave time."

"Oh yes, one final area, and this will probably be the easiest," Joseph Robinson said quietly.

"Go on."

"Sir, when my men and my officers are taken care of and plans are made for the handling of our "plates" bringing our country back, I am done! I've got someone waiting for me up near Two Rivers and desperately want to spend time with her. Sir, one final statement: it has been my deepest honor to have led the members of your Army. None of us, even in our worst nightmares, could have conceived of the Green Ghost and the nationwide anarchy and loss of our civilization. Facing such huge odds and hardships, I am incredibly proud of all my men and what we accomplished." At that, Joseph Robinson sat down.

The room broke out in applause for Joseph. He looked around in confusion, Jane Morris and Robbie Peterson hugging him. "Now I know why my sister fell for you."

After a few moments of cheering and applause, Coronel Blossitt managed to quiet the room, "All right, let's head over the mess hall. We'll eat and get a good night's sleep. Tomorrow is another day, wrong, it's going to be a great day. Dismissed."

After dinner, Coronel Blossitt called his Sergeant Major to him, "Sam, if I understand the "plates" correctly, we can take one and drive any vehicle, right?"

"Yes Sir, that's what Mr. Robinson's men told me."

"OK, do you know where our Commanding General, General Douglas lives?"

"Yes Sir, I've been there several times. Do you want him here?"

"Yes, take a van with a driver and two or three of the plates. He'll need his staff to start our recovery plans. I would like him here soonest. Oh yes, tomorrow morning, send a detail to Volk Field. Have them contact the National Guard Major and get a few of our biggest helicopters ready. We're going to try the "plates" to see if they'll work, but Joseph Robinson thinks that they will. Tell that Major there that I said to get a detail to find pumps to transfer fuel from airport underground fuel tanks to our helicopters. They'll land at airports and the larger airports should have tanks. I don't want to have our copters carry all their own fuel."

"Consider it done, Sir. I'll leave early tomorrow. He lives about an hour drive from here, Oh My God, how wonderful to be able to say that!"

Coronel Blossitt looked around the mess hall and motioned for Joseph Robinson and his officers to sit at his table. He also asked Dan Peterson and Lorraine Fairly to sit. Tom Peterson simply tagged along.

Coronal Blossitt sat with his hands clasped around a hot cup of coffee. "First, I, and our country, cannot thank each of you enough. With that being said, I need some information. You should know that my Commanding General is due here tomorrow. Sam is getting him."

"Who is the General?" asked Joseph Robinson.

"Major General George Owen Douglas, aka GOD to his loyal subordinates and troops, but don't ever, ever, call him that! He relieved General Grippand who was quite ill. Why?"

Joseph Robinson sat back in his chair, smiling and smiling, totally and finally relaxed.

"What? What?" came from nearly everyone the table including the Coronel. Dean Morris was quiet, not knowing the answer, but understanding that the answer would not surprise him. He knew his friend and leader!

"Of everyone here, Dean, you knew Colonel Regional Devonshirk III, the best, wouldn't you agree?" responded Joseph.

"Sure."

"Didn't you ever question where his orders, his information came from?"

"Of course, but I was a lowly Sergeant and Sergeants never question their Colonel. And most of the time, my-our assignments came from you. But. . . ?"

"Jim, you were a Captain in the middle of New Mexico, one of many? And as far as everyone was concerned, all you were was the aide to some General, right?"

"Yes, but occasionally I would get a phone call from an unidentified person telling me to orally pass on certain information," Major Jim

Wisnicki said. "I never knew who that was. Sometimes, I couldn't talk because of people in my office, and he would have to call back. But he would ask me a specific question and I would give him a specific answer."

"Like what?" Dean asked.

"I recognized the distinctive voice. He would say precisely, 'James,' he always called me James, 'there is a load of fatigues and female shoes being shipped to Iceland. Any problems with that?' My answer was also precise: 'No Sir, the palm trees' leaves are purple and pink.'" He sat back and smiled.

"But, that doesn't make any sense," exclaimed Dean.

"That's the point, but the operative words were purple and pink. If those colors changed to anything else, there was a problem. I was given a separate cell phone which was preprogramed for a specific number, but I never had to use it."

Jim continued, "I would get an order from someone, sometimes you, Joe, or a Coronel in Southern California, or my secret source to obtain certain supplies that came mostly from McCoy, but occasionally, from certain other highly classified sources for specialized explosives. They were repacked and forwarded to places, usually in Orange County, California, but occasionally to me. I was told to advise my General of certain tasks that only he could order such as sending C-130s and he was not to query why his planes used so many hours and he couldn't question certain of his flight crews. I did because I had to account for the bullet holes in some of the planes, but he never knew that, or at least I don't think he did."

Joseph Robinson replied, "There's a concept called plausible deniability. In other words, if one does not know something, that person can't divulge anything. There were cutoffs at every level. Required filing of certain paperwork was never accomplished and/or lost. Different bases were frequently utilized. Unknown to each person at each level, they were thoroughly investigated by the FBI and various military intelligence units. And of course, I and my men had to be paid. Jim, you did a helliva job handling our personal files and pay along with everything else."

He paused, the entire table was quiet, waiting. "And Jim, you found out way too much information on our 'medicine man.' Now, maybe much later, I'm sure I will be asked to follow up on that entire issue. I haven't thought about that for quite some time, but it may be an explorable future for our county. You, me, Dean and GOD and maybe one or two others."

Major Jim Wisnicki sat, stunned. "How, how the hell did you find out about that?"

Joe shook his head and finally finished, "I was the only civilian, and my unit was therefore a civilian unit, not answerable to the military. There are only two people who knew the entire system, from top to the grunts doing the actual work. It was specifically intentional that no one else would know about my men or that they even existed and especially what we accomplished. Not even our Coronel in Orange County knew everything. By the way, Jim, my deep personal thanks for your part in helping my men. I am telling all of you this because my unit will be dissolved after this and each man will go wherever he or the Army wants. This unit never existed! Oh, by the way, tomorrow, you'll meet GOD, the only other person who knew the entire concept. Good night all, I'm very tired." At that, Joe got up and left to find a bed.

The next morning, Coronel Blossitt searched out Dan Peterson and Lorraine Fairly. "Dan, Lorraine, I want to personally thank both of you for helping Joe Robinson. Lorraine, your animals helped Joe determine if the Green Ghost was present. We know now that the 'plates' keep that force away from our trucks, and probably any vehicle. However, we don't know, yet, what effect a plate will have in a helicopter. We'll be working to figure out a total spherical distance around a helicopter today at Volk Field. I'm asking if you and your animals would go over there, maybe even going up in a helicopter?"

Lorraine looked at Dan, "What do you think? They both went willingly into the school bus, and the kids kept them quiet. Our dog, Tom's dog, probably would go anywhere he went. I don't know about Baby."

"Baby? What's Baby?" Coronel Blossitt asked.

Loraine laughed, "That's the name our kids gave to my big cat."

Coronel Blossitt said, "I see. I have no way to repay you for what you did for us and our country. I do have a proposal for you. Assuming that we can use our helicopters, when my General arrives sometime today, we'll start planning to spread our information. My thinking is that helicopters will take a few of the plates and spread out to the local big cities to find more meteorites and blast furnaces to start getting our country back. Two of the first cities will be Milwaukee and Green Bay. How do you feel about getting a free ride to your home for your family, bikes and animals while the helicopter later continues on to Green Bay? It would be in one of our big helicopters that could carry about 35-40 men and equipment, and if so, it surely can carry you home."

Dan looked at Lorraine, "Remember when we fought that huge wildfire in Nebraska and sheltered under that bridge? Your cougar went out and gorged himself on whatever he could eat; when he returned, he could hardly walk, we had to carry him on our trailer, and he slept for a whole day? You sent him out getting his meal last night, didn't you?"

"Oh yes, I'd forgotten about that." Lorraine turned to Coronel Blossitt, "Sir, how is the wildlife around here? Would my "Baby" have enough to eat?

Laughing, Coronel Blossitt replied, "We have enough rabbits around here to feed a whole army of cougars. You would be doing us a favor to getting rid of a bunch of them."

"Dan?"

"If we can get Baby and Tom's dog on the helicopter today, I would say ok. It would depend on them. You understand that you would have to go too?"

"OK, Coronel, when?"

"This afternoon at the earliest. I'm waiting for my General to arrive and we can start."

Later that afternoon, several trucks with various military personal plus both Morrises, Coronel Blossitt, Major General George Owen Douglas, and Joseph Robinson in a yellow bus containing Dan and Tom Peterson, Lorraine Fairly, and two animals drove the 30 miles to Volk Field and parked next to a row of Army C-47 helicopters.

"Boy, those things are big," exclaimed Tom Peterson as he fondled his dog. "Mom, do you think Baby will ride in one of them?"

Lorraine Fairly smiled, both at the question and the reference to her as "Mom." In Tom's mind, she was *de facto* even if not *de jure* his mother. "Take a look at Baby," she replied referring to her full-grown cougar. Tom looked: the cougar's stomach almost dragged the floor. "He's had his fill of rabbits that are in the hundreds around McCoy. There's a good chance he'll sleep throughout the entire ride."

Two captains and a major approached Coronel Blossitt, General Douglas and Joseph Robinson who were standing apart from the Petersons. Salutes were given and returned and then all five approached the Petersons.

"We have two men going over to the tower with two plates to get the emergency generator working and to try to get the radio system working in the tower," Coronel Blossitt said. "Assuming that works, Major Scott Thurson here will be the pilot in command and Captain Josh McCann here will be the co-pilot. We think the first helicopter here, a C-47F, will start since there was nothing done to it when the Green Ghost came and shut everything down. They will have two plates. Mr. Robinson says that one should be enough, but I believe in a little more since this is a test flight."

He pointed at three men working on the C-47. "They're checking everything nonelectrical, and when you turn that Chinook on, and take it up, we want it in as good shape as possible."

General Douglas turned to Joseph Robinson, "Joe, do you have any idea how long the plates last?"

"I don't know, and I don't think my scientists, whom you met, know either. If I had to guess, George," Joseph paused thinking, "I would think the answer is quite a long time. The source, the meteorite has been around for eons and melting it didn't seem to change the substance's properties."

The expression on Coronel Blossitt's and Lt. Coronel Jane Morris' faces were priceless; they had never heard a commanding general being spoken to on a first name basis. Of course, they didn't know that the general was Joseph Robinson's secret contact within the military establishment and that they had become friends.

General Douglas turned to the pilot and co-pilot, "Good luck gentlemen. Mr. Robinson here said that the Green Ghost hovered over them about 150 yards above them on their way here. I understand that Dean and Jane Morris are going along as observers to keep an eye on the Ghost."

"That's correct, Sir," said Coronel Blossitt. "In addition to them going along, they're taking Lorraine Fairly with her big cat and Tom Peterson with his dog. Both animals are secondary observers of the Green Ghost. In addition, this is also a little experiment on if the animals can ride in the helicopter, I'm sending this ship to Green Bay, but it will take this whole family to Mr. Peterson's farm before Green Bay. I can't offer them anything for what they did, but at least, I can make their return trip home quicker, if possible."

"I totally approve!" exclaimed General Douglass. He turned to Joseph, "I understand that you're going with them to Mr. Peterson's farm, right?"

Joseph stood, surprised, "How the hell do you know that, George?"

General Douglas laughed, "Don't you know I'm a General and I know everything?" He reached out and clasped Joseph's shoulder like an old friend. "From a grateful nation, I want you to take as much time as you want. Maybe sometime later, after we get our nation back on its feet, I'll come up to see you about a certain jungle. You know what I'm talking about."

Major Jim Wisnicki thinking, had an epiphany and addressed the General, "Sir, with respect, Sir, are you sending women's shoes and fatigues to Iceland?"

"It took you a little time to figure that out, James; are the palm leaves still the same color?" General Douglas said smiling.

He reached over and shook Jim's hand with his other hand clasping Jim's shoulders, "Thanks are due to you too for a difficult duty well done! That orange leaf is well earned," General Douglas said, referring to Jim's new rank as Major.

"Anyway, let's get this show on the road."

Coronel Blossitt turned to Lt. Coronel Jane Morris, "You have the plates, why don't you sit up front while they turn the bird on? Everyone else, it will take them a little time to get it running and warmed up. I don't want anyone around until they're ready to lift and them everyone gets on board."

Lorraine Fairly interrupted, "General, I strongly suggest that I take my big cat and Tom take his dog around and through the helicopter before they start anything. Oh, you haven't met him yet. Give me your hands."

She rubbed the general's hands and then rubbed her big cat's face. "Come here, Sir, so he knows who you are. I need to do this with the pilots and anyone else around the helicopter. He is very protective of his area and you really don't want him suspicious or apprehensive of anyone."

"Nice kitty," said General Douglass rubbing the big cat's head; its rumbling could be heard over the entire area.

Tom Peterson laughed, "He doesn't know he's a cat, he thinks he's part people. And we are his people. Sir, I suggest that before you start the engines, that we be inside the helicopter. They wouldn't want to approach when the rotors and engines are running, but we should be able to calm them inside. I've got a leash for my dog, but Mom, er Lorraine, my dad, and I hope to keep our cat calm. You'll notice that he must have eaten a bunch of your rabbits here last night, look at his stomach. He just might sleep during the flight."

Everyone looked at the big cat's stomach. Lorraine interpreted the expression on the cat's face as "Ahhh, nice dinner! Thank you!"

"Ok, let's get started," General Douglas ordered.

Several hours later, after the requisite preflight checklist had been completed, a wave from the control tower indicated that they were up and working. Each passenger was supplied with their own earphones and microphones. The Green Ghost hovered over the tower, but the energy stayed about two hundred yards above it.

Major Thurson took a deep breath, "Well, let's see if this works. Give me power."

Master switches were flipped. Lights came on, dials registered, and they heard a pop in their earphone. "Volk Field calling Unit 1. How do you copy?"

"Volk, we copy you five by five. Request permission to start engines."

"Unit 1, permission to start. Minimal winds are south by southwest, there is no other traffic. Please advise when ready for lift."

After about fifteen minutes of letting the engines warm and paying close attention to various checklists, Captain McCann reported to Major Thurson, "Checklists complete, Major. We're ready for lift."

"Very good. Volk Field, Unit 1 ready for lift."

'Unit 1, you are cleared, God Bless!"

"Ok, crew and passengers, we're ready for lift. How is everything back there?"

Lorraine Fairly reported, amusement in her voice, "We're ok back here. My big cat woke up when you started the engines and then went back to sleep. Tom's dog barked a few times and then quieted. Have you seen the Green Ghost?"

Lt. Coronel Jane Morris broke in, "That's my job: looking for that thing. Right now, it's about two hundred yards above us and the same over the tower. We're not going far or very high, mostly up and down the runway, and about thousand feet in altitude. The people on the ground will spot the distance between us and the Ghost. Major Thurson, let's go!"

"Volk Field, Unit 1 lifting."

"Look, Look!" Coronel Blossitt exclaimed. "The Green Ghost moves up as our Unit rose. It stays about two hundred yards above them." He waved to the tower, motioning with his hands and arms up, up.

"Unit 1, Volk Field, increase your height slowly."

"Volk, roger, we'll slowly increase our height to a thousand feet. Watch what happens to the Ghost, especially around and under us."

"Unit 1, roger. As of now, it is staying about two hundred yards above you. We don't see any around or under you."

"Pilot to crew, what are the animals doing?"

"Lorraine speaking, my cat woke up again as you lifted and now, he's gone back to sleep. If that Ghost was around here, he will let me know, he clearly hates that stuff. Tom's dog is quiet too. Do you know where that thing is now?"

"Coronel Morris here, the ground tower reports that the Ghost is staying above us and most importantly, not around or under us."

"So, Joseph and his scientists are correct. Thank God!"

Lt. Coronel Jane Morris further reported, "It's interesting, the Ghost seems to divide, some moves with us and some stays above the tower. Obviously, both of us have electricity that it can't touch. Major, let's climb to a thousand feet just to make sure."

The beat of the rotors grew deeper, and the helicopter climbed. Lorraine Fairly reported, "Both animals are now awake, but not alarmed, just alert. I think they know it is out there, but it's not an immediate danger to them and us."

After about a half hour of back and forth and up and down, "Volk Field, Unit 1, we're landing. I think we've proved that we can operate now."

"Unit 1, roger. Congratulations on a job well done!"

After the helicopter landed and the rotors slowed and stopped, the back ramp came down. Everyone left. However, Tom's dog promptly trotted to one wheel and immediately deposited a large puddle on it. Tom Peterson, embarrassed, could not frame a reply, just shook his head while the entire audience laughed.

"All right," General Douglas said, "Major, Captain, thank you for a risky job done well. As soon as Coronel Blossitt writes it and I approve it, there will be a commendation in your file. You and your men can now start getting your base back. Every helicopter will need a plate to fly, and you need to experiment where you need to put the plates to get your electricity running again. Everyone else, let's head back to McCoy. I'd like to see Coronal and Lieutenant Morris, Coronel Blossitt, and Joseph Robinson in Coronel Blossitt's office when we get back."

That early evening, they met in Coronel Blossitt's office. General Douglas opened the meeting, unusually emotionally stating, "Joe, you and Lt. Dean Morris performed a service for our country that can never be repaid. Not only your secret assignment in California where you did a few things that we can't yet talk about, if ever, and where you stopped a lot of drugs and took care of a bunch of bad guys, but you stepped up to fight the Green Ghost. Joe, you want to go to someplace up north, but I don't know why."

Joseph looked at Jane Morris, she knew! "Sir, I met a girl up there, as a matter of fact, she is Dan Peterson's sister. I think, for me it is the real thing, George. She is a farm girl and has a farm a few miles from Dan's place. I would like a break from the heavy stress after months leading my great bunch of guys through unexpected combat and difficult conditions. It should be noted that I could not have done it without Dean Morris."

General Douglas responded, "For all of you, Joseph has requested, and I will approve the award of a Silver Star for each of you as well as Lt. Robbie Peterson and Major Jim Wisnicki. Joe also asked for a Silver Star for each of his enlisted men which I also will approve. I will also write commendations and set up Bronze Stars for the men from here who went to South Chicago for you. They knowingly went into probable harm's way."

"Sir, can I interrupt you for a second?" Joseph asked.

Upon receiving a nod, he turned, "Dean, Jane, do you remember our last conversation with our Coronel out in California?"

Getting a puzzled look and a shake of Dean's head, Joseph went on, "General, our Coronel in California gave me his opinion of Dean Morris. He said, and I quote, 'Joseph, between you and us, I am humbled beyond words to have led that man!'"

Surprised, something was in Lt. Dean Morris' eyes; his wife nodded agreement, proudly grasping his arm.

Joseph turned to the General, "George, with all respect, I totally agree with that statement; we could not have accomplished all we did without him guiding and helping lead our bunch! In addition, speaking of our bunch, I'm asking on their behalf that they be given time to make a decision about their individual future. They will make a great addition to wherever they go."

General Douglass nodded, "I totally agree. Lieutenant, Coronel, I truly hope you stay with us!"

He paused and took a deep breath, "Joseph, your assignment is now over, and your contract fulfilled. Oh my God, did you ever complete your contract! Your unit is now dissolved, and it never existed. Your men's jackets are clean with vague references to an Ultra Top-Secret assignment to account for their time. They know enough not to talk about what you and they did. I'm giving them the option to stay in the Army with any place they want to serve, or to be honorably discharged with their DD-214s showing great service. Their honorable ranks are now permanent as is yours, Lt. Morris. Major Jim Wisnicki and I will have a talk. He knows too much about certain subjects and I can use him. Now what are your plans?

"General, my husband and I would like to take some leave to visit Dan Peterson and his family up near Two Rivers. We will take the two little ones with us," Lt. Coronel Jane Morris said. "Later on, we'll figure out some way to legally adopt them."

"When did you want to leave?"

Jane Morris looked at her husband, Dean Morris, "Two things, General: Yes (!) we'd like to remain in the Army. That has been a large part of our life. My family is in New Mexico, and we'd eventually want to return there. For now, is tomorrow too soon for us to leave?"

"Yes, I would like you to stay one more day. Coronel Blossitt is ordering a helicopter, probably Unit 1, to take both of you, the Peterson family, their animals, bikes, trailers, to Dan Peterson's farm, stay there for a day or two, and then proceed to Green Bay. There they will meet another helicopter with additional plates and personal with portable pumps for refueling. Both will overfly the city, land at the Austin Straubel International Airport there and organize getting that city back with their own meteorites. We expect that will take about a month. Unit 1 will return to the Peterson farm, pick up you two and Robbie Peterson and return here. Each ship will carry plates, and enough food for about a month."

He turned to Coronel Blossitt, "Do you have any portable electrical generators here?"

"We are ahead of you, Sir. I have a whole warehouse of 7500 watt portable generators. They are being retrieved as we speak and we're hooking up a couple around here for us to have lights. The second helicopter to Green Bay will carry two of them, Unit 1 will carry one for the Peterson farm."

Joseph Robinson, who had been silent for a time, asked, "Coronel, can I ask a favor? Could we have two generators on Unit 1?"

Lorraine looked at Joseph for a moment, "Oh, I see why-you want one for your girl's farm, right?"

Joseph, a never-before seen blush on his checks, simply nodded.

Lorraine reached over and hugged Joseph, "I absolutely must meet this girl. General, this man is the second greatest man I've ever known." She smiled, "I married the greatest one!"

"Even if he can't count past his fingers and toes?" Joseph Robinson asked trying hard to not smile.

Her hands covering her blushing and smiling face, Lorraine mumbled, "You would remember that; just wait!

"A very personal joke, George," Joseph explained.

General Douglas smiled, "I think that's it. Anyone have anything else?"

Upon receiving shakes of the head, he said, "So Ordered."

Lorraine said, "Sir. Thank you very much."

"No, people, the thanks are the other way. If there is anything else I can do, simply ask."

Follow-up maintenance on Unit 1 and loading electrical generators, bicycles, trailers, food and water, and personal items comprised the next day.

Early the following morning, after a large breakfast, a large yellow bus and several trucks took the thirty-minute drive to Volk Field. Joseph Robinson's men also rode out to bid their leader good-bye.

He spoke to them, "Men, I can't tell you how proud I am of each of you. Every one of you, in your own individual way, has grown and accomplished much. As you know, our unit has been dissolved. For all purposes and records, it never existed. I don't know when, if ever, we'll meet again, but I must tell you it has been my rare privilege, my honor, to have led you. From the bottom of my heart, I, and our country, thank you. If there is ever anything you need, Dean, Jane or our General here will know how to contact me."

As Joseph boarded the helicopter, his men formed a line, requiring him and Dean Morris to pass in front of them.

Hugs and handshakes were exchanged; not a few turned away, water leaking from their faces.

Soon, CeCe and Douglas were seat-belted in, the animals were calmed and cared for and everyone else was ready. A somber Joseph Robinson, his face still wet, and Dean Morris sat quietly. The rear ramp rumbled up and the tower gave permission to start engines.

Joseph Robinson's thoughts turned to a certain farm in Wisconsin. He was surprised at the tension in his chest and depths and longing of his feeling. *"Did she mean what she said in her letter? OMG, I fought across our nation, but this woman scares me more than anything else, I've never felt this way before!"*

He leaned over to Jane Morris, his voice trembling, "Jane, do you think she'll be there when we land?"

She knew who he was talking about. "I don't know, but let's ask Dan, it's his sister."

"I don't know, but she spends much time at our home. Plus, she really loves my two little girls with the feeling mutual."

Pilot Scott Thurson came on the speaker, "We're about 140 miles away, or in other words, about an hour. Everyone relax and enjoy the view. Mr. Peterson, when we get airborne, please come up and show us where to land."

Nearly an hour later, as the helicopter slowed and hovered, Tom's dog barked; somehow, he knew he was nearly home.

At the Peterson farm north of Manitowoc, Wisconsin, Sarah, Dan's sister had come with milk for Dan's two little ones. More and more, she hung around the house, no one saying anything, but hoping against hope that their family was safe. Sarah had difficulty sleeping, Joseph Robinson was constantly on her mind, wondering, just imaging. She had never met a man like him, hoping that he received her letter.

Father Peterson had fed the cow and her calf, cleaned out the barn and was slowly walking back to the house carrying a pail of water. The day was bright, softly still, almost too quiet as if just waiting, only the lonely birds chirping in the trees, and a neighbor's dog barking a mile or two away.

The only thing he heard, faintly, was the sound of a helicopter south of him.

Helicopter??

Helicopter!!

He dropped the pail. He ran into the house, yelling, "Helicopter, Helicopter. Oh My God, a Helicopter!"

Pointing toward the southwest, the entire Peterson family ran out into the front yard. "There it is, coming from over Manitowoc," shouted Sarah.

The helicopter noise grew louder. Soon it was over the Peterson house, slowing. It was huge, its two engines shaking the windows of the house. It slowly moved over the barns to the road leading to the house. After hovering over the road, it turned completely around and then, facing east, slowly lowered itself to the road.

The Green Ghost following the helicopter remained hovering about two hundred yards above it.

All the Peterson family, including two little girls, and Sarah, ran up the road to the landing site. The whipping rotors slowed and finally stopped nearly striking a small crabapple tree in the roadway ditch.

Sarah clutched her mother's arm while holding Dan's little girls, "Do you think he's come back?"

Sarah's mother looked at her with wise eyes, "We'll know soon, sweetheart! I hope the rest of our family is on that helicopter, too."

Thoughts flowed through Sarah's mind, "*Will he come back to me? I'm, . . .I'm so scared!*" Her heart pounded within her.

Finally, the rear ramp slowly lowered. From the interior darkness, out bounced Tom's dog and Lorraine's big cat. The dog headed for a front wheel and watered it, the cat disappeared into the fields, it was home.

Dean and Jane Morris then walked out of the dark interior, leading a three-year old little girl, and carrying a two-year old little boy. Dan Peterson and Lorraine Fairly came out with Tom and Robbie Peterson. Sarah had been holding Dan's little girls, but they broke from her and ran to Dan, Lorraine and Tom, father and mother Peterson hustling after them.

Sarah stood alone, her heart pounding, her eyes brimming, "Did He Come Back?"

Little did she realize that Joseph Robinson was asking himself, *"Is she there? Oh my Lord, I hope so!"*

As he walked out from the dark interior of the helicopter, he saw her!

Sarah, crying, ran to him and nearly knocked him over.

"You came back, Oh Thank God, you came back!"

Arms grasped, two bodies and minds accustomed to harsh and severe loneliness clutched each other!

Lips needing lips touched softly, very gently, and then fiercely all over their faces.

Finally, Sarah laid her head on Joseph's chest, sobbing with joy. "I, I wasn't sure if you would come back."

"I couldn't stay away, my love, my darling, not after your letter."

They finally broke apart and turned to the pilot and co-pilot who had come around the side of the helicopter. Both were amused to see the meeting, "Geese, I wish my girl, any girl, would meet me like that," one drawled to the other with mutual grins.

Dan Peterson introduced his parents to Jane Morris. "You remember Dean Morris? This is Lt. Coronel Jane Morris, his wife. He came with Joseph Robinson, who I'm sure you remember. Sarah, Jane really wanted to meet you."

Jane walked to Sarah, grabbed her arms, looked her in the eyes and face, and instinctively hugged her. "I simply had to meet you, Sarah! Joseph is the second greatest man I have ever met, and for you to capture this man says that you are very special!"

Both shared looks and felt the same, *"I like this person. This is a warm woman I could respect."*

Dan Peterson turned to the pilot and co-pilot, "Introduce yourself to my parents, and that's my other sister, Sarah, who is hanging onto Joe Robinson over there."

Meanwhile, the Green Ghost, which had been hovering overhead, finally left.

Major Scott Thurson told the Petersons, "Folks, I have two little special gifts and one big one for you from my Coronel. He said to tell you what your son and Lorraine Fairly, and Tom and Robbie did for our country was a debt that could not be repaid. He said they were heroes and deserve thanks from a grateful nation."

He turned and retrieved a large package and a small package from the interior of the helicopter. The large package contained 30 pounds of whole coffee and the small package contained an old coffee grinder.

"There is a large gift too, but I'll need help with that. The Coronel said that this is a small token of appreciation from Fort McCoy. He knew that coffee was worth its weight in gold, and I have no idea where he got the coffee grinder."

After things quieted down, Dan turned to his parents, "Mom, Dad, our plans are that the helicopter will stay here for a day or two and then proceed on to Green Bay and get them organized. As you can see, Joseph Robinson's idea with Dean Morris helping was incredibly successful. We have small plates that came from a melted meteorite that keeps the Green Ghost away. We have ten of the plates, two for here, one or two for Sarah and a few for Two Rivers and Manitowoc. Dean and Jane with their two little ones plan on about a month leave here. More good news, Dad. With our plates, we can get your truck working again and that'll give us transportation."

He turned to Sarah, "I understand Joseph will be here for about a day."

"What?!" came from a shocked Sarah.

"Ha! Gotcha. I'm just kidding. I understand that he's going to be a permanent fixture around here and very welcome at that."

Father Peterson spoke, "All of you are certainly welcome here. This is a great day! But with Dan, Lorraine, Tom, and Robbie back, we are a little pressed for room."

Mother Peterson broke in, "Sure, but I have an idea. Dean and Jane, we have enough room on our living room if you don't mind sleeping on a floor for a day or so. Sarah, isn't that house across the road from you vacant?"

"Oh, yes, it is! No one has lived there even before the Green Ghost came. How about tomorrow, we'll go over and clean it. Mom, you have cribs up in the attic that we could give to Dean and Jane for their kids.

"Oh yes, I almost forgot," Dan Peterson said, "We have three portable 7500-watt electrical generators in the helicopter. One is for you, Mom and Dad, and one goes to Green Bay."

"And the third is my gift to you, Sarah," said Joseph. "It goes to your house."

"That's not the only gift you brought me," came Sarah's whispered thought. Jane Morris, overhearing the whisper, locked eyes with her. Jane nodded, knowing what Sarah was thinking. Thank you" were the louder words, but the look promised much more for her Joseph!

Co-pilot, Captain Josh McCann broke in, "Folks, in my other life, I was an electrician. I'll help you get the generators set up because that was the kind of stuff I did as a civilian. We can run wires across the road from your house, Sarah, to that vacant house. I'll need to look at the electrical systems, but they're probably a usual 120-volt hookup and I'm sure the generator will easily handle the charges."

"Thank you," said Dan Peterson.

"I almost forgot," mentioned Joseph Robinson, "I arranged for about a ton of canned and dried food in the helicopter for you, Mr. and Mrs. Peterson.

"Sir," Scott McCann said turning to Dan Peterson, "let's get your Dad's truck working and we can haul this stuff to your house. We'll use one plate and that should work."

"Great idea, that generator is portable but with the truck, we can clean out your bird."

Later that day, after needed repairs and modifications by Captain Larry McCann, for the first time in many months, there was lights in the Peterson house. As dinner was being served, Mr. Peterson stood aside with his arm around his wife, a tear winding down his seamed cheek, "Mom, our family is again home. All thanks to those two men," he nodded to Dean Morris and Joseph Robinson.

He spoke with deep feeling, "Dean, Joseph, I want you to know that this will always be your home. My wife and I can't thank you enough."

"Oh, you're very welcome" replied Joseph. "We couldn't have done it without your Dan, Lorraine, Tom, and Robbie. It took considerable courage to do what they did and we, with our nation, thank them for that."

Robbie Patterson interrupted, "Mom, Dad, I'll be home on leave for about a month. When Dean and Jane Morris return to McCoy, I must report back with them. Until then, I'm home!"

Tom Peterson's practical question for Joe, "Sir, what can we, as a family, and as a country expect?"

"Great question, Tom. We now know how to fight that Green Ghost. The Army is the only system that has remained organized and has the ability to spread required information. It will certainly take over a year and probably more to notify the entire country and then another year to recover our infrastructure. Dean and Jane will be part of that. What very few people know is there is a group of scientists outside of Chicago working on a way to capture that Green Ghost and turn it into some form of energy. Once they have electricity, it will be interesting to see what they accomplish. Probably in a year or two, they might successful."

Joseph paused for a moment, "As for me, my contract with the Army is over. However, General Douglas, our commanding general, and my secret friend, told me that maybe in six months or more, he and Jim Wisnicki might come up to see me. Jim and I know too much about an Ultra Top-Secret project involving our jaunt to a certain jungle. Dean, you were part of that, and you may be involved. Please keep in mind that that assignment was and still has that classification. We really don't know who, or more precisely what, was in that village nor does the people in Las Vegas have any credible information. Maybe, when you return to McCoy, you might want to keep our men involved and together. We'll need them whenever we hit that jungle again. Pass that on to our General, too please."

With a deep sign, Joe continued, "Now, frankly, I'm truly physically and emotionally exhausted."

He looked at Sarah, "All I want to do now is learn how to milk a cow."

Dan Peterson remarked causally, "She sure as hell will get you to do that," to much laughter.

She whispered so quietly that nearly no one heard, "You came home, my darling." Jane Morris heard; she understood and shared a glance with Sarah.

Later that day, Sarah asked her brother, "Dan, can Joseph and I borrow your bikes to get back to my house?" She hesitated, "I-we. . . we need to do chores."

"Of course, we'll load your generator on the truck, bring it over in the morning and hook it up."

"Good night, everyone, we'll see you all tomorrow morning," said Sarah.

At Sarah's farm, while helping Sarah milk her cows and feed the animals, Joseph thought, *"This is so strange, I feel like I've come back to a place I never knew was my home."*

Later, while making coffee for them, Sarah felt skittishly like this was a first date. They sipped their coffee with few quiet words. After they finished, she cleaned the table and was unnecessarily fussing with dishes and kitchen items, "Would, would you like some more coffee?"

"No." Joseph took a deep breath, rose, and approached her at the kitchen sink. Her back was to him. He moved her hair aside on her neck and gently kissed her on her neck.

She shivered and her knees wobbled as she felt faint. The dishtowel fell unnoticed into the sink water. He grasped her waist, turned her around and his hands cupped her face.

He bent his head and his lips gently touched hers. She moaned, "Oh, oh, oh, My Darling, for so long have I waited!" as her lips caressed his. He murmured, "Come sit with me." His eyes captured hers with something other than sitting on his mind.

Her heart pounding, she grabbed his hand, "I have a better place to sit," and she led him to her bedroom.

Again, there was little sleep that night, but if that old Wisconsin farmhouse could smile, it would-several times-no longer was it lonely!

Early the next morning after chores were done and after breakfast during which Joseph looked over the kitchen. His cup of coffee was warm in his hands. The thought came to him, *"Oh my Lord, I feel like I've looked my entire life for a place to belong, here I finally feel at peace, and the frosting is Sarah."*

Over a cup of coffee, Sarah asked, "My Joseph, can I ask you a question?"

"Of course, anything."

"This is your home. You know that as I wrote to you about my unknown search for you. How do I want to put this? I know a little. But, before that you were involved in a very secret area. It involved Dean Morris, some Major, and some General and them coming up to see you about that thing you did some months ago. I understand that meeting is not for maybe six months or more from now or until things get straightened out from the Green Ghost. Someone let it slip that thing involved something in Africa and an Air Force Base in Nevada and Area 51. So, can you tell me anything about that?"

"Jesus Christ, I know one of the reasons I love this woman so much: she is sharp as a tack," Joseph thought to himself. *The memory of farm callused hands clasping his back against the firmness of breasts with a sweetness of outstanding nipples coursed through his mind.*

After a moment's difficult thought and happiness, Joseph replied, "OK. You weren't supposed to hear anything about that. That entire assignment was so highly classified, it didn't even have a title. Yes, Dean, I and my men flew a classified-off the books mission to deep Africa.

We landed on a little used airport that was more road than airport. We hiked about ten or fifteen or more miles through heavy jungle to a village to retrieve a CIA operative. CIA had received rumors that the people in that specific village were extraordinary healthy. No diseases such as the typical stuff around there including AIDS, bad teeth, TB, Malaria, and so on. Rumor also said there were no old people there, at all! No one seemed to have aged."

Joe took a sip of his coffee, "So, the CIA had an undercover 'wandering medicine man' who spoke the language, looked the part, including scars and old tattoos, traveling from tribe to tribe, and after about three months eventually making his way to the village. He had an elephant's tooth that was a hidden camera, and a few of the things hanging from him, when pressed in a certain way, sent a signal to a satellite overhead, requesting immediate secret extradition. He spent about a week there and then signaled he wanted out, quickly. That's where we came in."

Joseph paused remembering the incident. "I had a couple of guys that could sneak in anywhere. We crawled up to that village and about O-dark hundred, or about three a.m., my guys crept in, figured out where he was and got him out. We walked the tough miles back through the jungle, notified our plane and we got out of there. He carried a small pack with him and refused to let anyone touch it.

Interestingly, he knew airplanes and MREs (meals ready to eat) and how to operate our microwave oven in our plane. He also refused to talk to Dean or any of my men. During the long flight over the Atlantic, including two re-fuelings in the air, while everyone else was asleep, he whispered to me in confidence that he was worried about what he found would be concealed and someone should know what he knew. He very quietly told me he found in that specific village three different men who looked much like the natives. They ran that village. These men always had turbans on their heads. One night when these three men were asleep, one had his turban off and our guy managed to get two photographs."

Joseph paused.

"Well, so what?" asked Sarah.

"According to our guy, they looked very normal in every way except..."

"Except what," demanded Sarah.

"Except that there was a third eye in the middle of the very large forehead."

Sarah looked at him with her mouth open. She shook her head, not sure if to believe this man she so loved or not.

"Let me finish, my darling. When we finally landed in Nevada at Homey Airport. . .."

He paused, "Know where that is?"

"I've never heard of it."

"It is also known as Groom Lake."

"I've never heard of that either."

"The more common name is Area 51, outside of Las Vegas."

"That everyone has heard of."

"Our C-130 pilot was directed to land on a specific runway and taxi to a designated location. He was told to stop, lower his back hatch, and then immediately leave. Our passenger jumped off the ramp, we closed it and directly left to our home base. Our passenger was met by three men and by the time we turned around, they had disappeared."

"In an absolutely off the record conversation with a totally confidential CIA informant, he guessed, and importantly only guessed, that these men were probably in a spaceship of some kind that had crash-landed there. Now, after we conquer the Ghost throughout the U.S., the very few people in the know, including the Major and General, want to send some of us back there to contact them. We believe that there are a tiny few in Area 51 that might know more.

"But, but why haven't anyone heard about this?" Sarah questioned. "We've got all those UFOs flying around, if you want to believe some of the stories."

"What would happen if these miracle men became public knowledge, especially their knowledge on health or longevity issues? The public and political response would be massive and certainly disastrous to our world society! Because of the Green Ghost, these natives/aliens or whatever they are probably have the same problem we have, and maybe we can work with them in fighting that truly alien life. We believe that they must be more advanced than us. And that my incredible lover," at that he looked at Sarah and she blushed," that entire story must never leave this kitchen."

"Why, why did you share this with me?" Sarah asked, her head shaking.

"The answer is simple: I want no secrets between us, particularly of this magnitude. When the Ghost issue is settled, I'll probably be part of the contact, probably in less than a year. It will take that long for our nation to get at least partially back on its feet and we'll have the ability to cross over to Africa by solving the refueling and communication problems. That General, that Major, Dean Morris and I, and my men are the only people, outside of Nevada, that know the story. And, importantly, my men don't know about whatever those 'people' are.

The only thing my guys know is that we had to pick up a medicine man, nothing else."

Joseph and Sarah were unaware of the rare profoundness of the level of unconscious trust and confidence in their exchange of thoughts, feeling, ideas and emotions.

Joe shrugged his shoulders saying quietly with deep emotion, "Why am I telling you? When I was down in Chicago working on fighting the Ghost, I could see your face in the clouds and nighttime stars. I could feel again your touch! Most men can't share this, but when *with* you, I have experienced a depth of feelings, of need and satisfaction, for lack of a better definition, a love; I guess the best way to say this is that my love for, with, and of you is absolute."

With tears running down her cheeks, she ran to him.

Later that morning, the sound of father Peterson's truck echoed down the road.

Rolling over in bed, Joseph exclaimed, "Hurry, we must get dressed before they get here."

Giggling like two teen-agers, they managed to get dressed, even if a button or two were slightly misplaced, after clothes were found scattered from the kitchen to the bedroom.

The truck arrived, carrying the Peterson clan, the Morrises and two helicopter pilots with a 7500 Watt Generator plus a week's supply of food.

Dean Morris looked at his leader, his friend, and quietly murmured, "Not much sleep, huh, boss? The least you could have done is get dressed before we got here!"

Standing next to Joseph was Sarah, her hands to her flushed face, giggling. She thought, *"I haven't blushed like this since I was a teenager. My God, I do love this man!"*

The response from Joseph was a dirty look with an involuntary smile, "Aw," knowing there was no real answer.

Dean quietly continued, "Do you recall the first night Jane and I spent in that pond. Remember, you embarrassed the hell out of me because of Jane's hickey on my neck. Ha! I see your neck is quite roughed up, too." he grinned as he hugged his friend.

"Sarah, you are going to have to remember to give him a high-necked shirt."

Sarah had to ask, "What on earth for?"

"Take a look at his neck. This poor guy has sunburn all over his neck."

Sarah had to look at Joe's neck and at that moment, she knew what caused "the sunburn."

More embarrassed giggling!

After a quick examination, Captain Josh McCann said the wiring on both houses were in fine shape, and that the vacant house had used Sarah's house current. He, within an hour, hooked up the generator. Surprisingly, the vacant house had most of the bulbs left and the propane gas stove had three nearly full tanks.

Sarah's two-hundred-gallon gas tank she had used for her farm machinery supplied the gas for the generator.

Josh stood next to the generator with a 5" by 5" piece on it, looked around and said, "All right, we need a countdown. Kids, count down from five to one. OK?"

Tom, feeling a little foolish, with his giggling sisters, "Five, four, three, two, One!" At which, Josh smiling widely, flipped a switch on the generator, the engine fired, started roughly and quickly, smoothed. Josh flipped another switch and suddenly, there was light where there had been all encompassing darkness. The Petersons shouted, grabbed and hugged Joseph Robinson. This was all because of him.

Almost a month later, the Wisconsin weather turned cold. Coming from Southern California, none of Dan Peterson's family nor the visitors had winter clothes. Dan's parents stepped in and heavy winter clothes and coats were found from loyal and pleased neighbors.

Joseph Robinson and Sarah Peterson found an abandoned nearly new pick-up truck on a side road. With the assistance of Father Peterson, a new battery, an examination of the engine, and a 5" by 5" plate, the vehicle was soon running despite the Green Ghost.

Joseph had found, the difficult way, that riding a bicycle in Wisconsin's early winter was not recommended. Frozen and rutted roads were hard on one's body!

A few days before the Morrises were planning to leave, Joseph suggested, "Dean, I want to experiment with our plates. I kept a half-dozen plates when we landed here. We now have 5" by 5" sized plates, but I want to see if a one square inch or two square inch plate would work, particularly on vehicles or even buildings. What do you think? "

"That's a valid point, Joe. I think Mr. Peterson has a couple of mechanical clamps to hold the plates. I would suggest that we use a chisel rather than try to cut them because that was what Kiko did in Illinois. I would recommend that we start with a two-square inch piece and if that works, try a one-inch square cut, all to see if they keep the Ghost away."

"Does Mr. Peterson have a lawn mower we can borrow?"

Dean laughed, "Of course he does! Don't you know that all Wisconsin farmers have lawn mowers? Their field equipment is too big to cut the family lawns. Mrs. Peterson would be terribly upset if her husband mowed her favorite petunias or rhubarb or whatever she's growing."

A day later, after chiseling a two-inch square piece and a smaller piece of a plate, they dragged Mr. Peterson's lawn mower about fifty yards away from the farm house and barns. The Green Ghost hovered over them.

"Will this start?" asked Joseph.

"Of course, it will," replied Mr. Peterson, "I renovated it last spring before that force came."

"Ok, everyone back away. I'm going to start with the two-inch," Joseph ordered.

He placed a two-inch piece of a plate on top of the lawn mower, bent and yanked on the starter rope. Nothing! The Green Ghost continued hovering over them.

Joseph bent again and pulled on the starter rope, the engine fired, sputtered for a few seconds and smoothed out.

Joseph retreated when the engine started. The force hovered angrily;

however it kept its distance! Tom's dog barked sharply, then quieted but kept an eye on the force.

The small group cheered; they understood the significance of what they had just witnessed.

After a few minutes, Joseph approached the lawn mower and shut it off. He then replaced the two-inch plate with a one-inch plate. He started the engine and again retreated, but closely watched the sky above the engine. The Ghost persisted its fuming and furious circling, but it came no closer.

"The smaller pieces work, Dean, they work!" exclaimed Joseph.

"Great!" Dean responded, "This will make the people at McCoy ecstatic: our nation's recovery will be much quicker than anyone thought." *All because of you, my friend*! he thought.

Shortly before the Morrises were due to leave, after things quieted down and the sound of helicopters and planes were frequent, Joseph Robinson drove over to Dan Peterson's home.

"Let's go for a walk." They put on heavy winter coats since the sky was overcast and snow flurries were floating through the 26-degree cold air.

"As you know, your sister, Sarah, and I have something special, somewhat like you and Lorraine and very much like Dean and Jane. I, I want to do something that I'd never thought I would do again, but I was thinking you might want to join me."

At that, Joseph handed Dan a small item. "I had one of our sergeants buy two for me at the McCoy PX. If you join me, it will be my gift to you."

"Ah yes! I've been thinking the same thing but didn't have this item. Absolutely, a great idea, thank you!" Dan hugged his friend; and plans were made.

Two days later, after Dan quietly talked with his kids, Mom Peterson invited Joe, Sarah, and the Morrises and children for coffee after chores.

In their ride in their pickup truck to the Peterson house, Joe was strangely quiet. Sarah was curious, but not alarmed.

When they arrived at the Peterson, they were surprised to see many friends and neighbors also visiting.

After coffee, when everyone was sitting in the living room, with the little kids and one friendly German Shepard on the floor, Dan looked at Joe and nodded, "Ready?"

"Oh yes!"

They took two straight back chairs from the kitchen and placed them side-by-side in the middle of the living room. Dan Peterson's children could hardly contain themselves with excitement, they knew!

Dan Peterson grabbed Loraine Fairly and guided her to a seat; Joseph Robinson grabbed Sarah Peterson and guided her to a seat. Both Loraine and Sarah were startled and confused.

"Sit!"

"What?"

"Sit!"

Both sat.

The room was deadly quiet, not even the kids were making any sounds.

"Oh my God," came a whisper from Jane Morris as she tightly grabbed her husband's hand. She knew!

Dan Peterson and Joseph Robinson had rehearsed how they would ask, and a flip of a coin determined who was the first speaker.

Dan Peterson knelt on one knee in front of Lorraine, from a trembling voice deep within him, he asked, "Lorraine Fern Fairly, will you marry me?"

Immediately after, Joseph Robinson, this veteran of combat and leader of tough men in dangerous assignments, also knelt on one knee in front of Sarah Peterson, his voice unsteady, "Sarah Peterson, will you marry me?"

Locking eyes with Lorraine, Dan continued, "I promise to love, respect, honor and care for you for the rest of my life!"

Joe continued, "Sarah, I promise to love, respect, honor, and care for you forever. With you, I am one!"

At that, both Dan and Joe each opened a small box containing a beautiful diamond ring. They took the rings out of the boxes and offered the rings.

Shaking fingers reached for the rings and they were gently slipped on needy fingers.

"Yes!" was the unanimous reply.

Both Loraine and Sarah's faces had tears flooding down. Both looked at each other, "You didn't know either, did you?"

Both strong women suddenly could not rise, their knees could not support them. Lorraine had kids hugging her while she tried to hold Dan. Sarah grabbed Joe and held him to her chest, both ladies murmuring unremembered phases of acceptance.

The room erupted in cheers and applause. The kids were ecstatic, jumping up and down and hugging their Lorraine, their new loving Mother.

Tom Peterson grabbed Lorraine with tears in his eyes, "At last, at long last, I can truly call you- Mom!"

After most neighbors left, the few who remained knew a local minister who could perform marriages and plans were made.

THE END